More Things
IMPOSSIBLE

EDWARD D. HOCH
(Photograph by Michael Culligan)

More Things
IMPOSSIBLE

Edward D. Hoch

Crippen & Landru Publishers
Norfolk, Virginia
2006

Cover painting by Carol Heyer

Cover design by Deborah Miller

Crippen & Landru logo by Eric D. Greene

ISBN (limited edition): 1-932009-48-5
ISBN (trade edition): 1-932009-49-3

FIRST EDITION

10 9 8 7 6 5 4 3 2 1

Crippen & Landru Publishers, Inc.
P. O. Box 9315
Norfolk, VA 23505
USA

www.crippenlandru.com
CrippenLandru@earthlink.net

For Steven Steinbock

CONTENTS

INTRODUCTION

I'm always pleased when I meet readers at Bouchercons or other fan gatherings who tell me that one or the other of my series characters is their favorite. It doesn't really matter to me which one they mention, and I've become aware over the years that a difference of opinion exists. Many people choose Nick Velvet, my most profitable series, as their favorite, while others prefer the intricate locked rooms and impossible crimes of the Dr. Sam Hawthorne tales. I usually hear from someone when it's been too long between my Captain Leopold stories, even though the good Captain has been trying to retire for years. And some old-time fans have stuck with Simon Ark almost from the very beginning — not easy to do since the character, and my professional career, are 50 years old this month.

I believe the stories about Dr. Sam Hawthorne have remained popular for two reasons. First, of course, is the eternal fascination with locked rooms and impossible crimes. When Fred Dannay, the legendary editor of *Ellery Queen's Mystery Magazine*, suggested that all the Dr. Sam stories feature some sort of impossibility, I readily agreed. I've now published 68 of them, and I don't believe I've ever duplicated an idea, or a solution. In fact, I sometimes find it easier coming up with a new impossible crime for Dr. Sam to solve than a new valueless object for Nick Velvet to steal.

A second reason for their continued popularity is that, taken together, they relate the life and times of my main character and tell the reader something of the world in which he lived. My previous volume of Dr. Sam stories, *Diagnosis: Impossible*, began with the good doctor's arrival in Northmont in January of 1922 and carries us up to September 1927. The present collection of fifteen stories begins in the Fall of 1927 and ends in December of 1931.

Eight of these stories have been reprinted in anthologies—"The Whispering House," "The Boston Common," "The Pilgrims Windmill," "The Pink Post Office," "The Octagon Room," "The Tin Goose," "The Hunting Lodge" and "Santa's Lighthouse." I have no special favorites among them, though it should be noted that "The Octagon Room" takes place on the day of Sheriff Lens's wedding, and "The Hunting Lodge" is the only story in which Dr. Sam's parents appear.

I do enjoy writing about Dr. Sam Hawthorne and Northmont's impossible crimes, and plan to continue the series for as long as I, and my computer, hold up. In later stories Sam finally finds a wife, just as the nation plunges into the Second World War. His 68th adventure is set in September of 1943.

For readers who wonder what Dr. Sam did after he finally retired: well, he poured himself a small libation and told these stories to his friends.

Edward D. Hoch
Rochester, New York
September 2005

THE PROBLEM OF
THE REVIVAL TENT

"**D**idn't I ever tell you about the time I was almost arrested for murder?" Dr. Sam Hawthorne began, reaching up to lift the de canter of brandy off the top shelf. "That was really something! Can't blame the sheriff, though, 'cause it looked like I was the only one there when the murder happened. Just me and the victim, alone in a big tent. The tent? Well, that was for the revival meeting. But maybe I'd better start at the beginning . . ."

I suppose the real beginning—the first time I heard about the revival meeting—was a week before it took place. A retired college professor named Hamus McLaughlin was writing a book on the rituals of American life, and he'd invited me to his home. McLaughlin was such a smooth talker and an ego-builder that I somehow got the idea I was to be the only guest. It was a bit of a surprise to encounter Madge Miller on the front porch, holding a thick scrapbook in her arms.

Madge was a schoolteacher, just turned 29 in that autumn of 1927. Since we were about the same age and both unmarried, there'd been a few unsuccessful attempts to get us together, in the heavy-handed manner of country folk. She was a good-looking young lady, with a shapely body, but we'd never really hit it off. Wrong chemistry, I guess. That's what somebody today would call it. Seeing her on the porch of Professor McLaughlin's house that evening, though, my first thought was of another marriage plot.

"Well, hello there, Madge. How's life treating you?"

"Dr. Sam! Imagine seeing you here!" She shifted the scrapbook nervously. "Are you part of Hamus McLaughlin's research project too?"

"It seems that I am."

"He's been interviewing people and gathering bits of material for this book of his. Honestly, he's such a wise old gentleman he really intimidates me! Once when he was touring our school he came into my classroom and I just froze. I haven't stood that still since I rode the sorority float in the homecoming parade. I just—"

The door opened and suddenly there was Hamus McLaughlin standing in front of us. I think we both felt like a couple of school kids caught talking in class. I was the first to recover and I held out my hand. "Good to see you again, Professor. How's the leg?"

"Much better, thanks." He'd been suffering from a bit of arthritis, but as he led us into the sitting room there was no evidence of his previous limp.

"I brought my scrapbook that I kept in college," Madge Miller said, laying it on the table. "You can keep it to look through if you want."

The professor smiled at her. He knew how to charm young women. "I'll put it safely away in my desk until I need it, Madge. Spending one's teaching career at Harvard isn't really a preparation for writing about student life on the average American campus."

"Ohio was about as average as you can get," she said. "Sororities, fraternities, football, homecoming parades, the works. The boy I went with had a ukulele and a hip flask—and that was only the first year of Prohibition!"

Professor McLaughlin glanced through the scrapbook and slid it into his desk drawer. "The rituals of college life—I'll find it fascinating." Turning to me he said, "That's to be a chapter in my book, you know. Another will be on the rituals of the rich. Sheriff Lens is helping me with legal rituals, and I want your help, Dr. Hawthorne, with the rituals of the sick and the dying."

"I don't know that I can—"

"I believe all of life to be made up of rituals. We pass from one set of rites to another, and I don't just mean in organized religion. The rituals of marriage, and business, and even sports—all of these need to be studied."

"Sounds like a massive task," I observed.

"Massive indeed! My publisher envisions a five-hundred-page book, and it could go even longer. I've already collected piles of research material." He cast a hand around the study and I noticed for the first time the stacks of manila folders, the correspondence waiting to be answered, the thick volumes with slips of paper marking important pages of text.

"I'm afraid that scrapbook is mostly just pictures of me," Madge said, a bit awed by the scholarly tomes.

"All the more reason for me to borrow it. A mixture of research and pleasure."

"I have no scrapbook to offer," I told him. "What do you want from me?"

Hamus McLaughlin picked up a handbill from his desk. "Have you seen these around town? There's to be a revival meeting in a tent out at the fairgrounds next Thursday night. Man named George Yester who travels around the northeast with his wife and seven-year-old son. He claims the child can cure people of illness by laying on of his hands."

"That's crazy!" Madge Miller exploded. "Do you believe such foolishness, Dr. Sam?"

"Certainly not."

"The man should be arrested!"

"I'm sure Sheriff Lens will keep an eye on him. But where do I fit in, Professor?"

McLaughlin shifted in his chair. "I'd like you to accompany me to that revival meeting, Dr. Hawthorne. I'd like your first-hand impressions of what goes on. The way I understand it, there's a great deal of religious fervor at these things."

"I'm no man of the cloth."

"But you're a man of medicine, and that's what I need. You can tell me if these so-called cures are real. You know everyone around here, especially the sick ones."

"And if they are real?"

"It will help support the thesis of my book that American ritual is a factor of immense psychological power."

"You're out of my depth," Madge admitted. "If you don't need me any more, Professor, I'll be running along."

He had a final smile for her. "Thank you, Madge. I'm certain your pictures and clippings will be a great help."

She glanced at me as she left, but if there was any special fondness in her look I ignored it. "Goodbye, Madge. See you around."

"Fine young lady," Hamus McLaughlin volunteered when we were alone. "Make somebody a good wife." I ignored that too.

So the following week I drove out to Hamus McLaughlin's house with my nurse April. "Imagine us goin' to this shindig, Dr. Sam," she said. "People see you there, they'll think you're gettin' ideas for new cures."

"I try to keep an open mind, April. Heaven knows I'd go along with anything that could cure someone like Phil Rafferty or Polly Aarons."

"I hear talk they're both goin' to be there tonight."

"I trust it's not raising false hopes." Rafferty was a man in his sixties with some sort of blood disease. Polly Aarons was almost crippled with back trouble. I hadn't been able to help either one, and I doubted if a seven-year-old child could. Still, there was McLaughlin's theory of rituals to consider.

"Here we are," April said. "Land sakes, you'd drive right by the house!"

"My mind was somewhere else."

"On the Miller girl, maybe? I hear you two were seen together the other night."

"On McLaughlin's front porch. Not exactly a trysting place." I left the motor of the Pierce-Arrow running as I hopped out and went to get the professor.

He answered the door on my first ring. "Good, good! I'm glad you could come early, Doctor. It'll give us an opportunity to speak with this man Yester before he starts performing."

The car only held two passengers, but April was used to straddling the bucket seats. "This is cozy," she decided. "Two handsome fellas."

McLaughlin chuckled. "Dr. Hawthorne, your nurse could make an old man young again."

"She's all talk," I assured him. "And speaking of talk, what's the word around town about Yester and his boy? Fill us in on the gossip, April."

She loved it. "Well, I hear tell his present wife isn't the boy's mother. First wife walked out on him after the kid was born. But the current one's something to see—all red hair and lip rouge. Flashy New York clothes too. He keeps her under cover at collection time." April was an entirely different person when it came to gossip.

The tent came into view, and I was surprised at the number of cars in the rutted parking lot a full hour before the meeting. We parked around back and followed Professor McLaughlin as he strode purposefully into the big top. There was no circus inside, only some local men arranging rows of chairs on the dirt floor while a slim fellow with a pencil-thin mustache worked at positioning a life-size silver statue of a nearly nude woman holding a sword.

"Hi there," he said, seeing our approach.

"George Yester?"

"That's me." He was both younger and handsomer than I'd expected, the sort of dapper city slicker we country folk were forever being warned against. I wondered how this man could possibly cure anything, except maybe an overweight wallet. But then I remembered the boy.

Hamus McLaughlin had introduced us all, and as I shook Yester's hand I asked, "Is your son around?"

"No, no—he has to rest before the revivals. They take a lot out of him. You'll see him later." He stepped back to eye the statue, then moved it a bit to the left. "Like it? I call it the Angel of Good Health. My first wife posed for it." He tapped the figure's left shoulder. "It's just plaster, covered with silver paint. Makes it easy to transport in the back of our truck. The sword is real, though."

I touched the weapon, held loosely in the statue's right hand with its point resting against the wooden platform on which we stood. It was indeed a real sword. "Shouldn't she have it raised over her head?" I asked. "Doing battle with disease?" I wasn't about to take any of this hogwash seriously.

But Yester gave me a serious answer. "Tried it that way, but the weight of the sword unbalanced the statue. So I have her holding it down. This way the sword helps support the statue. Toby likes it. Sometimes I let him play with the sword."

"I wouldn't think he could lift it."

"He's a big boy for his age. Looks all of eight or nine."

Professor McLaughlin turned and stared out from the platform at the rows of empty wooden chairs. "Expecting a crowd?" he asked. He seemed to be getting the feel of the place, and imagining how it would look from the boy's vantage point.

"We'll fill it," Yester answered offhandedly. "Toby really brings them in. The child of God and the Angel of Good Health. You seen our handbills around town?"

"We've seen them," I answered dryly. I could understand why his first wife left him, even if I couldn't imagine any sensible girl marrying him in the first place. "You'll forgive me for being skeptical."

"Medical men always are," he said, dismissing me with a wave of his hand. "Toby and me, we bring the cures you can't accomplish."

"And the rituals," the professor added. "Perhaps Dr. Hawthorne would be more successful if he performed like an African witch doctor. And I say that in all seriousness."

"I can't tell you how Toby does it," his father said. "I've been doing revivals for years, but it was only last winter that I brought the boy into the act—the service—and let him perform. He was born to it. Now he wears a little white suit and looks like an angel himself."

"I wonder if you'd have a photograph of him," McLaughlin asked. "Like the one on the handbill. Something for my book."

Yester glanced at his watch. "See me afterwards. He'll even autograph it for you. They're coming in now."

We retreated to front-row seats where Professor McLaughlin could have a good view of the proceedings. Yester started off the platform but was intercepted by a flashy red-haired woman who waved her hands as she talked. "That's his wife," April whispered in my ear.

I grunted an acknowledgement, wondering what the woman's problem was. Maybe she was having trouble with the boy. Maybe he'd got his white suit dirty.

The citizens of Northmont filed in, almost filling the place. A few looked guiltily in my direction, as if their presence lent support to this rival healer. I smiled and waved. It was a theater, not a church.

And presently the electric lights, hanging from the top of the tent, dimmed. The performance was about to begin. George Yester appeared on the wooden platform, billowing the side curtains as he came. He held his hands high toward heaven and proclaimed, "Today . . . is *Yester Day!*"

Nobody laughed.

I wondered if he'd managed to hypnotize them all while they stood in line. He'd barely appeared and he had the audience eating out of his hand. God help us all.

After a long introduction full of platitudes he directed our attention to the silver statue of the Angel of Good Health. The spotlight circled it while the rest of the platform went dark. Then, with a suddenness that was breathtaking, a boy in white stepped from behind the statue. Applause filled the tent. This was what they'd come for.

"Confess your sins," the boy intoned, "and I will make you whole again."

A phonograph record of some organ music came on, lending the proper mood to the event. I wondered if Yester's red-haired wife handled things like spotlights and Victrolas.

Then I saw them coming up the center aisle—the lame and the halt, the ill and the aged. My people, my patients. Coming to this child for the cure I could not find for them. And singing as they came.

It filled me with a fury I'd never known before, and it must have showed. I felt April's restraining hand on my arm. "Not now, Dr. Sam," she whispered.

Phil Rafferty was one of the first in line. He knelt as the boy laid on his hands, then struggled to his feet. I wondered if the blood disease that was wasting him had suddenly gone away. A few others came, even some I didn't know from nearby towns. Then I saw Polly Aarons, back bent with pain. She shrieked as Toby Yester's hands touched her.

And she straightened up.

Slowly, uncertainly—but she straightened up.

The audience went wild.

At my side Professor McLaughlin was busily making notes. "It's hardly surprising," he said above the roar of the crowd. "They always get one or two so-called cures."

The boy seemed unmoved by the demonstration. He went on to the others in line, resting his hands on them. Soon there came another scream and a woman fainted. The music grew louder.

Finally Toby finished. Without a word he bowed stiffly and walked off the platform. George Yester reappeared and gave a pitch for donations "to keep this fine work going." Then George and his red-haired wife passed along the rows of seats with collection baskets. I threw in a dime.

I figured that's what it was worth.

Outside, the crowd was still milling around, exchanging views on what they'd seen. I pushed my way through, leaving April and the professor behind, trying to reach Polly Aarons. Whatever had happened in there, she was still my patient.

When I found her she was leaning against a tree, head down, surrounded by a few friends. "What is it, Polly? What's wrong?"

"I . . . my back. It's not cured, Dr. Sam! It was only good for a few minutes and then it went out again. I didn't have enough faith!" She was starting to cry.

"Nonsense, Polly! He didn't cure you. The excitement of it—the anticipation—made you forget the pain and straighten up. But it was only temporary."

"I want to walk again like other people, Dr. Sam."

"And you will, I'm sure. But not with any help from that child." April had found us by then and I left her to comfort the woman.

"Where are you going?" Professor McLaughlin asked me.

"To find George Yester. Maybe I can't have him arrested for his performance in there, but I can certainly tell him what I think."

"Calm down."

I shook off his hand and strode rapidly across the rutted parking area. The cars and carriages were moving off now as people departed. I could see Sheriff Lens out near the road with a lantern, directing traffic onto the darkened lane, but I didn't stop to chat. Around the back of the big tent was a little trailer and a Packard car. I went directly to the lighted trailer and pounded on the door.

The red-haired woman came at once. "What is it?" she asked. Beyond her I could see the boy Toby stacking coins and bills from the night's collection.

"I want to see your husband."

"George is in the tent, packing up our things. What do you want with him?" She seemed frightened, and my anger had to be clearly visible. Without a word I turned toward the tent.

George Yester was in there all right, all alone, packing up the Victrola and spotlight that had been used in the performance. He turned to me, standing before the platform with its statue of the Angel of Good Health, and said, "Enjoy the show, Doctor?" The expression on his face made me want to hit him.

"Not particularly."

"Oh? Too bad. It was a good audience."

"Good for the collection baskets?"

"You saw a woman cured," Yester answered.

"And I saw her writhing in pain just now in the lot outside. Your cures don't last too long."

"Perhaps her faith was weak."

"I wish I could have you arrested for what you've done here!"

"Arrested? For bringing a little hope, a little comfort, to these ignorant people?"

Then I did hit him. I brought my right fist up and connected with his jaw, sending him over backward. He looked startled as he hit the ground. I turned without another word and headed down the aisle toward the rear of the tent.

I was almost to the entrance when I heard him scream. I turned, wondering what had happened, and saw him still lying there in front of the platform.

But now the silver sword from the statue's hand was embedded in his chest.

And there was no one else in the tent.

I ran to him, pulled the sword free, tried to dam the flow of blood with my handkerchief. His eyelids flickered once and then he was gone.

I stayed there on my knees, unable to believe what had happened. There was nothing but row upon row of empty chairs. No movement, no sound except the wheezing of air as it escaped from the dead man's chest. I looked at the sword and examined it, aware that my fingerprints were already on the haft.

There was nothing to do but call Sheriff Lens. I hoped he was still in the parking lot with his lantern.

I walked to the rear of the tent once more and lifted the flap. Yes, the lantern was waving away the last of the departing audience. No one but me had heard Yester's dying scream. "Sheriff Lens," I shouted, not wanting to leave the tent. "Over here—quick!"

"What's the trouble, Doc?" he called back.

"Come here and I'll tell you. It's important."

He trotted over, moving faster than usual. "What's up?"

"George Yester has been murdered."

"Come on now!"

"See for yourself." I held open the tent flap and he entered, giving a low whistle when he spotted Yester's body in front of the platform.

"How'd it happen, Doc?"

I told him everything I knew, starting with the revival meeting itself and my attendance with Professor McLaughlin.

"Where's the professor now?" he asked.

"Outside, I suppose. With April."

"Any possibility the sword was jarred loose from the statue when you knocked Yester down?"

"An accident, you mean? I wish it could have happened that way. But the point of the sword was resting against this platform. Even if it fell over on him the haft would have hit him. There's no way the blade could have gone into his chest accidentally. I pulled it out, remember. It was driven almost through him."

"You tellin' me the statue came to life and killed him?"

"Hardly. But someone removed the sword and plunged it into him as he sprawled there."

"An' your fingerprints are on it."

"I told you that. I pulled it out of the wound, trying to save his life."

"And you were angry with him. You admit hitting him and knocking him down."

"Yes."

"And there was no one else in the tent."

"No."

Sheriff Lens shook his head. I could see what he was thinking. He stepped onto the platform and put both arms around the silver statue, lifting it off to the hard ground. "Lighter than I expected."

"It's silver-painted plaster. Yester told us that. What are you doing?"

"Only place somebody could hide is under this wooden platform. I'm gonna have me a look-see."

The platform, about 12 feet square and 18 inches high, was enclosed on all sides. It merely rested on the ground and the sheriff lifted it easily. There was nothing underneath but more hard-packed earth. "I could have told you no one was hidden there," I said. "How could they have got out without toppling the statue on the platform?"

He stood up and looked around some more, his attention attracted now by the curtains on either side of the platform. "Could anyone have been hiding back here, Doc?"

"I'll admit I didn't look, but what if they were? I walked down that aisle for maybe fifteen seconds before Yester screamed. Then I turned instantly. There was no one in sight. It's doubtful the killer could have come out of hiding, crossed the platform, removed the sword from the statue's hand, and stabbed Yester—all in fifteen seconds. And it's absolutely impossible that he could have vanished into thin air as I turned around."

Sheriff Lens grunted, bending low to examine the ground. "Too packed down to show footprints. Maybe Yester killed himself, Doc."

"With a sword that long? Even if he could have managed it, he couldn't have driven the blade that deeply into his body. No, it was done by someone standing above him, thrusting downward." As I spoke my eyes turned up, toward the top of the tent, but there was nothing to be seen except the electric cords for the rows of dim hanging light bulbs.

"Doc, don't you see I'm tryin' to give you a way out? Hell, I don't want to arrest you!"

"Arrest me!" I hadn't seriously considered the prospect till that moment.

"You had the motive and the opportunity, Doc. And by your own account no one else coulda done it."

"But I'm innocent! I didn't kill—"

I was interrupted by the sudden appearance of George Yester's wife. She burst into the tent, obviously in search of him. "*George!*" she screamed when she saw the body. "George, what have they done to you?"

"I'm sorry, ma'am," Sheriff Lens said. "We were just coming to tell you. Someone's killed your husband."

She fell sobbing by the body then, and I had to gently pull her away. "There's nothing we could do," I said softly. "He died instantly."

She glared at me, her brown eyes flashing. "Nothing you could do, maybe. But his boy can do something! Toby can bring him back!" And she ran from the tent before we could prevent her.

"Stop her, Sheriff! We can't let her bring the boy in here."

"Come on."

We met them at the back of the tent, and Sheriff Lens barred the way. Young Toby simply stood there, trembling, not fully understanding what had happened. Finally the red-haired woman calmed down and led the boy back to their trailer.

No one could bring George Yester back. Not now.

"All right, Sheriff," I said with a sigh. "Now you can arrest me if you want to."

But he didn't arrest me, not quite yet. We'd been through too much together for him to seriously believe me capable of murder. He told me the case would be presented to the county grand jury, and I'd be free until an indictment was returned. That gave me a few days, at least, though I didn't know just what I'd do with them. The suspects were at once too many and too few. Anyone in the audience might have slipped back into the tent and killed Yester. But how? And why?

I started out with Phil Rafferty, because I hadn't seen him in the crowd outside the tent. Phil worked at the post office in town, when his blood condition didn't weaken him to the point of exhaustion, and I found him there the morning after the killing.

He looked at me a bit sheepishly and said, "I didn't really believe all that mumbo-jumbo last night, Dr. Sam. But my wife insisted I had to go."

"How are you feeling today?"

"About the same, I guess. I'm still able to work and I'm thankful for that."

"Tell me, did you notice anything unusual during or after the performance? Anything that might be a clue to this thing?"

"Sure did! In fact, I was goin' to tell the sheriff about it today. We were one of the last buggies out of the lot, because I wanted the cars to go first. Our horse Nelly shies at cars. Anyway, just before we pulled out I seen a figure runnin' from the tent, off toward the woods."

"Man or woman?"

"Couldn't tell. It was wearin' a long cape of some sort, reaching to the ground, and a hood over the head. You know, like monks wear."

"A cowl."

"Yeah, I guess so. Thought it was strange, and this mornin' when I heard about the killing I decided the sheriff should know."

"You tell him, Phil. And thanks for the information."

I went away thinking that the likelihood of a cowled monk sneaking around the tent was about as bizarre as the murder itself. Still, Phil Rafferty must have seen something.

Back at the office I talked to April and learned that she'd lost Professor McLaughlin in the crowd the previous night. She hadn't seen him at all after we reached Polly Aarons. "I should go have a talk with him," I decided. "He was looking around and making notes. Maybe he spotted something the rest of us missed."

I was to get there sooner than I'd planned. Not ten minutes later there was a call from Madge Miller. I hadn't seen her since the night at McLaughlin's home and now her voice was high and distraught. "Dr. Sam, I'm at the professor's house! He's been attacked—come quick!"

"Attacked?"

"He's unconscious and bleeding, and the house is a mess!"

"I'm on my way. Call Sheriff Lens."

The sheriff and I arrived at the house together. We found Madge in the professor's den, bathing his gashed forehead with a cold towel. He was conscious now, but still dazed. "I came over to see him and the front door was ajar," Madge said. "I found him like this."

I glanced around at the spilled papers and open desk drawers. His assailant had obviously been searching for something. "Can you talk now?" I asked as his eyes flickered open. I could see the wound wasn't serious.

"I–I think so. What time is it?"

"Ten thirty. How long have you been unconscious?"

"I heard a noise early this morning, before daybreak. I came down to see what it was and somebody hit me over the head. That's all I know."

"Did you get a look at him?" Sheriff Lens asked, making notes.

"Not a glimpse. I was hit from behind."

"This cut's on your forehead," I observed. "But you probably got it when you fell." I could feel a swollen bump under his hair. "You'd better get to bed till I can check you over."

"What did they take?" he asked, his eyes focusing finally on the strewn papers.

"I don't know. Maybe nothing. Maybe they couldn't find what they wanted."

Sheriff Lens helped me get McLaughlin to his feet. "Think it's connected with the killing, Doc?"

"That's a possibility." Though at the moment I couldn't see the connection. What was it the professor had observed that could endanger the killer? Hadn't I seen everything he had?

We got Hamus McLaughlin up to bed and I left him having a glass of bootleg whiskey. He seemed no worse for his encounter with the sneak thief. Sheriff Lens stayed on to examine a broken side window by which the thief had gained entry.

On the way back to my office I stopped by to see Polly Aarons. She was resting comfortably, but the momentary cure that ignited the revival meeting had not returned. Her back was no better. I left her and drove out to the fairgrounds once more.

Mrs. Yester was busy packing the trailer and it was obvious she and the boy would soon be leaving. "We didn't really meet last night," I said. "My name's Sam Hawthorne."

She looked at me dully and I noticed that her red hair was wild and uncombed. It had been a hard night for her. "I'm Sue Yester, but I guess you know that. Some say you killed my husband."

"No, I didn't kill him."

"You're a doctor, huh?"

"Yes. Could I talk to you about George?"

The boy Toby came to the door of the trailer but she chased him inside. "There's nothin' for him to hear. He's heard too much already. What are your questions?"

"Know anyone around here who'd want your husband dead?"

"Only someone like you. We always had trouble with country doctors."

"How long you been doing this?"

"He was holding revival meetings before I knew him. Got started back in Ohio when the boy was born. I hooked up with him four years ago, but Toby didn't get into the act till last year. He was a big hit—the greatest thing ever happened to George."

"Do you believe Toby can cure people of their ills?"

"I wanted to believe it last night. I wanted to believe he could bring George back. But I guess I never did really think so. Toby's just a boy, like other boys. He doesn't cure anyone, but sometimes in the excitement of it all they cure themselves."

She was a wiser woman that I would have believed. I had no more questions to ask her. She'd given me the final piece of the puzzle.

"We have to go back out to Professor McLaughlin's house," I told Sheriff Lens. "The answer is there."

He took a deep breath. "I'm gettin' a lot of complaints about not arrestin' you, Doc. If you don't clear this thing up quick I might have to take you in."

"I think we'll clear it up this noon."

The professor was sitting up in a chair when we arrived, supervising Madge Miller while she tried to straighten the study and sort out his scattered papers. "Still don't know what's missing," he told us. "A lot of these things were research materials I hadn't got around to yet. But who in hell would want them?"

I sat down opposite him. "Professor, I think I know who killed George Yester. I came here to tell you first, because you were there with me last night."

Sheriff Lens shifted uneasily. "Get on with it, Doc."

"Well, the big problem in my mind was *how?* How could Yester be stabbed with that sword almost before my eyes? I figured if I got the *how* I'd know the *who*. The killer had to be close enough that he could get the sword, stab Yester, and resume his hiding place all before I turned around. He might have waited till I left, but by killing Yester in my presence he had a ready-made suspect. Naturally he'd seen me punch Yester and knock him down."

"There was no hiding place," Sheriff Lens insisted. "You told me so yourself."

"There was one I never considered. Behind that silver statue! The killer stepped around it, took the sword, plunged it into the fallen man's chest, and stepped back behind the statue. He made his escape when I went to call you, Sheriff."

"Behind the statue!" Lens scoffed. "There's no room behind it! What was he—a midget?"

"No—a seven-year-old boy."

"Toby!"

"Exactly. Remember, Professor, how we saw him appear from behind the statue last evening during the performance? And remember Yester telling us how he played with the silver sword? I suppose the boy was rebelling against the life that had been forced on him, rebelling against a father whose love depended on the size of the nightly collections. There's no other way it could have been done. Only Toby Yester could have hidden behind that statue and killed his father."

And then I turned and looked directly into the ashen face of Madge Miller. Her mouth was working, but no words were coming out. "Did you want to say something, Madge?" I prompted. "Before the sheriff goes out to arrest Toby?"

"Damn you, Sam!" she screamed. "*You know!*"

"Know what, Madge?" I asked quietly.

"Toby didn't do it. I killed George Yester."

I told April about it later, back in the office. "I didn't feel any triumph when she said those words, April. I felt sad for us all."

"Dr. Sam, you mean she confessed just to save the boy from being accused? I don't understand it."

"She killed for him in the first place, so I knew she'd confess to save him. You see, Madge Miller is Toby's mother."

"My God! How'd you find that out?"

"Lots of guesswork, April. We knew Toby's real mother—Yester's first wife—had left him after the boy was born. Sue Yester told me today this was in Ohio, and I knew Madge went to college in Ohio. The dates were right too—Madge would have been twenty-one or twenty-two when the boy was born, since she just turned twenty-nine. Probably a senior in college when she got involved with George Yester. I suppose seeing what he was doing to her son was more than she could bear. Even though she'd walked out on them she felt she had to rescue Toby. And the only way to do it was to destroy George Yester like some avenging angel."

"How, Dr. Sam? You were right there. How could she have killed him without you seeing her?"

"Oh, I saw her, April. I must have looked right at her. But I didn't notice her. Sheriff Lens pegged it right last night when he asked me if that silver statue came alive. Because that's exactly what happened, you see. For a few crucial minutes Madge Miller became that statue."

"Dr. Sam!" Clearly she didn't believe me.

"It's fantastic, April, but not impossible. Once in Boston I saw models posed in a department-store window, standing for twenty minutes without moving a muscle. I remembered something Madge told me just last week. She said once Professor McLaughlin visited her classroom and intimidated her so much she just froze. She said she hadn't stood so still since she rode her sorority's float in the college homecoming parade. I remembered that later and thought it was odd, because people riding floats in parades usually wave to the spectators. If she was frozen on the float maybe it was because she was imitating a statue. I remembered seeing things like that in my own college days—a pretty coed painted gold or silver and imitating a statue. Sometimes the paint clogged their pores and made them sick."

"But certainly Yester and you would know a real girl from a statue!"

"Would we? The spotlight was already disconnected, remember. There were only the strings of dim bulbs at the top of the tent. And we had no reason to look at the statue. As for its size and general appearance, Yester told me himself that his first wife modeled for the statue. The Angel of Good Health was Madge Miller. I suppose seeing her on that sorority float gave him the idea for the statue in the first place."

"Did she tell you all this?"

"She told us enough. She first heard about Yester's appearance in Northmont last week at McLaughlin's house. I remember now how the news seemed to upset and anger her. She brooded about it all week and decided she had to kill her ex-husband to free Toby from this life as a false messiah. Among her college souvenirs she still had the tube of silver paint she'd used in the parade. Though the statue's face didn't look that much like her, the body was still hers. She was sure she could take its place after the performance, when she knew Yester would come back alone to pack up his gear. She wanted to kill him that way, like an avenging angel, like a statue come to life. She wanted to see his expression. I suppose the thought of her son, of abandoning him to Yester, had made her a little bit mad on the subject."

"Anyway, she rubbed herself all over with the silver paint and sneaked into the tent as the performance was ending. She wore a long robe with a hood, to hide her silvery near-nudity, and that's what Phil Rafferty saw as she made her escape. She hid the real statue behind the curtains—it was easy to lift—and took its place, sword in hand. Before she could kill Yester I walked in and started arguing with him. When I knocked him down she saw her chance and plunged the sword into him. He screamed, of course, and she had to freeze in position again when I turned around."

"She must have had some anxious moments then, but I was more interested in saving the man's life if I could. I never looked closely at the statue. When I went to call Sheriff Lens she lifted the real statue back onto the platform and made her escape."

"What about Professor McLaughlin? Did she attack him too?"

I nodded. "There were homecoming pictures in the scrapbook she left him, including one of her on the float. He hadn't looked at them yet, but she had to take back that picture before he saw it and connected it with the killing. He heard her in his study and she had to knock him out. Then she scattered everything around to make it look as if the thief had been searching for something. She didn't want to harm McLaughlin, though, so she returned this morning to find him and phone me for help."

April just sat there shaking her head. "And the boy, Toby?"

"I think it's best that he never knows about this. Sue Yester isn't a bad sort, and maybe she can get him back to leading a normal life."

". . . and that was all of it," Dr. Sam Hawthorne concluded. "Toby Yester grew up to become a successful night-club entertainer under another name, and he never knew his real mother had killed his father. Madge simply went to pieces after her confession. She was never well enough mentally to stand trial. And we didn't have any more revival meetings in Northmont. Funny thing, though— you know Phil Rafferty? His blood disease pretty much went away after that. I never understood why.

"Come by again, anytime. I've got a real ghost story for you next, with a haunted house and everything! And perhaps you'll have a small—ah—libation before you go?"

THE PROBLEM OF
THE WHISPERING HOUSE

"This time I promised you a story about a real haunted house," old Dr. Sam Hawthorne began, pouring the drinks as he always did. "And that's what I'm going to give you! It happened in February of 1928, and it came darned close to being the last case—either medical or mysterious—that I ever handled. But first I better tell you about the ghost-hunter, because the story really started the day he arrived in Northmont . . ."

The ghost-hunter's name was Thaddeus Sloan (Dr. Sam continued), and with a name like that I suppose I expected to meet a gray-bearded old professor with thick spectacles and a cane. Instead, he proved to be a man in his mid-thirties, not much older than myself, who immediately said, "Call me Thad."

"Then I'm Sam," I said, shaking his hand. He was taller than me, and thin to the point of being gaunt. A tiny beard—almost a goatee—helped to hide a weak chin, and it combined with his deep-set, intense eyes to suggest a sort of benevolent Satan.

"I suppose you know why I'm here in Northmont, Sam."

I scratched my head and smiled. "Well, I can't rightly say. We have our neighborhood haunts, certainly. Some years back there was talk that the bandstand in the town square was haunted, but it turned out to be a human spook. And then there's the—"

"I'm interested in the Bryer house."

"Oh, yes. I should have guessed." A Boston newspaper had recently run a Sunday feature on the old place, telling more than most of Northmont's residents had ever known.

"Is it true that the house whispers? And that it contains a secret room which no one has ever come out of, once they've entered it?"

"To tell you the truth I've never been inside the Bryer place. It's been empty for as long as I've lived in Northmont, and I only go where there are patients who need me."

"But surely you've heard the legends!"

"It was just an old empty house to me till I read that feature in the Boston paper. Maybe that reporter used his imagination a bit." He seemed so dejected by my words that I had to add, "I've heard people say it was haunted, though. And sometimes the wind made sounds as if the house was whispering."

That seemed to cheer him up. "I spoke to the reporter about his story, of course. He said he obtained most of his information from former Northmont residents now living in the Boston area."

"That's quite possible."

"Someone mentioned your name as one who has made something of a hobby out of solving local mysteries."

"I wouldn't say that," I demurred. "Things happen here the way they do in any town. Sometimes I help out Sheriff Lens, and if I'm lucky I spot a piece of evidence the others have missed."

"Nevertheless, you're the only one who can help me. I need someone who knows the area to act as a guide. I intend to spend a night in the old Bryer house, and I'd like you to join me."

"Ghost-hunting is a little out of my line," I said. "Ghosts don't need doctors."

At that moment my nurse April entered with the morning mail. She smiled uncertainly at Thad Sloan and said, "Dr. Sam, there's a telephone call from Mrs. Andrews. Her son Billy fell out of the hayloft and hurt his leg."

"Tell her I'll be right out." I smiled at my visitor. "Come with me if you'd like. You'll see how a country doctor practices. And Mrs. Andrews lives just down the road from the Bryer place."

He followed me out and climbed into my yellow Pierce-Arrow Runabout. "This is quite a car for a country doctor."

"A graduation gift from my family, seven years ago. It's getting a bit old now, but it still runs well."

I took the North Road, which got us to the Andrews place first. Mrs. Andrews hurried out to meet me, plainly distraught. "Dr. Sam, I'm so glad you came! Billy landed on a pitchfork! He's bleedin' pretty bad."

"Don't you worry, Mrs. Andrews. Just take me to him."

She led the way across the barnyard where vestiges of our February snow still lingered in spots. I could understand the reason for her concern. Her husband, a former carnival pitchman, had died of a heart attack the previous year. The job of running the farm and tending the livestock had fallen on 23-year-old Billy. A serious injury to the only able-bodied man on the place could be fatal to the future of the farm.

I found Billy lying on the barn floor, a crude tourniquet tightened around his left leg. His bloodied coveralls had been torn away from the wound, a messy thing where the prong of the pitchfork had gone clear through the fleshy part of his calf. "That's not so bad," I said reassuringly, after a moment's inspection. "The bleeding helped cleanse the wounds."

Billy Andrews gritted his teeth. "I was forkin' hay down for the cows when I lost my footing and fell. Damned fork went clear through me."

"Could have been a lot worse." Then I remembered Thad Sloan standing by the barn door and introduced him to Billy and Mrs. Andrews. He nodded a greeting but kept his eyes on me, apparently fascinated by my doctoring.

"Now I'm going to give you a little pain-killer," I told Billy. "Then I'll stitch up these holes in your leg." I cleansed the wounds with antiseptic and set to work. There was no point moving him to the house till I had him patched up, and he seemed comfortable enough where he was.

To make conversation while I worked, I said, "Mr. Sloan is a ghost-hunter. He's here to see the old Bryer house."

"Oh, there's no ghost in there!" Mrs. Andrews said with a flutter of her hand. "Them's just stories."

Thad Sloan was staring off across the fields at a house about a half mile away. "Is that the place?" he asked.

"That's it," I confirmed. "I'll get you there soon enough, when I finish with Billy here."

The ghost-hunter turned to Mrs. Andrews once again. "You mean you've never noticed anything strange there? No odd lights at night, or unexplained noises? It's said the house can be heard to whisper."

"Not by me, it can't. Billy used to play around there when he was a boy. Billy, you ever hear the Bryer house whisperin' to you?"

He shifted a bit on the barn floor as I completed my mending job. "Never heard a sound 'cept once when I found some hobos camped there. An' they did more than whisper. They chased me clear across the fields."

"Come on now," I said, helping him to his feet. "Just keep the weight off that leg and you'll be okay. We'll get you up to the house." I walked on his left side, keeping my arm around him as he hobbled along. Up at the house we got him into bed and I told him to stay put. "It'll be painful to walk on for a few days, but there's no serious damage. You'll be back in shape in no time."

Mrs. Andrews saw us to the door. "I can't thank you enough for comin' right out, Dr. Sam."

"That's what I'm here for."

"How much do I owe you?"

"Don't you worry. April will send a bill, and you pay me when you're able."

Back in the car, driving down the bumpy dirt road to the Bryer place, Thad Sloan said, "I thought country doctors like you only existed in books."

"There are a few of us left."

The driveway to the Bryer house, overgrown with weeds in summer, was rutted and muddy from the current thaw. One look at it decided me to leave the car on the road and walk up to the house. From the outside, even close up, it appeared in remarkably good shape for its seventy years. The shuttered windows seemed undisturbed, and though the gray paint was faded, there were no signs of peeling.

"I don't suppose we can get in," I said.

He smiled at me. "We can if the lock's working. I got a key from the real-estate man in Boston who has the property listed."

"Then you're serious about spending the night here?"

"Certainly."

Until that moment I hadn't really believed him. "If the place is for sale, does that mean the last of the Bryer family is dead?"

"There are some cousins, but they want to get rid of it." He inserted the key in the lock and opened the door with ease. I followed him into the darkened house.

"I'd suggest opening some shutters to let the daylight in. There's never been electricity here."

Thad Sloan produced a flashlight from his pocket. "I'd rather use this. You can see there's a good supply of candles here and that should do us. Sunlight isn't conducive to conjuring up ghosts."

Most of the furniture had been removed from the house long ago, and I was surprised to see the few pieces remaining. There was a shabby, moth-eaten armchair in the living room, and an empty cabinet standing next to the big old fireplace. There were two straight chairs in what might have been the dining room. In one corner of the kitchen we found a burned-down candle stub and an empty bottle which could have contained bootleg whiskey. "I guess Billy Andrews was right about the hobos," I remarked.

"No recent signs, though. This might have been here for years."

We moved on, through the other first-floor rooms, noting occasional pieces of furniture that hadn't been worth carting away. We went up the creaking stairs to the second floor, guided by Sloan's pocket torch and the sunlight that came from some unshuttered upper windows.

"Nothing here," I said at last. "Satisfied there are no ghosts?"

"Spirits hardly sit around welcoming noontime visitors. It's in the night that we'll find them, if there are any."

"I don't hear any whispering, either. And what about that room you mentioned, where no one ever comes out of, once they've entered it?"

Thaddeus Sloan sighed. "I don't know. We'll have to come back tonight."

I still wonder why I ever agreed to spend the night with a ghost-hunter in a supposedly haunted house. Now I can only blame it on the folly of youth, though at the time it didn't seem that wild an idea. I suppose I wanted to prove something to Thad Sloan, and maybe to myself. Northmont was my town, if only by adoption, and if there was a ghost to be revealed, I wanted to take part in the exorcising of it.

And so that night, shortly before ten, we drove back out to the Bryer place. Sloan had a good supply of candles and matches, along with some other equipment that puzzled me. "You see," he explained, "there are certain procedures which must be followed. Some ghost-hunters seal the doors and windows with seven human hairs, and wear a necklace of garlic. I don't go quite that far, but I do bring along a revolver—"

"For a ghost?"

He smiled at me. "Just a precaution."

We were in the largest of the downstairs rooms, and Thad Sloan stepped to the center of it with a piece of chalk in his hand. Without saying a word he drew a large circle on the wooden floor, and within it traced a five-pointed star. "A pentacle, you see. One is said to be safe inside it."

"A revolver and a pentacle!" I marveled. "You *are* ready for anything."

He had other equipment too—a camera and flashgun that he mounted on a tripod with a revolving head. "If any ghost comes here tonight, we'll be prepared."

I settled down for a long boring night, wishing I'd brought along the latest medical journal to catch up on.

It was about an hour later, not long before midnight, when we heard the whispering. At first I took it to be the wind stirring through the upper reaches of the old house, but soon it seemed to take on the sound and substance of speech.

"*Be gone from here if you value your lives . . .*"

"Did you hear it?" Sloan exclaimed.

"I think so. I can't be too sure."

"*Be gone from here . . .* ," the voice whispered again.

"It's some sort of trickery," I decided at once. "Somebody's trying to fool us."

"Come on, Sam. Let's have a look." He picked up the revolver and stepped outside the carefully drawn pentacle. I followed, a bit reluctantly for all my bravado.

"What do you think?" I asked. "Upstairs?"

"Let's see."

We went quickly up the front stairs and paused at the top to listen once more. Now there did seem to be a wind blowing outside, but we heard no sound of whispering.

Then suddenly the downstairs door opened. We froze in our tracks and Sloan signaled for me to hide. I stepped into one of the open bedrooms.

Someone was coming up the stairs. I saw the glow of a lantern and then I saw a man. A thin bearded man, not too tall, wearing a shabby winter coat and a fur hat. He moved quickly but carefully, holding the lantern high to light his way. Though he seemed familiar with the house, I was certain I'd never seen him before.

And yet, as the figure passed me, not five feet away, there could have been something familiar about it after all.

I expected Sloan to come out of hiding at any moment, but perhaps like me he was more interested in seeing where this man was going. We found out soon enough. He walked to the end of the hall, where a blank wall faced him, and touched a spot in the frame of an adjoining doorway. Immediately there was a click, and when he pushed the wall it swung open before him. It was the first time I'd ever seen a real secret panel in operation.

The hidden door closed behind him and the upper hallway was once more plunged into darkness. I waited a moment and then stepped back into the hall. Thad Sloan saw me and came out of his hiding place. "What do you think?" I asked.

"I think we've found our secret room," Sloan replied softly.

"The room no one ever comes out of?"

"We'll know soon enough. He went in, and he hasn't come out yet."

We waited for what seemed an eternity, though in truth it was no more than a half hour. At any moment we were prepared to leap back into our hiding places should the secret panel open, but it remained closed.

Finally, when the time was after midnight, Sloan said, "I'm going downstairs for my camera. Then let's open the damned thing and confront him."

"There's always the possibility of another exit," I pointed out.

"But where would it lead to? If he'd come out elsewhere on this floor we'd have seen him." He went down for his camera and tripod and returned in a few moments carrying them on his shoulder. "Do you remember what he pushed to open it?"

I'd been feeling around the door jamb and found a loose piece of molding. "I think this is it."

Sloan positioned the tripod and camera so that it pointed at the wall. He filled the flashgun with extra powder and gripped the shutter release. "All right," he said. "Open it."

I pressed the molding. The door in the wall gave a click and swung open. I wondered if we would find a startled man or an empty room.

We found neither.

The man was still there, seated upright by a table facing us. But our sudden appearance did nothing to startle him. "I think he's—" I began, stepping into the room and going to him.

"Dead?" Thad Sloan completed. He tripped the shutter of his camera and the small secret room was filled with an instant's glare from the flash powder. It was enough to show us there was no other occupant and no other exit.

"He's been stabbed," I said, pulling back the coat to reveal a hunting knife plunged deep into his left side, toward the heart. "And here's something." I pointed toward the floor, where a small .22 caliber automatic had apparently slipped from the dead man's fingers.

Sloan glanced around at the solid walls. He even looked behind the open door of the secret room. "But there's no hiding place, and no way out of here!"

"Exactly."

"You're saying, Sam, that he was killed by a ghost?"

I straightened up from my examination of the body. "No, what I'm saying is even more fantastic than that. I know quite a bit about rigor mortis and such things. This body is already cold and stiff. He didn't die within the last half hour. He's been dead for probably fifteen to twenty hours."

"But that's impossible! We just saw—"

I nodded. "It wasn't a ghost that killed him, but it certainly seems to have been a ghost that walked into this room tonight."

I stayed with the body while Thad Sloan ran down the road to use the phone at the Andrews house. He called Sheriff Lens as I instructed him, and most of the rest of the night was given over to the police investigation. We learned nothing new from it, except that a great many people entered the secret room during those hours and left it again without anything happening to them.

Sheriff Lens was fascinated with the workings of the secret door. "This place was built in the late 1850s," he said. "They say it might have been a station on the underground railway into Canada—for escaped slaves, you know."

"I suppose that's a possibility," I agreed. We'd been tapping at the walls and floor without finding a thing. I'd even allowed myself to be closed into the room alone while Thad Sloan and Sheriff Lens waited outside. I discovered to my horror that there seemed to be no way of opening the secret door from the inside.

"There you have it," Sloan said, obviously excited by the results of his ghost-hunting. "The room of no return! The room from which no one ever emerges! That's what it means—a secret cell in which someone could starve to death without ever being found."

"I'll admit these walls are thick," I said. "You could be right."

Sheriff Lens was examining the tiny automatic. "This gun has been fired. Looks like he took a shot at his killer."

I remembered a hole I'd noticed in the wooden table leg. "And I'll bet here's where it went. Do you have a pocketknife, Sheriff?" In a few moments I'd extracted the slug from the slender leg of the table. It was mashed a bit, but clearly identifiable as a bullet.

"What does that tell us?" Sloan asked.

"Nothing except that the dead man was a poor shot."

"The bullet would have passed through a ghost."

"Ghosts don't use huntin' knives," Sheriff Lens said. "I never believed in ghosts myself and I ain't about to start now."

"What about the thing we saw?" Thad Sloan asked. "It had to be a ghost!"

Sheriff Lens snorted. "That's your problem, not mine."

"Any idea who the dead man is?" I asked the sheriff.

"Never saw him before, and his pockets are empty. No cash, no identification, nothing."

We could do little more that night, but in the morning I was barely awake when Sheriff Lens was knocking at my door, bringing me some interesting news. "The coroner backs you up, Doc. Says he died sometime between three and nine yesterday morning. But there's somethin' else too. The dead man's beard is false."

"What?"

"A fake beard, glued on his face with spirit gum like actors use. What do you make of that?"

"I feel stupid for not realizing it. Did anyone recognize him with the beard off?"

"He looked a little familiar, Doc. I wouldn't want to swear to it, but I might have seen him hangin' around town."

"Funny—when he passed me in that hall I thought he seemed familiar too."

"You still onto that ghost story of yours?"

"I'm only telling you what we saw."

"How about telling me instead how you could see a dead man walkin'."

I thought about it. "That may not be the real problem, Sheriff."

"It's another one of them impossible crimes you like so much, ain't it?"

"Seems so," I admitted. "It certainly looks impossible."

"What are you goin' to do about it?"

"Go back to that house by daylight and start all over again."

I went alone, parking on the road as I'd done before, and made my way up the driveway to the house. The man last night, whoever he was, had apparently come without a car—or else someone had driven it away. I wasn't even considering the possibility of a ghost. The man I'd seen was flesh and blood, very much alive, and if that only deepened the mystery it was something I'd have to figure out.

I went around to the back of the house, walking over long grass still flattened by the weight of the recently melted snow. I didn't really know what I expected to find, but I had to look anyway. It was the drainpipe at the rear of the house that finally caught my attention. The spout at its bottom curved out about two feet above the ground, and there was something about it that reminded me of the mouthpiece for a particularly large trumpet. I cupped my hands around it and tried calling through it. My voice reverberated in the distance, but I couldn't tell if it was coming from inside the house.

"Back to the scene of the crime?" a voice behind me asked. I straightened up with a start and saw that it was Thaddeus Sloan, the ghost-hunter.

"Look, I think I've found something. Do you still have the key to the front door?"

"Yes." He produced it from his pocket.

"Go inside the house and stand about where we were standing last night when we heard the whispering. I want to try an experiment."

He followed my instructions, and I discovered I could see him moving about through the window above the drain spout. I tried calling again and he signaled that he heard. Then I lowered my voice to a harsh whisper. He hurried over and opened the window. "That's it, Sam! That's the whispering house! How did you know?"

"Just a guess. Our ghost last night entered the house right after we heard the whispering. That made me think there was some way of causing it from outside. I saw the drainpipe and tried it."

"Then you're saying our ghost is not a ghost?"

"I'm saying it's someone who knows that sounds from this drainpipe are somehow amplified in the attic and fed through the whole house, probably by way of the chimneys."

"How could that man have whispered into the drainpipe, opened the door, walked upstairs, and gone into the secret room if he'd been stabbed to death almost a full day earlier?"

"I don't know," I admitted. "There is one explanation, but at this point it raises more questions than it answers. It merely substitutes one impossibility for another."

"What's that?"

"Well, if the man we saw was the murderer, disguised as his victim, that would explain a lot."

"It wouldn't explain how he got out of that secret room."

"No, it wouldn't," I agreed glumly.

"I like the idea of a ghost much better. I only wish I'd gotten a picture of him walking."

"Did you develop the photograph of the room and the body?"

He nodded, reaching into a leather case he carried. "Here it is, but it doesn't help."

A photograph of the scene had once helped me solve a mystery, but this time I had to admit it showed me very little. The body at the table, the solid wall behind—that was all. We were still confronted with a nameless ghost. "I'm going back to the office," I said, handing the picture to Sloan. "You coming?"

He shook his head. "I want to look around some more."

I walked out to the road and climbed into my Runabout. I was just pulling away when something happened. There was a sputtering at first from under the hood, then a sheet of flame shot up, and suddenly the whole car was on fire.

Somehow I managed to jump free and roll around on the cold earth to smother the few flames that had clung to my clothing. But the car was a total loss. I stood and watched it burn as I might keep a vigil at the bedside of a dying patient. There was nothing I could do to save it.

Attracted by the smoke, Thad Sloan finally appeared from behind the Bryer house. He ran toward me. "What happened? Your car—"

"I don't know. There was something like an explosion, I think. I was lucky to get out."

"I'll drive you back to town."

"No, I think I want Sheriff Lens to look at this." I started down the road to the Andrews house. "I'm going to call him."

Mrs. Andrews greeted me at the door. "More trouble, Dr. Sam? Your clothes are all burnt."

"Car caught fire. I want to phone the sheriff, if I may."

"Go right ahead."

"How's Billy's leg coming along?"

"Slowly. I wish you'd have a look at it while you're here."

He was up in his room, trying to limp around as best he could. I saw at once that my stitches were a bit inflamed, but that didn't bother me. "You should be in bed," I told him sternly. "One day is too soon to be up on that leg."

"I feel so helpless when there's chores to be done. Momma can't do everything."

"Just get back in bed and let me put some salve on those stitches. Otherwise I'll send you to the hospital where you belong."

That seemed to scare him and he got back on the bed. "You don't look much better'n me, Doc. What happened?"

"Car burned up."

"Not your Runabout!"

"Yes. Needed a new one anyway, after seven years. Hated to see it go like that, though."

I finished up there and walked back to the car with Mrs. Andrews. The flames had died down and I saw that Sheriff Lens had arrived in answer to my call. He had a couple of our volunteer firemen with him and they extinguished the rest of the fire. "It sure is a shame," Mrs. Andrews said, looking at it.

"That was meant to cook your hide, Doc," Sheriff Lens said. "Somebody hid a can of gasoline under the hood, with a rag wick leadin' to the spark plugs. It was like a crude bomb."

"I suspected something like that."

"What do you think it means, Sam?" Thad Sloan asked. "You got any enemies around here?"

"The only enemy I've got is the person who killed our unknown man yesterday. And I guess this rules out a ghost, 'cause ghosts don't go around planting bombs in automobiles."

"The bomb had to be planted while we were out behind the house," Sloan said. "That means the killer must have been watching us."

"Maybe," I said, remembering that I'd been there first, before he arrived.

Sheriff Lens looked sadly at the smoking ruin and shook his head. "It was one beauty of a car, Doc."

"April will be heartbroken. Worse than me." The car had always been a special joy to my nurse.

Sheriff Lens led me aside. "I do have one bit o' news for you, Doc. I got a call this mornin' from the State Police. They managed to identify the dead man."

"Who was he?"

"Fellow named George Gifford. He was involved in some frauds during the Florida land boom a few years back. A grand jury indicted him, but the trial was still pending and he was free on bail. The state cops tell me Gifford was a real land promoter, always sellin' non-existent oil wells or gold mines to somebody."

"Interesting. I wonder what brought him to the Bryer place."

"Maybe he saw that newspaper article and decided to buy a real haunted house."

"Or to sell one," I said. The news had started me thinking, and on the way back to the office I asked Sloan for the name of the Boston newsman who'd written the story about Northmont's haunted house.

The news about the car had already reached April. "Oh, Dr. Sam!" she cried as I entered the office. "Are you all right?"

"I'm in better shape than the car, April. Any calls?"

"Nothing urgent."

"Good. I want to phone long distance to Boston."

The reporter's name was Chuck Yeager and I could barely hear him on the poor connection. Yes, he remembered the story about the haunted house, and he remembered Thaddeus Sloan asking him about it. "Sloan came after the article appeared?" I shouted into the mouthpiece. "You didn't see him before?"

"No, no—I never knew Mr. Sloan."

"Who was the former Northmont resident that told you about the house?"

"Well, it was a man named Gifford. He's in real estate."

"And under indictment for land fraud."

"I don't know about that," the reporter said, taken aback. "But I checked out what he told me. The house used to be a stopping place for runaway slaves, and there was a legend connected with a hidden room from which no one ever came out. You know that article caused me lots of grief."

"How's that?"

"The family was trying to sell it, and they claimed my story spoiled the deal. Some people don't like ghosts and other people don't like publicity. They especially don't want a house that's the object of curiosity. That's why the owners had to hire Sloan."

"Sloan works for the owners? Are you sure?"

"Sure I'm sure! They hired him to chase away the ghost or something. He promised to let me know what happened and give me an exclusive on the story. *Has* anything happened?"

"Nothing much," I assured him. "You'll hear about it when it does."

I hung up and decided I had things to do. But first of all I had to get out of my scorched clothing.

Late that afternoon I called Sloan at his hotel and told him I was going back to the Bryer house. "It's time I confronted the ghost," I said. "Want to come along?"

"Of course!"

"Then pick me up, will you? I haven't had time to replace my car."

It was already dark by the time we reached the house, and the weather had turned cold again, bringing a few snow flurries to the brisk February air. I waited while Sloan unlocked the door. "Does Sheriff Lens know you've got that key?" I asked.

"I mentioned it to him, but he didn't ask me for it."

"He should have."

"Then how would we get in?"

That set me thinking about something else, and I didn't answer him right away. Instead I followed him inside and up the stairs to the hidden room. "There has to be a way out of here," I said. "Those legends about the runaway slaves and the room no one ever comes out of must have a basis in fact. No one comes out because there's another exit, and I'm going to find it."

"How?"

I pressed the door jamb and then pushed in the unlocked panel. "I'm going in here and shut the door. Give me a half hour and then open it."

"Can't I come with you?"

"Then who would let me out if I don't find the other exit?"

He agreed with that and I entered the secret room alone. The panel swung shut behind me and I heard the lock click. I was alone in a room without an exit.

The lantern I'd brought along was set on the table, and I went to work on the walls first. They were all solid, but the back wall seemed more solid than the rest. I wondered why, and then I remembered that the fireplace would be somewhere below me. This solid stone wall would be the side of the chimney running up through the center of the house. It was the perfect place for a secret passage, but no amount of tapping yielded a clue. I tried the other walls next with the same result. And the wooden floor was just as solid.

But I'd been over all this before with Sheriff Lens. The one place we hadn't touched was the ceiling. It looked solid, and I climbed up on the table to make sure. It was solid. Even where the paint had chipped away here and there, I found no clue.

I climbed down off the table. It was a dead end.

I sat down on the chair, as the late George Gifford had done, and thought about it. Four walls, no windows, a solid floor and a solid ceiling. There was not even any ventilation when the door was closed. Had they all died like Gifford, here in this room? Was that why it was a room of no return? I could almost imagine the runaway slaves imprisoned here, dying of suffocation or starvation, whichever claimed them first.

No. No, no, no.

I had proved to myself that the killer left this room while it was locked. I couldn't be wrong about that. There was something I wasn't seeing—a door I wasn't finding.

My pocket watch showed that the half hour was up. I pounded on the locked panel to signal Thad Sloan for my release.

Nothing happened.

I pounded again, louder this time. Still nothing.

Thad Sloan. Had I misjudged him completely? Had I delivered myself into the hands of the murderer himself? I remembered him running down to the burning car, remembered that he was working for the owners of the house, remembered that he'd gone downstairs for his camera after the ghost entered this room.

The camera!

I'd been momentarily blinded by the flash when he took that picture. Could someone have sneaked past me, out of the room, in that instant?

I pounded louder, but nobody came.

It was a moment when all my certainties were called into question. If I'd been wrong, I'd put myself in the hands of a killer who'd already tried to burn me to death.

But I wasn't wrong. No one could have passed unseen in the instant that flash went off. Sloan and I were blocking the doorway. And some trace of him would have shown in the photograph itself.

But if Sloan wasn't in league with the killer, what had happened to him?

I stared at the blank solid walls, looking for the way out that didn't exist, growing more frightened by the minute.

And then I thought of something.

I'd been in here for close to 45 minutes, yet the air still seemed fresh and the lantern burned brightly.

The room was not as tightly sealed as it seemed.

I removed the glass chimney from the lantern and the flame immediately began to flicker. It took me only an instant to locate the source of the draft. Air was coming up from between the wooden floorboards.

Yet there was no way of lifting them, no trap door or panel. The floorboards extended beneath the solid wall on the chimney side.

And that stopped me.

How could the floor run *beneath* the wall, into what I was certain was the chimney itself?

I bent to examine the floor once more and noticed some gouges that could have been caused by the point of a knife. A few looked recent, but many seemed quite old. I took a penknife from my pocket and jabbed it into the floorboard that seemed to have the most gouges. Using it as a lever, I tried sliding the single board toward the chimney wall.

It moved. I tried a second and then a third. They all moved.

Each of the gouged floorboards slid away into the chimney wall, and I could only imagine them extending out into the chimney itself. When I'd moved four of the four-inch boards, there was a space in the floor wide enough for me to squeeze through. I dropped down, taking the lantern with me, and found myself in a crawl space above the first-floor ceiling. It was little more than a foot high, and difficult to negotiate, but I managed. Above me, I found that the wooden floorboards could be slid shut as easily as they'd been slid open.

I knew now there must be a way out of here, and I kept crawling—on my stomach—until I found it. Along the outside wall I came at last to an opening with a ladder running down to the first floor. I climbed down and found myself in a small pantry at the back of the house. This was the escape route the runaway slaves had used to avoid being trapped in the upstairs room. This was the exit from the room of no return.

I hurried through the house to the front stairs and went back up. Thad Sloan was sprawled on his back in the hallway, alive but unconscious. He'd been hit on the back of the head.

I straightened up and looked around, trying to see into the dark doorways of the other rooms. "You can come out now, Mrs. Andrews," I said. "I know you're in there."

She stepped into the circle of light from my lantern, holding a shotgun pointed at my chest. "You know too much, Dr. Sam. I'm sorry that I'll have to kill you."

The light danced off her face as she spoke, and I felt a chill of fear run down my spine. This was the real evil of the Bryer house, more dangerous than any ghost. "You've finally come out in the open, Mrs. Andrews."

She raised the shotgun an inch. "I didn't think you'd ever find the way out of that room, but I waited to be sure."

"You rigged that gasoline bomb in my car, didn't you?"

"Yes. I was afraid of your reputation for solving mysteries."

"My reputation almost went down to defeat tonight. It was only luck that I found the exit from that room—luck, and my certainty that there had to be an exit."

"How did you know?"

"Gifford's body had no identification. The pockets were all empty. But if the pockets were empty, what happened to the key he needed to enter the house? We saw him come in, pass us, and go into the secret room. Of course Gifford's body was already in that room, and it was you who passed us, wearing the hat and coat and false beard."

"But the absence of the key only added to the evidence of rigor mortis to convince me it was someone else who walked by us. You needed the beard and hat and coat, probably left over from your husband's carnival days, to disguise your own identity—and then you put them on the dead man to heighten the illusion that it was he who walked by us in the hall. Then you escaped through the floor-boards as I just did."

"George Gifford deserved to die," she said quietly.

"Why? I haven't quite figured out your motive."

"He came here months ago with some sort of land scheme. He wanted to buy this place and our farm too, and sell shares in a vacation resort of some kind. I made the mistake of telling him about the legends and the secret room, and he got a Boston reporter to write it up so's the value of the land would fall. When the Bryer family sent this ghost-hunter fella, Gifford hurried out here and started threatening us. We were dreadfully afraid he would take away the farm Billy and I worked so hard at!"

There was no need telling her that Gifford was more interested in bilking investors than in taking away her farm. It was the fear of losing the farm that had caused George Gifford's death. "I can understand that," I said gently. "But there's something else."

"What's that?" Her face was knotted with suspicion.

"Why did you take such a risk coming here last night in your false beard and coat? Why was it important that we see the dead man alive? We might never have found the body. You led us to it, at great risk to yourself. We might have grabbed you or burst into the secret room before you could escape."

She was confused now. "I—I don't—"

I shook my head sadly. "Out here in the country you don't get to know about things like rigor mortis, do you? You didn't know the police could tell the approximate time of death. You used Gifford's key, taken from his body, to come here in disguise after whispering into the drainpipe. Then you transferred the disguise to the dead man so we'd think he wasn't killed till last night. Tell me now, isn't that true?"

"You think too much, Dr. Sam." She raised the shotgun and I stared down the double barrels, knowing only that I had to keep on talking, keep on making her talk.

"You won't shoot me, Mrs. Andrews. You could plant the fire bomb because that was impersonal. You didn't have to see me die. But you won't shoot me because you haven't killed anyone yet and you're not going to start now. It was your son Billy who killed Gifford, wasn't it?"

The sound that came from her throat was all the answer I needed. "Whispering up a drainpipe to scare people," I hurried on. "Not the sort of thing a mother does, unless her son's told her how to do it. Her son who played here and stumbled on the secret room in his childhood. And found the way out too. It was Billy all the time, wasn't it?

"You didn't stab that man to death with a hunting knife—Billy did! And when Gifford pulled a tiny pistol during the struggle and shot Billy in the leg, it was your idea to pass the wound off as a barn accident. The small bullet, no bigger than a pitchfork's tine, made a clean wound through his leg and then lodged in the table leg. The fact that it didn't even have the power to go through that table leg hinted that it had gone through something else first.

"Of course Gifford's bleeding covered up the blood from Billy's leg, and I suppose Billy wrapped something around his wound till he managed to hobble home. He had too bad a limp to impersonate the dead man last night, so you did it for him. If we believed Gifford wasn't killed till last night, it gave your son a perfect alibi—in case Sloan and I found Gifford's body and Billy needed an alibi."

"My God, Billy stabbed him in self-defense! The man had a gun! Billy only stole the things from his pockets to delay identification."

"Then don't make it any worse for Billy than it already is, Mrs. Andrews. Let the jury decide. Sheriff Lens is at your house right now, arresting him."

It wasn't true but she didn't know that. The shotgun wavered for just an instant, and I took it away from her.

"Terrible case," Dr. Sam Hawthorne concluded, finishing his drink. "I almost lost my life twice over, and I did lose my car! That ghost-hunter fella Thad Sloan got a bump on the head and went back to Boston without his spook. The jury gave Billy the benefit of the doubt and only found him guilty of manslaughter, but the trial was too much for his mother and she died before it was over. And—oh, yes—April went with me the following week to pick out a new car."

He held up the bottle to the light. "Got time for one more small—ah—libation? No? Well, come again soon. Next time I'll tell you about when I went to a medical convention in Boston and found out that impossible crimes can happen in the big city too!"

THE PROBLEM OF
THE BOSTON COMMON

It was a warm summer's afternoon and old Dr. Sam Hawthorne was pouring a bit of sherry at a little table on the back lawn, obviously enjoying the opportunity to be out of doors. "The air is so clear and fresh today," he commented. "When I was young it used to be like this all the time, even in the cities. Sometimes folks ask me if I ever solved an impossible crime in the city, and there were a couple over the years when business of some sort took me away from Northmont. The first one—a terrifying case—happened in Boston, in the late spring of 1928 . . ."

I'd gone to Boston with my nurse April (Dr. Sam continued), to attend a New England medical convention. It was my first opportunity to take a long drive in my new car—a tan Packard Runabout that had replaced my beloved Pierce-Arrow. Though the roads weren't nearly as good as they are today we made the drive in under two hours, and I was quite pleased with the Packard's performance. It was warm enough to ride with the top down, which April especially enjoyed. Some years back I'd taken her with me to an engagement party up at Newburyport and she still talked about the excitement of that auto trip. Now she was equally excited as we drove up to the fancy hotel facing the Boston Common and the uniformed doorman hurried over to help us with our bags.

"Are you here for the medical convention, sir?" he asked.

"That's right. Dr. Sam Hawthorne from Northmont."

"Go right in and register at the desk. The bellman will take your bags and I'll park the car for you."

The first person we encountered in the lobby was gray-haired Dr. Craig Somerset, vice-chairman of the New England Medical Association. "Well, Sam Hawthorne! How've you been? How're things out in the country?"

"Fine, Craig. Good to see you again. This is my nurse, April. I brought her along to see the sights while I'm involved in all those dull meetings."

His look made April blush at once, but Craig Somerset was always the New England gentleman. "Nice to meet you, April. I hope you'll enjoy our city."

"I haven't been to Boston in ten years," she told him. "It's changed so much!"

"It has that," Dr. Somerset agreed. "This hotel wasn't even here ten years ago. There's a great view of the Common from the upper floors. A word of caution, though—don't walk across the Common in the early evening. We've had some trouble here in recent weeks."

"What sort of trouble?" I asked, assuming he spoke for April's benefit. "Someone molesting women?"

"More serious than that, I'm afraid." The lightness had gone out of his voice. "Three people have been murdered there, all in the early evening while it was still daylight. The killer seems to be absolutely invisible."

"I'll bet Dr. Sam could catch him," April said. "He's solved the most impossible-soundin' crimes you ever did hear of, back in Northmont."

"No, no," I protested. "I'm here for the convention, nothing more."

"And I want to talk to you about that," Somerset said. "I'd like you to fill a little gap in our program the day after tomorrow and speak to us on the problems of country medicine."

"I'm no public speaker, Craig."

"But you could do a fine job. It's an area of medicine most of these men know nothing about."

"Let me think about it overnight."

"How were the people killed?" April persisted, her curiosity aroused.

"It seems they were poisoned by a quick-acting substance injected into the skin," Somerset said. "The police are trying not to alarm the public, but I was called in as a consultant on the poison question."

"Back in Northmont I swear Sheriff Lens calls on Dr. Sam as much to solve crimes as the sick folk call on him to get healed."

"You're embarrassing me, April."

I'd completed the registration forms by that time and I could see the bellman waiting to show us up to our rooms. "We'll see you later, Craig."

In the elevator April remarked, "He thinks you brought me 'cause I'm your girl, Dr. Sam." Even the words made her blush.

"We won't worry about what he thinks." April was in her thirties, a few years older than me, and she'd been my nurse since I came to Northmont in 1922. She'd lost some weight since those earlier days but she was still a plain-looking country woman. I'd never thought about her romantically, though I did enjoy her company.

"Are you going to solve the murders for them?"

"No, I'm here to attend a medical convention."

But events were working against me. That evening, shortly after eight, the invisible killer claimed his fourth victim.

Dr. Somerset came to my door around 8:30, looking quite alarmed. "We'd like your help, Sam. There's been another killing."

"On the Common?"

"Yes, right across the street! Can you come down?"

I sighed. "Give me five minutes."

We crossed the street in silence to a spot just inside the Common where the body of a young woman lay sprawled against a tree. The police were busy photographing the scene, using flash powder in the beginning dusk. A burly detective who seemed to be in charge came over to us. "Is this your great sleuth, Dr. Somerset?"

"This is Sam Hawthorne, a physician from Northmont. He's here for the convention, and I understand he's had great success solving seemingly impossible crimes back home. Sam, this is Inspector Darnell."

I could see right away that this was no Sheriff Lens. Darnell was a big-city cop who obviously resented interference, especially from a country doctor. "Do you use a magnifying glass, Doc? Want to crawl around on the ground like Sherlock Holmes?"

"To tell you the truth I want to go back to my room."

Dr. Somerset was exasperated. "Look, Inspector, will it do any harm to tell Sam what you've got so far? He just might come up with an idea."

"Hell, we've tried everything else. What we've got now are four dead bodies. Two men, two women. This last one seems to be the youngest so far. One of the men was a drifter who panhandled in the park. Another was a young lawyer on his way home after working late at the office. Then there was a middle-aged woman out for a stroll in the early evening. And now this one."

"All poisoned?"

The detective nodded. "That's how Dr. Somerset got in on it. We needed a doctor's advice on the kind of poison. The autopsy showed the first three died of minute injections of curare, the South American arrow poison. That fact hasn't been released to the papers yet."

"Curare? On the Boston Common?" It was hard for me to believe. Even in medical school the subject of curare poisoning had been barely touched on. It wasn't something the average doctor ever encountered.

"Curare acts within a few minutes in humans, paralyzing the motor and respiratory muscles," Dr. Somerset explained. "The speed of death seems to depend somewhat on the size of the victim. A thousand-pound ox took forty-five minutes to die from curare in an experiment described in Charles Waterton's book *Wanderings in South America.*"

"You know a lot more about curare than I do," I admitted.

"That's why I was called in by Inspector Darnell." He was staring down at the dead young woman. "It's a particularly insidious poison for the killer to use, because there is no pain and very little warning to the victim. There is some double vision and inability to swallow, then asphyxiation as lung muscles are affected. Admittedly it's a painless death, but it's also one that gives the victim no opportunity to call for help."

"How was the poison administered?" I asked. "With a hypodermic needle?"

Inspector Darnell knelt by the body and turned back the collar of the dead woman's white blouse. A tiny feathered dart protruded from the skin of her neck. "It's so small she might never have felt it—or if she did she thought it was an insect bite. In two of the earlier killings we never found the darts. The victims must have felt them hit and brushed them to the ground as one would a pesky mosquito. In the first killing the dart was snagged in the victim's clothing."

"A dart gun of some sort?" I suggested. "An air pistol might have a fairly long range."

"In South America the natives use blowguns six feet long," Dr. Somerset said.

"I can't picture a murderer using one of those," I said. "He wouldn't stay invisible for long. Have all the killings been at this time of day?"

"All in the evening, but before dark. We doubled the police patrol after the second killing, and filled the Common with plainclothes men after the third one. Now I guess we should close it to pedestrians altogether."

"I'd advise against that," Somerset argued. "The killer would simply move elsewhere, or wait for the Common to reopen. You want to capture him, not scare him off."

"We're finished with our pictures," one of the detectives told Inspector Darnell. "Can we move her?"

"Sure. Take her away."

"Any identification in her purse?" I asked.

"Rita Kolaski, a nurse at Boston Memorial. Probably on her way to work."

The Inspector moved away from us without a goodbye, following the covered stretcher to the street. I turned to Dr. Somerset and said, "I really don't see how I can help here, Craig. Back home in Northmont I'm dealing with people and places I've known for six years. I know the way they live and how they think. I'm out of my element here. Boston people even talk different."

"I'm only asking you to look for something the rest of us might be missing, Sam."

"The killer is a madman, there's no doubt of that. And it's hard enough to catch anyone who's rational."

"Sleep on it, Sam. If you think you can help us in any way, see me after the first session in the morning."

They walked back to the hotel and Somerset asked the doorman to get him a taxi. "Aren't you staying here?" I asked, surprised.

The doorman ran down to the corner blowing his whistle for a cab, and Somerset fished a coin from his pocket for a tip. "No, I'm staying at home. My wife insists on it."

Up in my room I sat for a long time by the window overlooking the Common, watching the lights of the policemen as they searched the area of the killing. After a time I pulled down the shade and went to bed.

Another *Common Killing*, the morning paper screamed in a bold black headline. April read the story over breakfast and I admitted that Somerset had come to my room for help.

"You were over there, Dr. Sam? You saw the body?"

"I've seen a lot of bodies, April."

"But in the city like this—"

"She'd have been just as dead in Northmont."

"You've got time before the first session. Take me over and show me where it happened."

There was no talking her out of it, so we crossed busy Tremont Street and I showed her the spot where Rita Kolaski had died. We strolled farther into the park then, past the burying ground and all the way to the soldiers monument. Then we turned west, walking across Charles Street to the Public Garden that adjoined Boston Common.

"Look at the swan boats!" April exclaimed as we came to an artificial lake. "The people pedal them with their feet!"

She was like a child on Christmas morning, and I took her for a ride around the lake in one of the swan boats, knowing I'd miss the first session of the convention. Afterward we walked along the Arlington Street side, past the Washington monument and on up to Beacon Street. Presently, circling around the north side of the Common, we came to the State House with its golden dome glistening in the morning sun.

"The morning paper says the first body was found over on this side of the Common," April said.

"It doesn't concern me."

"Honestly, sometimes you can be so stubborn!"

"We're here to enjoy the city, not to solve murders. Come on, tonight I'll take you to the movie at the new Metropolitan Theatre. They say it's a regular palace."

We walked back across the Common, which was almost empty for ten o'clock on a weekday morning. The newspaper scare headlines were apparently having their effect. April left me at the hotel to do some shopping and I went upstairs just in time to catch the end of the opening session.

Dr. Somerset caught me on the way out. "I have a noon meeting with the Inspector. Care to sit in?"

"This business really isn't for me, Craig. April and I walked around the Common this morning. It's like a foreign country to me."

"There's one thing about the murders we didn't tell you last night," Somerset said, lowering his voice. "The killer has been in communication with the police."

"Just like Jack the Ripper."

"Exactly. Come along and you can see the letters."

Somerset knew how to pique my curiosity. There was no way I could turn down that invitation. I sat through the second morning session only half attentive, listening to a professor from Harvard Medical School discuss the latest polio research. The subject was much in the news that month, since Al Smith had just asked polio victim Franklin D. Roosevelt to run for governor of New York.

I offered to drive Somerset to police headquarters in my new Packard but he insisted we take a cab. They were easy to get at the stand near the hotel and during the day at least there was no need to tip the doorman. Riding up Tremont, I watched the faces of the people we passed, wondering if one of them might be the killer. In Northmont I would have known their names. Here they were strangers. In Northmont I might have had a half-dozen suspects. Here, the whole city of Boston was suspect.

"This is your city, isn't it, Craig?"

"Always has been. You should set up practice here and you'd learn what medicine is all about."

"Oh, I'm learning that."

"Six years in the country! Are you going to spend your life in Northmont?"

"Maybe."

"We've got three-quarters of a million people in Boston, Sam, and we need more good young doctors like yourself."

"Why?" I asked with a smile. "Is Boston the hub of the universe?"

"It could be. How many cities do you know that have daily steamship service to New York?"

"Maybe your killer comes up from New York by boat every week."

"No," Somerset answered seriously, "he's from this area."

We alighted from the taxi and walked up the steps of Police Headquarters. Off in the distance I could see the pointed tower of the custom house, the city's tallest structure. I had to admit that Boston had a certain charm. It was different from the simple country charm of a place like Northmont, but no less appealing.

Crime here was also different. The letters that Inspector Darnell spread out on the desk before me could only have been described as the work of a madman. *Last evening was the first of the Common killings! There will be more! Cerberus!* And another: *Two dead and more to come! Boston will remember me! Cerberus!* And a third: *Another must die because of what you did! Remember me! Cerberus!*

"And last night's killing?" I asked.

"Nothing yet." Darnell sighed and relit the stub of a dead cigar. "It's probably in the mail."

"These haven't been released to the press?"

The Inspector shook his head. "This sort of maniac thrives on publicity. We're trying to give him as little as possible."

"I agree completely," Somerset said. "The public doesn't even know the killings are connected, though it's bound to come out soon."

"The mayor wants to close the Common completely till this Cerberus is caught, but as you heard last night Dr. Somerset has advised against that."

"You need to capture him, not just send him into his hole."

I was studying the notes, but I could make nothing out of them. "I can't help you on this," I said. "I have no idea who he could be."

"That's not what we want you for," Craig Somerset said. "We want to know how he's doing it."

Inspector Darnell nodded agreement. "*How*, Dr. Hawthorne. We already know *who* he is."

I must admit their words took me aback. "You know who the killer is and you haven't arrested him?"

Craig Somerset smiled. "It's not like Northmont, Sam. In the city a man can hide out for months without ever being found."

"I didn't spend the whole of my life in Northmont, you know. Just the last six years. I know what city life is like."

But did I, really? Had I been away from it too long?

Inspector Darnell cleared his throat. "You must realize, Dr. Hawthorne, that what we tell you must go no further than this room. The lives of innocent people could be endangered if this Cerberus becomes aware that we know his identity."

"It was the curare that led us to him, of course," Craig Somerset explained. "It's not the easiest substance in the world to obtain, and once it was identified as the cause of death I began checking around at various hospitals and research centers in the Boston vicinity. As you may know, Sam, research is under way to find uses for curare as a muscular relaxant. It's a difficult task, because even in tiny doses it seems to cause nausea and a drop in blood pressure. But I found a research lab in Cambridge that's been running tests with the poison. About six months ago a quantity of curare disappeared from their lab, along with a part-time research assistant named George Totter."

"Why would he take it?" I asked.

It was Darnell who answered. "They laid him off. The research was being done under a grant from a local charity. When the money ran out, the research had to stop. Apparently Totter wrote to the city for more funds, but they ignored him. He made the remark to a co-worker that maybe they'd pay attention if a few people in Boston died of curare poisoning. Shortly after that he disappeared, and the lab discovered a vial of the poison was missing too."

"How much was in the vial?" I asked.

"Enough to kill twenty or thirty people. They didn't report it at the time because nobody believed Totter capable of murder. But when Dr. Somerset started checking for missing curare the story came out quickly enough."

"Is there any other possible source of the poison?"

Somerset shook his head. "It's highly unlikely. As you know, curare comes from the bark of various South American trees. The lengthy and laborious process is a deeply guarded secret among certain native families and tribes. Some attempt has been made to duplicate the process in a laboratory, but thus far researchers must depend on the real thing, brought in from the jungles. Our killer must be using a laboratory supply, and this lab in Cambridge is the only one that has it in this whole area."

"All right," I said, "I'll accept this man Totter as your killer. And I'll accept the fact that he could remain hidden in Boston for months. Now tell me why you can't stop him from killing these people."

Darnell ground out the stub of his cigar. "The darts are fired from either an air pistol or a blowgun. If he's using an air pistol of some sort he could probably be fifty feet away and still hit his target."

"Farther than that," I suggested.

"No, not with these hand-made wooden darts. We've tried it. After fifty feet they start wobbling and tumbling in the air. With a blowgun the effective range is only twenty-five feet. And there's our problem. These killings have been in broad daylight, in a park at the very center of a large city. There are no out-of-the-way trails or heavily wooded places in the Common. It's roughly an irregular five-sided park that's only seventeen hundred feet across at its widest point. You can see from one side to the other. There's no place to hide, except behind a tree or statue, and there are people constantly passing through—especially in the early evening hours on spring days like this."

"A blowgun disguised as a cane?" I suggested. "It would take just an instant for the killer to raise it to his mouth."

"Maybe for the first two killings it could have been something like that, but the park was filled with plainclothes police when the third victim got it. Yet nobody saw a thing." He picked up a folder on his desk. "Rita Kolaski, last night's victim, was actually under surveillance at the moment she was killed."

"What?" This was news to Dr. Somerset, and he reacted with surprise.

"I just learned of it this morning. She was suspected of being party to a Volstead Act violation. Two Treasury agents were following her in hopes she'd lead them to her boy friend who's been running boatloads of liquor in from Nova Scotia. She crossed Tremont Street at the corner beyond your hotel and entered the Common at exactly 8:10. There was still plenty of daylight and both agents had a good view of her. They were especially watchful of anyone who came close because they were waiting for a contact with the boy friend."

"But nothing at all unusual happened. No one even glanced at her. Nothing was pointed in her direction. She'd been walking in the park for only about two minutes when her walk became unsteady. She paused to lean against a tree and then collapsed. Our plainclothes men moved in at once, but it was too late. The Treasury agents filed a report with their superior and a copy was sent to me this morning."

"Surely she must have felt the dart hit her," I argued.

Darnell held up one of the feathered wooden shafts, half the length of a matchstick. "Notice there's the point of a common pin embedded in the wood. Don't touch it, there's still poison on it. When the dart hit it would feel like little more than a pinprick. She might have reached up to her hair, but the Treasury men would think nothing of that."

"I can't believe this pin point could carry enough curare to kill a person so quickly," I said. "Besides, what if she'd brushed it off her neck before the poison could act?"

"She didn't, and she died. We don't know how many people this Totter—or Cerberus—might have fired at. Maybe there's a dozen more that brushed the dart off and lived. All we know is that four of them died."

"Just where on the Common were the bodies found?" I asked.

Darnell referred to a large-scale wall map where four red pins dotted the green area of the Common. "The first one, Pete Jadas, was found on the other side of the Common near the State House. He was a former wrestler who'd fallen on hard times and taken to panhandling. Simon Falk, a young lawyer who'd been working late at his Tremont Street office, died right here, about in the middle of the Common. The third victim, a waitress named Minnie Wiser, died here, on the next walkway over from Rita Kolaski."

"Wrestler, lawyer, waitress, nurse," I mused. "I guess there's no pattern there."

"No pattern at all. He kills whoever happens to be handy."

I was staring at the map, but it wasn't telling me a thing. "What about that Cerberus signature?"

"A dog with three heads," Darnell snorted. "Greek mythology!"

"A dog from Hades," Somerset added.

"He must have chosen that name for a reason."

"What is reason to a madman?"

"All right," I said, getting up to leave.

"Where are you going?" Darnell asked.

"For another stroll on the Common."

It was the lunch hour now and the walks were more crowded. On benches people sat and chatted. One man was reading about the latest murder in the newspaper, but nobody seemed terribly concerned. They didn't know about the poisoned darts, or the letters from Cerberus.

I crossed over Charles Street to the Public Garden and went down to watch the swan boats again. That was when I noticed the man with the picnic hamper. He was dark and heavy-set, with unfriendly eyes, but the thing I especially noticed was the way he kept his right hand beneath the lid of the hamper at all times. He might almost have been holding something.

Like the trigger of an air pistol.

Whatever it was, he didn't look the sort who'd come here for a picnic. When he started walking back toward the Common, I followed, wishing that Inspector Darnell had shown me a photograph of George Totter.

The man's right hand was out of the hamper now, but still near its lid. I stayed just a few steps behind, watching that hand. When it moved, when the lid came up again, I ran forward. I needed only the briefest glimpse of the gun within and I slammed my fist down on the lid, pinning his hand inside. He let out a gasp of pain and released his grip on the hamper.

Then, before I knew what was happening, a second man spun me around from the rear. I felt a glancing blow to the side of my head and everything went black.

I must have been unconscious for several minutes.

When I finally came to, with a throbbing headache, I saw a circle of men bending over me. One of them was Inspector Darnell. "What in hell were you trying to do?" he demanded.

"I—"

"That was one of my plainclothes men you jumped on!"

"I'm sorry."

"You should be! If Totter was anywhere around you certainly scared him off!" He helped me to my feet and brushed the dirt from my suitcoat. "In the future you'd better stay off the Common, Dr. Hawthorne. If we need your help we'll call on you."

I mumbled more apologies and moved away, feeling like a fool. I just wasn't used to the ways of big-city police. Back in Northmont, Sheriff Lens could hardly be expected to fill the town square with deputies because he had only a couple of part-time men whom everybody knew. Here in Boston it was different, maybe too different for me. Had six years in Northmont changed my perceptions that much?

I found April in front of the hotel, asking the doorman for directions to Paul Revere's House. "I figured I might as well see some historical sights while I'm here," she said. "Want to come along?"

"I don't think so, April."

I turned my head and she noticed the bruise where the second cop had hit me. "What happened to you?"

"Just a little accident."

"Let me get you upstairs and wash that! Did you fall?"

"I'll tell you about it."

She listened to my tale with much clucking as she bathed the bruise with cold water. "You're not even safe from the police in this city!" she decided.

"Don't be too hard on them, April. It really was my fault."

"Well, a gun in a picnic hamper! What were you to think!"

"They called Inspector Darnell right away. They must have thought they had the killer." I told her what I'd learned.

"Don't they have a picture of this fellow Totter?"

I shook my head. "And only a general sort of description."

I opened my medical bag and found a powder to take for my headache. Then I settled down to relax. Almost at once there was a knock at the door. April opened it and Craig Somerset hurried in. "I just heard what happened. Are you all right?"

"I guess I'll live."

"Good God, they didn't have to slug you with a blackjack!"

"I suppose they thought I was the killer."

"Darnell is sorry about it."

"So am I."

"The afternoon mail brought another letter from George Totter."

I came alert at once. "If it really is Totter. What does it say?"

"Darnell let me make a copy to show you. Mailed just before midnight from the main post office." He held out a page from his notebook and I read: *Four down and more to come! I won't wait so long next time! Cerberus!*

"What is Darnell's plan to do next?" I asked.

"Keep watching the Common. Hope they can spot him the next time. What else is there to do, except close up downtown and throw the city into a panic?"

"There were two Treasury men watching the fourth victim and they didn't see a thing. What makes Darnell think he'll see the killer next time?"

"Sooner or later—"

"Sooner or later! Doesn't Darnell realize he's dealing with an invisible man? Someone like Chesterton's postman who's there but isn't there?"

Craig Somerset pursed his lips. "Could it be one of the plain-clothes men assigned to the park?"

"Stranger things have happened. But if Cerberus—"

"What is it?"

"Just an idea. That map on Darnell's wall showing the location of the killings—do you think we could borrow it? Or make another?"

"What for, Sam?"

"You asked me to speak to the convention on the problems of country medicine. Suppose I speak instead on curare poisoning."

"What? But you're no expert—"

"I think I've learned enough these last two days. Let's see, I'm scheduled to speak late tomorrow afternoon. Is that right?"

"Four o'clock."

"Good. I think I'll spend the morning out at that research lab, brushing up on curare." As an afterthought I said, "And be sure to post the topic of my talk on the schedule in the lobby. I want as large an audience as possible."

As the time for my speech drew near, April was beside herself. "What if the killer learns you're givin' this talk, Dr. Sam? He might pick you for the next victim!"

"Now don't you worry your head, April. I'll be all right."

But she stuck by my side all the way down to the second floor, where a big meeting room had been assigned for my talk. I looked out on the rows of chairs, just now receiving the first arrivals, and felt just the least bit apprehensive. But to be honest I think I was more afraid of speaking in public than of the murderer. Directly behind me the large curtained windows looked out on the Common across Tremont Street.

"He could be down there in the park, watchin' us through binoculars right this minute!" April said, obviously worried.

"I think he's a lot closer than that," I said, watching the doctors file in. I was surprised to see Inspector Darnell take up a position near the door. Somerset had obviously alerted him to the subject of my talk, in order to obtain the map I needed.

Exactly at four o'clock, with the room more than three-quarters full, Craig Somerset strode to the podium. "Are you ready, Sam?"

"Ready as I'll ever be."

He turned to the audience and spoke loudly so that his voice would carry through the room. "Gentlemen—and I note a few ladies with us today as well—our speaker this afternoon is Dr. Sam Hawthorne, a relatively young man who has spent his six years as a physician in caring for the ills of the people of Northmont, about two hours' drive from here. Yes, Sam Hawthorne is a country doctor—the backbone of our medical practice. He was planning to speak to us today on the problems of medical practice in a small town, but as most of you know he's chosen to change his topic. In recent weeks four persons have died on the Common across the street from this hotel. Only today the police admitted to the press that all four died of curare poisoning. And it is that poisoning—so rarely encountered in general practice—which is the subject of Sam Hawthorne's talk."

When he'd completed the introduction I stepped to the podium and began to read from my notes, covering a history of curare and the early experiments by

Charles Waterton in Dutch Guiana. Then I touched on the Boston-area experiments before getting to my main point.

"You see behind me, on my left, a large-scale map of downtown Boston. The points where the four curare victims died are clearly marked. But as you know from my previous remarks, curare does not kill instantly. You might say, the police have said, that a poison which kills within a few minutes is instant enough. But the truth is that a person can walk all the way across the Common in a few minutes. I've done it.

"The idea occurred to me that the invisible killer the police are seeking might not be roaming the park seeking out victims at all. His poisoned darts might all be fired from one location, and it might have been the dying victims who moved rather than the killer. Looking at this map, is such a possibility feasible?"

There was a stir of interest from the audience and I saw Inspector Darnell straighten up in the back row. I glanced over at April and hurried on. "We've already seen that the speed with which curare kills depends very much on the size and weight of the victim. An average person lives only a few minutes. A thousand-pound ox lives forty-five minutes. I checked the weights of the four victims this morning, but even without knowing them I could make certain guesses.

"The first victim, a drifter who'd been a wrestler, was found on the far side of the Common near the State House. My guess was that a former wrestler might be the heaviest of the victims—since the others were a young lawyer and two women. In that I was correct. He weighed the most, and therefore—assuming the curare doses to be about equal—would have taken the longest to die."

I could see I had them now. The doctors were hanging on every word, and all my early nervousness had vanished. "The young lawyer was found in the middle of the Common, and the two women closer to this side. The latest victim, being the smallest of the four, died the quickest. She was actually observed entering the Common from Tremont Street, just down at the corner here. The lawyer, we know, was coming from his office on Tremont Street. The waitress and the ex-wrestler both could have entered the Common from Tremont as well.

"I submit to you, Inspector Darnell, and to my distinguished audience, that the invisible killer is not in the Common at all, but right here on Tremont, hitting his victims *as they enter the park.*"

My wind-up after that was anti-climactic. I couldn't give them the name of the murderer, so I ended with a few generalities about police work in poisoning cases, and then stepped back while Dr. Somerset said a few words of thanks.

Doctors from the audience were grouped around me at the end, asking questions, but after a few pleasantries I made my escape.

"You were great, Dr. Sam," April assured me. "I can see Inspector Darnell coming our way."

"Come on, let's get out of here."

"Dr. Hawthorne!" Darnell called. "Let me have a word with you! I'm sorry about yesterday."

"That's all right."

"That was a very interesting theory. You seemed to be saying that the killer might be someone right around here. But how—"

"I have to go now." I broke away and headed for the elevator. If my idea was right, I could be in great danger.

Craig Somerset was hurrying after me too, but I jumped between the closing doors of the elevator and left him standing there with April and the Inspector. I knew it would be only a few moments before they caught the next elevator and came after me.

Downstairs I hurried across the lobby and out into Tremont Street. "Get me a cab, will you?" I asked the doorman.

"Certainly, sir."

He stepped behind me and blew his whistle and I felt the pinprick of a bite on my neck.

That was when I moved, as fast as I could, plucking the tiny dart from my skin and throwing myself on the uniformed doorman. Darnell and April and Somerset came through the revolving door as I wrestled the doorman to the sidewalk.

"Here's your killer!" I shouted. "Mr. George Totter, in person! April, there's a hypodermic needle in my right-hand pocket with an antidote for curare poisoning. I need it—hurry!"

What with all the police business and newspaper interviews after that, it wasn't till the drive back to Northmont the next afternoon that April and I had any time alone. "What a foolish thing to do!" she berated me. "Setting yourself up as a target for that madman!"

"Someone had to do it, April. The police were content to wait for the next victim, but I wasn't. I figured that the curare speech, advertised in the lobby, would attract his attention. But I probably wouldn't have risked it if that research lab hadn't given me a hypodermic full of an antidote they've been testing."

"Who would have thought of the doorman!"

"Once I established the victims had probably entered the Common from the Tremont Street side I started looking for somebody who was stationed there regularly. The doorman, whistling for taxis—sometimes even going up to the corner to get them—was in a perfect position to fire those darts at people crossing the street to enter the park. People saw him put something to his mouth and blow, but it was such an innocent gesture for him that they never noticed it. His whistle—a long slender one similar to the ones London bobbies use—had a tube like a short pea shooter taped to it. The tiny darts would be inaccurate at more than five or ten feet, but the point was he could get quite close to his victims before firing. He chose people heading for the Common so they'd die there. In his confession he said he'd fired more than a dozen darts in all, but some missed and the others were brushed off by the victims before the poison could take effect."

"Dr. Sam, you purposely ran ahead of us all in the hotel yesterday. You knew he was going to try for you and you didn't want us in danger."

"I was sure he would try. All the killings were in the early evening, so I figured it was the doorman who came on duty in the late afternoon. He knew I was the curare speaker and I thought I'd offer him a tempting target."

"You were that sure it was the doorman?"

"People like that want to be caught, April. Totter was telling the police who he was in those notes he sent, only they didn't understand him. Cerberus was a three-headed dog from Hades all right—he guarded the entrance! The word is sometimes used to signify a watchful guard or doorkeeper."

"You did pretty good in the big city, Dr. Sam."

"But it's good to be home."

"And that's how I caught the Boston Common killer," Dr. Sam Hawthorne concluded. "He was invisible only because nobody noticed him. But this sherry is invisible because the bottle is empty! Come inside and I'll give you another small—ah—libation. And if you have time I'll tell you about what I found back in Northmont that summer—an impossible murder right in our general store."

THE PROBLEM OF
THE GENERAL STORE

"Well, it's good to see you again," Dr. Sam Hawthorne said, supporting himself with his cane as he reached for the sherry bottle. "Would you like some of this, or maybe something a wee bit stronger? Let's see, I promised to tell you about the murder at our general store this time, didn't I? That was in the summer of 1928. The summer had started warmer than usual, with temperatures well into the eighties during June. The biggest news that month was Amelia Earhart's flying the Atlantic. She was the first woman to do it, and my nurse April took a special pleasure in that fact—"

"See, Dr. Sam!" April said, holding up the morning newspaper with the Earhart story. "I told you women can do anything that men can!"

"She wasn't alone like Lindbergh," I pointed out.

April merely shook her head. "You men! I think Maggie Murphy is right about you!"

"Maggie Murphy again! That's all I've been hearing lately."

Maggie Murphy was a woman of around 40 who'd settled in Northmont late the previous year. In younger days she'd campaigned for passage of the women's suffrage amendment. Now she was annoying the menfolk of our town with talk of women taking jobs and earning money just like men. It was a pretty radical idea for 1928.

Maggie generally held forth at one of Northmont's two general stores—the big one opposite the town square owned by Max Harkner. It was a popular place for young and old, with its great wheels of cheese, barrels of flour, and jars of taffy kisses. Not as cozy as the old days, since he'd knocked out the wall and expanded into John Clane's hardware store, but still it was as close as we came to a town meetin' place. There was even a cracker barrel near the pot-bellied stove, though Max had taken away the chairs since Maggie Murphy started hanging around. Not that it discouraged her, though.

61

Maggie was a handsome woman at an age when many of the farm wives, having given birth to a half-dozen children and toiled long hours in the kitchen and vegetable garden, were showing their years and then some. Maybe it was her attraction to men that kept them from running her out of town when she got started with her speeches. Maybe they secretly admired her, for all of their sputtering and sarcasm.

The little real-estate office Maggie had opened was right next door to Max's general store, on the opposite side from where he'd expanded. Some thought he should go the other way as well, and buy her out, but Max just couldn't afford that. And in truth I think he was sort of fond of her, for all her carryings-on. There are some men who spend their lives searching for a woman to dominate them, and Max Harkner was that sort. His wife Amelia filled the bill pretty well, but she lacked the physical attractiveness of Maggie Murphy.

As it happened, a few hours after my exchange with April I stopped in the general store to purchase some washers for a faucet in my apartment. Maggie was there, holding forth by the cracker barrel. The absence of the usual chairs didn't seem to bother her in the least. "What do you think about women in politics?" she was asking old John Clane. Since he sold his hardware store to Max for expansion he'd taken to hanging around the general store. Retirement was not going easily for him, and he looked tired.

"In politics?" he repeated, rubbing at his bristly gray mustache. "You mean like women mayors and governors?"

"That's right," she said. "And senators and presidents too! Now that we've got the vote it's the next logical step."

"Don't know about that," he grumbled, turning away. He didn't have much use for Maggie Murphy. "What do you think, Max?"

Max Harkner was busy arranging a new display of shotguns on the rack behind the counter. He took time out to reply, "Don't make no matter to me what they do. Long as they cook my meals an' raise my children, women can run for anything they like."

Maggie leaned back against the side of the big cracker barrel. "None of us might live to see it, but the day is coming when some men will do the cooking and raise the kids while the women go out to work."

This statement brought healthy guffaws from the assembled males, and she turned to me for support. "What do you say, Sam?"

"I don't meddle in those things," I told her. "Max, when you get a chance could you find me some washers this size?"

He came away from the shotguns and peered through his thick glasses at the object in my hand. "Got those around here somewheres," he said, and went in search of them, pausing to turn on the exhaust fan to clear away some of the cigar smoke.

"You should have," Clane spoke up. "You bought up my stock when you tore down the wall."

After several minutes of searching Max found the washers and I paid him. Maggie fell into step beside me as I left the store. "You didn't have much to say on my side, Sam."

"Look, Maggie, you've won April over. Don't you think that's enough?"

"I'll win that Max over too."

"You already have. But with a wife like Amelia I guess he's afraid to do anything about it."

She chuckled. "Can you imagine anyone being married to Amelia Harkner?"

I knew what she meant. Amelia was something of a shrew. "Some people probably couldn't imagine anyone being married to Maggie Murphy," I said in jest.

"One man could." She was suddenly serious. "I was married once, Sam. Back in New York, during the war. He was killed in France three weeks before the armistice."

"I'm sorry."

"You needn't be. Better men than he were killed in the war."

"You've never remarried?"

She shrugged. "There was always so much to do, getting the vote for women, and now trying to get them decent jobs."

"You can't do much stuck out here in Northmont."

"It's only temporary. If I can build my real-estate business into something profitable I'd like to move to Boston."

We'd reached my office and I said goodbye. It was the longest conversation I'd ever had with Maggie Murphy and it had been a pleasant one.

I hadn't thought old John Clane was looking all that well at the general store and I was right. He died of a heart attack at ten o'clock that night. His wife Milly phoned me and I hurried over, but there was nothing I could do.

"He's gone, Milly," I said.

She was a pleasant woman in her early sixties, younger than John, and his death had unnerved her. "He seemed all right after dinner, Dr. Sam. He went out for a walk and he stopped at Phil Sage's house. He came back just a while ago. I could see that he was flushed. He sat in that chair, complaining of a pain in his chest, and then he just died there." Her voice broke at the end and I tried to comfort her.

"Can I call the children for you, Milly?"

She stood up, shaking off the tears. "No, that's for me to do." She went to the telephone and then paused, as if remembering. "We had a good life together, but he was never happy a single day since his retirement. Working was everything to him, Dr. Sam."

I looked down at the figure in the chair. I'd never known John Clane well. He was only someone to tend my needs when I visited his hardware store. I wished now I'd had time for a conversation with him, like the one I'd had earlier with Maggie Murphy. "You call the children, Milly. I'll wait with you till they get here."

It was close to midnight when I got back to my apartment, and I found a strange greeting awaiting me. A tall man stepped from the shadows as I fitted my key into the door and said, "Don't be frightened, Dr. Sam. It's only me—Frank Bench."

"Oh—Frank! You did startle me."

"I've been waiting here for close to two hours." Frank was a slim boyish man in his early forties who'd held a number of odd jobs around town. Most recently he'd been working for Max at the general store, but I knew something had caused him to leave a couple of weeks earlier. I hadn't even realized he was still around town.

"Didn't I hear you'd moved away, Frank?"

"I did, but just over to Shinn Corners. I gotta talk to you, Doc."

I sighed. There'd be no sleep for a while tonight. "Come on in. I've been over to the Clane house. Old John died of a heart attack tonight."

"He did? Terribly sorry to hear that. I always liked him." He followed me inside and sat down. I noticed for the first time that his hands were trembling.

"Can I get you a drink or something, Frank?"

"No—no, thanks, Doc. I just wanted to talk. You probably heard that I lost my job at the store."

"I noticed you weren't around. But I didn't hear anything else."

"Max fired me. He was jealous of my attentions to his wife."

"Amelia?" The very thought of it floored me. "But surely there was nothing between you?"

"There was something, Doc, and that's why I had to see you. Amelia's forty-four years old. Gettin' pregnant at her age could be dangerous—"

"Pregnant?"

He hung his head. "I was afraid she might be. I couldn't stay away without knowing. You bein' her doctor, I figured you'd know as soon as anyone."

The news had stunned me so that I was speechless for a moment. When I recovered I said, "As far as I know Amelia's not pregnant, Frank. But you give me your address in Shinn Corners. If anything like that happens, I'll know where to reach you."

He hesitated. "You won't tell Max, will you? God, he'd come after me with a shotgun!"

"I won't tell Max. I won't tell anyone."

"Thanks, Doc. Maybe I'll take that drink now."

I poured him a stiff shot of Scotch and had one myself. The idea of Frank Bench and Amelia Harkner was still more than I could fathom. But I never was much good at understanding affairs of the heart.

Frank gave me his address and I watched him walk out to where his old jalopy was parked across the street. It was after midnight, but at last I was going to get some sleep.

Then the telephone rang. As I went to answer it my mind was running through the possibilities—a summer fever, an early delivery for Mrs. Johnson, an automobile accident—

"Dr. Hawthorne here."

"Sam, this is Sheriff Lens. Can you come down to the Harkner general store right away?"

"What's up, Sheriff?"

"Max has been murdered. An' it looks like that gal Maggie Murphy done it."

The place was ablaze with lights when I arrived. Sheriff Lens was inside and one of his new deputies was guarding the door, keeping out the small handful of curious townspeople who'd been attracted by all this post-midnight activity. I walked in and stopped dead. Max Harkner was sprawled on his back, the center of his chest bloody and tattered.

"What hit him?" I asked Sheriff Lens.

"Shotgun blast. From about six feet away, I'd judge, by the size of the pattern."

The shotgun itself lay on the floor nearby. It was a big double-barreled one from the rack behind the counter and I could see the price tag still on its trigger guard. Next my eyes went to a chair where Maggie Murphy sat holding the side of her head.

"You're hurt," I said, going to her.

"I fell and hit my head."

I took her hand away and saw some matted blood in her hairline. After washing it off I could see that the wound was not serious, but there was a bruised area around it. "You must have one heck of a headache."

She tried to smile. "It doesn't feel too good. I was unconscious for a couple of hours."

"You should be x-rayed at the hospital for a possible concussion. Are there any feelings of nausea or drowsiness?"

"I–I don't think so."

I glanced over at Max's body. Sheriff Lens had finally had the decency to cover it with a couple of burlap sacks. "Suppose you tell me what happened here," I asked Maggie.

"That's just the trouble–I don't know! I was working late–till around nine thirty–and as I closed my office I saw that Max was just closing up too. You know he's open late on these summer evenings. I came in to buy some cigarettes and I tripped over something–that sack of potatoes, I think. My head hit the cracker barrel and that's the last thing I knew."

"Who was here with you?"

"No one–just Max and me. That's why he was closing–because there were no customers."

I glanced at Sheriff Lens. "All right, what happened when you came to?" I asked her.

"It was much later, nearly midnight by the clock. Max was lying there just like that with the shotgun next to him. I thought he'd killed himself."

"Any chance of that?" I asked Lens.

"No chance. Even if he'd fired the shotgun with his toe–which he didn't– the barrel couldn't have been six feet away from his chest. It was murder, no doubt about it."

"Then someone entered the store while you were unconscious, took the shotgun from the rack, loaded it, and killed him."

"That's what I told the sheriff, but he doesn't believe me."

"I don't believe her for a good an' simple reason, Doc. If that's what happened, where'd the killer go? When we got here, every door an' window in the place was locked an' bolted–from the inside!"

I suppose I shouldn't have been surprised by that news. It seemed just about every crime Northmont had in those days involved an impossibility of one sort or another. "So that's why you phoned me," I said. "It's another locked-room murder."

Sheriff Lens shook his head in disgust. "Ain't no such thing, Doc, and don't you try to make it one! I called you 'cause the lady was bleedin' from that head cut. There's no locked room because the killer was right here when we arrived."

Maggie nodded sadly. "Max bolted the front door after he let me in for my cigarettes. When I came to and found him dead I phoned the sheriff. I was still dazed, so I just sat and waited. It never occurred to me that the door was still bolted from the inside. If I'd killed him do you think I'd be dumb enough to leave it like that?"

I went over to examine the door. It had a key lock with a separate bolt above it, for when Max was working around inside after hours. I checked the storeroom and the back door beyond it. This had a wooden bar bolt that went across the entire width of the door, and it was locked besides. No one had left that way. I glanced at the two storeroom windows but they were both locked and barred on the inside. The only windows out front were the big display ones on either side of the front door. There was the small exhaust fan halfway up the side wall, but I could see the blades were too close for a double-barreled shotgun to pass through between them, to say nothing of a flesh-and-blood murderer. I glanced up at the high wooden ceiling, painted black, but there was no skylight or opening.

"How about the cellar?" I suggested.

"We checked it first thing. Nobody down there. The coal chute is bolted shut from the inside. We checked everything and even looked inside the furnace. There's nobody here. Nobody except Miss Murphy and the dead man."

"There must be a dozen other hiding places in a place this big."

"Yeah? Find one," he challenged me.

I decided to change the subject. "May I examine the shotgun?"

"Sure. We took a couple of prints off it but near as I can tell with my magnifying glass they belong to Max."

I nodded. "He just put these guns on the rack today. I saw him handling them." I broke open the shotgun and saw that both barrels were loaded but only one had been fired. "Where's Amelia? Have you notified her?"

"Can't find her," he answered.

"What?"

"Can't find her. She's not at home."

"Isn't that odd?"

"Maybe, maybe not. She could be away visiting."

I admitted I hadn't seen her in a few days. "But I think we'd have heard if she was away."

"Oh, she'll turn up. Meantime, my business is with the living. Come along, Miss Murphy."

"Where are you taking her?"

Sheriff Lens stared me down. "Over to the hospital for that x-ray you suggested. Then I'm booking her for murder."

I was in the office early the following morning, but not early enough to beat April there. "Dr. Sam, did you hear what happened to Maggie Murphy?"

"I heard. I was there, April."

"I know it's terrible about Max Harkner being killed, but they can't really believe she did it. This is some sort of a trick to frame her."

"April, I doubt if anyone would kill Max just to frame Maggie Murphy for the crime. Murder needs a better motive than that."

"Then what do they say was Maggie's motive?"

"That's a good question." And it was one I decided to pursue.

I walked over to the jail and stopped at the sheriff's office. I had a dozen questions for him, starting with Maggie's head injury, but I was forestalled by the presence of Max's widow, Amelia. She sat straight as a ramrod on the chair opposite the sheriff's desk, her thin face tearless but unsmiling. Trying to picture her with Frank Bench was still more than my imagination could handle.

"Hello, Amelia," I said. "Terrible thing about Max. I'm sorry."

She nodded stiffly. "I've known all along that Murphy woman was no good."

"She hasn't been convicted yet," I pointed out. "Nor even indicted."

"But there's no one else who could have killed him!"

Sheriff Lens cleared his throat. "It certainly seems not, Mrs. Harkner. But we're investigatin' all angles."

I glanced at him. "Mind if I ask Amelia a question, Sheriff?"

"Go ahead."

"Amelia, where were you last night at the time of the killing?"

"I don't rightly know what time the killing was."

I looked at Sheriff Lens again but all I got was a shrug. "No one's come forward who heard the shot, Doc. The coroner figures he died somewhere between nine thirty and eleven thirty, but that's a pretty long time."

"Look at it this way," I suggested. "Maggie came in around nine thirty, tripped, and hit her head. Max must have been shot soon afterward or he'd have done something to revive her."

"That's if you believe her story, Doc. I don't. This business of trippin' over a potato sack just don't hold water."

"Anyway, Amelia, where were you? The sheriff tried to reach you shortly after midnight."

"I was right at home. When Max didn't come I went to bed. I can sleep through anything when I first go to sleep, and I never heard the phone. He called back around three and finally roused me."

"Any idea why Maggie Murphy would want to kill your husband?"

"He probably disagreed with her crazy ideas. That would be enough for a woman like her."

I turned back to Lens. "Sheriff, how is Maggie's head? Did the x-rays show a concussion?"

"They couldn't tell for sure. She's supposed to take it easy for a few days. That won't be hard, in a cell upstairs."

"May I see her?"

"I don't know, Doc." He glanced at Amelia Harkner. "Can't give her any special treatment, you know."

"She should be examined by a doctor. That's not special treatment."

"Oh, all right. Here, I'll get my keys and take you up there."

As I followed him up the narrow stairs to the upper cell block, I asked, "What do you think of Amelia Harkner?"

"God, that woman's cold as a fish. She hasn't showed a bit of emotion about poor Max."

"Maybe she had a gentleman friend on the side," I suggested.

"Her? You kiddin' me, Doc?"

"Stranger things have happened."

Maggie Murphy was sitting in her cell writing a letter. "It's to my mother," she said. "I wanted her to hear it from me, to know that I'm all right."

"Where is your mother?"

"Home. Pittsburgh, or at least a little farm just outside of Pittsburgh. That's where I came from. I haven't been back there in years."

I sat down on her bunk as Sheriff Lens locked the cell door behind me. "You got ten minutes, Doc," he called out as he went back downstairs.

"You're in big trouble, Maggie," I told her.

"I know."

"Every door and window in that place was locked from the inside. Max might have unlocked a door to admit his killer, but then how did the killer escape?"

"I wish I could tell you, Sam, but I can't. It's as much a mystery to me as to everyone else."

"Suppose you start by telling me the truth about what happened to you."

"What?"

"I don't see how you could have tripped and hit your head on that cracker barrel in exactly the way you described. If you had, the wound would have been on the left side of your head instead of the right."

She looked away, staring at the wall for a moment. Then she turned back to me. "It was like I said, except that I went over backwards. That's why I hit my left side instead of my right."

"You were backing up when you fell?"

"Yes."

Then suddenly I knew what had happened. "You were backing away from Max. He was coming at you."

She nodded, head down. "He was coming right at me. I don't know what got into him, what he intended to do. He reached out and grabbed at me. I jumped back out of reach and my foot got caught on the potato sack. I hit my head just like I said, and that's the last thing I know."

I sat and thought about it. Then, very quietly, I said, "Maggie, if he was trying to attack you and you shot him, that's a defense any jury could understand."

"*I didn't shoot him!*"

"All right. Calm down. I believe you, Maggie."

"You don't sound as if you do!"

"I'm sorry. Look, do you remember anything at all during the time you were unconscious? Any sound, any voices?"

"No. Nothing."

"Had Max ever made advances before?"

"Not serious ones. He'd say things sometimes, just kidding around. I suppose when I came there last night he thought I wanted more than kidding."

"Did you ever hear any talk about Max's wife and another man?"

"Amelia? You must be joking!"

"Maybe." I got to my feet. "I think I hear the sheriff. My time must be up."

"Can you help me, Sam?"

"I'll try, Maggie."

But I went out of there without any idea as to how.

Northmont's only funeral parlor was busy that afternoon as both Max Harkner and John Clane were being prepared for showing. Will Watson, the undertaker, had always been philosophical about death. "Funny thing," he said to me, "these two men had stores next to each other for all these years, and now they both die on the same night."

"A coincidence," I told him. "Unless you think there was something funny about Clane's death."

"No, no—it was a heart attack just like you said on the death certificate, Doc. A good way to go, I suppose, if you have to go at all."

"I suppose." I was remembering the time I'd spent at the Clane house, at the very time of Max's murder, while Frank Bench claimed to have been waiting for me at my apartment. There was no one's word but his that he'd been there.

". . . fixed them both up lookin' real natural," Will Watson rambled on. "That was a terrible chest wound!"

"Shotguns do that," I answered absently. I was still thinking about Bench. Could he have murdered Max so Amelia would be free?

"As for John, except for a little shoulder bruise where he fell, there wasn't a mark on him."

"Is either of the widows here yet?" I asked Watson suddenly.

"Amelia Harkner is upstairs."

I went up to find her sitting alone in the family room. Max hadn't had much in the way of relatives. "Hello again, Amelia."

"Hello, Dr. Hawthorne."

"It used to be Sam."

"I'm not myself today."

"I know, and you must forgive my intruding on your grief with more questions. But I know you're anxious to find Max's killer."

"Max's killer is already in jail."

"Maybe. Tell me, Amelia, have you seen anything of Frank Bench lately?"

"Frank?" She grew a bit pale at my question. "No—why do you ask?"

"He came to me late last night with a crazy story. He asked me if you were pregnant."

She closed her eyes and swayed a bit, and I hurried to steady her. "I'm sorry, Amelia, but I have to know the truth."

"I'm not pregnant," she said, her voice low.

"Did Frank have a motive for killing Max?"

"Frank wouldn't hurt a fly."

"All right," I said. I was getting nowhere with her. "I'll see you later, Amelia."

The outer rooms were already filling with mourners. I recognized Phil Sage, the local gunsmith, and his wife at the door. Some of the other regulars from Max's store were drifting in too. I decided if they were here I should go back to the store itself.

I walked over to the town square and strolled around the building, noting the boxes and barrels piled in the side alley. The door of Maggie's real-estate office on the other side carried a simple *Closed* sign. Outside Max's store a deputy stood guard.

I got him to let me in and looked around once more. Nothing had changed. I sat in a chair and stared at the ceiling, waiting for some notion to hit me.

And then I saw something I hadn't noticed before.

I found a stepladder and climbed up for a closer look. The black-painted wood of the ceiling seemed splintered in one area, and there were tiny holes like worm holes covering the same area. The rest of the ceiling was untouched. I got out my jackknife and probed in one of the holes.

"What you doin' up there, Doc?" a voice asked from below. I looked down to see Sheriff Lens standing there.

"Checking the ceiling for worm holes," I said.

"Deputy called to tell me he let you in."

"That was very efficient of him."

I climbed down the ladder and faced him. He was looking just a bit smug as he said, "Thought you'd want to know I solved the case."

"You said you solved it last night when you arrested Maggie Murphy."

He dismissed that with a wave of his hand. "No, the Murphy woman didn't kill Max. I know who did do it, though, and for once I've solved a locked-room mystery ahead of you, Doc!"

"Let's hear it, Sheriff."

"I've got a neighbor of the Harkners who saw Amelia leave the house alone before midnight. She wasn't sleepin' at all when I phoned. She wasn't there."

"Where was she?"

"Hiding. Hiding right here in this store after killin' her husband."

"But you said you searched the place," I protested.

"Didn't look in one hidin' place. It was so obvious, right here in front of us, that I never thought of it."

"Where's that?"

He pointed it out dramatically. "Right there, Doc, in the cracker barrel! Amelia Harkner killed her husband an' hid in the cracker barrel."

"A clever idea, Sheriff. But you're trying to tell me that Amelia killed Max, climbed into that barrel, somehow buried herself in crackers, and remained absolutely motionless for several hours. You and your deputies were here, I was here. The slightest rustle of those crackers would have attracted our attention. And how could she have left the store afterward, with a deputy guarding the door? She'd never risk something like that when she could simply leave the scene before Maggie came to and found the body. After all, Maggie would still have been a likely suspect even if the store wasn't locked."

Sheriff Lens was downcast. "Then the thing's impossible, Doc."

"Maybe not," I said. "Come on, let's go for a walk."

I led him down one of the side streets, away from the center of town. We'd walked about ten minutes when I paused before a house and glanced in both directions. "I'm going to look around here, maybe enter that garage without permission. You'd best look the other way, Sheriff."

"But what—?"

"No questions now."

Once in a while you get lucky. I found what I was looking for almost at once, hidden among the rakes and garden tools at the back of the garage. I took it out and showed it to Lens. "What does it mean?" he asked.

"I'll explain later. Right now we're going to the funeral parlor."

It was crowded now, and Sheriff Lens, preceding me, headed for the room where Max Harkner's body was on view. "Not there," I said. "The other room."

Milly Clane rose to greet us, and Lens-muttered a few words of sympathy. "So good of you both to come," she said.

"Milly, there's something I have to tell you," I said. "Could we talk in private?"

She glanced from Lens to me. "Certainly. There's a room for the family."

When we were away from the mourners I came right to the point. "Milly, we've just come from your house. I found the shotgun in your garage."

"What?"

"The gun that killed Max Harkner, Milly."

"Are you accusing me of killing him?"

"No, but I'm accusing your husband. It was John who killed Max, and the excitement of it brought on his heart attack."

Sheriff Lens was taken by surprise. "Doc, are you telling me a dead man killed Max?"

"He wasn't dead when he pulled that trigger, Sheriff. He was very much alive. You told me, Milly, that he went out for a walk after dinner, that he was going to stop at Phil Sage's house—Phil Sage, the gunsmith. He picked up a shotgun there, didn't he? Maybe one that Sage was repairing for him, and he bought some shells too. I don't think he intended to use it on Max—not then, at least. But he was passing the store and he saw Max, the man who'd bought him out and put him into retirement, the man who had trouble finding something as simple as washers in his big new store. Moreover, he saw Max in the act of attacking a woman, Maggie Murphy. He must have tried to go to her aid, more out of a hatred for Max than any love of Maggie."

"But what about the shotgun we found inside the store?" Sheriff Lens wanted to know.

"John Clane probably shouted at Max through that locked front door. Max saw Clane with a shotgun and loaded one of his own in self-defense. He wouldn't open the door, but that didn't stop Clane. He remembered the exhaust fan and went around to the side alley. He stood on one of the boxes there, stuck the barrel of his shotgun between the blades of the fan, and fired at Max, hitting him in the chest. Max's finger pulled his trigger in a reflex action, and his load of buckshot hit the wooden ceiling. I found the pellets embedded there this afternoon. One trouble with shotguns is there's no way of checking pellets for identifying marks. We saw the gun near the body, noticed it had been fired, and assumed it was the murder weapon. That meant the killer had to have been inside the store, but in truth he never was."

"Wait a minute now, Doc," the sheriff protested. "I saw you examine that exhaust fan myself, an' the barrel of the shotgun wouldn't fit between those blades."

"A double-barreled shotgun is so called to distinguish it from the single-barreled variety. Max's double-barrel wouldn't fit, but John Clane's single-barrel did."

Through all of this Milly Clane had remained silent. Now she spoke. "You've built up a theoretical case against John, but where's your proof?"

"The shotgun I found in your garage, Milly. Once I dug that buckshot out of the store's ceiling I knew there had to be a second gun. Your house is only a ten-minute walk from Max's store, so John could easily have reached home by ten o'clock when he suffered his fatal heart attack, but there wouldn't have been time for him to get rid of the shotgun. I thought we'd find it at your place."

"I need more than that to accept him as a murderer."

"I'm sorry, Milly. I'm just as sorry as I can be. But if you want more, I can give you more. When I was here earlier today, Will Watson mentioned something about a bruised shoulder being the only mark on John's body. We all know you can get a slightly bruised shoulder from the recoil of a shotgun. The undertaker thought the bruise was from John's falling, but you told me he died sitting in his chair."

She only nodded. And turned away.

"I'm convinced," Sheriff Lens said. "The case is closed. But tell me one thing more—if Amelia wasn't at the store killing her husband, where in hell was she?"

"I imagine she was meeting her lover," I said. "Frank Bench left my house shortly after midnight. She must have been waiting somewhere for him, not knowing he'd gone to see me."

"So that was the end of it," Dr. Sam Hawthorne concluded. "But surely you've time for another—ah—small libation before you depart. No? Well, come by next time and I'll have another story for you—about what happened the time I was called to jury duty at the old courthouse."

THE PROBLEM OF
THE COURTHOUSE GARGOYLE

"**I** promised to tell you about the time I was called to jury duty down at the old courthouse," Dr. Sam Hawthorne said, as he poured two glasses of white wine. "It was in September of 1928, when the presidential race between Hoover and Al Smith was really heatin' up, that I received my first and only summons to jury duty in Northmont. Ordinarily I wouldn't have been chosen for a criminal case, since everyone in town knew of my long friendship with Sheriff Lens and my interest in solving local mysteries. But this case had actually occurred in a neighboring town. The defense requested a change of venue because of all the bad publicity, so the trial was moved to Northmont . . ."

Summer had lingered in our area that year (Dr. Sam Hawthorne continued), and the leaves had not yet begun to turn as I strolled down Main Street and entered the courthouse. It was a large vulgar building of darkened stone, built at the turn of the century by some town fathers who envisioned a growth for Northmont that never occurred. Though only two stories high it covered a small block near the town square, its peaked roof guarded by four honest-to-goodness gargoyles that were the delight of small children and the embarrassment of their elders.

Twenty-five men and women had been summoned to the second-floor courtroom where Judge Bailey presided. Mostly they were men, because in those days only a few women were on the juror rolls in Northmont. We were shepherded in by the court clerk, Tim Chaucer, an old duffer who walked with a limp he had got in the Argonne. He was so ugly that some folks called him the courthouse's fifth gargoyle, but old Tim didn't seem to mind.

The case to be tried involved the murder of a farmer in the neighboring town of Cudbury. He had been a popular man, the largest landowner in the county, and he'd been killed in his barn by a single shotgun blast. The man accused of the crime was a young hired hand who'd drifted into the area and been hired to help with the chores. His name was Aaron Flavor, and he was 23 years old.

I hadn't known the dead man, Walt Jostrow, except by name, and I was a natural one to be chosen for the jury. Before the day was out I found myself impaneled along with nine other men and two women, with an extra man chosen as an alternate. Judge Bailey informed us that we would not be sequestered during the presentation of evidence, but only during our deliberations. He said he expected the trial to last about a week, and hoped we wouldn't be inconvenienced by it. As he spoke he sipped some water from a glass at his elbow. A water pitcher and two other glasses stood ready for use on a small tray between the judge's chair and the witness stand.

Under ordinary circumstances a week away from my medical practice would have been an inconvenience, especially to my patients. But that summer another doctor had set up practice in Northmont, relieving some of the pressure. This fellow, Bob Yale, was just out of a Boston internship, attracted to Northmont by plans for a new small hospital. He reminded me of myself six years earlier when I'd arrived to set up practice, and we were close enough in age to become fast friends. He volunteered to look after my patients while I was on jury duty.

Though my medical practice was being tended to, I still made a habit of dropping by the office during the noon recess, to check with my nurse April and look at the morning mail. By Thursday, the fourth day of the trial, she barely glanced up as I entered. "How'd it go this morning?"

"Middling," I replied. "The prosecution rested its case. After lunch it's the defense's turn."

"Do you think he's guilty?"

"Can't talk about that. No one's denying he fired the shotgun. It's just a matter of deciding whether it was murder or an accident. The prosecution tried to prove Aaron Flavor was having an affair with Jostrow's wife. That would establish a motive for the killing."

April nodded smugly. "I been hearing stories of some pretty juicy testimony."

"Sometimes I think these small towns are made of rumors! I suppose it was even worse over in Cudbury if they had to move the trial away." I glanced through the mail but there was nothing of interest. "Guess I'll grab a sandwich and get back to the courthouse."

"Can't you even give me a hint of the testimony?" April pleaded.

"I'll tell you all about it after the trial," I promised. "Till then I'm not supposed to discuss it with anyone."

At the coffee shop where I usually ate lunch I saw one of my fellow jurors, Mrs. Landsmith. She was a stout woman in her fifties who'd been a clerk at the dry goods store for as long as I'd been in Northmont. "Come sit with me, Dr. Sam," she invited. "It's good to get out of that stuffy courtroom for a bit."

"Well," I said, sliding into the cramped wooden booth opposite her, "it should only last a day or two more."

"I hope so!"

Sheriff Lens came in at that moment, pausing at the cigar counter to buy a plug of chewing tobacco. He saw us in the booth and strolled over to chat. "How do you like bein' a juror?"

"It's a change."

"Your patients will learn to get along without you," he said with a chuckle.

"I hope not."

The sheriff walked back to the courthouse with Mrs. Landsmith and me. Then he waved goodbye as he cut across the dusty, cindered parking lot to the jail in the next block. "That's Judge Bailey's car," Mrs. Landsmith said, pointing to a black Packard sedan. "They say he earns good money for a small-town judge."

"He's impressed me during the trial," I said. "Never had too much dealing with the man before."

The afternoon session opened with a defense statement by Aaron Flavor's attorney, a man from Cudbury named Simmons. He seemed good enough at his job, though there was something just a bit too routine about his presentation, as if he was going through the motions in a case already decided. I wondered whether he thought he had it won or lost, because as a juror I certainly didn't know.

After the opening statement Simmons called his only witness, the defendant himself. Aaron Flavor was a handsome young man with sandy hair, his face and arms deeply tanned by a summer's work in the fields. He'd sat with his lawyer during the whole week, rarely changing expression. Even when the dead man's wife testified that Aaron had often paused in his chores to talk with her, the young man only allowed himself the hint of a smile, as if remembering those days in the warm July sun.

"Now then," Simmons said, rubbing his hands together in a nervous gesture he'd used before, "tell us in your own words what happened on the afternoon of Monday, July 23rd."

"Well," Flavor began, scratching his forehead, "I'd been working in the field since early morning, bringing in the hay. There was just me and Walt—Mr. Jostrow—'cause the other field hand was sick that day."

"You were living at the Jostrow house at the time?"

"Right. I'd been there since the spring planting season, helpin' with chores."

"Was there any unusual relationship between you and Mrs. Jostrow during this time?"

"No, sir! She was the wife of my employer and that was all. She prepared the meals and sometimes I'd help her with chores around the house."

"We have seen that Mrs. Jostrow, widow of the deceased, is a woman in her late twenties—closer in age to yourself than to her husband. And we have seen that she is quite an attractive woman. We have heard reports—town gossip—to the effect that there was something illicit between you. Was there any truth to these stories?"

"No, sir!" Aaron Flavor's voice was loud and firm as he replied, though I noticed he ran his hand nervously along the seat of the witness stand as he spoke, in a gesture similar to one Mrs. Jostrow had used. Husbands and wives often picked up each other's nervous habits and I found myself wondering if lovers did the same.

"Please continue with your account of the afternoon in question, Mr. Flavor."

"Well, I was in the barn when Mr. Jostrow came in from the field and said there were some pesky crows in the north forty. He told me to bring the shotgun from the house so he could scare 'em away."

"And you did that?"

"Yes."

"Mrs. Jostrow was in the house at the time?"

"Yes."

"Did you have any conversation with her?"

"Not so's I remember." He rubbed his sweating hands against his pants and glanced over at us in the jury box.

"Was the shotgun loaded when you fetched it from the house?"

"I loaded two shells of birdshot on the way to the barn."

"Why did you do that?"

"Just to help Mr. Jostrow. If he was goin' after them crows I wanted him to have the shotgun all loaded and ready."

"What happened when you reached the barn?"

"He was right there inside the door. I came in out of the sunlight and I didn't see a milk stool settin' there. I tripped on it and as I tried to catch myself the gun went off. It hit him right in the chest. I swear to God I didn't mean to shoot him."

"What did you do then?"

"I ran to the house and got Mrs. Jostrow. He was a terrible mess, bleedin' all over. By the time we got back he was dead."

Judge Bailey had been following the testimony with interest. Now he leaned forward to signal the court clerk with an empty water pitcher. Old Tim Chaucer hobbled forward to get the pitcher, and every eye in the courtroom followed him. Apparently he'd neglected to fill the pitcher during the noon recess, and now he took it to the water fountain in the far wall, opposite the jury box. He let the water bubble out and caught it in the pitcher, filling it about three-quarters of the way up. Then he hobbled back and set it on the tray, right next to the three glasses.

"Excuse the interruption," Judge Bailey said. "The throat grows dry after so many hours."

I glanced toward the rear of the courtroom and noticed that Bob Yale, the new young doctor, had slipped into a seat in the last row. For a moment I thought he'd come with some urgent message for me, but he seemed as intent on the proceedings as everyone else.

My attention was drawn back to the bench, where Judge Bailey seemed to ignore the renewed questioning by Simmons while he picked up the water glass nearest him and peered through his spectacles at the rim.

". . . and then Mrs. Jostrow called the sheriff," Aaron Flavor was saying.

Judge Bailey ran his finger around the rim of the glass and apparently detected a chip or crack. He set it back on the tray and took one of the remaining glasses. Lifting the pitcher, he poured the water until his glass was half full.

"The shooting was completely accidental?" Simmons asked the defendant.

"Completely! I swear it!" Aaron Flavor's face was twisted with emotion, as if he were reliving the awful moment. I decided in that instant he was either an innocent man or a good actor.

Judge Bailey lifted the water glass to his lips and drank.

He made a face almost at once and put down the glass. Then, as I watched from the jury box with unbelieving eyes, he grabbed at his throat and uttered a gasp of pain.

I was still young enough to swing myself over the railing of the jury box and that's just what I did. I was a doctor first, and Judge Bailey needed me. The courtroom was in a turmoil when I reached him, with both lawyers and Tim Chaucer close behind. I caught him as he slumped from his chair and smelled the deadly odor of bitter almonds on his breath.

"He's been poisoned!" I shouted over my shoulder. "Get help!"

Judge Bailey tried to speak, and as I leaned forward I heard him say, quite distinctly, ". . . gargoyle . . ."

Then I realized I was holding a dead man in my arms.

The courtroom turmoil continued and it took several minutes to restore order. By that time Bob Yale had joined me at the judge's side. "What do you make of it, Sam? Heart attack?"

I shook my head. "Poison. Bitter almonds. That makes it some form of cyanide."

"My God! In the water?"

"Where else?"

"But everyone in the courtroom saw Tim Chaucer fill the pitcher from the fountain over there! How could it be poisoned?"

"I'm telling you *what*, not *how*."

Sheriff Lens pushed his way through the crowd to join us. "Doc, you draw corpses like flies, I swear!"

"Better get your prisoner out of here and clear the courtroom, Sheriff. We've got a murder on our hands—one that's a lot more mysterious than the case we were trying."

"Who'd want to kill Judge Bailey?"

"That's what we have to find out."

An alternate judge was brought in long enough to declare a mistrial, and we were dismissed as jurors. The defendant, Aaron Flavor, was remanded to a jail cell in lieu of bail. The victim's widow, Sarah Jostrow, seemed to be devastated by this latest act of violence and had to be led from the courtroom in tears.

"Where are we?" Sheriff Lens said to me later, when we were finally alone in the courtroom. "You've helped me on these crazy cases before, Doc, an' I sure need your help on this one! The voters'll have my scalp for lettin' a judge be poisoned in his own courtroom."

I stood back and stared at the empty seats. "There's always the possibility he poisoned himself. He might have had some cyanide salt crystals concealed in his hand and swallowed them with the water."

"You believe that for a minute, Doc?"

"No," I admitted. "Far as we know he had no reason for suicide. And if he did he'd more likely perform the act in private. It's almost certainly murder."

"How?"

I thought about that. "Three forms of cyanide exist—the gaseous, which some states are starting to use as a method of execution, the colorless liquid called prussic acid, and the cyanide salts. I think we can rule out gaseous, and liquid seems the most likely. I can still smell bitter almonds in this water glass the judge used."

"How about the pitcher?"

I sniffed it and shook my head. "I don't think so, but you'd better have it analyzed."

"How could anyone have poisoned the glass or the pitcher? From what you've told me, everyone was watching Chaucer while he went for the water, and everyone watched the judge when he drank it."

"The judge may have felt that Chaucer did it. His dying word was *gargoyle*."

"Meaning Tim Chaucer?"

"Who else?"

"Let's go talk to him."

We found Chaucer in the little office reserved for the court clerk. He was bent over a desk drawer, cleaning out an accumulation of pencils and notepads, stacking them on the desk next to a picture of himself in his wartime master sergeant's uniform. He looked up and said, "You don't have to tell me. I know I'm fired."

"What gives you that idea?"

"Judge Bailey was the only friend I had here. Maitland hates my guts. But Bailey was a real gentleman. He's the one who kept me on the job when people started callin' me names behind my back."

"Names like gargoyle, Tim?" I asked.

"Yeah, that's right. Why you gotta have a pretty face for this job is more than I know!"

"How'd the poison get into the water, Tim?" Sheriff Lens asked.

"Beats me!"

"Did you put it there?"

"I just told you the judge was my friend."

"But maybe you thought he'd stopped being your friend. Maybe you poisoned him."

"No, no!" It was almost a wail. "Go away, leave me alone!" He limped over to the coat rack. "You can see I'm goin'. You don't have to drive me out."

I placed a kindly hand on his shoulder. "We might want you to stay, Tim, if we can get to the bottom of this case. Tell me something—did you catch the odor of bitter almonds any time while you were filling that pitcher?"

"Don't know what bitter almonds smell like," he answered. "Don't even know what plain almonds smell like. Never had any in my life."

"The judge's last word before he died was *gargoyle*. Could he have meant you?"

"No, not him! He never called me that! I was always Tim to the judge."

"One more thing. Did you forget to fill the water pitcher during the lunch hour, before court resumed?"

"No, I didn't forget. Always filled it whenever the judge asked me to."

Sheriff Lens told him to stay on the job for the present and we went out into the hall.

I spotted my fellow juror, Mrs. Landsmith, talking with the defense lawyer, Simmons. "Wasn't that a terrible thing?" she asked, shaking her head sadly. "And to happen right there in front of our eyes!"

"It's terrible for my client," Simmons interjected. "Now he sits in his cell till they decide to retry him. I'm going to move that the indictment be dismissed, or that he be freed on his own recognizance."

"Not much chance of that," Sheriff Lens said. "Young Flavor's unmarried, without any family or roots in the community. He's a wanderer, and once they let him out of jail that's the last we'll see of him."

Simmons tucked his briefcase under his arm. "I hope the courts take a different view, Sheriff."

As he strode away down the hall, Mrs. Landsmith asked me, "Now that we're dismissed, you can tell me, Dr. Sam. How would you have voted on the case?"

"I honestly hadn't made up my mind."

"I'll tell you what I think," she said. "I think that Mrs. Jostrow killed her husband and Aaron Flavor is taking the blame for it. All during her testimony she was chewin' gum. I don't never trust a woman who chews gum in public."

"You may have a point there—I mean, about Flavor's taking the blame," I admitted.

"How do you think the judge was killed? Is the whole water system poisoned? I've been afraid to drink out of the fountains since it happened."

"The fountains are safe." The first thing I'd done after Judge Bailey died in my arms was to check the fountain in the courtroom. The water was pure, and there was no evidence of funny business with the spigot.

"Thank heaven for that!" Mrs. Landsmith said, and went off to try one.

Our other local judge—the one who'd dismissed us—was Bruce Maitland. He was a stout friendly man closely identified with local politics. While Sheriff Lens went back to the jail to check on Aaron Flavor, I decided to pay a call on Judge Maitland in his chambers.

"Well, Dr. Hawthorne." He waved me in. "You were on that jury I dismissed, weren't you?"

I nodded. "My one chance for jury duty in this town. I'll probably never get another one."

"I don't know about that. Northmont is growing. We'll need more doctors, and more juries too. What's on your mind?"

"The same thing that's on yours, I'm sure. Judge Bailey."

He shook his head sadly. "Poor fellow. Who'd want to kill him like that?"

"I came to ask you the same thing."

"He had no enemies—except perhaps criminals whom he'd sentenced in the past. We all have those. It goes with the job."

"I spoke with old Tim Chaucer. He seemed to think you'd fire him as clerk of the court now that Bailey is dead."

"Well, I can't pretend I'm fond of Chaucer. The man's ugly!"

"He was wounded fighting for his country."

"And that's the only reason we've kept him as long as we have." He lit a cigar, plucked carefully from a box of Havanas on his desk. "I hope the sheriff is investigating his connection with Bailey's death."

"Tim claims he had nothing to do with it."

"But he filled the pitcher, didn't he? He was the only one who could have poisoned it."

"We don't know the pitcher was poisoned. In fact, it probably wasn't."

Maitland looked confused. "But—"

"Maybe Bailey was killed some other way, and the poison slipped into his glass when everyone was milling around the bench afterward." It sounded good but I knew it wasn't true. I'd been the first one to reach that glass and sniff it, before anyone else arrived. Still, Maitland looked worried enough for me to push on. "You were on the bench yourself, Judge, when you ordered the mistrial."

"Do you suspect me of killing my dear friend? I was here in my chambers when it happened."

"As he was dying he mentioned the word *gargoyle*. Do you know what he meant?"

"No idea, unless it was a reference to Tim Chaucer."

"He never called him that. It's not likely he'd do so as he was dying."

"Perhaps you misunderstood him. He might have been trying to say *gargle*, or *car girl*."

"No, he said *gargoyle*. There are some on top of this building, you know."

"Of course. On each corner. Bailey and I had our picture taken with one when they brought it down for cleaning last summer."

"I remember that."

Judge Maitland stood up, signaling an end to the conversation. "Feel free to drop in any time, Dr. Hawthorne. And take a cigar with you."

"I never smoke them." I paused at the door. "Will you be firing Tim Chaucer now?"

Judge Maitland sighed. "I expect so."

I went outside and spent the next few moments staring up at the courthouse gargoyles. They were four ugly beasts, with elongated necks and open mouths to serve as water spouts. These had been plugged up when the gargoyles were repaired the summer before, because people complained of the streams of water they ejected during a storm. Now rooftop gutters caught it all, and pipes conducted it to the ground. The fabulous beasts were merely a decorative reminder of the past.

While I was standing there, Sheriff Lens came along the sidewalk from the jail across the street. "Damn it, Doc, I just had a call from the state police. They're offering to move in an' take over the investigation if I can't handle it!"

"Calm down, Sheriff. You know how they get sometimes. After all, the poisoning of a judge in his courtroom during a murder trial is going to be big news. There's no way you can limit it to Northmont alone. Tomorrow morning it'll make the Boston papers, and even the New York ones."

"But this is my town, my investigation!"

"Let's try to keep it that way. If we can solve the mystery within the next few hours that should satisfy everyone."

He gave me a puzzled look. "How we goin' to do that, Doc? You know how the judge was poisoned?"

"No, not yet. But I know he was trying to tell me something about one of those gargoyles. Is there any way we could examine them?"

"Not unless you want to climb out on the roof. Remember last year? They had one hell of a time gettin' them down for repairs."

"I remember. Still, the slant of that roof isn't too steep. A young agile man could reach them without any trouble."

"You thinkin' of yourself, Doc?"

"I'm thinking Bob Yale might be even better, with me along to hang onto him."

I phoned Bob at his office and he came around quickly. Happily it was a healthy time for both his patients and mine. But when he saw the old courthouse roof he balked a bit. "You want us to climb up there, Sam?"

"Sure. A few years back you'd have thought nothing of it. Pretend you're still a kid. I'll have a rope attached to your belt so's you can't fall."

He chuckled. "Tie us together like mountain climbers. If I go I want you right behind me."

"Fair enough."

"What do you expect to find in those gargoyles?"

"I don't know. Even though they were plugged up last year, something may be inside them."

He stared up at the roof. "Have we got to check all four of them?"

"Not if we get lucky."

He took off his jacket and rolled up his sleeves. "All right, Sam. Which one do we try first?"

I thought about that. Finally I said, "Bailey had his picture taken next to one of the gargoyles. We should be able to figure which corner it's at by studying the background of the photo. That's the one we'll try first."

We could make out the front door of the courthouse in the picture, over on the right side. That meant the gargoyle on the ground between Bailey and Maitland was the one from the left-front corner as you faced the building. Once we were out on the roof that's the one we headed for. Bob Yale had a rope around his waist, looped around one of the big old courthouse chimneys, but to tell the truth it wasn't very dangerous.

"I used to climb apple trees that were tougher than this," he called back to me as he edged along the slate roof.

"Just be careful when you're out at the edge. I don't want to lose Northmont's only other doctor."

He straddled the gargoyle and began feeling the crevices of the stone monster. "What am I supposed to be looking for?"

"They were plugged with something, to close the spouts."

"Sure were—cement!"

"Oh."

"No way I can get through this, Sam." He twisted his lean body to gain better leverage, but the blockage still resisted him. "You'd have to lower this to the ground and go at it with a pickax."

Standing by the chimney with a firm grip on the other end of the rope, I wondered if it had been a waste of time. I could see people in the street below looking up and pointing at us, and I felt just the least bit ridiculous. "Try the mouth," I shouted back.

"What?"

"Try the mouth. They sealed the back of the spout with cement, but you should be able to reach into the open mouth."

He stretched out as far as he could along the gargoyle's neck, and I prayed it would support his weight. "I've got something!" he called. I saw his hand emerge from the monster's mouth with a small packet, and I sighed with relief. Maybe it hadn't been a crazy idea after all.

I hauled up on the rope and he scrambled over the slate to join me at the chimney. In his hand he clutched a thick packet wrapped in oilskin and tied with heavy cord. "His own private time capsule," I remarked, weighing the thing in my hand. "He probably figured it wouldn't be found till the next time the gargoyles were cleaned."

"What's in it?" Yale asked.

"Let's get off this roof and have a look."

With Sheriff Lens peering over our shoulders we carefully unwrapped our discovery. There were papers inside, legal documents showing that Bailey and Judge Maitland had been secret investors in a Boston speakeasy. "I'll be damned!" the sheriff snorted. "Who'd of thought it of those two?"

Bob Yale looked up at me. "A motive for murder?"

I shrugged. "Could be. Obviously Bailey felt guilty enough about it to entrust these confessional documents to posterity. Let's go call on Judge Maitland."

"Do you still need me?" Yale asked.

"No. You did nobly up on that roof."

"I just wonder where they'd have found a doctor if we both fell off, Sam."

Judge Maitland listened distastefully as I told him what we'd found in the gargoyle's mouth. When I'd finished he said, "Obviously Bailey felt he was doing something wrong by investing in that club. I feel just the opposite. A judge can invest his money just like anyone else. Owning part of a restaurant in Boston certainly doesn't conflict with my responsibilities on the bench in Northmont."

"It's not a restaurant, Judge Maitland. It's a speakeasy, operating in violation of the law."

"If Al Smith gets elected that might all change."

"I didn't come here to argue politics. I'm helping Sheriff Lens investigate a murder."

"And you think I killed Bailey to keep our business venture a secret?" He snorted at the idea. "First of all, I don't consider I'm doing anything wrong. Second, I wish you'd tell me how I could have poisoned Bailey's water when I wasn't even in the courtroom at the time."

I had to admit he had me stumped there. Bailey had died with the word *gargoyle* on his lips, but maybe it had nothing to do with his murder. Maybe it was simply that his last conscious thoughts had been of the guilty secret he'd hidden away for posterity.

"All right," I said, heading for the door. "I'll talk to you later."

"Hawthorne—"

"What is it?"

"What are you going to do with those papers you found?"

I turned and stared at him. The mask had dropped away. He was a frightened man. "I'll see," I told him. "I haven't decided yet."

There were people outside standing in little groups in front of the courthouse. Maybe they'd seen me on the roof with Dr. Yale and wondered what was going on. It was my nurse April who spotted me and came running up. "Dr. Sam, come quick! Sheriff Lens has found something!"

I followed her on the run without asking more. Lens was waiting in my office and what he produced couldn't have surprised me more. "Take a whiff of this, Doc," he said, holding out a tiny vial of colorless liquid.

"Prussic acid," I said. "Where'd you find it, Sheriff?"

"In a trash barrel down the street. I was walking behind that lawyer fellow, Simmons, and I seen him toss it in."

"Very interesting."

"Do you think Simmons did it?" April asked. "But he wasn't anywhere near the judge, was he?"

"We'll ask him about it," I said. "But first I have another suggestion—one that might wind up this case in a hurry. I want a reenactment of the crime in the same courtroom this evening."

"What's that?"

"You heard me, Sheriff. I want the lawyers and the defendant and as many of the jury and spectators as we can round up on short notice. I want everything the same as it was this afternoon, including Tim Chaucer and the water pitcher."

"You mean you can solve the case tonight, Doc? You can show us how Judge Bailey was killed?"

"Maybe, if my luck holds."

"All right. When it comes to these crazy impossible killings you're the expert, Doc. But even if I can round these people up, the most important one's goin' to be missing."

"Judge Bailey."

"Right. I can't produce his body for your reenactment."

"I just might be able to persuade Judge Maitland to sit in for that role."

"Maitland!"

I nodded. "Have everyone there at eight o'clock, Sheriff . . ."

Promptly at eight o'clock I entered the jury box and took my seat next to Mrs. Landsmith. Almost everyone was there—the jurors, Tim Chaucer at his clerk's desk, the prosecuting attorney, the accused, Aaron Flavor, seated next to Simmons for the defense, the victim's widow in the front row, a scattering of spectators, and even Bob Yale occupying a seat at the rear just as he'd done that afternoon. Only the judge's bench was empty, but almost at once Tim Chaucer leaped to his feet to announce the arrival of Justice Maitland.

We all stood up as Maitland took the bench, glaring down at us. Then he said, "I have been persuaded to lend my presence to this charade only because I'm told it could result in a solution to the terrible crime which took place this afternoon. However, this is still a court of law, and I will allow no antics that might in any way influence the forthcoming second trial of the accused, Aaron Flavor." He turned toward the jury box and said, "You may proceed, Dr. Hawthorne."

I stood up and left the box, taking charge of the proceedings. It had been a struggle to get Maitland there, and only my possession of the so-called gargoyle papers gave me the leverage to demand his presence. Now, seeing his cold dark eyes on me, I wondered if it had been the wisest course of action.

I began by holding up the tiny vial of poison that Sheriff Lens had seen Simmons throw away. "This, ladies and gentlemen, was the weapon used to murder Judge Bailey in this courtroom a few hours ago. Hydrocyanic acid—or to give it the more common name, prussic acid."

Tim Chaucer stirred uncomfortably at his desk, eyeing the empty pitcher. "Would you care to tell us, Mr. Simmons, how it came into your possession?"

The little lawyer was on his feet. "No, sir! I have nothing to say!"

"Thank you, Mr. Simmons." I turned back to Judge Maitland, directing my remarks to him. "Now, with your indulgence, I intend to demonstrate exactly how Justice Bailey could be poisoned in full view of the roomful of spectators."

"I trust the demonstration will not result in my becoming a stand-in victim," Maitland said grimly.

"There's nothing to fear," I told him, hoping it was true. "Now if the witness will take the stand exactly as he did this afternoon, we may proceed."

When Aaron Flavor was in the witness chair and Simmons was poised in front of him, I continued. "Tim, please get the pitcher and fill it exactly as you did this afternoon."

Tim Chaucer rose reluctantly from his chair and approached the bench. He reached up for the empty glass pitcher, on its tray with the three glasses, as if he expected it to bite him. Then he took it and limped across the front of the courtroom to the water fountain. Every eye was on him, just as they had been earlier. He carefully filled the pitcher and returned to the bench with it, placing it on the tray.

"Thank you, Tim," I said. "You all saw it, ladies and gentlemen. Was there any chance he could have poisoned that pitcher without being noticed?"

"Not a chance," Sheriff Lens said from the front row. "Besides, I got the word there was no poison in the pitcher, only in the glass."

"As I suspected. Now how could the glass have been poisoned, and by whom? By Judge Bailey himself? No, this was obviously not a suicide. Yet *no one* but Bailey could have poisoned the glass after he poured water into it. We are faced with an impossibility, unless—" I left them hanging on my words for an instant as I unstoppered the tiny vial and reached over to the tray of glasses. "Unless the poison was already in the glass."

Judge Maitland watched with widening eyes as I poured the contents of the vial into the glass by his elbow. It barely covered the bottom. "Invisible even from a few feet away, and if Bailey noticed it he'd have thought it was a little water—a melted ice cube, perhaps."

"But—" the sheriff started to protest.

"He only filled the glass halfway, so the poison still kept enough strength to kill. And Bailey never noticed the odor until it was too late."

"Then anyone could have poisoned the glass during the noon recess," Maitland said, perhaps concerned that I was shifting suspicion back to him.

"Anyone at all," I agreed. "And that's why it becomes so important to learn where Simmons obtained this vial of poison."

The lawyer looked uncertainly at the row of spectators. I lifted the pitcher and filled the glass halfway, as Judge Bailey had done. Then I walked past the lawyer to the railing and pointed toward a woman in the first row. "The poison was yours, Mrs. Jostrow, wasn't it?"

"I—" She tried to speak but couldn't. Then she stood up, as if seeking escape, but Sheriff Lens was quickly at her side.

"Simmons found the poison and took it from you, didn't he?"

The lawyer started to protest, but Sarah Jostrow interrupted. "He's right. I wanted to kill myself after Walt's death. Mr. Simmons found the poison and took it away from me. But I swear he didn't have anything to do with the judge's death!"

"I know he didn't," I said. "I've demonstrated how the poison could have been in Bailey's glass before he added the water. But how many of you remember the exact sequence of the events you witnessed this afternoon? You see, the poison could have been in Judge Bailey's glass—except that it wasn't. The judge examined one glass, noticed a chip or crack in the rim, and set it aside. The glass he finally used—the glass which must have contained the poison in its bottom—was one of the two remaining glasses on the tray. One of the glasses nearest the witness stand."

Aaron Flavor turned to me as I spoke. "Are you saying the poison was meant for me?"

"Exactly, Mr. Flavor. Meant for you and supplied by you. While all our eyes were on Tim Chaucer filling his pitcher, you passed your hand over the glass and emptied the vial into it. You meant the poison for yourself, though when Bailey took your glass and filled it with water you kept silent. Why, Mr. Flavor? I suppose in that split second you were imagining a mistrial and some sort of freedom. There was always the chance you wouldn't be tried again. Bailey was drinking the poison meant for you, and you kept silent."

"That's crazy!" the defendant protested. "Where would I get a vial of poison?"

"You had a vial of poison and Sarah had one too. The implication is obvious—a suicide pact, in case you were found guilty."

"She never went near him!" Sheriff Lens protested. "How could she slip him a vial of poison?"

"As one of my fellow jurors observed, she was chewing gum during her testimony. And I noticed Aaron Flavor running his hand along the bottom of the witness stand in the same gesture she had used. She stuck the tiny vial to the bottom of the chair with gum, and Flavor retrieved it. While we watched Chaucer filling the pitcher, Flavor emptied the poison into the glass nearest him—and then allowed Judge Bailey to die in his place. No wonder Mrs. Jostrow was so distraught at the judge's death—she knew what must have happened!"

"The evidence of a suicide pact," Judge Maitland intoned from the bench, "is certainly a strong presumption of guilt in the earlier death of Walt Jostrow. It can be used as evidence in the second trial."

"There won't be no second trial!" Aaron Flavor shouted, and scooped up the half-filled water glass, downing it before any of us could move. I think all the persons in the courtroom were frozen to their seats, waiting for the poison to claim its second victim.

But I shook my head and took the glass from his hand. "You won't escape justice that easily, Aaron. I emptied the second vial and refilled it with water."

"Well now (Dr. Sam Hawthorne concluded), they held a second trial all right, and this time I wasn't on the jury. Aaron Flavor was convicted of murdering Walt Jostrow and sentenced to twenty years to life. That seemed to settle the matter, and they never did try him for letting Judge Bailey drink the poison he'd meant for himself. And Mrs. Jostrow changed her mind about committing suicide . . . You're leaving so soon? Another small—ah—libation before you go? And come back again—I'll tell you about the opening of the Northmont hospital and how Dr. Bob Yale became its first casualty."

THE PROBLEM OF
THE PILGRIMS WINDMILL

D r. Sam Hawthorne filled the glasses and settled back in his chair. "This time I promised to tell you about what happened when we opened the new Pilgrim Memorial Hospital in Northmont, back in March of 1929. I'd been practicing medicine in the town for seven years by that time, and the idea of a hospital all our own was something to fill me with wonder and delight. Dr. Bob Yale, who'd come to Northmont the year before the hospital opened, landed a job on their staff. I was offered one myself, but I told them I wanted to keep on bein' a plain old G.P. As it turned out, though, I was summoned to the hospital before it had been open a week, to investigate one of the strangest crimes I ever encountered. It was like something Mister Chesterton might have written about, and if he had I suppose he would have called it *The Devil in the Windmill* . . ."

O n March fourth (Dr. Sam continued) Herbert Hoover was inaugurated as the 31st President of the United States. On the following day Pilgrim Memorial Hospital opened its doors for the first time. It was located just outside of town on land that had belonged to the Collins family for generations. When they donated the land for a hospital there was only one stipulation—the old Dutch windmill on the property should remain standing.

People are always startled to see windmills in New England, but there are still a few around. You pass one on Cape Cod, on the road to Provincetown, and I think the one at Northmont is still standing too. When people passing through town asked about Northmont's windmill they were usually reminded that the Pilgrims had come to America by way of The Netherlands, and the *Mayflower's* companion ship, the *Speedwell*, actually sailed from The Netherlands before being forced to turn back. I suppose that had something to do with the Collins family windmill being called the Pilgrims windmill, though to tell the truth it wasn't built till the middle of the 19th Century and had mighty little to do with Pilgrims.

Anyway, it looked right nice standing there in front of Pilgrim Memorial Hospital. Its four wooden vanes still turned slowly when the wind blew, even though the mill was no longer in use. Inside was a good-sized room where an exhibit of Northmont history had been prepared. The building itself was made of fieldstone, which helped to give it an aged look that might have dated back to Pilgrim times. Some of the windmill's gears and wheels were still in place overhead, and I glanced up at them as I toured the place with my nurse April and half a hundred other honored guests.

"Was this place ever used as a mill?" I asked her.

"I guess so, long before I was born." She grinned at me. "Folks say Randy Collins's pa hid a fortune in gold somewhere in the windmill, but no one was ever able to find it."

"If you believe that story I'll tell you the one about the little green men. Randy Collins isn't the sort who'd give anything away that belonged to him. When he donated the land and this windmill, he was darn sure there was no gold or anything else around."

"I suppose you're right," she agreed. We passed through the historical exhibit and left the windmill, starting up the curving driveway to the hospital itself. It was a low two-story brick building that had a wide front and two wings on the back. Some folks had snorted at the idea of an eighty-bed hospital in Northmont, but the town planners figured you had to build for tomorrow's needs and there was no doubt the region was growing. Of course all the beds weren't in use yet, so they'd opened with a limited staff of doctors and nurses—but even here there was a problem, and as April and I approached the hospital's main entrance I saw the problem standing in the doorway to greet us.

His name was Lincoln Jones, and he was the first black doctor the people of Northmont had ever seen.

It was not a good time for blacks in the north or the south. The Ku Klux Klan was once again active and I'd heard about a cross burning just a month earlier in another part of the state. But Lincoln Jones was a good doctor, a young man who specialized in children's illnesses. There weren't too many specialists around in those days, and I figured we were mighty lucky to have him in Northmont.

Dr. Bob Yale was standing at Lincoln Jones's side to greet us. "Welcome to Pilgrim Memorial, Dr. Sam. How's it look?"

"The windmill exhibit was fine. Now I'm looking over the hospital."

"You know Dr. Jones?"

I shook hands with the black man. He was tall and handsome, probably in his early thirties like me. "We met briefly the other day but we haven't had a chance to talk. I hope you'll find the community to your liking, Dr. Jones."

He smiled. "I guess you'd better be calling me Lincoln. I think we'll be working close a lot of the time."

"I hope so." Then, while Lincoln Jones chatted with April, I took Bob Yale aside. "Any more trouble about him, Bob?"

"Nothing we can't handle here. The hospital administrator, Dr. Seeger, had a few telephone calls complaining about a black doctor. You know the sort. But I think it'll blow over."

I nodded and walked on with him across the hospital lobby. It was tastefully decorated with a few landscape paintings, and there was an admissions desk that made the place look like a hotel lobby. I recognized bald-headed Dr. Seeger standing behind it. Seeger was around 60, a businessman first and a doctor second. I didn't much like him but I had to admit he'd been mainly responsible for getting Randy Collins to donate the land for the hospital.

"What do you think of it, Dr. Sam?" he asked.

"I think you're off to a great start. A place this size, you'll be able to treat patients from three counties."

Seeger laughed without mirth. "We'll have to if we want to cover the overhead. This is an expensive place to run, and it's even more expensive with eighty empty beds."

Randy Collins and his wife Sara Jane came down the stairs from the second floor. Seeing Randy was no treat—his big broad-shouldered figure and glowering face were familiar sights at the town council meetings where he'd been known to argue half the night over some minor resolution. But Sara Jane was indeed a treat. She was slim and cool and lovely, a honey-blonde with never a hair out of place. I could have looked at her all day and dreamed of her all night. They were familiar figures on whatever small social scene Northmont possessed.

Randy was a man in his early forties, conservative and set in his ways. "Can't say I approve of all your new gadgets," he told Seeger, "but then I don't have to approve. I only donated the land."

"Let me show you our operating room," Dr. Seeger said, leading him off down the first-floor corridor.

"Operating rooms aren't for me," Sara Jane decided, lingering close to me. She was a good ten years younger than her husband, and that along with her fresh openness had led to the usual small-town rumors. Some of the older women had even called her a "flapper," a word they'd discovered from reading the magazines of the day.

"Me neither," I agreed. "I'm just a country doctor."

Suddenly she tugged on my arm. "Damn! There's Isaac Van Doran and I don't want to see him!"

I steered her down a corridor before Van Doran could spot us. He was a muscular if slow-witted young man who ran Northmont's only gas station. Tongues had been set wagging when he'd been seen once riding in Sara Jane's roadster, but she insisted later he was only checking out her steering wheel.

"What have you got against Van Doran?" I asked with a smile.

"He and Randy don't get along. When Randy goes in there for gas they hardly talk."

"And you don't want to upset your husband."

"Well, Randy is very good to me." She fluttered her lashes as she said it, and I decided she'd been seeing too many moving pictures. Next thing I knew she'd be pulling a whiskey flask out of her stocking top.

We'd reached the end of the corridor and turned back. I could see there was some sort of commotion in the lobby and I wondered what the trouble was. "It's probably my husband," Sara Jane said with a resigned sigh, but we quickly saw that it wasn't.

A shabbily dressed woman, whom I recognized as Mabel Foster from up on Hill Road, had confronted Dr. Jones and was pointing a knobby finger at the black doctor. "You get rid of this man!" she screeched. "He's in league with the Devil! If he stays here Satan himself will come!"

Her words sent a chill down my spine, not for Lincoln Jones or for the coming of Satan but only for this poor deranged creature. I'd treated her off and on over the years, listening calmly to her claims of psychic power. But now, confronting our new black doctor, the hatred of generations had come boiling to the surface.

Luckily for everyone, April moved quickly to her side, comforting her with murmured reassurance as she moved her out the door. Dr. Seeger tried to laugh it off. "Did you put her up to that, Randy?" he asked Collins.

"Hardly!" Sara Jane's husband answered, visibly shaken. "Too bad something like that had to spoil the opening. Let's hope Mabel's psychic powers are all in her imagination."

"I'm sure they are," Lincoln Jones said with a smile. "Things like that don't disturb me, and I trust they won't disturb anyone else. It's something I learned to live with a long time ago."

April came back in after a bit. "I managed to get her in her carriage and headed for home," she said. "That woman should be locked away, Dr. Sam."

"Sometimes she's as sane as the two of us. I wish I was better equipped to help her."

We left the hospital shortly after that. I never did get up to the second floor that day, but it didn't matter. Within a week I'd be spending a great deal of time there.

The call came late on Sunday night, close to twelve. Pilgrim Memorial Hospital had been open five days by that time, but the word around town was that it had yet to admit its first patient. A pregnant farm wife had delivered her baby at home, as she had on three previous occasions, and a man who broke his leg had insisted on being driven to the old hospital in the next county because, he said, they knew him there.

So I was a bit surprised to hear Bob Yale's voice on the line, summoning me with something close to panic. "You'd better come over to the hospital mighty quick, Sam. We need you here."

"What's happened?" I asked. "A train accident?" It was the first thing that popped into my head.

"A fire. I'll tell you when you get here."

Winter had delivered a late blow that night, and about an inch of snow covered the ground. That wasn't too unusual for the tenth of March, but we'd been spoiled by a relatively mild season and I'd thought we'd seen the last of the snow. When I reached the hospital I saw lanterns in the road and the town's fire truck pulled up by the Pilgrims windmill. The building itself didn't appear damaged, and the vanes with their canvas covering were turning slowly in the night breeze.

Bob Yale came running up to my car and I saw that his hands and arms were bandaged.

"What happened to you?" I asked.

"Burned myself. Not serious."

"You're the hospital's first patient!"

There was no humor on his face when he replied. "No, I'm not. Randy Collins was badly burned. We don't know if he'll live."

"Randy! What's been happening here?"

His face reflected the flickering red glow from the firemen's lanterns. "I was coming off duty about an hour ago, and as I went out to my car I saw a flash of light through the window of the windmill. It looked like a fire and I walked out to investigate. I thought some kids might have gotten in there, and I saw a single set of footprints in the fresh snow leading to the door."

As he talked we moved through the crowd of firemen and hospital staff to the door in question. I saw Dr. Seeger come out of the building, stepping nimbly over a fire hose. "Hello, Sam. Is Bob filling you in on what happened?"

I said he was, and for the first time the thought struck me that I wasn't here as a doctor. Seeger and Yale had phoned me because of something else—some mystery they couldn't explain. "What about Collins?" I asked Bob.

"I heard him scream before I reached the door. I pushed it open and saw him standing in the center of the room, covered with flames."

"The room was on fire?"

"Not the room—just Randy Collins. He staggered around, smashing the glass on some of the historical display cases. I was close to panic myself. There was nothing to wrap him in, to smother the flames. Finally I just grabbed him and yanked him out the door and rolled him in the snow. There was nothing else I could do."

"That was a brave act," I told him.

"Brave or foolish. That's how I burned my arms."

"Is he up at the hospital now?"

Bob Yale nodded. "We had to give him a sedative. The burns on his body are terrible."

"Did he say anything?"

"Just one word—Lucifer. He kept repeating it."

"Lucifer. He must have remembered what old Mabel Foster said about the devil."

I looked around at the inside of the windmill. The floor in the center of the room was badly scorched, and there was evidence that Randy's flailing body had set fire to some of the display cases as well. But the firemen had extinguished it quickly. The stone walls of the mill were undamaged, of course. I stepped carefully around some broken glass from the display cases and peered up toward the high ceiling. There was enough lantern light to make out the wind shaft and gears—and enough light to see that no one was hiding up there. I thought I saw a tiny piece of something red, but I couldn't be sure. "I checked with Dr. Seeger, who was in charge of the exhibit. He assured me nothing inflammable was left inside."

"What do the firemen think?"

Bob Yale shrugged. "They don't know either. He just caught fire."

The room had been wired with electric lights for the exhibit, but no one had thought to turn them on. I flicked the switch now and the bulbs lit. "It's not the electrical wiring," I said.

"One fireman thought he smelled gasoline."

I frowned. "Do you think someone tried to kill Collins by burning him to death?"

"I'd think that except for one thing."

"What's that?"

"There were no other footprints in the snow, Sam. Randy Collins was alone in this windmill when it happened."

We waited at the hospital until Dr. Jones finished dressing Collins' burns as best he could. Then he came into the corridor to talk with us. "I thought you specialized in children's illnesses," I said.

"I treated a few burn cases in children. Seeger figured I was the burn expert on the staff."

"Will he pull through?"

Lincoln Jones ran a hand through his thick black hair. "It's in the hands of the Lord now. But I'm hoping he'll make it."

"Is he conscious?" I asked. "Could I talk to him?"

"He's heavily sedated but he was talking a bit. I'll give you one minute with him if it's absolutely necessary." He wagged a finger at me to emphasize the point. "Not a second more—he's my patient!"

I entered the room and stood by the bed, looking down at the burned man. Randy Collins must have sensed my presence because he opened his eyes. "Dr. Sam . . ." His voice was barely a whisper.

"What happened to you, Randy? What happened at the windmill?"

"I . . ."

"You kept saying *Lucifer*."

"Driving by . . . saw light in the windmill . . . flickering light like a fire . . . went in and . . . it was the Devil, Dr. Sam . . . just like that woman said . . . a ball of flame just enveloped me . . ."

Lincoln Jones tapped me on the shoulder. "Sorry, Sam. Your minute's up. Let him sleep now."

Randy Collins closed his eyes and I followed Jones out of the room. Sara Jane was in the corridor, her eyes swollen with tears. "What happened to him? Will he be all right?"

Yale filled her in on what little he knew. Then she turned to me again. "What happened to him, Sam?"

I could only hold out my hands helplessly. "We just don't know, Sara Jane. We just don't know."

By Wednesday Randy Collins had recovered enough to have visitors, and Lincoln Jones was grinning broadly as he studied the chart at the end of the bed. "You're out of danger, Mr. Collins. You're going to live."

Collins shifted his gaze from the black doctor to me and asked, "What about my face, Sam? And my skin?"

"They can do amazing things these days. As soon as you're strong enough Dr. Jones plans to send you by ambulance to a hospital in Boston that specializes in burn cases. They'll use plastic surgery and skin grafts to make you as good as new."

"I'll be like this for years!"

"But consider the alternative," Jones pointed out. "If Bob Yale hadn't rushed in to save your life, we'd be burying you today."

"How are his hands?"

"Not as bad as yours. You were both lucky there was snow on the ground."

"Have you remembered anything else about the fire?" I asked.

"Seems like I've told it a hundred times around. It was a ball of fire floating there, just enveloping me. All I could think of was Mabel Foster's predictions of Satan." He glanced pointedly at Lincoln Jones.

"Well, the Devil's not going to drive me away from this job," Jones responded. "I've seen the Devil wearing a white sheet and delivering a speech, and that didn't scare me. I guess a ball of fire doesn't scare me either."

During those first days when he could have visitors, it seemed that half of Northmont trooped out to the hospital to see Randy Collins. While Sara Jane hovered near his bed, most of the town council put in an appearance and even Sheriff Lens drove out to pay a visit. We hadn't needed his services yet because no one could figure out if there'd been a crime or not. If there was a criminal involved—one who'd tried to murder Randy Collins—he'd have had to be invisible.

"Think somebody slipped one of them there infernal devices into his pocket?" Sheriff Lens asked as we left the hospital building and strolled down toward the windmill.

"Without his knowing it? That's hardly possible, Sheriff. Besides, he insists the fireball was already inside the place when he entered it."

"Don't they keep it locked at night?"

"It was left open because of the exhibit. There was nothing to steal here."

We went inside and I saw that the fire damage had not been repaired since Sunday night. The floor was still scorched and broken glass still littered the area. Something caught my eye and I stooped to pick it up. It was a thick piece of curved glass.

"What's that, Doc?" Sheriff Lens asked.

"Just a piece of glass. This place should be swept out before someone cuts himself."

"Who's in there?" a voice called suddenly from outside. I walked to the doorway and saw it was Isaac Van Doran.

"Just us, Isaac—the sheriff and me."

"Thought it might be that devil Randy seen," Van Doran said with a chuckle.

"What brings you out here?"

"Come to visit him. That's the least I can do."

I was surprised by that. "Didn't know you two were all that friendly."

"Hell, we're not enemies. He's been a customer of mine for years—him and Sara Jane both. It's good business to come see him."

I knew Sara Jane had gone home for lunch and I wondered if Isaac had purposely chosen a time when she wouldn't be there. We watched him walk up to the hospital and Sheriff Lens asked, "What do you make of him, Doc? Think maybe he tried to kill Randy so's he could run off with Sara Jane?"

"You've been listening to the town gossip too much, Sheriff. If Van Doran had tried to kill him I'm sure Randy Collins wouldn't be covering it up."

"Then you believe this devil business?"

"I don't know. But I think it's time I called on Mabel Foster."

I was driving along the highway toward Mabel's place on the hill when I happened to spot her horse and buggy. I wondered where she was going and decided to follow along at a short distance. It wasn't easy making the car run that slow but I managed—and I was rewarded for my patience when I saw her turning into the driveway of the Collins house. A few snow flurries were just beginning to fall.

I parked down the road and went the rest of the way on foot, arriving just in time to see Mabel Foster confronting Sara Jane at the front door. "I warned them all—I warned them and they laughed at me! Now your husband is on his bed of pain—and that won't be the end of it!"

"Get away from here!" Sara Jane screamed. "I'll call the police!"

Mabel made a pass with her fist as I hurried up to grab her. "Time to go home," I told her quietly.

"Let go, Dr. Sam! Let go!"

But I managed to get her back to her buggy. "You've got to behave, Mabel, or people will want to lock you away."

"The Devil will guide me! Satan is my master!"

"And it was Satan that burned Randy Collins?"

"Of course! I warned you all it was coming!"

"Why Collins?"

"Don't you see? Because he donated the land for the hospital!"

"And who will be burned next?"

"Seeger!" She almost spat out the name. "He's the one who hired the black doctor—Seeger is next!" She raised her buggy whip and I thought for an instant she would strike me. But her target was the horse's back and the blow galvanized him into action. Horse and buggy took her down the road with the snow flying around her.

I walked back to the doorway where Sara Jane stood. She was trembling so bad she had to hold the door for support. "God, she frightened me half to death! I'm so glad you came by, Dr. Sam. Come in and have some coffee."

"You need something to calm you down."

"Do you think she tried to kill Randy? To make her crazy prediction come true?"

"I doubt if she'd be capable of it."

Sara Jane poured two cups of coffee and then nervously picked up a box of friction matches to light a cigarette. Not many women in Northmont smoked, but for Sara Jane it was part of her flapper image.

"If someone did try to kill Randy they might try again at the hospital."

Her words reminded me of something. "Isaac Van Doran came to visit him this noon. Did you know that?"

She shook her head. "I only see Isaac at his station. Those stories about us were foolish."

"I'm sure they were." I finished my coffee and stood up. "I have to be going. I was on my way over to see Mabel Foster but I guess I've seen her now."

"If you go back to the hospital tell Randy I'll be over in a little while."

I didn't go back to the hospital right away, though. I had my own patients to consider, and April was waiting for me back at the office with a sheaf of phone messages. It was late afternoon before I returned to Pilgrim Memorial. Bob Yale told me they'd admitted two more patients that morning—a broken leg and an appendix case—but neither was a patient of mine. People in the surrounding towns were beginning to realize that the new hospital was open at last, and I had no doubts about its future.

"How are your arms?" I asked, because I hadn't seen him that morning when I chatted with Sheriff Lens.

He patted the bandages. "Coming along. I'm going to unwrap them in a day or so and see if the air will help them heal faster. It's more a nuisance than anything else."

Sara Jane was visiting with Collins, so I didn't disturb them. Instead I went down to Seeger's office on the ground floor. He looked up from a mass of paperwork as I entered. "Hello, Sam. What can I do for you?"

I told him about my encounter with Mabel Foster and her threat against his life. "That woman should be locked up," he muttered. "But thanks for the warning. I won't go anywhere near the windmill—or any fireplaces, for that matter."

"How's the hospital coming?"

Seeger shrugged. "Three patients, with another coming in tomorrow. I've no doubt some people are staying away because of Lincoln Jones, but I think they'll come around sooner or later. We have a good hospital here, with modern equipment, and that's what will win them over."

I left Seeger's office and spent some time chatting with a couple of nurses. Then I decided it was time to be on my way. Though the days were growing longer as spring approached, it was still dark before six o'clock in mid-March, and I turned on my headlights as I drove out of the parking lot. In their searching beams I caught a sudden glimpse of someone by the side of the road near the windmill. It wasn't till I was some distance away that I realized it had been Isaac Van Doran.

I slowed the car and made a U-turn in the road. By the time I returned to the spot, Van Doran had disappeared. There was no place he could have gone except into the windmill. Though much of the earlier snow had melted, the few flurries earlier in the day still clung to the grass. There was enough for me to trace his footprints leading up to the windmill door. I saw no other prints nearby.

Then, almost at once, I heard the scream. It was the drawn-out scream of a man who might have been falling from a great height—falling all the way to Hades itself. I burst through the door into an inferno of flame. Isaac Van Doran lay in the middle of it, trying to rise from the floor, stretching out his hand toward me. This time the flames were not confined to the body but seemed to fill the windmill's interior, shooting high into the mechanism above.

I tried to beat at the flames with my coat, but it was useless. With his dying screams still in my ears I was forced to retreat before the fire.

The town's fire engine came again, and Seeger and Bob Yale ran down from the hospital with some of the nurses. The whole scene could have been a duplicate of Sunday evening's, except this time there was no survivor. When the flames had finally been extinguished, they wrapped the blackened remains of Isaac Van Doran in canvas and carried the body away. Then the rest of us trooped up to the hospital and went into Seeger's office. "We'd better report this to Sheriff Lens," Seeger said, reaching for the telephone.

"As what? Another unexplained accident?" I asked.

Bob Yale looked at me. "You were there, Sam. What do you think it was?"

"I'm damned if I know. We've had two fires, with one man badly injured and another dead. Both men were alone when it happened. Randy Collins entered the windmill because he thought he saw a glow of some sort. We don't know why Van Doran went in."

"You saw no one else around?"

I shook my head. "There were only Van Doran's footprints going in. And anyone hiding inside from earlier in the day would surely have been consumed by those flames. We have to face it—both men were alone in that windmill when they suddenly caught fire for no apparent reason."

"Did Van Doran manage to shout anything as he was dying?" Yale asked me.

"Just screams. If he thought it was the Devil he didn't say so."

Sheriff Lens drove out and talked to us, then went to look over the windmill as best he could in the dark. The electric wiring, undamaged in the first fire, was burnt out now, and everyone agreed a better inspection could be made in the morning. I went home to bed and dreamed of Isaac Van Doran's final moments in the fire, screaming and reaching out his hand toward a salvation I could not give him.

In the morning I drove back to the hospital. I parked my car in the gravel lot, and as I started down the hill toward the windmill Lincoln Jones intercepted me. "There's something I thought you'd want to know," he said.

"About last night?"

He nodded. "I gave Van Doran's body a cursory examination before it was removed. The man had a broken leg."

"What?"

"A compound fracture of the left tibia."

"You couldn't be mistaken?"

"The bone was protruding through the skin."

"I see. Why are you telling me this?"

"Because you said he walked into the windmill. He couldn't have, with that leg. You must have seen someone else."

I considered that. "Or Van Doran broke his leg after he was inside."

"During the fire? It was a pretty bad break to get from just falling down."

"Anyway, thanks for the information. It may be a big help." I left him and continued down the hill.

Sheriff Lens was already on the scene, standing in the doorway. After this second fire the wooden floor was almost burned through in spots, and the display cases for the exhibits were all but consumed. Even the windmill mechanism above our heads was charred and unmoving. The wind shaft on which the outside vanes revolved had become jammed in the fire, freezing the blades in position. "Like a cross to keep away the Devil," Sheriff Lens observed, and his words surprised me. I'd never known him to be a particularly religious man.

"I want to go up there," I said, standing in the doorway and pointing above our heads at the blackened gears.

"What for?"

"Van Doran died with a broken leg. If he walked in here by himself he must have broken his leg here, in the instant the fire started. When I heard him scream I had the impression he might have been falling. Maybe I even heard him hit the floor without realizing it. And if he fell, it was from up there."

Sheriff Lens grunted. "I got another idea. The body was pretty badly burned, wasn't it?"

"Yes."

"Maybe Van Doran had injured someone else, broken his leg. When he saw you coming he returned here and set fire to the body, then managed to escape out one of the windows. The dead man might not be Van Doran at all."

"You've been reading those mystery novels again, Sheriff. There was only one set of prints coming in here. And I saw his face clearly in the flames before he died. I even dreamed of it last night. Besides, I would have seen anyone trying to climb out a window, even that high one over the wind shaft."

"Then the thing's impossible, unless you're telling me he committed suicide."

"I'm not telling you anything of the sort. But I do want to climb up there and take a look."

We got a ladder from the hospital groundskeeper and carried it over between us.

Sheriff Lens snorted as I lifted it into position. "If you need a ladder to get up there, Doc, how in hell you figger Van Doran got up there—flew?"

"He could have stood on one of the display cases." I went halfway up the ladder until I was within reaching distance of the blackened central wind shaft.

Certainly nothing was hidden up here, and there was no sign of what had caused the fire. But over to one side, at the edge of the charred area, I did find something of interest.

A tiny piece of—what? rubber?—half melted from the heat and stuck to the wood. The unmelted part was red, which earlier had attracted my attention. But I couldn't for the life of me figure out what it had been. Had the killer hung from the roof by a giant rubber band that snapped him up out of sight when the fire started? No, I'd as soon believe in the Devil as in that idea.

I came back down the ladder. "Any luck, Doc?"

"Not much," I admitted.

"What now?"

"Let's go up to the hospital."

Bob Yale was in Seeger's office and he was just hanging up the telephone as we entered. "Mabel Foster's at it again. She was down in the town square creating a disturbance, warning people the Devil has come to Northmont. One of your deputies picked her up, Sheriff, and he's bringing her out here."

"Don't know what in hell we'll do with her," Seeger muttered.

I walked to the window and stared out at the windmill. "How's Collins coming along?"

"Better," Seeger said. "I think we can move him to Boston by the first of next week."

"His spirits are good," Yale added, confirming the diagnosis.

"The fire damaged your windmill," I said. "It doesn't turn any more."

"We can get that fixed," the hospital's director assured me.

I remembered something that Sheriff Lens had said. I had to think about it for a few moments, sorting it out in my mind, but then I was certain. "I know who did it," I told them.

"What?"

"I know who caused Randy Collins' injuries and then murdered Isaac Van Doran."

"Not the Devil?" Dr. Seeger asked with a slight smile.

"No, not the Devil. It was a very human killer." I started for the door. "Where's Lincoln Jones now?"

Yale glanced at the wall clock. "Probably up with Collins, changing the dressing on his burns."

"I'm going up there," I said, and though I didn't tell them to, the others trailed along.

Sara Jane was seated next to her husband's bed as we entered the room. Dr.

Jones looked up from his task of spreading salve over the burned flesh and said, "I really don't know if it's good to have so many people in here at once."

"This is very important," I said. "I want to explain who caused Van Doran's death and how it was done."

Sara Jane came forward in her chair. "Was it the same person who did this to my husband?"

"Yes."

"Who was it?"

I leaned over the bed. "Shall I tell them, Randy? Shall I tell them who did this terrible thing to you and Isaac?"

"It was Satan," he rasped. "The Devil."

I shook my head. "No, it was only the Devil that dwells within each of us. You set fire to yourself, Randy. It was an accident, of course, but it was no accident when you sent Isaac Van Doran out to his death last evening."

They were all trying to talk at once, but it was Sara Jane's voice I heard above the rest. "What do you mean he set fire to himself? How could that be?"

"He was filling rubber balloons with small quantities of gasoline from a glass jug. The balloons were attached to a long fuse wound around the wind shaft up above. The gasoline ignited, breaking the jug and setting fire to his clothes. The wind shaft was turning at the time, and lifted some of the gasoline-filled balloons up out of the way of the fire."

"Why would Collins want to burn down the windmill?" Dr. Seeger asked, clearly unconvinced.

"He didn't want to burn the whole windmill," I explained. "Look out at it now, with those four vanes frozen in position. Sheriff Lens said it looked just like a cross, and it does. Randy Collins was going to burn a giant cross in front of this hospital because you hired a black doctor."

Lincoln Jones never looked up at my words. He kept on ministering to his patient as if none of this concerned him. Collins just lay there with his eyes closed as I hurried on. "The day the hospital opened and we had that scene with Mabel Foster, Seeger asked you, Randy, if you put Mabel up to it. Sara Jane wondered too if you were causing the disturbance. Even though they spoke in jest, I should have known from that—and from your conservative reputation—where you stood on hiring a black doctor at Pilgrim.

"The Ku Klux Klan has been active near here, burning crosses and so forth. Whether you're an active member or merely a KKK sympathizer, it must have struck you as fitting that the canvas-covered vanes of your windmill could be set afire for a cross burning. So you got a gallon jug of gasoline from Isaac's station. The idea, I suppose, was to attach the gasoline-filled balloons to the vanes of the windmill as they turned, then light the fuse and scoot away while the balloons burst and that flaming gasoline spread itself over the canvas. You were filling the balloons, letting the turning wind shaft carry them up above your head, when the accident happened."

"What about this business with the Devil?" Sheriff Lens asked.

"When it first happened, Randy didn't use the words *Devil* or *Satan*. He said *Lucifer*, though no one else including Mabel Foster used that name. Once he knew what he was saying, Randy's talk was of the Devil and fireballs. He didn't mention Lucifer any more either. But if he didn't mean the Devil when he first said it, what else could *Lucifer* have meant? What else is Lucifer a name for? Common friction matches.

"They're still called Lucifers by some people, and I know Randy used them because I saw a box at his home. He was simply telling us that a friction match accidentally ignited and caused the fire. But when he came to his senses and decided on a coverup—he changed Lucifer to the Devil."

"But Collins hasn't left his hospital bed," Bob Yale protested. "How was he able to kill Isaac Van Doran?"

"When I figured what must have happened to Randy, the rest was easy. After the first fire I found a piece of thick curved glass—not from the flat display cases, more like from a glass jug. That helped me, same as finding bits of rubber today helped me make a good guess about the balloons. If Randy brought the gasoline out in a glass jug, where'd he get it from? Only from Isaac Van Doran, who operates the town's only gas station.

"So what happened a few days after the fire, when Collins could have visitors? Van Doran comes to see him, at noon when Sara Jane's not around. How come, when the men have always been cool to one another? Because Van Doran knows damn well that Randy burned himself up somehow, with that gallon jug of gasoline he bought at Isaac's station." I turned to the man in the bed. "Van Doran came to blackmail you, didn't he, Randy?"

The eyes were still closed, but after a moment's silence he spoke. "Yeah, he wanted money. Said he'd tell them I was probably setting a fire with the gas. I told him where he could get money."

The scorched lips twisted into a sort of smile.

"Of course!" The final piece of the puzzle dropped into place. "The old stories about money hidden in the windmill! You told him the money was there—where? In little balloons full of gold dust? Something like that, I suppose.

You knew the fire hadn't consumed the gasoline-filled balloons already wrapped around the wind shaft. You knew you had to get rid of them somehow, before the gasoline leaked through or they were otherwise discovered. Because if they were found, everyone would realize what you were trying to do.

"So here was Van Doran presenting himself at your hospital bed. A man you already disliked because of the rumors about him and your wife. A man threatening blackmail. What better way to destroy the last evidence of your disastrous mistake? I suppose you told him where the money was supposed to be, told him to light a match or take a candle so he didn't need to turn on the windmill lights.

"Van Doran worked around gasoline every day, so he probably didn't even catch the odor of it when he climbed up there and lit his match. The fumes would have ignited, or one of the balloons would have burst. Whatever happened, Van Doran was immediately enveloped in flames and fell screaming to the floor, breaking his leg as he did so. Isaac Van Doran, and the evidence of the first fire, were destroyed together."

Sara Jane reached out her hand toward the man in the bed. "I can't believe it. Tell them it isn't true, Randy! Tell them!"

But he didn't say anything at all. He just lay there on the bed with his eyes closed, as if he couldn't stand the sight of the black doctor who was ministering to his wounded flesh.

"It was an odd sort of murder case," Dr. Sam Hawthorne continued, "difficult to prove in a court of law, since Randy Collins was helpless in a hospital bed at the time the victim died. They never did bring it to trial, but I guess he suffered enough anyway, what with all the operations to rebuild his body after the fire. They took him off to Boston and he never did come back, and I hear tell that Sara Jane finally left him and married someone else. It was the last of the trouble over Lincoln Jones, though, and over the years he proved to be one of the most popular doctors on the Pilgrim staff."

Dr. Sam got to his feet, leaning heavily on his cane. "Sorry you haven't time for another—ah—small libation. But come by again and I'll tell you about the boat on the lake, and our own miniature version of the *Mary Celeste* mystery."

THE PROBLEM OF
THE GINGERBREAD HOUSEBOAT

"This was in the summer of 1929," Dr. Sam Hawthorne began, warming to the subject as he always did. "My leg's bothering me a bit today, but you can help yourself to a small libation. Oh, and fill my glass again too, will you? Thanks. Now where was I? Oh, yes, the summer of '29. I suppose in a way it was the end of an era, because the country was never really the same after that summer. October brought the stock market crash and the beginning of the Great Depression. But for that summer, life went on as it always had . . ."

We had a little lake not far from Northmont (Dr. Sam continued), and some of the people had cottages where they went in the summer. It was called Chester Lake, after one of the area's early landowners, and it was about a mile wide by maybe five miles long. As it happened, that was the summer I fell in love—with a dark-haired girl named Miranda Grey who was just out of college and spending the summer with her aunt and uncle.

It was my eighth summer in Northmont, my ninth since getting out of medical school, and as my nurse April kept reminding me at every opportunity, it was about time I settled down and got married. The trouble was, in a town as small as Northmont where most families were my patients, it was difficult to work up any romantic interest in someone I'd treated for mumps or chicken pox just a few years earlier. I suppose that was why Miranda's arrival became such a big event in my life. The fact that she was ten years younger than me didn't seem important at all.

Her aunt and uncle, Kitty and Jason Grey, spent the summer at their Chester Lake cottage. Jason was a teacher over in Shinn Corners, so he had the whole summer off. I knew them slightly, though they'd never been my patients. Not, at least, until that day in late June when April announced that Kitty Grey was in my waiting room with her niece Miranda. She'd been giving Miranda a quick tour of Northmont when a windblown speck landed in the young girl's eye. My office was close by and they'd come to me for relief.

I was glad to give it. Miranda's big brown eyes teared up as I rolled back the lid and removed the offending speck. I guess it was pretty close to being love at first sight, at least on my part. "Thank you, Doctor," she said, and her voice was like music.

During the next few weeks I saw a great deal of Miranda Grey. I took her for rides in my tan Packard Runabout, and even escorted her to a barn dance on the weekend following the Fourth of July. On Sundays we picnicked at the lake and I found myself becoming a familiar figure at the Grey cottage.

The identical cottage next door was owned by a rather odd but friendly couple, Ray and Gretel Hauser. I knew little about them except that they were from Boston and had some money. Ray was a handsome man in his early forties who dabbled in real estate and stocks. His wife was small and flighty and a bit overweight. They were friends of the Greys and the two couples often dined together. But the Hausers' chief claim to fame was a flat-bottomed houseboat, the *Gretel*, which they launched each spring on the lake's placid waters. It had a shingled roof, fancy windows, and all sorts of gaudy ornamentation on the outside. The first time Miranda saw it she'd remarked, "It looks just like a gingerbread house!"

Mrs. Hauser liked that. "Ray and I are like Hansel and Gretel. When my money runs out we'll start eating the houseboat."

Her husband merely scoffed. "The way the market is climbing we won't have to worry about that!"

On that first day Miranda and I strolled down to the dock to get a better view of the houseboat. Of course Kitty and Jason had been on it plenty of times before, but Miranda hadn't, and Kitty urged Ray to take her aboard. "Come on, Ray, I want Miranda to see the inside!"

Jason, wearing a red jacket that seemed to be his summer uniform, tried to quiet her, but Kitty was insistent. She was a pretty brown-haired woman in her late thirties, with a sparkling smile, and not at all shy. Despite her age she was closer to the twenties' idea of a flapper than her niece Miranda. Ray Hauser smiled obligingly, as if he was used to her demands, and said, "Sure, let's all go for a cruise."

I followed along, feeling just a bit like an outsider. A month earlier I hadn't known any of these people, except for a nodding acquaintance with the Greys. Suddenly I was like one of the family. "Watch your step," Jason Grey instructed, guiding me up the wobbly wooden gangplank. Even on summer vacation he seemed like a slightly stodgy teacher.

I had to admit the houseboat's interior was impressive. A large central room had comfortable chairs and a table, plus a small pot-bellied stove for chilly evenings. There was a galley for preparing light meals, and a smaller room with bunk beds and a closet. "We can sleep four on board," Hauser said, "though we don't take many overnight cruises on Chester Lake."

"What kind of motors do you have?" I asked.

He led me to the stern. "Here—twin outboards. I did most of this work myself, a few years back. Bought a used flat-bottomed barge in Boston and built this on it. Picked the motors myself too. I have to keep extra gasoline on board, and they don't push it very fast, but it's better than being towed everywhere. I figure if you own a houseboat you're not out to break any speed records."

Gretel brought out a bottle of good Canadian whiskey and mixed drinks for everyone. A bit to my surprise, Miranda declined. "I don't think we should be violating the law," she said, and her primness was something new to me.

"Oh, come on," I kidded. "Prohibition is ignored by everyone these days."

"Then it should be repealed, shouldn't it?"

I felt oddly embarrassed disagreeing with her in front of her aunt and uncle. Somehow I was too old to be having a lovers' quarrel with this girl just out of college. But I pressed on nevertheless. "Didn't you ever break the law in your whole life?" I asked.

"Oh, everyone's broken the law," Aunt Kitty said, jumping to her defense, trying to soothe things before a real argument developed. "But I can see Miranda's point. She has a principle and she should stick to it."

Hauser changed the subject. "Come on, we'll go out for a little ride."

I helped him start the motors and cast off the lines, and the gingerbread houseboat drifted away from the dock. He'd been right about its slow progress. It took us a good fifteen minutes to cross the lake to the other side. But I was enjoying it, and so was Miranda.

"I'm sorry I kidded you about not drinking," I told her when we were seated alone on the deck. The others were inside, having another round.

"I went through four years of college confronting things like that, Sam. I didn't think I'd have to face it with someone as mature as you."

"You won't, ever again." I took her hand and held it. We'd started back across the lake and the breeze was in our faces. "Too cool for you?"

"No, I like it."

"Your aunt and uncle are fine people, Miranda. I wish I'd known your dad before he died."

"I was only ten when he went off to war," she said, looking away toward the shoreline. "Some day I hope you can meet my mother in Chicago."

"I hope so."

"Wouldn't you like to sail away like this on a boat some day, and just disappear?"

"What do you mean? Like the people on the *Mary Celeste?*"

"Who were they?"

"It's a famous unsolved mystery—I read about it just recently. It seems that back in 1872 a small sailing ship was found adrift in the Atlantic. Though the seas were calm and there was no evidence of damage or violence on board, the captain, his wife and child, and the crew of seven had all vanished. The mystery of what happened to them has never been solved."

"I think I did read about it once."

"I've helped the local sheriff with a few crimes that were every bit as strange. Sometime I'll tell you about them."

Kitty came out to join us. "You two all friendly again?"

"Sure," I told her. "Your niece is going to make me stop drinking."

"Good! Maybe we should all stop."

When Hauser docked the houseboat we thanked them for the ride and went ashore. I watched Gretel Hauser go up to their cottage and push open the door. Then Miranda and I followed her aunt and uncle up to their cottage for dinner.

In those days April had started to question me about Miranda. Especially on Monday mornings, after my weekends at Chester Lake, she'd ask, "Any wedding bells in the future, Dr. Sam?"

"Too soon to tell, April. I got called out twice over the weekend for emergencies. Plays havoc with my love life!"

"Come on, now. I think you like doctoring even more than women!"

"Maybe so. Maybe I should find me a woman doctor."

In truth Northmont's new hospital had taken some of the pressure off my weekends. If people couldn't reach me, there was always someone to help them at the hospital. So on Saturday afternoon, seeing my last patient and closing the office for the weekend, I was ready to drive up to Chester Lake and visit the Greys' cottage again.

Miranda met me at the door, and seemed really glad to see me. "Sam, it seems we've been apart forever!"

"It was a busy week at the office. I'd hoped to drive up and surprise you on Wednesday, but Mrs. Rodgers decided to have her baby."

"Come in. Aunt Kitty and Uncle Jason are next door with the Hausers."

"Good. I'd rather be alone with you anyway."

We settled down to flirtatious small talk, and the next half hour passed quickly. It was nearly six o'clock when the screen door opened and Aunt Kitty came in. She was wearing a colorful summer dress and carrying a sweater. "Miranda," she said breathlessly, "your uncle and I are going out on the houseboat with the Hausers. Can you and Sam find yourselves something to eat?"

"Sure, Aunt Kitty."

I glanced out the door and caught a glimpse of Jason's bright red jacket vanishing inside the houseboat. There was no sign of the Hausers. "We'll walk down with you and say hello," I suggested.

Kitty smiled at me. "We'd ask you along, but I'm sure you love-birds would rather be alone."

Miranda and I strolled along as Kitty hurried nervously out on the dock and up the gangplank. Ray Hauser came to the ornate latticework door and waved. Then he called to me, "Sam, help me with these mooring lines, will you?"

"Sure thing!" I unhooked the lines and tossed them aboard while Hauser started the engines. I thought I heard Gretel's laugh from somewhere on board, and I imagined they were going out on the lake to do some more drinking—free of Miranda's criticism.

Kitty turned to wave at us once more and then went inside to join the others. Ray Hauser stayed on the deck until finally we waved goodbye and strolled back to the Greys' cottage. "The four of them seem to be getting on well," I said, holding open the screen door.

"Aunt Kitty could get along with anyone, she's so friendly. I am a bit surprised that Uncle Jason likes them too."

I stood at the front window watching the houseboat drift slowly near the middle of the lake. There were no other boats nearby, though a couple of sails could be seen far down at the other end of the water. "Well, they've pretty much got the lake to themselves. Everyone else must be eating dinner."

"Is that a hint, Sam Hawthorne?"

I laughed and tossed a pillow at her. "Unless you'd rather smooch for a bit."

"Oh—you!"

She busied herself preparing something to eat, while I continued watching the Hausers' houseboat.

I noticed a pair of binoculars hanging from a hook by the window and tried them out. They were powerful ones, army issue from the war, and I could see the houseboat easily with them. No one was on deck, though I could see Jason's red jacket through the window. "That's odd."

Miranda came up beside me, resting her hand on my back. "What is?"

"The motors are off and they're just drifting."

"They often do that. I think they go out there to drink."

One of the sailboats from the other end of the lake had come up this way, and as I watched, the drifting houseboat seemed to head straight for it. Through the binoculars I saw the man on the sailboat maneuver it away just in time, than stand up to shout and shake his fist as the *Gretel* passed him by.

"Could they all be drunk on there?" I wondered.

"Hardly! They've only been out for fifteen minutes."

"Still . . ." I took the binoculars and went outside, walking out to the end of the Hausers' dock. As I watched the houseboat turn slowly in the water I could see that no one was steering or controlling it. And there was no sign of any of them.

Miranda came out to join me. "What's the trouble, Sam?"

"I don't like it. There's something wrong. That day we were out Hauser seemed very careful about handling the boat. Today he's just letting it drift."

"They're busy drinking," she scoffed, dismissing my concern.

"Could they all be swimming?"

She shook her head. "My uncle doesn't swim a stroke."

"And there's no sign of them in the water." I lowered the binoculars and glanced over at the Greys' own dock where a little motorboat was tied up. "Let's take a ride out there and see. You're probably right that they're just sitting around with drinks, but I'd feel better taking a look."

"Oh, all right. Let me turn off the stove."

I started the motor with some difficulty and we headed out toward the houseboat. We still had about two hours of daylight and a few more boats were taking advantage of it. None had come near the Hausers' craft, though, except for the sailboat which brushed by it. I said nothing as we approached, but Miranda spoke softly. "It seems deserted. Do you think they're . . . in bed?"

"You stay here. I'll go on board for a look."

I got a grip and boosted myself on board. Glancing through one of the windows I could see Jason Grey's red jacket draped over the back of a chair. The door was unlatched and I stepped inside. Surprisingly, there were no glasses or liquor bottles in evidence. Nothing seemed to be disturbed. I had an awful feeling that Miranda had been right. I would find them in the bunk beds.

But these were empty too, as was the little galley and the toilet. The entire houseboat was empty.

The Greys and the Hausers had vanished, leaving the *Gretel* to drift aimlessly in the center of Chester Lake.

We covered the lake, back and forth, for the next hour. I was certain we'd find swimmers or bodies or something that would furnish a clue, but there was nothing. It was as if the lake, or the sky, had swallowed them up.

"Four people! Miranda, what happened to them?" I was pacing the deck nervously. "It's like another *Mary Celeste!*"

"You're letting your imagination run wild, Sam. I'm sure they'll turn up. Let's tow the houseboat to shore and wait."

We attached a tow line and brought it, with some difficulty, back to the Hausers' dock. The little motorboat wasn't built for that sort of work but somehow we managed. The Hauser cottage was locked and there was no sign that any of them had returned. "I'm going to search the houseboat one more time while it's still daylight," I decided. "Maybe there's a hiding place we missed."

I quickly discovered that the high ceiling of the main room left no space unaccounted for beneath the roof. There was some storage space below the deck, but in the dim light I could find nothing except a half-dozen cans of fuel and some old rags. I checked the narrow closets but they were empty. There were two half-empty bottles in the whiskey cabinet—apparently the same ones we'd used on my earlier visit. A little icebox in the galley was empty. Except for Jason's red jacket there was not a sign that any of them had been on board the *Gretel.*

I came down the gangplank just as the sun was setting. "I think I'd better telephone Sheriff Lens," I said.

"Do you really think that's necessary?"

"They're gone, Miranda. Your aunt and uncle, and the Hausers. And I don't know what happened to them. If they're in the lake we have to get a search party organized."

"I suppose you're right," she admitted reluctantly. "I just can't bring myself to believe any of this. It seems they must be playing a joke on us."

"I hope so. But they've had plenty of time to show up if it is a joke."

Very few of the cottages had telephones, but there was one at the Greys'. I used it to call Sheriff Lens and tell him what had happened.

Chester Lake was nearly 20 miles from Northmont but it was still in the county, and therefore still the province of Sheriff Lens. He responded to my call with two cars full of deputies and townspeople ready to join in the search. Despite the darkness one boatload set out immediately, lighting its way with lanterns, to search the shoreline for washed-up bodies.

"They musta gone swimmin' and got cramps," the sheriff speculated, staring down at the shoreline as the lanterns moved along it in the dark. "We'll find their bodies."

Miranda, who'd stood up amazingly well to all this, shuddered at his words. She shook her head and argued doggedly, "My uncle doesn't swim. And my aunt is too good a swimmer to drown on a calm lake like this. Besides, Sam was watching the boat through binoculars. He'd have seen them in the water."

"You wasn't watchin' it every minute, was you, Doc? You couldn't see the other side of it now, could you?"

"No," I admitted. "I suppose they could have sneaked off. I suppose a submarine could have surfaced and taken them off the other side when I wasn't looking, but I doubt if that happened. I'll grant you there are ways the four of them could have gotten off that houseboat without attracting attention, but why would they do it? Why would four perfectly normal, sensible, middle-aged people want to disappear and hide from us? It isn't April Fool's Day, you know."

"They'll turn up," Sheriff Lens assured me. He dropped his voice a bit so as not to upset Miranda again. "Or their bodies will."

I stayed up most of the night with the others, until the search parties had covered the entire shoreline. There were no bodies. Around midnight we forced open the door of the Hausers' cottage, searching for a note or clue of some sort, but there was nothing. Everything had been left in perfect order for their return.

Finally, toward dawn, I wakened Miranda long enough to kiss her and say, "I'm going home for some sleep. I'll be back before noon."

It was the sheriff who awakened me a few hours later. I stood aside to let him enter my apartment, at the same instant remembering what he must be there for.

"You've found them!" I said.

"No such luck, Doc. I had people searchin' again first thing this mornin', but there's no sign of them. We went over the houseboat again too."

I sank into a chair, not fully awake yet. "It really is beginning to look like another *Mary Celeste*."

"What's that?"

"A ship that was found in the middle of the ocean, drifting without its crew. No one ever discovered what happened to them."

Sheriff Lens grunted. "Was this recent?"

"No, a long time ago."

"And they never solved it, huh?"

"Something drove the people off the ship, but what? The sea was calm, just as the lake was calm yesterday."

"Could another boat have attacked 'em?"

"A ship might have attacked the *Mary Celeste*, though there was no evidence of it. I don't see how another boat could have gotten close to the *Gretel* yesterday without my noticing it."

"Come on, Doc. I'll drive you back up there. Maybe in the daylight we'll get an idea."

"This isn't like the other cases I've helped you with, Sheriff. In the past there's always been a body, or a crime of some sort. This time we just don't know what happened! And there aren't even any suspects—they've all disappeared!"

"All but one. Miranda Grey's still around."

I glanced at him, thinking he must be kidding me, but his face was dead serious. "Miranda was with me the whole time! How could she have caused their disappearance?"

"Don't know *how*, Doc. But I know *why*. The word is that she stands to inherit a tidy sum with her aunt and uncle both dead. They had some stocks that're showing a good profit these days, an' they got no family. I hear that Miranda is the only heir."

I tried to keep my temper under control. "Sheriff, even if that's true, Miranda couldn't collect a cent unless their bodies were found. Otherwise she'd have to wait years for them to be declared legally dead. It makes no sense to suspect her, even if she hadn't been with me all the time. I think you're jumping to the conclusion there's been foul play when all we really know is that they've disappeared."

"Maybe so," Sheriff Lens admitted. "Anyway, let's get goin'. My deputies might have turned something up."

But when we reached the lake it was much as it'd been the previous night. Miranda came running out to meet me, and I thought for an instant she might throw her arms around me. "Have you heard anything?" she demanded of the sheriff.

"Not a thing, Miss. We got more people comin' in today to search the shoreline, an' we're going to start dragging the lake."

"I can't believe they're dead!"

We went through the Hausers' cottage again, searching for anything that might be a clue to the mystery. I examined bills from Boston department stores and a Cape Cod tourist court and even one from a plumbing-supply house, but I came up with nothing.

Sheriff Lens, looking over my shoulder, asked, "What sort of plumbing supplies?"

"A hot-water heater they installed themselves."

He grunted and went on with his own searching. The cottage's tiny rooms yielded nothing, and there was no basement to be searched. We trooped back to the place next door more dejected than ever. "There are no clues," I complained to Miranda. "Nothing I can get my teeth into! They're simply gone!"

All afternoon long deputies and other searchers brought back reports, but they always added up to the same thing. No bodies had been washed up on shore and the men in the rowboats with their grappling hooks had snagged nothing but a fisherman's wading boot and a splintered beer keg.

Finally Sheriff Lens said, "Miranda, we should have photographs of your aunt and uncle to send around to the newspapers. Do you have any good ones?"

She thought for a moment, then her face brightened. "Aunt Kitty showed me a picture of them with the Hausers. It was taken last summer at that amusement park down near Winslow."

"Could you find it?"

"I'll see."

She searched around in the Greys' house without success, then suddenly remembered an attic crawlspace that was reached through a trap door in the bedroom ceiling. "They used it for storage," she explained. I stood on a chair and lifted down a cardboard box as she directed. Inside we found a photograph of the four missing people, smiling at the camera and standing before a sign that read *Sea Serpent Ride–1001 Thrills!*

I showed it to the sheriff and he gave a customary grunt. "You think a sea serpent swallowed them up?"

"No. The picture was taken last year at an amusement park. But it's a good likeness of all of them."

He took it and promised to give it to the papers. I noticed that Miranda seemed a bit more cheerful, as if finding the picture had given her renewed confidence that the four of them would be found as well. Maybe she was right. I just didn't know.

Late in the afternoon I telephoned April at home, just in case some patient had been trying to reach me with an emergency. But everything was quiet. "Any sign of the missing people?" she asked.

"Not a trace."

"Dr. Sam, I happened to think of something I read in one of them magazines we got around the office. Don't remember if it was true or not, but it was about people jumping overboard from a motorboat for no reason at all and drowning. Turned out there was a big spider hidden on the boat that came out and scared them into jumping."

"A spider?"

"That's right. You think there's something like that hidden on board the *Gretel?*"

"April, it's worth thinking about. Thanks for the tip."

I hung up and went outside, standing there staring at the fancy houseboat and thinking about a horrible creature that might be lurking somewhere inside. I turned and hurried back to the cottage.

"What's up, Doc?" Sheriff Lens asked.

"Sheriff, I need some heavy gloves and a canvas sack. And a flashlight."

"Won't a lantern do?"

"A flashlight would be better. I'll be in cramped quarters."

"On the houseboat?"

"Yes, I'm going on a spider hunt."

The sheriff and Miranda stood on the shore and watched as I boarded the houseboat once more, carrying the flashlight and sack in my gloved hands. I made my way directly to the back of the boat and opened the access door to the storage space in the hull. The gasoline cans and old rags were still there, and at first my slowly moving flashlight picked out nothing else.

But then I saw it, slim and still and very deadly.

I reached out a careful hand, hardly daring to breathe.

Another inch—

I had it, and I placed it carefully in the canvas sack.

"You find somethin'?" Sheriff Lens asked as I came ashore with my prize.

"I found something."

Miranda stared at the sack in my hand, unable to tear her eyes away. "What's in there, Sam?"

"The solution to the mystery. And I'm afraid it isn't a very pleasant solution." I opened the sack carefully and showed them what I'd found. "You see, we had the wrong legend. It wasn't the *Mary Celeste* after all. It was *Hansel and Gretel.*"

The hours that followed were sad and distasteful. There was business to be done at the cottage, and when that was over Sheriff Lens had to find a judge to swear out a warrant. Then we drove half of the night to rendezvous with other law officers at a town hall on Cape Cod.

We reached the tourist court just before dawn. There was enough light already to make out the semicircle of little white cabins grouped around the central kitchen and bathroom facilities. As we parked on the road and fanned out across the grass, one officer asked me, "Are you armed, sir?"

"No, I'm just along for the ride."

Saying it, I wondered why I had come all this distance just to see the sad conclusion of a sad story. Then I stood aside as Sheriff Lens pounded on the door. "Police! Open up in there!"

After a few minutes the door of the little tourist cabin opened and a tired face peered out at us in the dawn light. He seemed to recognize me rather than the sheriff. "Hello, Sam," he said quietly. It was Ray Hauser.

"We have a warrant for your arrest," Sheriff Lens announced.

I didn't wait for the rest. I already heard the window squeaking open at the rear of the cabin.

I sprinted around in the direction of the sound and caught her as her feet touched the ground. "I'm sorry," I said. "You didn't make it."

"Oh, Sam—" She collapsed sobbing against my chest as Sheriff Lens came up behind us.

"I have a warrant for your arrest," he intoned, "on two counts of first-degree murder. Do you have anything to say?"

Miranda's Aunt Kitty shook her head. "Take me back," she told us. "I'm ready."

L ater, at the local police station where we waited out the legal formalities, I talked with Ray Hauser. He sat handcuffed and grim on a hard wooden bench, occasionally taking a puff from a cigarette someone had given him. "We found their bodies last night," I said. "Your wife Gretel and Kitty's husband Jason, both in the attic crawl-space of your house, where you'd hidden them."

"Yes," he said simply. "You're a smart fellow, Sam. When it didn't work we knew it was only a matter of time, but somehow we were hoping for more time than this."

"When it didn't work," I repeated. "I found it yesterday on the houseboat, and that told me the whole story. We thought it was another *Mary Celeste*, with everyone disappearing from the houseboat, but it was only Hansel and Gretel all over again. Or Jason and Gretel. Remember how the wicked witch tried to bake them in the stove? That was the whole plan. The houseboat wasn't supposed to be found deserted at all—it was supposed to explode and burn and sink. What I found yesterday was a single stick of dynamite with a fuse that had sputtered out before it did its job. Had it gone off as planned, it would have blown a hole below the waterline and ignited those six cans of gasoline you'd stored there. The *Gretel* would have sunk in flames."

"It would have been so simple that way," Hauser said glumly.

"The people from shore, searching for survivors, would have pulled you and Kitty Grey from the water. There'd have been no sign of Jason or your wife Gretel, but their bodies would have washed ashore after a few days. The key to it all, of course, was that Jason and Gretel were never on the houseboat Saturday afternoon. You and Kitty killed them—"

"I did it," he insisted. "Kitty had nothing to do with the actual killings. I gave them a sleeping powder in some whiskey and smothered them. It was supposed to happen on the houseboat, so their bodies would be found soon after the explosion, but Jason drank the whiskey at the cottage and fell asleep. We couldn't carry them onto the boat, so we hid the bodies. After we were rescued we planned to dump the bodies out in the lake in the middle of the night, to be found later."

"It wouldn't have worked, you know. The time of death would have been correct, but an autopsy would have shown neither smoke nor water in their lungs."

"We figured after a few days in the water that wouldn't have mattered. We'd have scorched their clothes to make it look like they'd died in the fire." He took another drag on his cigarette. "Tell me how you know it all, Sam."

Kitty had collapsed and been given a sedative. Though I barely knew Hauser, he seemed to be the one to tell. "There was one thing bothered me from the start. You locked your cottage Saturday, but you hadn't bothered to lock it before when we all went out on the boat. I remember Gretel simply pushing the door open when you returned the day I was along. That got me wondering if the disappearance and the locked cottage were connected. Wondering if you'd planned to disappear all along, or if there was something in the cottage you didn't want found."

I remembered the gasoline cans on the houseboat—far more than you'd need for extra fuel. I went searching and found the dynamite with its scorched fuse, and then I knew. We never actually saw Gretel or Jason board the boat. I caught a glimpse of Jason's red coat, which you could have been wearing. I thought I heard Gretel's laugh, but it could have been Kitty. We had only Kitty's word, and your word, that they were aboard when you cast off.

"Kitty was nervous and breathless when she told us you were all on the boat—not surprising since she'd just seen the murders committed. Jason and Gretel were already dead, hidden in your cottage crawlspace. We missed the trap door when we searched your cottage, because we weren't looking for it. But I knew it had to be there because the Greys' cottage had one and the two cottages were identical."

Hauser stubbed out his cigarette. "I lit the fuse and we went into the water on the side away from the cottage, in case you were watching. When the boat didn't explode we swam to the opposite shore. I had to steal a car." He made it sound like the worst thing they'd done.

"Miranda told me Kitty was a good swimmer. But why didn't you just get back on the houseboat?"

"Kitty was still afraid it might explode any minute. Besides we couldn't have explained the absence of our spouses."

I nodded. "You and Kitty—the handsome man and the flapper. A better pair than the stuffy teacher and the overweight Gretel. I can understand your attraction to each other, but did it have to cause murder?"

He lifted his sad eyes to mine. "You have to realize we're deeply in love. We did this for love."

"For love and a bit of money too, I imagine. Gretel referred to it that first day as her money, and Jason had made money in the market. You and Kitty had to kill them both to inherit it from both sides, and a staged accident was the safest way to do that."

"I told you she had nothing to do with killing them."

"You never lifted their bodies into that attic crawlspace by yourself. She must have helped you with that part, at least."

He didn't even argue the point. "How'd you find us at the tourist court?"

"I figured you two ran away after the boat failed to explode. The question was where. It wouldn't be too close because you had to know the bodies would be found within a few days, when the odor became noticeable. I remembered a bill I came across from the tourist court. You'd gone there once, and maybe you'd gone there again. The sheriff phoned and they confirmed there was a couple fitting your description. You know the rest."

He shook his head sadly. "I don't know the rest. What happens to us now?"

But that was for a judge and jury to answer. Four months later Hauser was found guilty and sentenced to life in prison. Kitty was never brought to trial. She hanged herself with a torn bedsheet in her cell.

"You're wondering what happened with Miranda and me?" Dr. Sam Hawthorne concluded, pouring himself another drink from the bottle. "Well, that's another story—another mystery, really. It involved a strange happening at the Northmont post office on the very day of the big stock-market crash. But I'd better save that one for next time."

THE PROBLEM OF
THE PINK POST OFFICE

"Now this is what I call a summer's day!" Dr. Sam Hawthorne said as he poured the drinks. "Makes me feel young again! We can sit out here under the trees without a care in the world and reminisce about the old days. What's that? I promised to tell you about the Northmont post office and what happened back in 1929 on the day of the stock market crash? Well, I guess that was a memorable affair, all right—and it presented me with a problem unique among all the cases I helped investigate during those years. Unique in what way? Well, I suppose I should start at the beginning . . ."

The date, I well remember, was Thursday, October 24, 1929, (Dr. Sam continued), and in future years it would be known as Black Thursday, though several of the days that followed were even worse for the stock market. In the morning, though, it was just another autumn day in Northmont. The sky was cloudy, with the temperature in the low fifties, and there was a threat of rain in the air.

It was the day that Vera Brock finished painting her new post office, and since business was slow at the office my nurse April and I strolled down to see it. Until now the post office had always been located in the general store, and we viewed it as a sign of progress that the old sweet shoppe opposite the town square had been taken over by the government for a post office.

"Now we've got our own hospital *and* our own separate post office!" April exclaimed. "We're growin' bigger all the time, Dr. Sam."

"Boston better start worrying," I said with a smile.

"Oh, now you're makin' fun of me, but it's true. Northmont's going to be on the map."

"The post-office map, at least." I spotted our postmistress, Vera Brock, hurrying along the street with a can of paint. She was a solid woman in her forties who'd run the post office in the general store for as long as I'd been in Northmont. "Vera!" I called out to her.

"Morning, Dr. Sam. You an' April coming for your mail?"

"We wanted to see the new post office."

She hefted the can of paint. "This is opening day and I discovered one whole wall I forgot to paint! Can you believe that?"

She unlocked the post-office door and we followed her inside. "It's pink!" April gasped, and I don't think she would have been more startled if the walls had been covered with tropical vines. "A pink post office!"

"Well, the paint was cheap," Vera Brock admitted. "Hume Baxter ordered it by mistake and he gave me a good price on it. I figured I'd save the government some money. Just last month the Postmaster General estimated this year's deficit at a hundred million dollars and said the cost of a first-class letter might have to go up to three cents."

"I can't believe that," April scoffed. "The two-cent letter is a tradition."

"We'll see. Anyway, I figured a cheap coat of paint wouldn't do any harm."

"But pink, Vera!" April exclaimed.

"It don't look so awful to me, but then I guess I'm a bit color blind anyhow."

The new post office was a good-sized room about twenty feet square, which had been split across the middle by a counter where people could go to pick up their mail or purchase stamps and post-cards. The back wall was lined with the usual wooden pigeonholes where the mail was sorted for pickup. In those days, of course, there was no home delivery. Everyone had to come to Vera Brock's post office for their mail.

"Well, I don't think it looks half bad, Vera," I said. "This town could stand some perkin' up."

The words were hardly out of my mouth when the door opened and in came Miranda Grey, the perkiest thing to hit Northmont in many a moon. I'd met Miranda the previous summer, during the business on Chester Lake, and we'd dated regularly for a few months. With the coming of autumn and the reopening of school, there was the usual increase in illness, and in my house calls. What with one thing and another, Miranda and I saw less of each other, though I suspected the fact that she'd stayed on in Northmont past the end of summer meant she had serious intentions. Maybe they were more serious than mine.

"Hello, Sam, how are you?" she greeted me. "I haven't seen hide nor hair of you since last Saturday night. I was beginning to think you'd moved to Boston."

I tried to see if her eyes were laughing as she spoke to me, but they weren't. She was downright upset at my not having called her for five days. "This damp weather's brought on a lot of illness, Miranda. I've been busy day and night."

"I thought the new hospital was taking some of the load off you."

"It is, for serious illness. But they still call on me for the flu and the chicken pox. I just don't have as much free time as I had in the summer, Miranda."

Through all this exchange April stood to one side, eyeing Miranda with something like apprehension. I think April saw her as a threat to the office, and to my ability to devote all my time to our patients. For whatever reason, Miranda was a danger in April's eyes, and I'd become increasingly aware of it with each passing month.

About that time Vera Brock must have realized she wasn't going to get any painting done on the opening day of her new post office. We were there and more people were coming by all the time, no doubt attracted by the pink walls seen through the front window. She stood for a moment contemplating the unfinished job—the righthand wall as you entered was still a dull yellowish-tan from the counter to the front. "I'm gonna ask Hume Baxter if he can close up his store for an hour and come paint this for me," she said. "I just don't have time to do it today."

"I can't believe you forgot to paint that whole part of the wall," April said.

"This big cabinet with all its pigeonholes was out there against the wall when I painted. They moved it back here yesterday and I discovered I'd forgotten to paint behind it."

"Wish I had the time, Vera," I said. "I'd do it for you."

"No, no, Dr. Sam, I wouldn't hear of it! Hume can be over here in ten minutes if he's not busy."

The idea of Hume Baxter ever being busy almost made me chuckle. He'd opened his paint, hardware, and farm-supply store right in the center of town about a year earlier, but how he managed to keep going with the small amount of business he did was more than I could figure out. Farmers didn't like to get all dressed up for a trip into town when they needed supplies in a hurry, and the amount of business he got from the townsfolk was minimal.

Still, everyone liked Hume Baxter because he tried so hard to please. And sure enough, within ten minutes he appeared at Vera's post office, paint brush in hand. He was a sandy-haired fellow in his mid-thirties, just a little older than me, and he was barely in the door when Miranda began flirting with him.

"Oh, Hume, I'll bet you have plenty of time for your lady friends, don't you?"

He blushed and glanced around, as if seeking a quick exit. "Well, now, sometimes it gets busy at the store."

"Don't pay any attention to her, Hume," I told him. "That's just for my benefit. I've been neglecting her lately."

Hume Baxter spread out his drop cloths and opened the can of pink paint. "Well, now," he replied, entering into the banter, "I don't rightly see how anyone could be too busy for you, Miss Miranda."

"Thank you, Hume. You're a sweetheart!"

"You send me a bill for this paintin'," Vera told him. "I'll see to it the government pays."

"Sure will, Vera. I pay enough taxes. If I can get something back from them I'll take it."

He set to work with his paint brush while Vera opened the sack of morning mail and began sorting it into the pigeonholes behind the counter.

"Guess we'll be going along," I said, "and leave you to your work, Vera."

"Might as well wait another few minutes, Doc, and you can take your mail along."

"That's a good idea," I said, "if you don't mind us cluttering up your new place."

"I think I'll wait for my mail too," Miranda decided. She was working afternoons at the hospital as a nurse's aide, but I knew her mornings were free.

Hume Baxter had started painting at the front, working back toward the counter. "What did you think of the World Series, Doc?" he asked. "Never thought them Athletics would beat the Cubs." Philadelphia had defeated Chicago in four out of five games the previous week.

"I only got to hear part of one game on the radio," I admitted. "It was a busy week for me."

Our conversation was interrupted by the sudden arrival of Anson Waters, the town banker and one of our most distinguished citizens—except that he wasn't looking too distinguished at the moment. He carried a thin manila envelope as he hurried up to the counter.

"Land sakes, Mr. Waters," Vera Brock said, "you certainly look flustered this morning."

"Haven't you heard the news? The stock market is collapsing again! My broker just telephoned me from New York."

I was vaguely aware from the newspaper that there'd been heavy losses in the market on Monday, and again on Wednesday, but it had seemed then to be a world apart from my existence. I couldn't help thinking that while Baxter talked of the World Series and Waters of the stock market, my world was different from theirs.

"What's happening?" Miranda asked him.

"It's a panic down on Wall Street," the banker informed her. "The scene on the stock exchange floor is so wild they've closed the visitors' gallery. And the ticker tape is so far behind actual sales that nobody knows what's happening. My broker needs cash from me to cover some stock I bought on margin."

"I can't help you there," Vera told him in her joking way. "This here's just a post office. Unless maybe he'll take stamps."

"It's nothing funny, Vera." He handed her the envelope. "This is addressed to my broker. It contains a railroad bearer bond in the amount of ten thousand dollars. I want to register this and mail it. He must have it by tomorrow—"

"I can't promise that," Vera told him.

"—or by Saturday morning at the latest. It's a short session on Saturday, so he'd need it before noon."

Vera was busy stamping the envelope and making an entry in her register. "This bond is negotiable?"

"That's right. My broker can cash it at once."

"Dangerous thing to send through the mails."

"That's why I want it registered."

"You said the value was ten thousand?"

"That's correct."

She totaled up the postage and registry fee and he paid them. Then Vera turned and placed the envelope on the desk behind her for special handling.

"You think the panic will last?" I asked Waters.

"If it does the whole country's in trouble. It could even throw us into a depression. The banking structure of this country is in bad shape, and I'm the first to admit it."

"I hope you're wrong," I said.

"I hope so too." He pocketed his registry receipt and headed for the door. "I have to get back to the telephone. I only pray things haven't gotten worse in the last half hour."

Vera bustled around behind the counter, sorting more of the morning's mail. "Land sakes, people like Anson Waters spend so much time watchin' their money they don't have time to enjoy it."

"That's the most unsettled I've ever seen him," April admitted. "In the bank he's usually like an iceberg."

"Maybe we should be glad we're not rich," Hume Baxter said. He was making good progress with the painting and was over half finished already.

Vera completed the last of the sorting. "Well, now, I can give you your mail, Doc. And yours too, Miranda. Just one letter for you today."

I took the little stack she handed me and glanced through it. There was nothing of importance, only a couple of bills and an announcement that a new salesman would be calling on me from one of the pharmaceutical houses. "This too," Vera said, and reached across the counter with a weekly medical journal to which I subscribed. My parents had given me my first subscription when I graduated from medical school, and I'd been getting it ever since.

April and Miranda and I were starting for the door when it opened to admit the formidable bulk of Sheriff Lens, carrying a large cardboard box tied with stout cord. "Morning, folks," he greeted us, making for the counter. He stopped almost at once and stared at the walls. "Pink?" he asked of no one in particular.

"Yes, pink!" Vera shot back. "I'm not taking any guff from you today, Sheriff. State your business and be gone!"

"I gotta mail this box off to Washington," he said meekly. "It's got some bottles in it that're evidence in a bootlegging case."

Vera lifted the middle section of the counter and opened a doorway that allowed him to pass through.

"Bring it back here," she ordered. "I'm not goin' to be lifting heavy boxes around."

He did as he was told and set the box on her desk. "This okay?"

"Not on my desk, you old fool!" Her voice was so sharp that Sheriff Lens jerked the box off her desk and took a few steps back the way he'd come, almost tripping over Hume's drop cloth. Vera sighed and said, "I'm sorry. Put it on this back shelf, Sheriff."

He followed her instructions and deposited his burden on the shelf by the pigeonholes. "Sorry I offended you, Vera. I'm just tryin' to do my job."

"I'm too edgy this morning," she admitted. "Opening this new place and all is a lot of work."

"That's all right, Vera," Sheriff Lens told her with uncharacteristic restraint. "I understand."

"I finished your paint job," Hume Baxter announced, gathering up his drop cloths. "Don't get too near the wall till it dries." He bent to touch up a spot that he'd missed just above the floor level and near the counter as Vera came out to inspect his work.

"A right fine job, Hume, and much faster than I could ever have done it. What does the government owe you for it?"

"Couldn't charge more than five dollars, Vera. I was here less than an hour."

"Bill me for ten—it's worth it. I'll see that you get it."

Once more the women and I started to leave, but this time we found the doorway blocked by the return of Anson Waters. The little banker seemed even more distraught than before. "I'm being wiped out!" he screamed. "U.S. Steel's down twelve points!" In his hand he carried an engraved bond of some sort.

"You need an envelope to mail that," Vera pointed out.

He looked at it in surprise. "No time for another envelope! I'll put it in the first one. I have to send my broker another ten thousand."

"Can't," Vera said simply. "The first one's been mailed."

"It's still here, isn't it?"

"Well, yes."

"Then I'll add this to it. It's my own envelope. These people are witnesses." He turned to us for support, and Vera turned to Sheriff Lens.

"Don't you have some sort of form he can fill out to retrieve an envelope he's mailed?" the sheriff asked.

"Well, yes," Vera Brock admitted.

"Then have him fill it out, give him the envelope so's he can add to it, and then take it back again."

"All right," she agreed, turning toward the desk. "Except—"

"Except what?" the banker wanted to know.

"Except where in heck is that registered envelope?"

"You put it right on your desk," I said. "I saw you do it."

"I know I did, and I didn't move it off of there." She bent to peer under the desk, then straightened up. Her face was white as chalk. "It's gone!" she said, her voice breaking.

"Now wait a minute," I said, trying to calm everybody down. "If it is gone it's not gone very far because nobody's left this post office since you mailed it, Mr. Waters." I turned to look at April and Miranda and Vera and Hume and the sheriff and Waters. "There are seven of us here. Either the envelope got misplaced somehow or one of us has it."

"I was never anywhere near it," Miranda protested. "You certainly can't include me as a suspect, Sam."

"None of us are suspects," Sheriff Lens decided as Vera filled him in about the missing envelope. "It's gotta be here someplace."

The rest of us just stood there while Vera and the sheriff conducted a careful search, but the missing envelope was nowhere to be found. Anson Waters watched it all with growing impatience, glancing from time to time at the big clock on the wall. "Now it's noon—I'm probably ruined by now! You can be darned sure the Post Office Department owes me ten thousand dollars!"

"It'll turn up," Vera said, though she didn't sound too certain.

Finally Sheriff Lens turned to me. "Doc, what do you think?"

"We have to go about this systematically," I decided. "The envelope was either stolen or misplaced. What was the size of it, Mr. Waters?"

"About nine by twelve inches, I think. It contained a bearer bond just like this one, with a covering letter. I wanted to send them flat, so I used a big envelope."

"So it's too big to have fallen into a drawer or behind the desk without being seen. The floor is covered with brand-new linoleum, so it couldn't have fallen through a crack or anything like that. We've just finished searching for it without turning it up anywhere. I think we can conclude that it wasn't misplaced. It was stolen."

"The purloined letter!" Miranda exclaimed, though I could see the reference meant nothing to the others.

"That's right," I agreed. "In the Poe story the letter was in plain view all the time, only nobody noticed it. If, as Chesterton wrote, a wise man hides a leaf in a forest and a pebble on a beach, what better place to hide a stolen letter than in a post office?"

"Look here," Vera said, "only the sheriff and I were behind the counter with that letter. Are you saying one of us must have stolen it?"

"You were sorting the morning's mail, Vera. It would have been a simple task for you to slide the letter into one of those pigeonholes, to be retrieved later."

April unwrapped a stick of chewing gum and popped it into her mouth. It was her one bad habit, but I usually let it pass. "You really think that's where the missing letter is, Dr. Sam?"

"I think it's worth a look."

So we looked.

But we didn't find the letter. It wasn't with any of the other mail, either in the pigeonholes or the incoming and outgoing sacks.

"I told you so," Vera announced, restored to grace. "I wouldn't steal my own letter."

"It's my letter, not yours!" Anson Waters insisted.

"While it's in this post office it's mine," Vera responded. "Even if I don't know where it is."

"All right, Sheriff," I said. "You're next."

"What? Me?"

"Vera's right, you know. You were the only other one to step behind that counter, and none of us could have reached the desk from this side."

"But how could I have—"

"With that box. I read somewhere that the police in New York caught a shoplifter using a special box with a false bottom. You set your box on that desk, right on top of where the letter was."

"I didn't see no letter!"

"Nevertheless, I'm going to have to ask you to unwrap your box."

"Come on, Doc!"

"Look, Sheriff, we've been friends a long time. But you're a suspect like everyone else this time. I'm sorry about it."

Sheriff Lens continued to grumble but he unwrapped the package. A close examination showed there was no false bottom, and nothing inside but some carefully wrapped jars that had contained moonshine liquor. There was no envelope.

"What does that do to your theory?" Waters asked, growing impatient. "You've offered two solutions but I haven't seen you produce my missing envelope yet."

I was still young and cocky in those days, and very sure of myself. "Don't worry, Mr. Waters. There are seven of us here, and I can offer seven solutions. If Vera and Sheriff Lens didn't steal your envelope we'll have to look further afield."

"But they were the only ones behind the counter," Hume Baxter protested.

"But not the only ones who could have stolen the envelope. Let's take you next, Hume. Suppose the sheriff pulled that envelope onto the floor when Vera yelled at him and he retreated a few steps with his box. It could have fallen just outside the counter opening, onto your drop cloths."

"I didn't—"

"And it could be hidden in one of the folds of those drop cloths right this minute. Suppose we have a look."

So we searched the drop cloths, and just for good measure we had a careful look at his brushes and paint bucket too.

There was no envelope.

"This gets more impossible all the time," April observed. "You think I might have stolen it too, Dr. Sam?"

"I'm afraid you're a suspect with the rest of us, April. Once again, if the envelope fell just outside the counter opening, you might have picked it up while our attention was distracted by the sheriff and Vera."

"And did what with it?"

"You're chewing gum, April. You might have stuck the envelope to the underside of the counter with a wad of gum."

It was such a likely explanation that they all bent down to look at once. But there was no envelope under the counter. There was nothing under the counter.

The little banker snorted. "You're striking out every time, Hawthorne. Who's next—your girl friend?"

I'd avoided looking at Miranda till now, but there was no way out of it now. "You could have picked it up and hidden it under your skirt, Miranda," I said very quietly.

"Sam, the very idea! What do you intend to do, search me?"

"I want April and Vera to search you."

"Sam!" She seemed close to tears. "Sam Hawthorne, if you make me do this I'll never speak to you again!"

"I'm sorry, Miranda. I have to rule out every possibility."

"Come on," Vera suggested. "The three of us womenfolk will search each other. Then it won't be so bad. You men turn your backs!"

Miranda calmed down a bit and we did as Vera suggested while the women carefully searched each other. Miranda wasn't hiding the envelope and neither were the others.

"That's everybody," Anson Waters said. "Now what, Hawthorne?"

"It's not everybody, it's only five people. There's still you and me, Mr. Waters."

"You think I stole my own letter?"

"You registered the letter, insuring its value for ten thousand dollars. Now suppose there was never a bearer bond in it. Suppose it was just an empty envelope and the only bond was the one you brought in to *add* to the envelope. The post office loses ten thousand dollars, which could be a big help to you with the market plunging."

"An empty envelope! That's absurd! Even if it were true, how would I make an empty envelope disappear?"

"You might have written the address with disappearing ink. If Vera noticed an empty envelope on the floor with no address on it, she might have put it in a drawer or thrown it away."

But of course Vera spotted the flaw in my reasoning at once. "Even if the address faded away, it would still have its stamps on it, and the registry notice. I'd have known it was the same envelope."

She was right and I had to admit it. "That still leaves me," I said. "I know I didn't steal the envelope, but the missing bond could have been removed and folded into a small packet. It might have been slipped into my pocket without my knowing it. I think it's time somebody searched me, and I guess you're the most likely one, Sheriff."

While he was at it Sheriff Lens searched Hume Baxter and the banker too. There was no envelope and no bearer bond, except the second one Waters had brought with him. I searched the sheriff in turn, with the same result.

"Seven people," Anson Waters snorted, "and seven solutions to the mystery! Only trouble is, all seven of them are wrong! What do you do next, Hawthorne, examine us with a stethoscope? Maybe one of them ate my bond."

"I hardly think so," I answered seriously. "Paper would dissolve in the stomach acids and the bond would be destroyed."

Waters turned toward Vera. "I'm holding you personally responsible for my bond!"

"Do you want to mail the other one to your broker?"

"I wouldn't trust you with it! I'll take the train to New York tonight and deliver it personally!"

With those words the banker stormed out, leaving the rest of us standing there. For the first time the strain of the morning began to show on Vera Brock. She seemed close to tears as she said, "And I wanted my opening day to be such a success. Now it's ruined."

April seemed embarrassed by this sudden show of emotion. "I'd better be getting back to the office, Dr. Sam," she decided. "A patient might have been tryin' to reach us."

"Good idea," I agreed. It was time for me to leave too. There was no solution to this mystery of the missing envelope.

I fell into step beside Miranda as she walked along Main Street. "I'm sorry the way things went in there," I said quietly. "I didn't really think you stole the letter."

"Oh, didn't you? Your performance certainly fooled me! I felt as if I were on my way to jail."

"Miranda, I—"

"It's all over between us, Sam. I think I knew it before today."

"It's not over unless you want it to be."

"You're not the same man you were last summer, Sam."

"Maybe you're not the same either," I answered sadly.

We parted at the corner and I crossed over to my office. Sheriff Lens came around the back of the building and headed me off. "You got a minute, Doc?" he asked me.

"Sure, Sheriff. I just finished apologizing to Miranda, so I'd better do the same with you. I didn't really think you hid that letter in your package, but I had to look everywhere."

"I understand," he assured me, "but Vera's plumb upset about the whole business. She's afraid Washington might even remove her as postmistress if she loses a ten-thousand-dollar letter on opening day."

"Does it concern you that much, Sheriff?" I asked him.

"Well, yeah. You know, Doc, Vera's a mighty attractive woman for her age. An old coot like me gets lonesome after all these years as a widower."

A light began to dawn. "You mean you and Vera Brock—?"

"Oh, she loses patience with me sometimes, like this morning, but most times we get along fine. I been over to her house a few times . . ." His voice trailed off and then started again. "You know I'm not much of a detective, Doc. Not much of a sheriff, either, if the truth be known. Maybe the town's gettin' too big for the likes of me."

"You're an important part of the town, Sheriff."

"Yeah, but I mean now Vera's in trouble an' I don't know no way of gettin' her out of it. Damned if I know who stole that envelope, or how. We searched everywhere."

"Yes, we did," I agreed. "We searched the floor and the desk and all those pigeonholes and the mail sacks. We searched Baxter's drop cloths and painting gear. We searched under the counter and even under Miranda's skirts. We searched every single one of us. I'm ready to swear there's no place in that post office where the letter could have been hidden, and yet there's no way it could have left the post office either. There were no mail pickups while we were there, and no one left the place during the crucial period."

"Then you're as baffled as I am, Doc?"

"I'm afraid so," I admitted. "Maybe I do better with murder cases when you have a motive staring you in the face. This theft has a universal motive—anyone can use ten thousand bucks, even banker Waters."

"Well, if you think of anything that might help her, Doc, we'd sure appreciate it. Both of us."

"I'll try, Sheriff."

As I went on into my office I thought that was the most human moment I'd spent with Sheriff Lens in the seven years we'd known each other.

And maybe if one romance had died at the post office that morning, another had been strengthened.

The worst of the Wall Street panic was over by noon, as banks decided to pool their resources and support the market. Stock prices even rallied a bit in the afternoon, and April returned from a trip to the bank with the report that Waters was actually smiling.

I had only one appointment scheduled after lunch, and when my patient had been sent on her way I got my collection of Edgar Allan Poe down from the shelf and reread "The Purloined Letter." But it told me nothing.

In Vera's post office all letters were suspect and all had been examined. There was no letter in plain view that we had missed.

I'd failed Vera Brock and Sheriff Lens. Most of all, I'd failed myself.

At the end of the day April came in to say good night. It was starting to drizzle outside and I hardly recognized her in her new raincoat.

"You look so different," I said.

"Coats do that sometimes."

Coats.

After she'd gone I sat at my desk and thought about coats.

Was it possible?

Already it was growing dark outside, and night would fall within the hour. If I was right this time, there was an easy way to prove it before I told anyone else and made a bigger fool of myself. I locked up my office and walked down Main Street through the damp drizzle.

When I reached the post office I peered through the big front window and wondered how to go about getting inside. Vera had left a small light burning toward the back and it cast an eerie glow over the fresh pink walls. I supposed there might be an alarm system on the doors, though I could see no evidence of one.

But if I was right about the hiding place of the stolen letter, the thief would return tonight too. Maybe all I had to do was wait.

"Still looking for the thief, Hawthorne?" a voice behind me asked. I turned and saw Anson Waters, his collar up and hat pulled down against the rain.

"I had another idea I thought I'd check out."

"I've already filed a claim for the missing bond."

"I thought you were taking the train to New York tonight."

"I am. The 10:45 to New Haven. I'll change trains there."

He was starting to say something else when I thought I heard the muffled breaking of glass. The light in the post office had gone out. "Quick!" I told the banker. "Get Sheriff Lens!"

"What—?"

"Don't ask questions!"

I left him standing there and ran around the back of the building. A pane of glass had been broken and a window raised. I climbed over the sill and searched around for the light switch. The overhead lights went on, blinding us both for an instant, but then I saw him.

"Hello, Hume."

Hume Baxter stared at me, the stolen envelope in his hand. "How'd you know, Sam? How in hell did you know?"

"It took me a while, I'll admit, but I finally tumbled to it. The only place we didn't look. Like Poe's purloined letter, it was right in front of us all the time and we didn't see it."

Later, after Sheriff Lens had arrived to take charge of Hume Baxter and the stolen envelope, I explained, "I got to thinking about how coats can cover up things and change their appearance, and that made me think of a coat of paint. You see, what happened was that you set your box right on top of Anson Waters' envelope. When Vera yelled and you yanked it back up, the envelope got caught in the cord around the box and hung there. You stepped back a few paces, just outside the counter, and the envelope fell to the floor."

"How could that happen without someone seeing it?" Sheriff Lens wondered.

"But someone did see it," I reminded him. "Hume Baxter saw it. Think about our various positions in the room and you'll realize he was in the best position to see it. You were holding a large box that blocked your view of the floor. And once you'd moved back a few paces the counter was between you and Vera, obstructing her view. Miranda, April, and I were near the door, on our way out, and your back was to us. Waters wasn't present at that point. Only Hume Baxter, off to the side with his paint brush, was likely to see what happened. While you followed Vera's instructions and carried the box to that back shelf, Hume tossed one of his drop cloths over the envelope and then managed to pick it up."

"In a single quick gesture he stuck it to the freshly painted wall just above the floor level and near the counter, where the shadow of the counter top kept the light from falling directly on it. And then he painted pink over it. I remember him bending to touch up a spot by the counter. The face of the envelope was against the wall of course, so the stamps didn't show through. And the buff color of the manila envelope wasn't that different from the original yellowishtan brown color of the walls before they were painted, so the pink was about the same shade on the envelope."

"But how come we didn't see it even so, Doc?"

"Several reasons. For one, Hume warned us not to get too close to the wet paint and nobody did. For another, down near floor level, partly under the counter, it didn't show. A freshly painted wall is always wet and streaky looking till it dries, so the edges of the envelope weren't noticeable. It was a large envelope but very thin, remember. There were only two unfolded sheets of paper inside—the bearer bond and a letter."

"What about when the paint dried?"

"Exactly! The envelope might fall away from the wall, or at the very least its edges would come loose and be more visible. That's how I knew he'd have to come back for it tonight. He'd even brought along a little pink paint to touch up the spot again after he removed the envelope."

Sheriff Lens shook his head. "What people won't do for money."

"Or love," I added and gave him a wink. Vera Brock was coming through the post-office door.

"I said at the beginning it was a unique case," Dr. Sam Hawthorne concluded, "and it was. For one thing there was no murder, and for another my solution showed that it was Sheriff Lens himself who actually aided the thief by snagging that envelope with his box. I guess in a way they both paid for their crime because Hume Baxter went to jail and Sheriff Lens went to the altar. That's right—it didn't work out for Miranda and me, but it sure did for Vera and the sheriff. It was one of the happiest weddings I ever attended, despite a locked-room murder on the very day of the ceremony that almost—but that's for next time!"

THE PROBLEM OF
THE OCTAGON ROOM

Old Dr. Sam Hawthorne answered the door on the second ring, and stood blinking into the harsh afternoon sun. He recognized at once the person who stood there, even though they hadn't seen each other in fifty years. "Come in, come in!" he urged. "It's been a long time, hasn't it? A long time since that day in Northmont. No, no, you're not disturbing me. I was expecting someone else, though—a friend who often drops by to hear my stories of the old days. Funny thing, I was going to tell him about you, and about all the others and what happened on the day Sheriff Lens was married. I often think about it, you know. Of all those old mysteries I helped solve back then, the business with the octagon room was unique. Would you like to hear about how it seemed from my viewpoint? Fine, fine! Settle down there and let me pour you— ah—a small libation. We're both old now and a little sherry is good for the circulation. Or would you like something stronger? No? Very well. As you know . . ."

It was December of 1929 (Dr. Sam Hawthorne began), and a mild December it was in Northmont. By Saturday the 14th, the day of the wedding, we'd had no snow at all. In fact, it was a sunny day as I remember it, with the temperature hovering around sixty. I was up early, because Sheriff Lens had asked me to be his best man. We'd grown to be close friends during my years in Northmont, and even though he was nearly twenty years older than me he still liked the idea of me being at his side during the wedding service.

"Sam," he'd told me earlier, "it was back in October, that day at the post office, when I realized how much I really loved Vera Brock." Vera was our postmistress, a spunky, solid woman in her forties who'd run the post office in the general store and now had a building of her own. Vera had never been married, and Sheriff Lens was a widower without any children. They'd drifted together out of companionship more than anything else, and now it had blossomed into love. I couldn't have been happier for them both.

139

Vera Brock, it turned out, had a hidden streak of sentimentality. She told Sheriff Lens that more than anything else she wanted to be married in the famous octagon room at Eden House, because her mother and father had been married at an octagon house on Cape Cod forty-five years earlier. Now the sheriff was a religious man, even if it didn't show too often, and he wanted to be married at the Baptist church just as he'd been the first time. They had a little disagreement about that until I solved the problem by talking to the minister, Dr. Tompkins, who reluctantly agreed to perform the ceremony in the octagon room.

Eden House was a fine old place on the edge of town. It had been built by Joshua Eden in the mid-1800's, during the so-called "octagon craze" that swept the nation and was especially prevalent in upstate New York and New England. His fascination with octagon houses caused him to install a mirrored octagon room on the main floor of his new home. Its construction had been quite simple. He'd taken a large square room, originally designed as a study, and cut off each of the four corners with a mirrored cabinet that reached from floor to ceiling. The width of the mirrored doors was the same as the sections of wall between them, so the shape of the room was a true octagon. When you entered through the room's only outer door you faced the large sunny window on the south side of the house. The walls to the left and right, between the mirrored segments, were hung with 19th Century sporting prints. It was an odd but cheerful room, if you didn't mind the mirrors.

Behind each of those mirrored doors was a cabinet with shelves reaching from floor to ceiling. There were books and vases and tablecloths and silverware and china and every sort of knickknack crowded onto the shelves. The room itself was almost bare, with only a small table by the window holding a vase of fresh flowers.

At least that's how it looked when I came to inspect it a few days before the ceremony. My guide was young Josh Eden, grandson of the builder, a handsome young man well aware of the family's tradition in Northmont. He unlocked the thick oak door of the room and pulled it open. "As you know, Dr. Sam, we occasionally rent out the octagon room for weddings and private parties. A lovely place like this should be shared by the community, and the sheriff's marriage is an event that deserves the best setting."

"I'm too young to know much about octagon houses," I admitted.

He grinned at that. "I'm younger than you by a year or two, but I'll try to enlighten you. The eight-sided shape was both functional and efficient, but superstition had something to do with it too. Evil spirits were believed to lurk in right-angled corners, and an octagon house without right-angled corners was believed to be free of them. For this reason the houses were popular with spiritualists. In fact, it's said that seances were held in this very room by friends of my grandfather. Seems to me the spirits they conjured up might have been just as bad as the ones they were avoiding."

I glanced at him. "The room is haunted?"

"Some old ghostly stories," he said with a chuckle. He showed me the crowded cabinets and the view from the window as we discussed the wedding. Before we left I noticed him check the window to make sure it was latched on the inside. The heavy wooden door had a key lock and an inside bolt. He couldn't work the bolt from outside, but he did turn the lock with a long slender key.

"Keeping the ghosts locked in?" I asked with a smile.

"There are some valuable antiques in those cabinets," he explained. "I keep the room locked when it's not in use."

Josh's wife Ellen met us at the front stairs, coming down with a load of laundry to be washed. Her blue eyes sparkled as she greeted me. "Hello there, Dr. Sam. I was wondering when you'd come by. Good to see you again!"

She was flushed with the health and beauty of youth, and a bright cheerfulness that always made me envious of Josh Eden. They'd met at college and married soon after, and though they were both a few years younger than me they seemed somehow to be in full charge of their lives. Josh's father Thomas deserted the family after the war, preferring to remain in Paris with a dancer he'd met there. The shock had been too much for Josh's poor mother, who'd died from it, and from the influenza outbreak of 1919.

Josh went on to college and in time the courts ruled his father was dead too, though there was no evidence of it except his continued silence. Eden House had passed to Josh, along with a small inheritance. He'd wisely invested in land rather than stocks, and the recent Wall Street crash had left him virtually unscathed. Still, there was money to be made from renting out the octagon room on occasion. Ellen even talked of converting the entire house to a restaurant if an amendment to repeal Prohibition was ever passed. There was already talk that mounting unemployment might be countered by the jobs created through the rebirth of the liquor industry.

"We're getting ready for the big day on Saturday," I told Ellen. "I just came over to look at the room."

"I'll bet Sheriff Lens is nervous," she said with a grin.

"Not so's you could notice. After all, he's been through it before. It's the first time for Vera."

"I know they'll be very happy," Ellen said.

She seemed quite pleased by the prospect of the wedding, and when we trooped over for the rehearsal on Friday evening she surprised Vera and the sheriff with a hand-made quilt as a wedding present.

"That's so nice!" Vera exclaimed. "We'll have it on our bed!"

"It's just a little something from Josh and me," Ellen murmured. She seemed more subdued than on my previous visit, possibly because of the intimidating presence of Dr. Tompkins.

The minister arrived dressed in a gray suit, greeted Sheriff Lens and Vera with somber good wishes, and then turned to me. "You understand, Dr. Hawthorne, that the service tomorrow morning must be at ten o'clock sharp. I have another wedding over in Shinn Corners at noon. In a church."

"Don't worry," I assured him, beginning to feel a bit sorry I'd ever become involved with such a pompous man.

We ran quickly through the rehearsal in the octagon room, with Josh and Ellen Eden watching from the doorway. The sheriff and Vera had wanted only two attendants. I was the best man and Vera's close friend Lucy Cole was the maid of honor. Lucy was a charming Southern girl in her late twenties who'd moved to Northmont a year earlier. She helped out sometimes at the post office and had become a close friend of Vera's in the past year.

"You know, Sam," Vera had told me earlier, "if it wasn't for Lucy's encouragement I never could have agreed to marry the sheriff. Once you pass forty, gettin' married for the first time is an awesome decision."

"But she's never been married, has she?"

"No, not unless she's got a husband down south she's not talkin' about."

Lucy was an open, attractive young woman—not unlike Ellen Eden in some ways. I couldn't help feeling they were the vanguard of a new age. The books and magazines might be filled with stories of big-city flappers, but I preferred women more like Lucy Cole and Ellen Eden.

After the rehearsal Josh carefully locked the door of the octagon room and walked out with us to my car. "We'll see you all in the morning," he said. A wedding breakfast for a few close friends would be held nearby, followed by a reception later.

I drove the wedding party back to my apartment and opened a bottle of genuine Canadian whiskey. Sheriff Lens sputtered some about breaking the law, but after all it was the night before his wedding. We toasted the bride, and we toasted the groom, and then we toasted Lucy and me for good measure.

I was up early in the morning because I'd promised my nurse April that I'd drive her to the wedding in my car. She was chatty and excited, as she always was at the prospect of weddings and parties. We picked up Sheriff Lens on the way, and I had to admit I'd never seen him dressed so handsomely. I adjusted his formal morning coat and straightened his tie.

"Keep your stomach in and you'll be fine," I said as we walked to the car. "You look great."

"You got the ring, Doc?"

"Don't worry." I patted the pocket of my own coat.

"You both look handsome enough to be on the wedding cake!" April exclaimed as we climbed in the car. "Can I marry the one that's left over?"

"Being a doctor's wife is even worse than being a doctor's nurse," I told her with a chuckle and started the car.

As we pulled up to Eden House, Vera was just getting out of Lucy Cole's little sedan. "Oh, look!" April pointed. "There's the bride!" Then, remembering our passenger, she quickly added, "Don't you look, Sheriff Lens. You're not supposed to see her till the ceremony."

Vera Brock was all in white, with a fancy lace wedding gown that trailed to the ground. She held it up with both hands as she ran to the door of Eden House. In that moment she was a girl again, half her age, and I could see why Sheriff Lens loved her. I parked the car and walked over to meet Lucy.

"Beautiful day for it," I remarked, looking at the cloudless sky. "Maybe this'll be the year without a winter."

Vera had reappeared at the front door, looking slightly exasperated. "They can't get the door of the octagon room open. It's stuck or something."

This seemed to be yet another job for the best man. "I'll go see about it," I said.

Inside I found Ellen Eden and her husband standing together at the thick oak door of the octagon room, looks of bafflement on their faces. "The door won't open," Josh said. "This has never happened before."

I took the key from him and tried it in the lock. It turned, and I could tell the lock was working properly, but still the door would not open. "There's a bolt inside, isn't there?"

"Yes," Josh replied, "but it could only be worked by someone inside the room. And there's no one inside."

"Are you sure about that?"

Josh and his wife exchanged glances. "I'll go around and look in the window," she said.

At this point Dr. Tompkins walked in, already glancing at the large gold pocket watch in his hand. "I hope we're on schedule. As you know, I have a noon wedding in—"

"Just a short delay," I told him. "The door seems to be stuck."

"That doesn't happen in churches."

"I'm sure not."

Ellen hurried in through the back door, out of breath. "The shade is drawn, Josh! You didn't leave it like that, did you?"

"Certainly not! Someone's in there."

"But how could they get in?" I asked reasonably. "I saw you lock up and latch the window."

"The window's still latched," Ellen confirmed.

The minister began to sputter and Josh said, "Please bear with us. We'll break down the door if necessary."

I tapped it with my fist. "That's pretty thick oak."

Josh joined me and pounded on the door. "Open up in there, whoever you are!" he shouted. "We know you're there!"

But there was only silence from behind the door.

"A burglar, probably," Sheriff Lens reasoned. "Trapped and afraid to come out."

"We can break in the window," I suggested.

"No!" Ellen said. "Not unless we have to. We couldn't replace it before Monday and it's December, after all. A sudden storm could damage the room. Look, can't you all pull on the knob? That bolt on the other side of the door isn't very strong."

We followed her advice, turning the knob and yanking. The door seemed to move a fraction of an inch. "April," I called over my shoulder, "bring the tow rope from the trunk of my car."

She returned with it in a few moments, grumbling about getting her hands dirty. We attached the stout rope to the doorknob, made sure again it was unlocked, and Josh and I tugged.

"It's giving!" he said.

"Sheriff," I called out. "I know it's your wedding day, but could you lend us a hand?"

The three of us gave a mighty pull on the rope. It was like the games of tug-of-war I'd played as a child, and we were rewarded by the screeching of screws being pried from wood. The door sprang open, sending us backward, off balance for an instant. Then Josh and I ran into the octagon room together, with Ellen close behind.

Even in the dim light from the shaded window we could make out the man in the center of the floor, arms and legs thrown wide. His clothes were the shabby costume of a tramp, and I'd never seen him before. But with a slim silver dagger in his chest, I had no doubt that he was dead.

Behind me, Lucy Cole screamed.

I stepped around the dead man and crossed the dim room to raise the shade. The single window was indeed latched, and though it was only turned half-way that was enough to lock it firmly. The latch turned easily and I tried to see if it could have been operated somehow from outside, but the window frames fit together snugly, leaving no gap. The panes themselves were unbroken.

I turned back to the room. The door had opened outward, so there was no hiding place behind it. The mirrored cabinets—

"Aren't you going to examine the body?" Josh asked.

"I can see he's dead. Right now it's more important to examine the room."

I was especially interested in the inside bolt which had been pried from its wooden moorings by our tugging. It hung now from the door jamb, the twin screws having been pulled from the door itself. But examining the holes and the traces of wood shavings on the screw threads, I was convinced the bolt had been firmly screwed into the wood of the door.

I noticed a piece of string knotted around the doorknob and tried to remember if it had been there the previous evening. I didn't think so, but I couldn't be sure.

"He's dead, all right," Dr. Tompkins was saying.

I turned from the door. "Dead several hours, judging by the color of his skin. I didn't mean to seem heartless but sometimes you can tell by looking. Does anyone know him?"

Ellen and Josh shook their heads and the minister grumbled, "A tramp passing through town. Sheriff, you shouldn't allow—"

"I recognize him," Lucy Cole said quietly from the doorway.

"Who is he?" I asked her.

"I didn't mean I knew him, just that I recognized him. There were two of them yesterday, walking near the railroad tracks. Both hobos, I suppose. I remember that long stringy hair and the dirty red vest, and those little scars on his face."

Josh Eden came forward to kneel beside the body. "That dagger looks like a silver letter opener from one of our cabinets. Ellen, see if it's missing."

She walked carefully around the body and opened the mirrored door to the left of the window. After rummaging for a moment she said, "It's not here. There may be other things missing too. I can't be sure."

"While we're at it," I suggested, "we'd better check all four of these cabinets."

"What for?" Josh asked.

I was staring down at the body. "Well, unless the killer is hidden inside, on one of those big shelves, it looks like we've got ourselves a murder committed in a particularly impenetrable locked room."

So many things happened in those next few hours that it's hard now to remember them all. But we searched each of the four mirrored cabinets with care and found no one hidden there. I also took measurements to make sure no cabinet had a false back. When we finished I was convinced the killer was not hiding in the room—nor was there any secret passage or trap door out of the room. There was only the single door, bolted from inside, and the single window, latched from inside.

I'd already studied the window latch. Now I went and knelt on the floor by the door, examining the piece of string I'd found knotted around the knob. "Is this string usually here?" I asked Ellen Eden.

She stared at it. "No, it's not ours—unless Josh tied it there for some reason."

But he hadn't. That left the killer or the victim as the likely possibilities. A year or two earlier I'd read S.S. Van Dine's mystery novel, *The Canary Murder Case*, which included a diagram of how a pair of tweezers and a piece of string could be used to turn a door handle from outside a room. It was a clever idea, but it didn't apply to this situation.

I tried to imagine a way in which the string could have been looped around the bolt and pulled to close it, but for one thing the string wasn't long enough. And for another, the door fit so snugly to the jamb that there was not even room for a string to pass through. Even on the bottom, a small strip of wood was nailed to the floor inside the door, apparently to cut down on drafts. I found a longer piece of string and tried shutting the door on it. The fit was so tight the string could not be pulled.

My preoccupation with the locked room had made me forget everything else. Sheriff Lens came to me presently and said, "Doc, it's almost eleven o'clock. The minister's about to leave for Shinn Corners."

"My God! The wedding!"

For all Vera's enchantment with the octagon room, she refused to be married in a room where the blood was not yet dry on the floor. The wedding guests, kept waiting in the cool outside air, were told of the change in plans. We all piled into cars and drove to the nearby church. Though he was miffed by the delay, Dr. Tompkins felt some sort of triumph in getting the ceremony moved to the church. He hurried through the ceremony, paused long enough to shake the groom's hand and peck at the bride's cheek, then vanished toward his noon appointment in a cloud of dust.

"How's it feel to be married again?" I asked the sheriff.

"Wonderful!" he said, hugging his bride with an uncharacteristic display of emotion. "But it looks like we'll have to delay the honeymoon."

"How come?"

"Well, I'm still the sheriff here, Doc, and I got a murder on my hands."

For the moment I'd forgotten about that. "You go ahead on your honeymoon, Sheriff. Your deputies can handle things."

"Them two?" he snorted. "They couldn't find a skunk in a suitcase!"

I took a deep breath. "Don't you worry, I've got it under control."

"You mean you know who killed that guy? And how it was done in a locked room?"

"Sure. Don't you worry about it. We'll have the killer in a cell by nightfall."

His eyes widened in admiration. "If that's true we can leave on our honeymoon right after the reception."

"By all means. Don't give the murder another thought."

I turned away, wondering how I'd go about fulfilling that promise.

I started out by taking the maid of honor for a ride in my car. "This isn't the way to the reception," Lucy said after a few minutes. "You're heading back toward town."

"Right now this is more important than the reception," I told her. "You said you saw the dead man walking with someone else."

"Another hobo, that's all."

"Would you recognize the other man if you saw him again?"

"I don't know. I might. He had a bald spot on the back of his head. I remember that much. And a plaid scarf wrapped around his neck."

"Let's go looking."

"But the reception—"

"We'll get there."

I drove down by the railroad station and then followed the street that ran parallel to the tracks. Chances were the dead man's friend was miles away by now, riding some fast freight, especially if he'd been involved in the killing. Still, it was worth the time to try to find him.

A few miles the other side of Northmont we came upon a hobo camp in among the trees. "Wait here," I told Lucy. "I won't be long."

I made my way down the worn path, moving openly through the trees in hopes that the men around the campfire wouldn't panic and flee. One of them, warming his hands near the flames, turned as I approached. "What you want?" he asked.

"I'm a doctor."

"Nobody sick here."

"I'm looking for a man who passed this way yesterday. Wearing a plaid scarf, with a bald spot on his head." I added, "No hat," since that seemed obvious.

"Nobody like that," the man by the fire said. Then he asked, "What you want with him? He ain't got a disease, has he?"

"We don't know what he's got. That's why we're trying to find him."

One of the other men came over to the fire. He was small and nervous and spoke with a southern accent. "It sounds like Mercy, don't it?"

"Shut up!" the first man growled. "This might be a railroad dick for all we know."

"I'm not any sort of dick," I insisted. "Look here." From my pocket I produced a pad of blank prescriptions with my name and address printed across the top. "Does this convince you I'm a doctor?"

The first man looked suddenly sly. "If you're a doctor you could write us a prescription for some whiskey. They sell it in drug stores."

"For medicinal purposes," I said, beginning to feel a bit uneasy. A third man had appeared and was moving around behind me.

Then suddenly Lucy began blowing the horn on my car. The three men, realizing I wasn't alone, backed away. One of them broke into a run toward the tracks. I grabbed the little one, nearest to me, and asked, "Where's Mercy?"

"Let go!"

"Tell me and you're free. Where is he?"

"Down the tracks by the water tower. He's waiting for his friend."

"You know who the friend is?"

"No. They're just travelin' together."

I let go of his collar. "You'd better clear out of here," I warned. "The local sheriff's a mean one."

I ran back to the car and climbed in. "Thanks for blowing the horn," I told Lucy.

"I got scared when they started circling you."

"So did I." We drove down the road along the tracks. "The man we want may be at the water tower."

The tower came into view, outlined against the sky, and suddenly we saw a man in a long shabby coat break from cover and run toward the woods. "I think that's him!" Lucy exclaimed.

I followed after him as far as I could in the car, keeping the bald spot and the flapping plaid scarf in sight. Then I was out of the car and chasing him on foot. I was a good twenty years younger than he was, and I ran him down quickly.

He squirmed in my grip and whined, "I didn't do anything wrong!"

"Are you the one they call Mercy?"

"Yes, I guess so."

"I'm not going to hurt you. I just want to ask some questions."

"What about?"

"You were seen with another man yesterday. He had long stringy hair, turning gray, and was wearing a dirty red vest. Man in his fifties, about your age, with some scars on his face."

"Yeah, we rode up from Florida together."

"Who is he? Tell me about him."

"Name's Tommy, that's all I know. We shared a boxcar from Orlando to just outside New York, then we hopped another train up here."

"Why'd you want to come here?" I asked. "Why travel from Florida to New England in December? Do you like snow?"

"He wanted to come here, an' I didn't have anything better to do."

"Why was he coming here?"

"Said he could get a lot of money up here. Money that belonged to him."

"And he told you to wait here?"

"Yeah. He left me last night. Said he should be back by noon, but I haven't seen him."

"You won't be seeing him," I said. "Someone murdered him during the night."

"God!"

"What else did he say about the money that belonged to him? Where was it?"

"He didn't tell me."

"He must have said something. You were with him all the way from Florida."

The man called Mercy looked away nervously. "All he said was that he was coming home. Coming home to Eden."

I dropped Lucy Cole at the restaurant where the reception was being held and then drove back to Eden House. It was almost dark when I pulled up in front, the brief December sun already vanished beyond the line of trees to the west. Josh Eden came to the door, looking tired and troubled.

"How did the wedding go?" he asked.

"Very well, all things considered. They'll be leaving on their honeymoon soon."

"I'm glad this terrible event didn't ruin the day for them."

"I was wondering if I could see the octagon room again. Sheriff Lens asked me to assist his deputies in the investigation."

"Certainly." He led the way into the house. The door stood open and I could see he'd been working on repairing the damaged wood-work where the bolt had been torn loose. The room itself was in semi-darkness, with the drawn shade admitting only a single spot of fading light through a pinhole in its middle.

"I had to draw the shade," Josh Eden explained. "The neighborhood kids were all coming to look in at the murder scene."

"Kids will do that," I agreed. "But the shade was usually left up at night, wasn't it?"

"Oh, yes—you saw me lock up yesterday. The shade was up."

"Then either the victim or his killer had to lower it."

"Seems so. If they had a light on they might not have wanted outsiders to see what they were doing."

"Which was—?"

"Why, robbing me, of course! It seemed obvious enough. Lucy Cole said she saw the dead man with another tramp yesterday. The two of them got in here to rob me, had an argument, and the other one stabbed him with that dagger letter opener."

"How'd they get in without forcing a door or window? More important, how'd the killer get out?"

"I don't know," he admitted.

"The dead man's name was Tommy."

Josh raised his eyes to meet mine. "How'd you find that out?"

"He traveled north from Florida to come here, to Eden House, to regain his fortune."

"What are you saying, Sam?"

"I think the dead man was your father. The father who never came back from the war."

It had grown so dark in the octagon room that we could barely see each other. Josh reached for the wall switch and snapped on the overhead light. Instantly our mirror images were reflected in the cabinet doors. "That's insane!" he said. "Don't you think I'd know my own father?"

"Yes, I do. You might have known him enough to kill him when he returned after twelve years to take back your house and inheritance. He wasn't your father any more. He was merely the man who'd deserted you and your mother all those years ago."

"I didn't kill him," Josh insisted. "I didn't even know him!"

I heard a movement behind me in the hall. "I know you didn't," I said with a sigh. "Come in, Ellen, and tell us why you murdered your father-in-law."

She stood there, pale and trembling, in the doorway of the octagon room. I had seen her reflection in the glass, knew she'd been listening to every word. "I–I didn't mean to–" she gasped, and Josh ran to her side.

"Ellen, what's he saying? This can't be true!"

"Oh, it's true enough," I told him. "And she'd have had a much better chance convincing a jury it was an accident if she hadn't gone to such lengths to cover her traces with this locked-room business. Your father, Tommy, came here last night to take back what was his. You slept through it all, but Ellen heard him at the door and let him in. I suppose she took him into this room so their voices wouldn't awaken you. And there he was, this tramp insisting he was your father, saying he wasn't dead at all and he'd come to take back Eden House. She saw her plans for the place–the restaurant and all the rest of it–going up in smoke. She went to the cabinet, seized that silver letter opener shaped like a dagger, and plunged it into his chest in a moment of insane fury."

Josh was still shaking his head in disbelief. "How could you know that? How could she have killed him and left the room locked from the inside?"

"I didn't know how it was done until I came back here just now, until we walked in here and I saw that pinhole of light in the center of the shade."

"There is a hole in the shade! Funny I never noticed it before."

"I'm sure it wasn't there until last night. You see, this octagon room is different from many rooms in two respects–the door and the window are exactly opposite each other, and the door opens outward."

"I don't see–"

"Ellen tied a string to the doorknob and attached the other end to the window latch. Then she went out the window. When we yanked open the door this morning, the string turned the latch and locked the window. It's as simple as that."

Josh's mouth fell open. "Wait a minute–"

"I examined the latch as soon as we entered the room. It worked very easily and it was only turned halfway–just enough to lock the window. She'd put a loose loop of string around it, and when the latch reached the halfway mark, pointing into the room, the string slid off just as she'd planned. Of course I never thought of anything like that because the shade was drawn. That's why she made the tiny hole in the shade—for the string to pass through. After she climbed out the window she had to lower the window and the shade together to keep the string in position, but that wasn't difficult. The slight slack in the string was taken up quickly enough when we opened the door."

"If this is true what happened to the string?"

"The loop was yanked off the latch and through the hole in the shade. It probably trailed along the floor somewhere. We didn't notice it in the dim light when we burst into the room. I went immediately to the window to examine it, and you two were right behind me. Ellen simply grabbed the string and snapped it off the doorknob. She'd have liked to get it all, but it broke and she had to leave the piece around the knob."

"Even if I believe that, why does it have to be Ellen? There were several of us present. Myself, Lucy Cole—"

He wanted so much to believe in her innocence. I hated to shatter his last hope. "It had to be Ellen, Josh—don't you see that? It was Ellen who went around the back of the house and told us the window was latched. It was Ellen who persuaded us not to break in through the window but to pull on the door—that was the only way her scheme would work. It had to be Ellen and no one else."

"But why make it a locked room in the first place? Why go to the trouble and risk?"

"He was too big for her to carry the body off somewhere. Ideally she should have left the window open so he would look like a burglar killed by his partner. But you see Ellen didn't know about any partner until Lucy mentioned seeing two hobos together. That convinced me Lucy wasn't involved—because she surely would have left the window open to implicate the other hobo. No, Ellen had to leave the body where it was, so she wanted it locked away from the rest of the house, cut off from you and her. She bolted the door and set the string to latch the window, perhaps imagining the death would be blamed on the old ghostly stories about the room."

Finally he removed his protective arms from his wife and stepped back to ask, "Is this true, Ellen?"

Old Dr. Sam Hawthorne leaned back in his chair and reached for his glass. "And of course it was true, wasn't it, Ellen?"

The woman across from him was almost as old as he, but she held herself erect and proud. Her face was lined and her hair was white, but it was still Ellen

Eden, not that much different, considering the passage of fifty years. "Of course it was true, Sam. I killed the old man then and I would do it again. I don't blame you for helping send me to prison. They were long years but I never blamed you for that. What I blame you for is my loss of Josh."

"I had nothing to do with—"

"I went to prison and after a time he divorced me. That was the blow—to know that I'd never be going back to Eden House. And then I heard he married Lucy Cole."

"Those things happen. The two of you were very much alike. I'm not surprised he turned to her after you were gone."

"But you see I killed the old man to save Eden House, to preserve my dream of its future. And that was what you took away from me—Eden House and Josh."

"I'm sorry."

"After I was released from prison I moved across the country. But I never forgot you, Sam. Sometimes I thought I wanted to kill you for ruining my life."

"You ruined your own life, Ellen."

She sighed and seemed to slump in her chair. The life, the fight, had almost gone out of her. But not quite. "I killed a man who deserted his family for another woman, who came back a bum to steal from his own son. Was that such a bad thing for me to do?"

Sam Hawthorne studied her face for a long time before replying. Then he said, very quietly, "Tommy Eden never left his family for another woman, Ellen. He stayed in France after the war because his face was terribly disfigured by a wound. To me as a doctor those little scars meant plastic surgery, and that explained why Josh didn't recognize his own father's body. I never mentioned it at the trial because Josh had enough grief already. But the man you killed didn't deserve to die. And the sentence you served in prison was a just one."

She took a deep breath. "Ten years ago I might have killed you too, Sam. Now I'm too tired."

"We're all tired, Ellen. Here, let me call you a taxi."

"Well," Dr. Sam Hawthorne said, "come right in! I was expecting you earlier. That old woman getting into the taxi? Funny thing, I'd planned to tell you about her this very day. Settle down while I pour us a little refreshment. If you've got the time, after I tell about the octagon room, I'll give you another story that happened soon afterward—a baffling medical mystery at Pilgrim Memorial Hospital, about a man who died with a bullet in his heart but not a wound on his body!"

THE PROBLEM OF
THE GYPSY CAMP

"I promised you another story today, didn't I?" old Dr. Sam Hawthorne told his visitor, rising to refill their glasses. "About the medical mystery at Pilgrim Memorial Hospital, and the man who died of a bullet in the heart but had no wound on his body. Really, though, it's also the story of a gypsy curse—and of a weird mystery that confronted me with not one but *two* impossibilities . . ."

The new decade of the 1930s dawned in Northmont (Dr. Sam continued) much as the old one had ended. It was an especially mild winter in the northeast, with some days warm enough even for an afternoon ball game at the new field in Pilgrim Park. Sheriff Lens was just back from his honeymoon, and I hadn't even seen him since the happy day. There were the usual wintertime complaints among my patients but by and large it was a quiet time, both medically and criminally, in our town.

"I never felt so lazy," I told my nurse April one fine January morning. "I think spring fever's starting early this year."

She was busy sorting through the inactive files. "That's not the only thing that's starting early. The gypsy camp is back at the old Haskins place."

"It is?" Somehow the news surprised me. It had been just over four years since the gypsies were last in Northmont, and I'd assumed they were gone for good after that Christmas steeple murder. But here they were back again at their old campsite. Mrs. Haskins had died a year or so earlier, at the age of eighty, but her property was still in litigation. Meanwhile, the fields had become overgrown and the old barn was sagging dangerously on one side. It had become something of an eyesore for the town, but apparently the gypsies didn't mind. "When did they show up?"

"I drove in that way this morning and noticed their wagons. Mrs. Peachtree down the road said they came over the weekend. She's trying to get Sheriff Lens

154

to evict them, but I guess there's some legal problem unless the owner of the land requests their removal."

"And the courts can't decide who the owner is."

"That's the trouble."

I got to my feet and stretched. "Well, April, I've got to get moving before I fall asleep. I think I'll take a run over to Pilgrim Memorial and check on Mrs. Ives."

"Good luck," she called after me, knowing I'd need it. Mrs. Ives was a grouchy woman in her sixties who was convinced all doctors were trying to poison her.

I thought about stopping by to see Sheriff Lens on the drive over, but decided that could wait till later. It was his first full day back in the office and I knew his work would be piled high. Besides, I really did want to speak with Abel Frater about the future of Pilgrim Memorial Hospital. Opened in March of the previous year with much fanfare, the eighty-bed facility had never been more than one-quarter full, and now an entire wing had been closed off to save fuel and electricity.

There were three doctors on the staff now. The hospital's founder, Dr. Seeger, and its black resident, Lincoln Jones, had been joined by Dr. Abel Frater, a skilled surgeon out of Boston. Seeger had given over the business end of things to Frater and it was his reluctant decision to close a wing of the building. Even a non-profit hospital had to watch the pennies.

Frater saw me as I entered the building and called out, "Making your morning rounds, Sam?"

"I have to check on my patients, Abel. Can't just abandon them to your care forever."

Abel Frater was a tall slender man who walked with a slight limp, the result of a leg wound suffered in the trenches of France during the war. He had a little mustache that was beginning to gray, and a way of smiling that made even the most pessimistic diagnosis somehow acceptable to the patient. "Who is it this time?" he asked. "Mrs. Ives?"

"The one and only."

"Better you than me. The woman accused us of neglecting her yesterday."

"I'm not surprised." I dropped my voice a bit so we wouldn't be overheard by the nurse at the front desk. "How are things going here, now that you've cut back to forty beds?"

"Oh, a little better. We have sixteen patients today, and that's about average for the past few weeks. I think Seeger's resigned to the fact that he built too large a facility for present needs. Still, who knows what tomorrow holds, eh?"

"Any danger of closing entirely? I'd hate to see Northmont lose this place."

"Oh, we'll be around. I—"

He stopped suddenly, staring over my shoulder at the hospital's entrance. I turned my head and saw a black-haired, mustached man coming through the door. He wore a short dark jacket that hung open to reveal a colorful sash around his middle in place of a belt. And as he drew closer I could see a single gold earring worn in his left lobe. It was one of the gypsies from the encampment.

"Can I help you?" Dr. Frater asked the man.

"I have been cursed," he told us, looking terrified. "I will die of a bullet in the heart—"

"You need the sheriff," I suggested, "not a hospital."

But the words were hardly out of my mouth when he clutched his chest and toppled over. Frater was at his side at once. "Get a stretcher, Sam! It looks like a heart attack!"

We rushed him to the nearest empty room while one of the nurses came to assist us, but it was too late. Frater had bared the man's chest and was massaging his heart when suddenly he stopped and said, "It's no use. The man is dead."

I placed my stethoscope to the hairy chest and listened. There was no heartbeat. Remembering a time when I'd once been fooled into thinking a man was dead while he was still alive, I performed a number of other tests. I even held a mirror to his nostrils, but it did not cloud.

"Trying to bring him back to life, Sam?" Dr. Frater asked.

"No, just making sure he's dead. He went pretty fast, even for a heart attack. It was almost as if he'd been shot as he seemed to fear."

"You believe in gypsy curses now, Sam?"

"Hardly. There's no wound on the body—not even a scar from an old wound."

Abel Frater corrected me. "Knife scar on his arm, but it's an old one. That certainly didn't kill him."

"Could I be present when you do the autopsy?"

"Certainly. But first we'd better notify his family, if he had one."

The dead man had carried no identification, but I quickly established his identity at the gypsy camp. There were about twenty brightly decorated wagons drawn up in the field at the old Haskins place, about a mile from the house and barn which were now deserted. The horses had been tied to a line at one end of the camp, and as I arrived a young man in his early twenties was feeding them. He'd seen my car drive up and asked, "Are you a lawyer?"

"No, I'm a doctor. We have one of your people at the hospital."

His eyes widened in panic. "Edo Montana! He feared the curse!"

"Does he have relatives here?"

The young man nodded. "I will take you to his sister, Teres."

Teres Montana was a tall angular girl about the same age as the young man. When she saw us approaching her wagon she jumped to the ground to confront us. "What is it, Steve? Who is this man?"

"I'm Dr. Sam Hawthorne. Your brother is Edo Montana?"

"Yes."

"A man died at the hospital this morning, apparently of a heart attack. I'm sorry, but it might be your brother."

She let out a long high-pitched wail, and I feared she might topple over as her brother had. Others came running at the sound, and one powerful gypsy grabbed me in a bear hug. "Did he offend you, Teres?" he asked.

"Release him, Rudolph—you have done enough already! Your curse has killed my Edo!"

My arms were freed at once and I turned to stare into Rudolph's stricken face. "How is that possible?" he asked. "I did not shoot him!"

"But did you threaten him?" I asked.

"I heard him," Steve said. "It was only this morning that they fought, and Rudolph told him, 'May you die with a gypsy bullet in your heart!'"

"Shut up, you!" Rudolph snarled. "I did not kill him!"

"We need someone to identify the body," I said. "The hospital will have to do an autopsy."

"I will go," the girl said quietly.

We left the others and walked across the field to my car. To put her at ease I asked about the others in the camp, mentioning names of those I remembered from previous visits of the gypsies to Northmont. But she seemed to know none of them. "Edo and I only joined this tribe recently, near Albany," she explained.

"Who is the king of this tribe?"

Teres took a deep breath. "Rudolph Roman. That is why his curse carried such power."

"Why did he curse your brother?" I asked, but she did not answer. The hospital came into view and she was reminded of her task. It had only been a few minutes' drive from the Haskins place, with its overgrown fields surrounded by woods, but overland it would have taken Edo Montana ten minutes of running to reach Pilgrim Memorial.

I escorted her through the front door and back to the autopsy room where Dr. Frater awaited us. He shook hands solemnly with the girl and offered his sympathy. Then he lifted the sheet from the dead face just enough for her to see it and cry out, "Edo, Edo!"

I took her by the arm, steadying her. "Come on, I'll drive you back."

She stared as if she'd forgotten who I was. "There is no need. The gypsies will come for me."

I wondered why she said "the gypsies" rather than "my people," but I had no time to think about it further. Dr. Seeger burst into the room, looking anxious. I could see drops of sweat on his bald head.

"There's fifty or sixty gypsies outside, heading toward our front door. Should I get the gun from my office?"

"I hardly think that's necessary," I told him.

Seeger had been the founder of Pilgrim Memorial, and in that instant he must have feared they were storming his building to destroy it. Teres Montana turned to him and said, "They come to honor the dead."

"We have to do an autopsy before we can release the body," Dr. Frater said. "Go talk to them and calm them down."

"They are calm," she replied, but she went out as instructed.

"They'll probably stay outside till we release the body to them for burial," I said. "Maybe we'd better get to that autopsy, Abel."

Seeger followed the girl outside and Frater and I slipped into surgical gowns and masks. He pulled on his rubber gloves and selected a scalpel for the initial incision. I rolled back the sheet from Edo Montana's naked body.

As soon as Frater parted the flaps of skin and exposed the chest area I saw the torn tissue and muscle. The heart itself had been pierced, and we only had to probe a few seconds to discover the small-caliber bullet that had done the damage.

I let out my breath slowly, not believing what I was seeing.

"You'd better phone your friend Sheriff Lens," Frater said quietly. "This is murder—the man was shot through the heart."

Sheriff Lens began grumbling as soon as he saw the autopsy room. "You might know I'd just be back from my honeymoon when you'd get yourself involved in another impossible murder, Doc! What is it this time?"

"The impossibility seems to be more medical than anything else. If there's a locked room in this killing it's the skin of the victim. Dr. Frater and I both examined the body at the time of death. There was no wound on it, front or back, and the only scar was that old one on his arm. I was here when Dr. Frater cut into the body, and I saw the damage caused by the bullet. I helped him probe for the slug myself."

Sheriff Lens stared distastefully at the body with its unveiled chest cavity. "Not much blood."

"He's been dead over an hour," Abel Frater explained. "The blood seeks the lowest level after death, like any liquid."

"So somebody murdered him?"

"It seems so," I agreed. "All we have to figure out is who and how."

"You mentioned something about a gypsy curse. Are those the gypsies standing around outside? The ones Mr. Peachtree phoned about?"

"That's right. They're camped over on the old Haskins place, just like last time. Apparently the one who cursed the dead man is their leader, Rudolph Roman."

Sheriff Lens nodded. "I'll go get him. I always believe in starting with the most likely suspect."

A few moments later he reappeared with the powerful gypsy who'd grabbed me in the bear hug. He identified himself as Rudolph Roman, leader or king of this gypsy tribe since the death of his father. He admitted to having heard from other gypsy tribes that the old Haskins land was good camping ground, free from police harassment.

"But Mrs. Haskins is dead now," I informed him. "That land is in litigation." I wasn't too familiar with the court case, but I knew it involved a nephew who claimed the land should go to him rather than to charity. Mrs. Haskins' will had been ambiguous.

Rudolph Roman merely smiled at my words. "We recognize no litigation. The land is for the people's use. We camp there, but we do not damage it."

"What about Edo Montana?" Sheriff Lens asked. "You sure damaged him!"

"I spoke without thinking," the gypsy leader admitted. "We were having a violent argument and I spoke the curse. 'May you die with a bullet through the heart!' I shouted. He turned pale at my words, and ran off."

"And died with a bullet through the heart," the sheriff said. "Are your curses always that effective?"

Rudolph Roman sighed. "I am the leader of this tribe, as was my father before me. My people expect me to do as my father did. He once cursed a man who died the following day. That curse has become a legend with us, and when I spoke those words unthinkingly my people remembered. They warned Edo of my power."

I nodded. "And he ran."

"But I did not kill him! I did not mean to kill him!"

"What did you do after he ran away?" I asked.

"Went back to my wagon to be alone."

"And why did the two of you argue?"

"I—I cannot say."

"This is a murder investigation," Sheriff Lens reminded him.

When Roman answered his voice was very soft. "It was about the girl Teres," he told us.

"What about her?"

"I wanted to take her for my wife. My request threw Edo into a rage. He called me vile names, and that was when I cursed him."

"I'd think he would have considered it an honor to have his sister wed to the leader of the tribe."

Roman started to reply but then thought better of it. His mouth closed and he would say no more. "We should talk to Teres again," I suggested.

While Sheriff Lens went to get her, I returned to the autopsy table where Frater was preparing to sew up the body. "The sooner we turn it over to them for burial, the sooner they'll be gone," he said. "We can learn nothing more by keeping it here."

But something in the dead and torn heart caught my eye. I slipped on a rubber glove and extracted a thin sliver of wood. "What's that?" Frater asked.

"I don't really know. Looks like a tiny piece of wood, but I can't be sure."

I helped him sew up the autopsy incision. "What are you going to list as the cause of death?"

"Hell, Sam, the man had a bullet in his heart! That's the cause of death. It's not up to me to figure out how it got there."

Sheriff Lens took Teres Montana to one of the offices for questioning, so she would not be confronted with her brother's body again. I joined them as he was saying, "Rudolph Roman has admitted he fought with your brother when he asked to marry you, but he would say no more about it. Were you present when this happened?"

"Yes," she admitted, with head bowed.

I decided to ask a question of my own. "There was a great age difference between you and your brother, wasn't there? He appears to have been in his late forties."

She hesitated. "Yes, he was forty-seven. I am twenty-two. He was my stepbrother, really."

"Was he your brother at all?" I asked. "Or was he something more?"

"What do you mean?"

"His anger at Rudolph's offer of marriage makes me wonder. What was your true relationship, Teres?"

She burst into tears then, and Sheriff Lens looked dumfounded. He started to speak but I waved him to silence. "Tell us the truth, Teres," I said softly. "You and Edo were married, weren't you?"

She nodded, trying to control her tears. "We were married last summer in Albany, before we joined Rudolph's tribe. Because we had not gone through the traditional gypsy wedding ceremony, Edo wanted to keep it secret."

"It seems you kept the secret too well, at least from Roman. But why couldn't you simply tell him the truth and have a gypsy ceremony?"

She merely shook her head, unable to answer for a moment. Finally, bringing herself under control, she told us in a soft voice, "I'm not one of them. I'm not a gypsy. I ran away from home and met Edo in Albany. He said I was dark enough to pass for a gypsy and so we joined the caravan. He told them I was his sister, so no question would arise about my blood. He was known to some others of the tribe, and nobody questioned it until Rudolph decided he was in love with me. If Edo told the truth about our relationship it would have come out that I wasn't a gypsy, and I would have had to leave the camp."

"Do you have any idea how Roman might have killed him?"

"No—unless it really was a curse."

"Did Edo run away from the camp immediately after his argument with Roman?"

"I think so, yes. I tried to get Steve to find him—you remember, the young man you met this morning?—but he couldn't. Steve said once he had a capsule containing a potion that could be taken to ward off curses."

"A capsule?" Something stirred in my brain. "How large a capsule?"

"He showed it to us once. It looked big enough to give to a horse."

The door opened and Dr. Frater stuck his head in. "Thought you'd want to know that I've finished with the body and turned it over to the gypsies. They're going back to their camp."

I turned to Teres. "Will you go with them?"

She lifted her head, brushing the hair from her eyes. "I don't know."

In that instant she looked very young indeed. "You said you ran away from home. You're not twenty-two, are you? People who are twenty-two don't need to run away from home."

"I'm seventeen," she admitted.

"Damn!" Sheriff Lens was on his feet. "And you were livin' at that gypsy camp with a man thirty years older than you? I'm takin' you into custody till we can get you back to your parents!"

Abel Frater was still in the doorway. "What should I tell them outside?"

"She's detained for questioning," the sheriff responded. "Don't tell them anything else."

I walked to the window and watched as the men of the gypsy tribe hoisted Montana's body onto a stretcher and started off the way they had come. "I hope we did the right thing releasing the body," I said. "We've no idea how he was killed."

"A bullet in the heart." Sheriff Lens answered. "That's good enough for Frater and it's good enough for me. I told him he could release the body, just to get rid of them."

I went in search of Dr. Seeger and found him by the front door, watching the gypsies depart. "Thank God they're gone, Sam. If I never see them again it'll be too soon."

"Maybe you can answer a question for me."

"Sure. What is it?"

"Those gelatin capsules they're starting to use for drugs—is it possible a small bullet could be placed in one and swallowed without the person realizing it?"

"Sure, but the bullet would just pass through his stomach and out the intestinal tract. It wouldn't end up in the heart, if that's what you're thinking."

"I know that much. I was just wondering about it. How about this—is it possible an old bullet could remain in the body for years, lodged near the heart, and finally kill a person after some exertion or fright?"

"It's possible, but not in this case, Sam. Frater showed me the body before he sewed Montana up. There's no doubt a bullet was fired into the body. The damage was too recent and too extensive to have been caused by an old wound. Besides, the only scar was on his arm."

"I know. Don't mind me. I'm just trying to rule out every possibility."

"And whatever remains, however improbable, must be the truth?" Seeger asked with a smile.

"That's just the trouble—nothing remains! But I did find a tiny splinter of—"

"Doc! Help me!"

We turned and saw Sheriff Lens staggering down the corridor toward us. There was blood on his nose and face.

"What happened?" I asked, running to him.

"He punched me and took the girl! They ran out the back way."

"Who punched you?"

"One of them gypsies! I heard her call him Steve."

It was late afternoon, beginning to grow dark, by the time I'd stopped the sheriff's nosebleed and accompanied him to the gypsy camp. Steve and Teres were nowhere to be found, and Rudolph Roman denied any knowledge of where they might be. "You'd better turn them up by morning," Sheriff Lens told him, "or I'm arresting everyone here!"

Roman merely smiled. "You believe you can do that?"

"Damn right I can do it! And I'll get the state police to help me!"

"Gypsies can fade away with the night."

"You just try it! I want that girl back, and I want Steve too, for assaultin' me!"

The others in the camp merely watched us as we walked back to the car. Already some men and boys were gathering wood for evening bonfires to ward off the chill of the January night. "I wasn't fooling, Sam," the sheriff told me. "I'm calling the state police." He started the car and headed back to town.

"Roman implied they might be gone by morning."

"They're not goin' nowhere till I get my hands on that Steve and the girl! I'll make sure of that if I have to watch the camp all night!"

I could see he was furious, considering the attack on him to be a personal affront. He telephoned the state police from the jail and requested that three cars be sent to help him round up the gypsies in the morning. Then he called his deputies and ordered them in too.

I checked with April and learned I had a patient to see on the way home. I drove out past the Haskins place and saw the silhouettes of the caravan wagons against the glowing gypsy bonfires. They seemed to be settling in for the night. Lens and one of his deputies pulled up behind me and parked off the road with a good view of the camp. I waved a good night to him and continued on my way.

I'd always been an early riser, and the following morning I came awake while it was still night, not much after five a.m. The gypsy camp was very much on my mind, and although there were still a couple of hours before daylight I decided I should get dressed and drive over to the Haskins place. I didn't want Sheriff Lens, or the gypsies, doing anything foolish.

Downing a cup of coffee and a piece of toast quickly, I went out to the car, shivering a bit in the morning air. It took me ten minutes to reach the old farm, and I saw the sheriff's car still where I'd last seen it. A state police car was parked down the road about twenty feet away. I tapped on the glass and opened the door. "Keeping awake, Sheriff?"

"Oh, it's you, Sam. I was hoping it was more state police. It'll start gettin' light any minute now, and I want to move in on them."

"You been awake all night?"

"All night," the deputy with him confirmed. "Sheriff don't want any of them slippin' away."

I stared through the darkness in the direction of the campsite, wondering if any of the bonfires were still burning. But there was nothing to break the curtain of night. Headlights appeared on the road in front of us and I saw another state police car pull up and park. Sheriff Lens got out to greet them.

"They're trespassing and possibly harboring a criminal as well," I heard him explain. "One of them punched me yesterday afternoon and helped a suspect escape. There's also been a killing that almost certainly involves them." He led them back to the car and I shook hands with the uniformed officers. I wasn't happy to see their hands resting on the butts of their service revolvers, or to note that one of the men in the other car had produced a shotgun from the trunk.

"I don't think guns will be necessary," I told them.

"We heard somebody got shot yesterday."

"Well, yes," I admitted. "But—"

I stopped talking as my eyes became more accustomed to the gradual approach of dawn. A mist seemed to hang over the fields, and I saw now that a bit of smoke still rose lazily from one of the almost dead campfires. But more than that I saw something that boggled the mind.

Where last evening twenty wagons had stood with their horses, now there was nothing. Only the remains of the bonfires testified to the fact they'd ever been there. Somehow during the night, with Sheriff Lens and his deputy standing guard all night, the gypsy camp had vanished.

"It's the devil's work!" Sheriff Lens growled, striding back and forth across the empty field. The rising sun had only confirmed what they could already see—somehow the entire caravan of gypsies had disappeared during the night.

"Or another gypsy curse," I suggested quietly, only half in jest. Looking at our surroundings, I had to admit the thing seemed impossible. The Haskins field was bordered on three sides by tall stands of trees, and fenced to keep cattle from wandering too far. The only exit to the highway was the narrow rutted lane where the sheriff's car had been parked. "Could you have dozed off?"

"I might have, once or twice, but my deputy Frank was awake the whole time. Besides, we were parked right across the end of the lane. Even if we were both asleep they couldn't have gotten twenty horses and wagons past us. There's no room. They'd have ended up in the ditch!"

I had to admit he was right. I strolled past the ashes of the bonfires and made a circuit of the field, inspecting the fence for signs of passage. "A man could go over that easy," Frank said to me, a bit sheepish about the whole thing.

"Sure," I agreed, "but what about the horses and wagons? There aren't any breaks in the fence, and the wagons couldn't get through those trees anyway."

The state police were taking a dim view of the entire matter. "You sure they were here in the first place?" one officer asked the sheriff.

"Sure, I'm sure! And Doc here saw them too. You think we're crazy or something?"

I poked around at the charred remains of the fires. They had been here, all right, and now they were gone. They had vanished as easily as that bullet had appeared in Edo Montana's heart.

"Where you goin', Doc?" Sheriff Lens called to me as I headed back to my car.

"To work. And I'm going to make a phone call or two."

"Can't you help us out on this? We got *two* impossibilities in this case, Doc!" His voice was pleading.

"Go back home to your new bride, Sheriff. You shouldn't have left her alone last night anyway. I'll phone you when I have something."

"What about the gypsies?"

"Have the state police send out a general alarm. Vanishing from this field might have been easy for them, but staying out of sight on the public highways will be a real miracle if they can pull it off. Look for them about a hundred miles from here, possibly heading northwest toward Albany."

"But how—?"

"Later, Sheriff."

It was still early when I reached my office, and I was able to catch up on the previous day's mail before April arrived. She looked startled when she saw me already at my desk. "You been here all night, Dr. Sam?"

"Not quite. I wanted to stop by the gypsy camp on my way in."

"I heard the sheriff was going to run them all in."

"They beat him to it. They up and vanished."

"The whole camp?"

"The whole camp."

"What are you going to do?"

"Make a phone call," I said. I flipped through the address book on my desk, searching for a number I'd called once, two years earlier, when I was treating old Mrs. Haskins.

I caught her nephew as he was about to leave home for his Boston office. Explaining who I was, I told him about the gypsies that had camped on his aunt's land. "I know about them," he answered curtly. "My lawyer says to leave them there."

"Why is that?"

"We're trying to convince a judge the property should come to me instead of some charity. My lawyer figures as long as the gypsies are camped there it creates a bad impression. I promise to use the land, while the charity would let it stand idle for future use, attracting more gypsy caravans."

"What sort of will did Mrs. Haskins leave?"

"The land was to be left to me or to the charity, whichever could demonstrate its use was in the best public interest of the citizens of Northmont. A crazy will, but the judge has to decide the issue. Which is what he's doing right now."

"Well, I can tell you the gypsies are gone, as of this morning."

"What?"

"You heard me. They just vanished overnight."

"I'm sorry to hear that."

"Tell me something, Mr. Haskins—which charity was mentioned in your aunt's will?"

"Some non-profit hospital you got there. Pilgrim Memorial?"

"Yes," I said quietly. "That's the name."

"I have to go to work now, Dr. Hawthorne. Just what was it you called about?"

"You've answered all my questions, Mr. Haskins."

I was driving toward the hospital ten minutes later when I passed the sheriff's car on the road. He honked at me and I pulled to a stop as he backed up. "That was a good guess, Doc," he yelled out the window. "The state police picked up the gypsy caravan just this side of the New York state line. How'd you know?"

"As you said, it was a good guess. Follow along with me to the hospital and we'll wrap this thing up."

Things had quieted down considerably at Pilgrim Memorial from the previous day. Dr. Seeger was anxious to see us, and when I asked that Dr. Frater be present too he buzzed him immediately. "What is this?" Frater asked as he came in. "A final confrontation, the way it happens in mystery novels?"

"Something like that," I admitted.

As usual, Sheriff Lens was more direct. "We've got the gypsies in custody and now we've come to arrest a murderer," he announced.

"Not quite, Sheriff," I corrected. "There's no murderer here."

"Huh?" His mouth dropped open. "Doc, you told me—"

"That we'd wrap this thing up, and that's exactly what I intend to do. But there's no murderer simply because there was no murder. And we've had two impossible crimes without any real crime at all."

"No crime?" Frater asked. "But what about the bullet in Edo Montana?"

"The closest thing to a crime might be the desecration of a dead body. And I doubt if the sheriff will bother to charge you with that, Dr. Frater."

He simply stood there facing me, saying nothing. It was Seeger who finally spoke. "What do you mean, Sam?" he asked.

"We have to remember that Edo Montana came running to the hospital from the gypsy camp. Why? Because someone had uttered a curse? That's not very likely, unless Montana was suffering some symptoms along with the curse. A chest pain, for instance, just after Roman's words, might have scared him into seeking medical assistance. And then what did he do? He ran ten minutes to the hospital, the worst possible action if he was experiencing the beginning of a heart attack. He arrived here, collapsed, and died—a natural death."

"But—"

"It was just before he died that Abel Frater heard his dying words about the curse, about the bullet in the heart, and decided to make it come true. He took the gun from your office, Seeger, and while I went off to visit the gypsy camp he fired a bullet into the dead man's chest and heart."

"There was no wound," Sheriff Lens argued.

"I found a tiny splinter of wood in the heart. I think Frater fired through a thin board held against the dead man's chest. This would have served two purposes—to slow down the small-caliber bullet enough so it wouldn't exit through the back, and to shield the chest from powder burns that might have singed the hair and left other marks."

"Firing through a board, Frater left only a small entrance hole which was easily hidden by flesh-colored putty or makeup. The body was covered by a sheet and I had only a glimpse of the chest before Frater cut into it—making his incision directly over the bullet hole, of course. The victim's hairiness helped to hide the wound too."

"Why would he do a crazy thing like that?" the sheriff asked.

"I think we should let him tell us that. It was the Haskins property, wasn't it, Abel?"

His shoulders sagged a bit then. Perhaps he'd thought I was only guessing up to that point. After a moment he said, "I didn't harm anyone. The man was already dead of natural causes. But here was a judge in Boston about to decide whether Mrs. Haskins' nephew or the hospital got the land. I'd been on the phone to our lawyer just yesterday and he said the judge knew about the gypsies camped there. It looked bad for us. It looked as if the community would be better served by Haskins farming it than by our owning the land and letting it stand idle for another few years, attracting gypsies. I wanted that land, for the hospital's future. By firing a bullet into a dead man's chest I knew it would spread talk of the gypsy curse. They'd either be arrested or forced to make a quick exit from Northmont, which is exactly what happened. I wrapped the gun in a towel to muffle the sound, but a .22 doesn't make much noise anyway. And I fired through a board just as Sam said."

"How'd you know it all?" Seeger asked me.

"I eliminated the impossible, just as you said. And if the bullet was fired into the corpse after death, only Frater could have done it and hidden the wound."

"What about the gypsy camp?" Sheriff Lens wanted to know. "How did that disappear?"

"The question really is *when* did it disappear, Sheriff. Roman moved his horses and wagons out quickly, between our late afternoon visit to the camp and your return in the evening to watch it."

"But the wagons were still there! I saw them!"

"What we saw were *silhouettes against the campfires*. They were pieces of cardboard cut to the size of the wagons. It's probably a trick Roman has used before in tight spots, and I imagine each wagon carries its own piece of cardboard for just such an emergency. A few of the gypsies stayed behind, tending the fires and giving evidence of normal activity so the caravan would have time to escape down the highway. Then after nightfall they simply burned the cardboard silhouettes in the bonfires and escaped over the fence to rejoin the caravan. If you look closely at the remains of the fires you'll find evidence of the cardboard pieces."

"I'll be damned!" Sheriff Lens muttered. "But you knew right where to look for them, Sam."

"A good guess, as I said earlier. If they left before dark last night I figured they could cover about a hundred miles in their wagons. Montana and Teres had joined them near Albany and I figured they might head back in that direction."

The sheriff merely shook his head. "I still can't believe it. Two impossible crimes, and yet there was no crime."

"Some days are like that," I said with a grin.

So that's the way it was (Dr. Sam Hawthorne concluded). Dr. Frater left the hospital staff the following week and moved out west somewhere. Roman's gypsies were released without charges when the sheriff discovered that Teres and Steve had never rejoined them. The two ran off together, telling Roman they were getting married. I suppose you can say the story had a happy ending, though perhaps Rudolph Roman wasn't too happy with the loss of Teres.

"I see our bottle is empty, and it's past my bedtime anyhow. But come back again and I'll have another story for you—about the time when gangsters and bootleggers fought a regular war in Northmont, and even a bizarre impossible crime seemed mundane by comparison."

THE PROBLEM OF
THE BOOTLEGGER'S CAR

"Wait till I open a new bottle," Dr. Sam Hawthorne was saying. "We can't have a story without a small—ah—libation. You know, looking at this bottle brings back so many memories. You were too young for Prohibition, of course, but I was around for it. You might think we'd escaped the worst of the gang wars up in Northmont, in the peaceful New England countryside, but let me tell you—in the spring of 1930 we had a dilly of a one! It was all over a shipment of empty barrels—yes, I said empty—and it involved an impossible disappearance from a bootlegger's car that I had to solve, quite literally, to save my own life."

"But it all began with my kidnaping . . ."

It was a Saturday morning in early May (Dr. Sam continued), and I was down at my office getting out some bills. My nurse April had gone off to visit her sister in Florida—a journey of some magnitude in those days—and I'd been left to cope with things as best I could for three weeks' time. I was just finishing up my chores, putting stamps on some of the bills I wanted to mail out, when I heard the little bell on the outside door signal the arrival of a patient. Since none was scheduled, I went to see who it was.

A man in a pin-stripe suit and a brown fedora hat stood in the center of my waiting room, pointing a long-barreled revolver at me. "Dr. Hawthorne?"

"That's right. What's the gun for?"

"You're comin' with me, Doc. We got an injured man."

"If there's an injured man you don't need a gun. I'll get my bag."

He followed me into the inner office, the gun still in his hand. I collected some extra rolls of bandages and stuffed them into my bag, having a pretty good idea of the nature of the injury. But I asked anyway. "What's the matter with him?"

"Gunshot wounds."

"More than one?"

"Just one that's bad. Come on, cut the talk!"

I snapped my bag shut and walked out the door in front of him. "Make sure you lock it," I cautioned him. "There are lots of crooks around these days."

"You being a wise guy?" he asked.

"Not a bit."

There was another man waiting outside at the wheel of the car, a closed black sedan. I could see that his right hand was inside his jacket, no doubt clutching another gun. I didn't feel scared. I felt more like a character in a Class B gangster movie.

"Get in!" the one behind me ordered, giving me a shove.

I glanced around, but the alley behind my office was deserted on a Saturday morning and I didn't really expect anyone from the nearby houses would notice my predicament. I slid into the back seat of the car as ordered, and said to my captor, "Do you have a name I can call you? It looks as if we'll be together for a few hours."

"Phil," the man with the gun said. "That's Marty behind the wheel. He don't talk much."

"Where are we going?"

"A farmhouse just outside of town. Fat Larry rented it."

"Fat Larry?"

He nudged me with the revolver. "Your patient. But don't ask too many questions, Doc. It's not good for your health."

I remembered a name from the newspapers. "Would that be Fat Larry Spears? The bootlegger?"

"I told you not to ask questions, Doc. You want to come back from this trip alive, don't you?"

I fell silent, thinking about Fat Larry Spears. He controlled most of the illegal whiskey flowing into Boston and Providence, according to the press, and was rumored to have killed a half-dozen men. His own life had been on the line countless times, and it was a known fact that the New York mobs had a price on his head. They wanted control of bootlegging in the entire northeast, with no interference from independent operators like Fat Larry.

We were some miles out of town, bumping along the Old Ridge Road in the spring sunshine, when Marty finally turned off into a weed-choked driveway. I recognized the farmhouse at once as the old Haskins place, abandoned since the death of the last unmarried brother a year earlier. If Fat Larry Spears was renting it he probably wasn't paying much. The house was near a crossroads, and I supposed it might make a good meeting place for bootleggers.

I entered the place between Marty and Phil, with the gun still at my back. As we approached, the door was flung open by a slim dark-haired woman with a pretty face. "He still won't let me look at the wound," she told them, "but there's blood all over! Is this the doctor?"

"I'm Sam Hawthorne," I said. "How long ago did it happen?"

She glanced at the gunman. "What was it, Phil? Around nine?"

"Yeah. They were waiting for him in the bushes near the road. When he came out the door they started firing. We came for you right away."

"Let's see him." I was already opening my bag as I followed her into a first-floor bedroom.

It was Fat Larry Spears, all right, though at the moment he didn't look much like the dapper newspaper photos. He was curled into a ball on the bed, clutching at his stomach and abdomen, writhing in pain. There was blood on the sheets and on his shirt, and I could see an additional flesh wound in his upper left arm.

"I'm the doctor," I announced. "Let's take a look at you."

He rolled over, grimacing, and told the woman, "Leave us alone, Kitty. I don't want you to see it."

"For God's sake, Larry—"

"You heard me!" he shouted. "Out!"

She went out with the two men and closed the door, leaving me alone with my patient. "Take your hands away and let me see it," I instructed him.

He straightened out at once and his shirt fell open, revealing a hairy but unmarked stomach. There was no wound.

But there was a little .22 automatic just inches away from my head.

"Don't make a sound," Fat Larry Spears cautioned me. "No yelling."

"I didn't intend to," I answered quietly. "I came to fix your wounds."

"There's one in my arm, that's all. It's just a flesh wound. Take care of that and then we'll talk."

"You don't need that gun."

But he kept it there. "How do I know you're a doctor?"

"Hell, how do I know you're a bootlegger?"

"Wise guy, huh?"

"No wiser than you." I went to work on the arm. "You're thinner than you look in the papers. How come they call you Fat Larry?"

"I used to be fat. I lost weight. That's what saved my life this morning." He rolled over on the bed, revealing a thickly padded vest he'd hidden beneath his body. "I started losing weight a year ago, but I decided to keep it a secret. In this business, with half the guns in New York after me, I figured I might need to change my appearance in a hurry some day. So I started wearing padding around my stomach and stuffed a little cotton into my cheeks. I looked about like I had before, except that I was fifty pounds lighter."

The bullet had passed through the fleshy part of his arm, and it was only a matter of taking a couple of stitches. "This'll hurt," I warned. "You should go into the hospital."

"Go ahead and do it, Doc. I won't shoot you."

"I certainly hope not." I went to work as he gritted his teeth. "But why keep your weight loss from those people outside?"

"Because one of them is an informer. One of them has been tipping off the New York mob to everything I do. That's why there was a gunman waiting in the bushes this morning. Only those three knew I was up here. Luckily my stomach padding stopped the bullet, but the impact knocked me over and I decided to pretend I was badly wounded. If they think I'm on the way out I might be able to catch the guilty one off guard. Understand?"

"Kitty must know you've lost weight," I said.

He snorted. "You think I sleep with her? That was over a year ago. She just hangs around now for what she can get outa me. Maybe she decided she can get more outa the New York boys."

"All finished," I announced, patting his arm. "You were lucky. When you get back to Boston or wherever, you should have that checked by your own doctor."

"One more thing, Doc."

"What's that?"

"I gotta keep you here with me, till tonight."

"What?"

"You heard me. You know I'm here and you know I'm not badly wounded. The police would be interested in the first fact, and the people who shot me would be interested in the second. You've got to stay here till my business is finished tonight."

"What business is that?"

"I have to take delivery of a shipment of barrels."

"Booze?"

"No, just barrels. All I'm promised is that they'll be here by sundown." He paused and looked at me. "They're valuable."

I buttoned his shirt up again and remarked on all the blood. "Did this all come from your arm?"

The familiar waxen face actually smiled. "Yeah. I soaked the blood into my shirt so it would look more like a chest wound. That was fast thinking if I say so myself."

"If it keeps you alive I won't disagree."

"What's the local police setup here, Doc?"

"Sheriff Lens has a few deputies, but they never patrol up this way. You shouldn't be bothered."

"Good! Now you tell the others I'm gonna pull through but I'll have to stay in bed. Got that?"

"Yes."

"I'll tell them not to let you go till the truck gets here. You play your cards right and you'll get out of this alive." He raised his voice and shouted, "Marty! Phil!"

The driver and the gunman immediately appeared. "How you feelin', Larry?"

"I'll live, the doc tells me."

I nodded, getting to my feet and starting to gather up my equipment. "He's a lucky man. He's very weak and he'd better stay in bed, but the bullet missed any vital areas. If he doesn't develop an infection he should be back on his feet in a month or so."

"Keep the doc here till the truck arrives," Spears told the two men, making his voice sounding suddenly weak. "I said we'd let him go after that."

"Right, Larry," Phil said. "Let's go, Doc."

"And send Kitty in here," the man in the bed ordered.

The farmhouse was sparsely furnished, but there were a table and chairs in the front room. Phil motioned me to sit down and then said to Kitty, "Your turn. He wants you."

She turned to me. "How is he?"

"Weak, but he'll live."

Her face was a mask as she turned and went into the bedroom, closing the door behind her. Phil sat down at the table. He'd taken off his suit coat and returned the revolver to its shoulder holster. "How about some cards, Doc? You play gin rummy?"

"Sure," I replied, "but what about Marty?"

"He don't play."

"Does he ever speak?"

Phil looked up at the burly driver. "Say something for the doc, Marty. He don't think you can talk."

"I can talk," a voice rasped.

"My God, what's the matter with his throat?"

"He got some bad booze. Burned his throat and nearly killed him. Back in the early days they were selling anything they could put in bottles. Some still do, for that matter."

I couldn't help wondering if Marty might blame Fat Larry Spears somehow for the booze that had ruined his throat. Had he kept on working for Spears only until he could get his revenge by betraying Fat Larry to the New York crowd?

But here I was acting like a detective again, and there was no reason to. The truck loaded with the mysterious barrels would arrive soon and then everyone would depart. Since they hadn't killed me yet I was pretty sure Spears meant it about letting me live.

As Phil dealt the cards I asked, "Who do you think shot Larry?"

He shrugged. "Some hired gun from the New York mob."

"How would he know Larry was up here?"

"Followed us, I suppose. Or else he heard it from Tony Barrel."

"Who?"

"Tony Barrello. Everybody calls him Tony Barrel because that's what he sells—barrels. He's makin' the delivery today."

"Tell me, what's in these barrels?"

"Nothing. Nothing but air."

"Larry said they were valuable."

Phil scooped up his cards, but Marty was standing there peering over his shoulder. "Go outside, Marty," he ordered. "Watch for the truck." When the burly man had gone, he said, "Guy gets on my nerves. Always so damned quiet. Never know what he's thinkin'. Where were we?"

"The barrels."

"Yeah."

"Larry said they were valuable."

"Well, they cost sixty bucks each and there are supposed to be two hundred of them on the truck. That's twelve thousand dollars."

"Sixty dollars each for empty barrels?"

"These are special," Phil said with a smile. "You'll see."

We played two games of gin and he won both times. We were just starting a third game when Kitty came out of the bedroom. "He's hungry," she said. "I'm going to make him a sandwich."

Phil glanced at me. "You're not supposed to eat with a stomach wound, are you?"

"Well, the bullet didn't actually hit his stomach. It's all right if he eats a little."

She went off to the kitchen, where they apparently had a small stock of cold meat and bread. "Make me one too," Phil yelled to her. "And Marty's probably gettin' hungry. It's after one already."

Kitty brought in a plate of sandwiches, moving with a languid grace that made me guess she'd once been a cocktail waitress. "Where were all of you when Larry was shot this morning?" I asked casually.

"Kitty was fixin' breakfast," Phil replied, studying his cards with a frown. "Marty and I were still in bed. We didn't get in till past midnight. I was just wakin' up when I heard the shots."

"How many?"

"Three or four, I guess."

"Four," Kitty said. "There were four shots. By the time I got to the door Larry was down on the steps, trying to crawl back inside. There was no sign of the gunman. Larry said the shots came from the bushes near the road."

"He must have been expecting trouble if he brought you guys along," I commented.

"Larry always expects trouble," Kitty agreed. "Especially when he's dealing with people like Tony Barrel. Tony deals with the New York mob. You never know whose side he's on."

As the afternoon wore on I began to get restless, wondering if anyone had yet noticed my absence. Probably not, I decided. It was a Saturday, when I only had limited office hours, and April was on vacation. Sheriff Lens might drop by to see me, but he'd think nothing of my absence.

At three o'clock I got to my feet, saying, "I'd better have a look at my patient."

"I think he's sleeping," Kitty said.

"I'll just peek in."

I opened the door and looked in. Fat Larry was in bed with his eyes closed, but they snapped open at once. I knew his hand beneath the covers would be clutching the .22 automatic. "What is it?" he asked. "Is the truck here?"

I stepped inside and shut the door behind me.

"Not yet. I just wanted to see how you're getting on."

He gave me a hard smile. "Pretty good for a man with a bullet in his belly. Are they suspicious?"

"They don't seem to be. But where is all this leading? Do you think one of them might try to finish you off?"

"Might be. Let's see what happens when Tony Barrel arrives."

I went back out to join the others. By that time I think we were all getting tired of waiting, but before Phil could deal another hand of gin rummy Marty came in from outside.

"Car and truck coming," he said in his raspy voice.

Phil was on his feet at once, reaching for his holstered weapon. "Cover the back, Marty—just in case it's some sort of trick." Then, to Kitty, "Tell Larry they're coming."

Kitty went into the bedroom and returned at once with a message. "He says we're to bring Tony Barrel in there so he can close the deal and give him the money for the shipment."

Phil nodded and went to the door. I looked through the window, watching a rise of dust approach us along the dirt road. A car pulled into the driveway first, followed by a large long truck with a tarpaulin-covered cargo. Interested as I was in this mysterious cargo of empty barrels, it was the car that caught my attention. It was a black Packard limousine with shades drawn on the rear windows. A thin man of medium height with a pock-marked face slid out from behind the wheel. Like Phil, he wore a dark suit and a wide-brimmed fedora, but the suit seemed somehow too big for him.

"That's Scoop Turner, Tony's driver," Phil told me. "And there's Tony Barrel himself."

Scoop opened the rear door and a stout bearded man emerged. If he wasn't quite shaped like a barrel, he was certainly large, and somehow the bushy black beard and slouch hat gave him an undeservedly squat appearance. While his driver lounged against the car, Tony Barrel walked quickly up the steps to the front door.

Phil holstered his gun and opened the door. "Hello, Tony. Good to see you again."

Tony Barrel's steel-gray eyes covered the room at a glance, passing quickly over Kitty and stopping at me. "Who's this?" he asked.

"A local sawbones. Larry got hurt."

I extended my hand. "Dr. Sam Hawthorne. Pleased to meet you, Tony."

"Yeah." He took my hand and gave it a limp shake. I couldn't help noticing that he wore a diamond ring shaped like a barrel. "What's the matter with Larry?"

"Somebody shot him," Phil answered before I could reply. "But the doc says he'll pull through. We got him in the back room here and he wants to see you about the shipment."

"He better do more than see me. He better give me twelve grand plus the fee for the truck."

"He's got it for you."

"He bring a driver?"

"Marty's around back."

Tony Barrel snorted. "That hophead!"

"Is your guy any better?" Phil glanced out the window. "What in hell's he doin' wavin' that shotgun around?"

"Protectin' the cargo," Tony Barrel said.

I went to the window to take a look. The driver of the truck had gotten out and was standing like a soldier on guard with a double-barreled shotgun. Kitty came over to my side. "That's Charlie Hello with the gun. He's part Indian or something. About like Marty. They're good with a gun and that's all."

"What makes those barrels so valuable?"

"Come on out and I'll show you."

We waited while Tony Barrel was shown into Larry Spears's sick room. I heard Larry greet him in a weak voice. "Tony, my old friend! They tried to kill me but I'm a tough one." Then Tony closed the door.

I followed Kitty outside while Phil went around back to get Marty. Barrel's driver, Scoop Turner, was still lounging against the Packard, but he stirred as we approached. "Why do they call him Scoop?" I asked Kitty.

"He used to be a reporter out in Chicago, but he decided he could make more money working for the mob. He's always after the bucks." Then, in a louder voice, she greeted him. "How's tricks, Scoop?"

He gave her a sleepy grin. "Hello, Kitty. Still knocking them dead?"

"Sure, Scoop." She explained to me, "I was in burlesque for a while in Chicago. Scoop reviewed my act one night, didn't you, Scoop?"

"I loved it."

"Can we look at Tony's car?"

He shrugged and opened the back door. With the shades drawn the interior was dim, but there was a ceiling light that cast a soft glow over the fancy leather upholstery. Tucked into the pocket behind the front seat was a sawed-off shotgun. Scoop opened the driver's door and rested his arms on the back of the front seat, watching Kitty's reaction. "Pretty classy, huh?"

"Why does he ride with the shades down?"

"Too many people tryin' to get a shot at him. This way they can't tell if he's in the car or not. See, my side glass in front is smoked too. Only the front windshield is clear glass."

"Bulletproof?"

"So they say, but I wouldn't like to try it with a Tommygun."

Kitty and I continued walking toward the truck and Scoop Turner closed the car doors. He wandered off toward the side of the house. "I'm sorry you had to get involved in this business," Kitty told me as we walked. "But I made Larry promise you wouldn't be harmed. We'll release you as soon as Tony Barrel and his men leave."

With Phil and Marty both around the back of the house, I wondered if I could make a run for it then, but I decided against it. The truck driver, Charlie Hello, still had his shotgun out and I didn't know when he might decide to use it. He might like to practise on a running target.

"It's me, Charlie—Kitty. You remember me, don't you?"

If he did he showed no sign of it. Instead, he slipped his finger through the trigger guard of the shotgun and said, "Stay away from the truck."

"We just want to look at the barrels, Charlie. We won't hurt anything."

His eyes were sleepy, possibly from drugs. They followed our movements around the truck but the warning was not repeated. Kitty lifted the tarpaulin and showed me the wooden barrels. One row was upended and I could see they were empty. "They're not even new," I commented. "The insides look like they've been charred."

"Of course they're charred, silly! That's what makes them so valuable. Tony Barrel buys them from distilleries in Canada. They're charred barrels in which whiskey has been aged. You fill them with denatured alcohol and let it stand for a few weeks. It absorbs the flavor of the whiskey and comes out tasting like Scotch or rye or bourbon or whatever was in the barrels originally."

"Where does the denatured alcohol come from?"

"The government allows it to be sold to certain manufacturing firms. In some cases poisonous chemicals are added, but the alcohol used in making hair tonic—for example—is nauseating but not deadly. A chemist can rectify or purify it by repeated distillation, removing the nauseating substance. The pure alcohol is left in these barrels a few weeks, and it tastes just like the real thing."

"Amazing!"

"Just one of the tricks of the trade."

"I thought Larry Spears was selling whiskey he smuggled across the border."

"He is, but demand is outstripping his supply. Besides, he needs more money, the way his gambling debts keep rising."

"There comes Tony Barrel," I said. The door of the farmhouse had opened and the stout bearded man emerged just as Phil and Marty came around the corner of the house.

"Get the money, Tony?" Phil called out.

"Yeah," he mumbled. "The truck's yours." His bare right hand reached out and opened the limousine's rear door. He climbed inside.

"Take the truck, Marty," Phil ordered, and Marty started trotting toward it. Then something happened.

Charlie Hello, his mind fogged with drink or drugs, saw Marty running toward him and must have thought he was being attacked. He swung the shotgun around and fired in Marty's general direction. Marty hit the ground, skidding in the dust, and pulled a snub-nosed revolver from under his coat. He fired three fast shots from the ground as another booming roar came from Charlie's shotgun.

Then Charlie Hello toppled backward against the fender of the truck and went down. "Stop shooting, for God's sake!" Phil yelled, running forward with his own gun drawn. Kitty and I were still on the far side of Tony Barrel's limousine, between it and the farmhouse. Scoop Turner was coming out from the driver's seat, pulling a gun of his own. For an instant I feared he'd open fire on Phil and Marty from behind, but he hesitated, unsure of what to do. He was staring down at the left hand front tire of his car, and I could see from my side that it was flat. One of Charlie's shotgun blasts had hit it.

"Doc, I think he's dead," Phil yelled at me. "Come take a look."

"Stay here," I cautioned Kitty and started forward.

Marty was still standing with his gun out, staring at the body on the ground. "He shot first," he rasped. "He tried to kill me."

"All he hit was my tire," Scoop Turner said. "Let's everybody put the guns away."

I confirmed that Marty's bullets had killed Charlie Hello and then straightened up. I was staring at the limousine, but Tony Barrel hadn't yet emerged. Remembering the shotgun he had in the back seat, I decided we should speak to him before he did something foolish over the death of his truck driver.

"Where you goin'?" Phil asked me.

"Just to see Tony," I answered, and opened the rear door of the car.

The back seat of the limousine was empty.

The front seat was empty.

While Charlie Hello and Marty were shooting it out, Tony Barrel had disappeared.

"Where is he?" Kitty asked. "He didn't leave the car."

"He left it, all right," I said. "He's gone."

"He can't be gone!" Scoop Turner insisted. He pushed by me and looked for himself. Phil and Marty came up for a look too.

"He musta gone back in the house when the shooting started," Phil suggested.

"He didn't go in the house because I'd have seen him!" Kitty insisted. "So would the rest of you, shooting or no shooting! It's thirty feet to the house and Tony's not exactly the invisible man, you know."

"I'll settle this by taking a look inside," I said, and ran toward the house. I went in through the front door, fully expecting to see Tony Barrel cowering behind a chair. But the front room was empty.

I went into the ground-floor bedroom, wondering if Larry Spears would be among the missing too. But he was sitting up in bed, pointing his little .22 at the door. He looked pale and frightened. "What was that shooting?" he asked. "Cops?"

"No such luck. Marty killed their truck driver, Charlie Hello."

"Small loss."

"But this is a big loss. During the shooting Tony Barrel vanished from his car."

"What do you mean, vanished?"

"Just that. We saw him get into the car and now he's gone."

Larry Spears lowered his gun. "Well, go find him. I can't come out and let them know my stomach wound was a fake. One of them is still trying to get me."

"I'll be back," I promised.

Outside, Kitty was pawing at the car's upholstery, looking for any sort of hidden compartment large enough to hide a man. But the limousine seemed solid enough. I had Scoop unlock the trunk but there was nothing in it except a spare tire and some tools.

"Where is he?" Phil asked me.

"I wish I knew. He's not inside the house and Larry doesn't know a thing."

We walked around the house and then around the truck, looking for a clue, but there was none. We searched Larry's car and then began looking through the empty barrels on the truck. There was no way he could have gotten inside them without someone seeing him, but we looked anyway.

Twenty minutes later we were ready to admit defeat. Tony Barrel was gone.

"I know the fast way to find out where he is," Phil said, drawing the gun from his shoulder holster. He turned and pointed it at Scoop. "We all saw him get in the car, Scoop. You gotta know what happened."

"Nothing happened!" the ex-reporter insisted.

"Did he say anything to you?" I asked.

"He just told me to pick up Charlie and get moving. But then the shooting started and my tire got hit."

"Charlie was going back in the limousine?"

"Sure, up front with me. Spears bought the truck and everything."

"For twelve thousand dollars cash," I reminded them all. "Tony Barrel had that money in his pocket, and it might have been enough of a motive for any one of you."

"You're saying one of us killed him?" Kitty asked. "But how?"

"I don't know," I admitted.

"To hell with Tony," Phil decided. "Whether he's dead or alive, Charlie Hello is dead. And we've got to make tracks out of here before someone comes along. That truckload of barrels is still worth money."

The others agreed, but Scoop Turner asked, "What about the body?"

"We'll take it with us," Phil decided. "Inside one of the barrels. It'll be a lot easier to dump along the way, off a bridge somewhere."

Turner pointed at me. "And what about him?"

"I guess he knows a little too much," Phil said bluntly.

"Wait a minute!" Kitty spoke sharply, stepping in front of Phil before he could draw his weapon, if that was his intention. "Larry promised he wouldn't be harmed!"

"For all we know Larry might be dying. And where will that leave us?"

"The doc doesn't know anything. He doesn't even know our last names."

"He knows mine," Scoop Turner said. "What am I supposed to do? Charlie is dead and the boss has disappeared."

"What are you supposed to do?" Phil said. "Tell us what you did with him, that's what!"

I held up my hands to quiet them. "You won't get anywhere fighting among yourselves. The way things stand now, the police would probably arrest the whole bunch of you. They've got Charlie's body and they might come up with Tony's too if they look hard enough."

"Is he dead?" Kitty asked.

"I expect he is. Now do you all want to go to prison for it or do you want me to name the murderer?"

"It's one of us?"

"It's the same person who shot Larry Spears at that front door this morning. In fact, you might say that Larry's shooting was part of the same crime."

"Do you know where Tony's body is?"

"Yes."

"All right," Phil agreed. "You produce Tony's body and tell us who killed him—and how—and we'll let you go. How's that for a deal, Doc?"

I nodded. "Let's go into Larry's room. He's well enough to hear this too."

They all followed me inside, leaving Charlie Hello's body sprawled where it had fallen. There hadn't been another car along the road all afternoon, but I knew that Sheriff Lens sometimes drove up this way late in the day. There was always a chance someone might have heard the shooting and called in a report of illegal hunting.

Larry Spears brought his gun out as we entered. "What is this? What do you all want?"

"We made a bargain," I explained. "I go free if I can produce Tony Barrel's body. And his murderer."

"How can you be sitting up with that terrible wound?" Kitty asked him. "When I was in before you were half dead."

"There's a lot of things that need explaining," Phil agreed. I could see his fingers twitching to draw his gun. "But if Tony Barrel is dead this is the only person who could have killed him." He pointed at Scoop Turner, who was beginning to look frightened.

Larry Spears shifted his gun in Turner's direction. "And he could have driven up here this morning and taken that shot at me!"

I saw his finger whitening on the trigger and knew I had to move fast. I threw myself on the bed, knocking his arm aside just as the gun went off. The bullet hit the ceiling and I wrested the gun free before he could fire again. "Phil!" Spears shouted from beneath me. "Kill him! Kill them both!"

"Oh, no!" I said. "Phil won't kill me or Scoop, because he wants to hear where the body is."

"Where is it?" Kitty demanded.

I kept a firm grip on Larry Spears. "Under this bed, and Spears is the one who put it there!"

As I spoke, Scoop Turner was edging toward the door. But Marty moved in silently to block his passage. "That's right," I said. "Hang onto him. We'll be needing him."

"Then Scoop is involved too?" Kitty asked.

I nodded, pulling up the rumpled bedclothes to reveal Tony Barrel's body where I said it would be. "Larry killed him, but he couldn't have worked it without Scoop's help. You said Scoop was always after the bucks, and Larry must have bought him out some time back. Tony Barrel was murdered in this room." I looked more closely at the newly revealed body. "Strangled with a thin wire. He never left the house. It was Scoop, wearing a false beard and stomach padding, who walked to the car and got in. He and Tony were wearing a similar suit and hat, and I'd noticed earlier how loose-fitting his clothes were."

"I don't understand this at all," Kitty protested. "You said the same person killed Tony that shot Larry this morning."

"Exactly! Larry shot himself. I've known since I first arrived that there was no stomach wound, but I didn't guess until a short time ago that the arm wound was self-inflicted. There never was any gunman in the bushes."

"But why?" Kitty asked. "What was his motive in shooting himself, killing Tony, and arranging this vanishing-man act?"

"He shot himself as a means of luring Tony to the bedroom where Tony could be killed. Otherwise they would most likely have met outside or in the company of the rest of you. And he killed Tony, quite simply, because he didn't have the twelve thousand dollars to pay for the shipment of barrels, which he desperately needed. As for the vanishing man, it was never planned that way."

"What do you mean, never planned that way?" Phil wanted to know.

"Maybe I'd better describe the crime from the beginning," I suggested, "so you can see what was planned and where it went wrong. Larry needed those barrels to manufacture artificial whiskey, which could be sold at a big profit. He arranged to buy them from Tony, as we know, for twelve thousand dollars. But somewhere along the line he ran out of money—right, Larry? Kitty said you've been gambling heavily lately. There's no way you short-change a man like Tony Barrel without starting a gang war, so you knew you had to kill him—in such a manner that you'd be completely free from suspicion.

"You arranged to bribe Scoop at some previous time, probably for a thousand bucks or whatever you could scrape together. This morning you walked outside the door and shot yourself in the fleshy part of the arm with that .22. There was plenty of blood and you pretended you'd been hit in the stomach as well. It was easy to fire the pistol through a cloth of some sort so there'd be no powder burns around the wound. And you knew a .22 slug wouldn't do much damage."

"He told you his stomach wound was a fake?" Kitty asked.

"He had to. There was no way he could keep you from summoning a doctor. The superficial arm wound alone wouldn't keep him in bed, and being in bed was essential to his plan. He had to lure Tony Barrel into this room, alone, to strangle him. Meanwhile he told me he suspected one of you three of tipping off the New York mob to his whereabouts, but that was just a red herring for my benefit. So Tony came in here alone to get his payment, and maybe Larry even asked him to bend over the bed to hear his whispered voice. He strangled Tony with this wire—"

"Strangled a strong man like Tony when he had a bullet wound in one arm?" Kitty asked.

"The wound is in his left arm, and he still had all the strength of his right arm. And with the element of surprise this wire noose wouldn't need that much strength."

"Where did Scoop Turner come in?"

"Through the window, to give you a literal answer. Remember after he showed us the limousine he strolled around the side of the house. He came in through the window, put on a false beard and the padded vest that Larry wore to conceal his weight loss, maybe helped Larry slide the body under the bed, and then went out the door to the car. He only had to mumble a few words, you'll remember. Once in the back of the car he shed the beard and padding, probably stuffing them in the glove compartment. When we searched for Tony, no one bothered to look in so small a place.

"Scoop climbed over the front seat and started to drive away. He was going to pick up Charlie Hello and be gone from the scene. Later you people would leave and maybe Larry would arrange to burn down this house before Tony's body could be found. But Charlie Hello spoiled the plan. He started shooting, blew out the tire on Scoop's car, and we quickly discovered that Tony Barrel had disappeared. Otherwise, instead of an impossible disappearance here we'd have had Tony disappearing fifty or a hundred miles away. Maybe the car would have gone off a bridge into the water. In any event Larry would be in the clear. Charlie was so doped up he might not have even noticed his boss wasn't in the back seat. If he did notice, Scoop probably could have convinced him he dropped Tony off somewhere."

"How'd you know all this?" Phil asked.

"When Tony climbed back into his car, I noticed that he didn't have the barrel-shaped diamond ring on his right hand. And though we all saw Tony get in, I hadn't seen Scoop come back to the car. With that smoked glass we couldn't tell if he was in there or not—but if he had been in there wouldn't he have gotten out and opened the door for his boss, as he did when they arrived? If the bearded man wasn't Tony it had to be Scoop, and if Tony hadn't left the bedroom his body must be still here. Under the bed was the logical place, and

Larry was the logical killer. Everything else, including the motive, sort of flowed from that."

Phil looked down at the man on the bed. "You got anything to say, Larry?"

"So I killed him! He's not the first person I killed. Let's just get out of here like I planned."

"What about the doc?"

"Kill him."

"And Scoop?"

"Him too."

"You tried that a few minutes ago," I pointed out. "Tried to kill the only witness to your crime. And next you'll have to kill Kitty and Phil and Marty, or the word will leak out and the mob will really be after you."

Suddenly Marty stepped to the window and rasped, "Car coming."

"That'll be the police," I said confidently, hoping I was right. "Someone must have heard the shooting and reported it."

Then Scoop broke free and lunged for the door. He was already outside when I heard Sheriff Lens bellow. I relaxed and smiled. Everything was all right . . .

"Kitty and Phil and Marty had no desire to share the blame for Tony Barrel's killing," Dr. Sam Hawthorne concluded, "so they threw down their weapons and surrendered without a fight. The sheriff caught Scoop Turner outside and Scoop quickly confessed to his part in the killing. A few months later Fat Larry Spears, then thinner than ever, was tried and convicted of first-degree murder."

"After that the bootleggers seemed to steer clear of Northmont, but we had other troubles. In the summer of 1930 a flying circus of barnstorming pilots came to town, one of our local girls fell in love, and we had ourselves a locked room in the sky! But that's for next time. Another small—ah—libation before you go?"

THE PROBLEM OF
THE TIN GOOSE

"What was I goin' to tell you about this time?" old Dr. Sam Hawthorne asked as he poured two brimming glasses of sherry and then seated himself in the worn leather armchair. "Oh, I know—it was the flying circus that visited Northmont in the summer of 1930. That was a wild time, I'll tell you, with murder committed in what could be called a flying locked room. It all began, I suppose, with a romance that blossomed quickly between a barnstorming pilot and a local girl . . ."

It was a hot, cloudless July afternoon (Dr. Sam continued) when I strolled over to the offices of the *Northmont Bee* to place a classified ad in their week-end edition. I was trying to sell my tan Packard runabout that I'd owned for a little over two years. It was a fine car but it had never replaced my beloved Pierce-Arrow that was destroyed by fire in a botched attempt to kill me back in February of '28. Now I'd been lucky enough to purchase a beautiful 1929 Stutz Torpedo, almost like new, from a doctor in Shinn Corners who'd lost a bundle in the stock-market crash. The Packard would have to go, so I decided to run an ad offering it for sale.

"That's sixty cents," Bonnie Pratt told me as she finished counting the words. "This sounds like a good deal. I should come out and take a look at it myself."

"Why don't you?" I urged her. "It's over at my office now."

"Oh, I've seen you driving it," Bonnie said. She was a pert young redhead who'd been working at the *Bee* since she'd dropped out of college when her father died about a year before. The Pratts were good people, and though I didn't know Bonnie well she was the sort of pretty girl who got noticed in a town as small as Northmont. "But maybe I will come over later," she added.

Because I enjoyed chatting with her I lingered a while after I'd paid my sixty cents. "What's the latest news, Bonnie? Give me a scoop."

187

She returned my grin and said, "You have to buy the paper, Dr. Sam. You don't give out free diagnoses, do you?"

"No," I admitted, "but can't I have a peek at the headline?"

"Oh, all right." She relented and held up the afternoon edition. "It's all about the flying circus that's coming to town on the weekend."

"We don't have an airport," I protested. "Where are they going to land?"

"At Art Zealand's Flying School. Look at these pictures. There's a Ford Trimotor, the one they call the Tin Goose because of its all-metal body. They'll actually be taking passengers up in that one, for a twenty-minute ride across the county and back. And this is their stunt biplane. They'll take you up in that too if you're brave enough—five dollars for five minutes. They've got the Ford Trimotor and two of these biplanes in the circus. It's quite a show."

"Those barnstormers have been popular for years," I said. "I wonder why they never came here before."

"Because Art Zealand didn't have his flying school till now," she answered reasonably. "They had no landing field. But aviation's the coming thing. People are flying across the country. I have an aunt who traveled from Los Angeles to New York last year in forty-eight hours! They flew by day and transferred to trains at night because it's too dangerous to fly after dark. She was on the maiden flight and Charles Lindbergh himself piloted the plane."

"You're really excited about this, aren't you?"

"I sure am," she conceded. "They're going to let me interview Ross Winslow for the *Bee*. He's the head of it. Look how handsome he is."

The head of Winslow's Flying Circus was an attractive fellow with curly black hair and a pencil-thin mustache. Looking at his picture on the front page of the paper I was struck by the notion that men like Ross Winslow were the forerunners of a whole new world. They were the ones that girls like Bonnie Pratt hankered after, not dull country doctors like myself.

"I'd like to meet him," I said. "The only experience I've had with fliers was back in 'twenty-seven when they shot part of a moving picture here."

She nodded, remembering. "I'd just gone off to college. Look, if you're interested you can come with me Friday to meet him. They're flying in around noon."

The idea intrigued me. "Let's see how things go. If Mrs. Haskel doesn't have her baby I should be able to get away for a few hours."

So that was how I happened to accompany Bonnie Pratt out to the Zealand Flying School on Friday noon to watch the big Ford Trimotor and the two smaller planes settle down for perfect landings on the grassy field. Art Zealand was there to greet them himself, of course, looking like his idea of a World War flying ace with a white silk scarf wrapped around his neck. Art was in his mid-thirties, about my age, and like me he was unmarried. He'd moved to Northmont a year or so earlier to start his flying school and there were unconfirmed rumors of an abandoned wife and children somewhere down south. He was pleasant enough when the need arose but kept to himself much of the time.

"Good to see you again, Sam," he greeted me as we drove up in my new Stutz Torpedo. "The doctoring business must be pretty good these days," he added, patting the car's shiny black fender. The body itself was tan, the contrasting red upholstery on its twin seats matching the red wheels. It was a flashy car for a country doctor, but it was my one extravagance.

"I figure I need something good for these bumpy country roads," I replied.

"I'll bet you could buy an airplane cheaper than that car."

We went off across the field to welcome the barnstormers. Ross Winslow was easy to spot climbing down from the lead plane, waving and walking forward to shake hands. Bonnie Pratt was highly excited as she introduced herself and me. "Hope we don't need your services, Doc," Winslow joked, shaking my hand with an iron grip. "But then I don't guess we will. If I fall off a wing up there, you won't be able to do much for me."

Art Zealand had met Winslow before and he pointed out the area where the three planes should be parked. There was some discussion about the crowds that might be expected and a low-keyed conversation about Winslow's share of the gate. Apparently Zealand guaranteed him a flat sum of a few hundred dollars plus anything he earned from the plane rides.

I turned my attention to the other members of Winslow's Flying Circus, who seemed to be three in number. Two were men a bit older than I—a blond fellow with a scar on his cheek, whose name was Max Renker, and a short jolly fellow named Tommy Verdun. But my real interest centered on the fourth member of the team, a longhaired blonde named Mavis Wing who gave me a slow smile like nothing I'd ever seen in Northmont.

"I can't imagine women barnstorming and walking on wings," I said when I'd found my tongue.

"Oh, we do it, Dr. Hawthorne." The slow smile was back. "Lillian Boyer has her own plane with her name in big letters on the side. That's what I'm aiming for. My name's really Wingarten, but that wouldn't look good on the side of a plane, would it?"

"You could just use your picture. That would be enough," I replied gallantly.

"Oh, come now, Dr. Hawthorne—you're something of a flirt, aren't you?"

Before I could pursue the subject, Winslow gave them instructions for parking the planes and Bonnie and I went off with him for the interview. Art Zealand had provided a table and chairs in the hangar, where Bonnie took rapid notes as Winslow spoke.

"Max and Tommy both flew in the war," he explained, "So they're a leg up on me. I took pilot training but it was all over before I ever got to France. The three of us got together nearly ten years ago and decided to try barnstorming. You've probably read about Sir Alan Cobham, the famous European barnstormer. His circus has performed all over the Continent and we hope to do the same thing on this side of the Atlantic. There's a lot of competition, of course, and we try to outdo each other dreaming up wild stunts."

"What about your planes?" Bonnie asked without looking up from her notes.

"In this country we all use Jennies, those little biplanes with the double set of wings. They're JN-4D trainers the Army built near the end of the war. By the time they were finished the war was over and the government started selling thousands of 'em for as little as three hundred dollars each. A lot of us who flew in the war, or who trained to fly like me, went out and bought ourselves a plane. Max and Tommy and I started with three Jennies but last year we traded one in for that Ford Trimotor transport. We found out that after watching our stunts the crowd was really ready to fly. We'd have thirty or forty people lined up for a five-minute ride in a Jennie, so we decided that if we could take up ten at a time, for a slightly longer flight they'd still pay five dollars and we'd make a lot more money."

"Tell me about your stunts," Bonnie urged. "That's what'll get the people out."

"Well, we start out by buzzing the town with the two Jennies while Max and I walk out on the wings. Then Mavis does her wild act, actually hanging by one arm from a wing while I fly the plane. That's been known to make people faint. Tommy Verdun is our clown and he's liable to do anything. Sometimes he dresses up like a woman and waits in line for a ride in one of the Jennies. The pilot gets out and Tommy gets in and pretends the plane is taking off with him at the controls, out of control. It's guaranteed to get screams out of the spectators. Then I wind things up by transferring from one plane to the other, either using a rope ladder or walking across, wingtip to wingtip."

"Do you make good money at this?"

Ross Winslow snorted. "Hell, no. We do it because we love it. Somebody said the most dangerous thing about barnstorming is the risk of starving to death, and he's right. We were going to give it up this year, but they say the country's heading into a depression and where would we find jobs? We figure if we can keep at this for another year or two, till the airlines really get established, they'll take us on as commercial pilots. Then maybe we'll start making real money."

"What about Mavis Wing?"

"She's great. Wait till you see her up there. Mavis joined us last summer and business shot up right away. There's nothing like seeing a girl hanging from that plane to get the crowds cheering and biting their nails. I make her keep her hair long so they know she's a woman from a distance, and she wears knickers so they see a little bit of leg."

"It sounds like a great show," Bonnie said. "I'll be here bright and early tomorrow."

As we were preparing to leave Winslow asked her, "What's there to do in this town at night? Got any good bars?"

"With Prohibition?" she asked in mock horror.

"Come on—I'll bet you know the places to go."

"There's a lunch counter where you can get a shot of whiskey in a coffee cup. Will that do?"

"For starters. Will you go with me?"

She hesitated only a second. "Well—sure, I guess so."

"Fine. Can I pick you up at your office?"

"In your plane?"

He chuckled. "Art said I could use his car while we're in town."

So it was decided. I drove her back to the *Bee* office in my Stutz, amazed that Ross Winslow had gotten a date with her so easily and wondering why I'd never thought to ask her for one myself.

The *Northmont Bee* was published on Monday, Wednesday, and Friday afternoons, with the Friday edition being designated for the weekend. Of course, back in those days most people worked at least a half day on Saturdays, but the Friday edition still had the most readers of the week, which is why I'd run the ad for my car in it. Friday evening brought several interested callers, and one of them—the son of the town banker—came by on Saturday morning to close the deal.

With the car sold I felt I could relax for the weekend. Mrs. Haskel's baby still hadn't made it into the world and showed no signs of doing so before Monday, so I decided to close the office early and take my nurse April out to the flying circus.

"You mean to say I'll get to ride in your new car?" she asked. I think that was a bigger treat for her than the prospect of seeing the barnstormers.

"It's the only car I've got now," I told her. "I sold the old one this morning."

"If I'd had the money I'd have bought it myself. You take good care of your cars, Dr. Sam."

She was thrilled by the ride in the Stutz, holding down her hair as the wind whipped through it on the way to the flying school. When we arrived a little before noon, I saw that the adjoining field was already crowded with parked wagons and automobiles. Their noise made the horses nervous, but as the planes flew back and forth in their opening salute the crowd roared its approval.

"Everyone in town must be here," April said.

Sheriff Lens and his new wife Vera were there, and I was pleased to see them. Married life had made the sheriff almost a stranger, though I was glad to see he was still his old self. "Doc, Vera was just sayin' the other day we gotta have you over for dinner some night. We been back from the honeymoon six months and the only time we seen you was at that church social in the spring."

Vera took up the urging. "How about next week, Sam? What evening is best for you?"

I knew Vera was still working at the post office and I was reluctant to force dinner preparation on her at the end of a working day. "Maybe Sunday would be good. A week from tomorrow?"

"Perfect," she agreed. "Do I get a ride in your new car?"

"Of course."

April tugged at my sleeve. "Look, Sam!"

The two Jennies had landed but now one had taken off again, and I saw a figure with long blonde hair, a white blouse, and knickers edging out on the wing. It was Mavis, beginning her act. I left April with the sheriff and Vera and walked around the fringes of the crowd for a better view. I'd reached the hangar area, nodding now and then to familiar faces in the crowd, when I encountered Bonnie Pratt standing beside Ross Winslow. He was wearing a short leather flying jacket and had his arm lightly around her waist. "Hello, Bonnie," I said.

"Hello, Sam." She edged free of his arm.

"That was a nice opening," I told Winslow. "I thought you'd be up there flying for Mavis."

"Max is flying her today. After Mavis does her stunts I'll take some passengers up in the Tin Goose."

Zealand came into the hanger, looking troubled. "Can I see you alone, Ross?"

They walked back to the office together and I said to Bonnie, "So you showed him the town last night. Did he enjoy it?"

"I think I'm in love with him, Sam. He's so handsome and dashing. I feel like he's a war hero. The local boys just don't compare to him."

"He's only here for the weekend, Bonnie. Don't get your hopes too high."

"He talks about settling down, maybe here in Northmont. He says he may have had enough of flying."

I wondered how many girls in how many towns had heard that same line over a weekend. But I said simply, "I hope it works out for you, Bonnie."

Zealand and Winslow returned, and I heard the school owner mutter, "I didn't know what I was getting into when I booked your crew." Winslow didn't reply but flashed his familiar smile when he saw Bonnie.

"Will you be going up again?" she asked him.

He nodded, glancing at the sky. Mavis was hanging from the plane by one arm as the crowd screamed its delight and apprehension. "She'll be finishing soon. Come on, I'll show you the inside of the Trimotor." The invitation seemed to include me so I tagged along with Bonnie.

It was a big plane by any standards I knew then. The body was covered with corrugated metal and the high wings supported two of the three engines, the third being at the front of the plane. Inside were two rows of wicker-backed chairs separated by an aisle. I sat down in one of the chairs. It felt about like a lawn chair. "Not too comfortable," I commented to Winslow.

"The wicker saves weight, but the airlines are deciding the same thing. Comfort is important. We were able to get this plane fairly cheap because they're phasing it out in favor of a new Douglas aircraft. These things are noisy, and if you fly too high they're cold."

"When will the new planes be flying?"

"Not for a few years, unfortunately, but when they are they'll probably put Ford out of the flying business completely. Ford owns the Detroit airport, you know, but Henry Ford won't allow it to be open on Sundays." He patted the side of the metal craft affectionately. "Still, this is what we've got today and it gets you where you're going most of the time. Would you like to go up for a spin?"

I wanted to, very much, but I felt guilty going without April. "I should take my nurse along," I explained. "We'll go later."

"How about you two?" he asked Bonnie and Zealand.

"Sure," Art Zealand answered. "Let's go up. I want to see what the customers get for their five dollars."

I left the plane as Winslow went up a few steps into the cockpit and closed the door behind him. He called out the window to a ground crewman to move the blocks from under the wheels and then started all three engines. I watched him slide the window closed and taxi out to the grassy runway. Then he gunned the motors and the plane shot ahead, lifting its wheels from the ground with ease.

I glanced up and saw the Jennie still circling the crowd. Mavis had lifted herself onto the wing again, and was climbing back into the front cockpit. The second Jennie was still on the ground and I wondered what had become of the other team member, Tommy Verdun.

I strolled back to where April still stood with Sheriff Lens and Vera. "Were you on that plane?" April asked. "I thought I saw you."

"I just took a look. Winslow is taking Art Zealand up, and Bonnie Pratt from the *Bee*. When he lands they'll start taking paying passengers."

"I'd like to go up," April said.

"I figured you would."

The spectators were pointing toward the sky again and I saw that the Jennie piloted by Max Renker had moved into position quite close to the larger Ford Trimotor. They were flying almost wingtip to wingtip, and Mavis waved to the crowd as she started walking out on the Jennie's upper wing again.

"What in hell is that gal goin' to do next?" Sheriff Lens wondered.

"I think she'll try to walk over to the other plane's wing," I said, remembering what Winslow had told us of their stunts.

And that she did, stepping over as easily as she might cross the street. The crowd cheered as the planes flew overhead, so low I could see Bonnie's face at one of the Trimotor's windows, straining for a view of the wing above her head. "The passengers are missing the performance," Vera remarked.

Then Mavis hurried back, hopping onto the wing of the Jennie, and the two aircraft drifted slowly apart. I watched her climb into the open cockpit of the Jennie as it circled one more time and came in for a landing at the far end of the field. The Trimotor landed right behind it, taxiing to a stop near us.

We waited for the door of the passenger compartment to open, but nothing happened. I couldn't see Winslow through the cockpit windows, although there was movement inside the passenger compartment. Finally, after another few moments, the passenger door was shoved open and Bonnie's head appeared. "Dr. Sam!" she shouted.

I trotted across the trampled-down grass of the field, already sensing that something was wrong. "What is it, Bonnie?"

"Ross is still in the cockpit with the door locked. We've been calling him and he doesn't answer. I think something's wrong!"

I climbed through the door and hurried up the aisle between the wicker seats. Art Zealand was pounding on the cockpit door, shouting, "Winslow! What's wrong? Open up!"

"Should we put a ladder up to the cockpit window?" Bonnie asked.

I tried the door myself. "If it's something like a heart attack every second counts. This feels like a flimsy lock." I glanced at Zealand for permission. "Should I force it?"

"Go ahead."

I hit the cockpit door with my shoulder and the door started to give. Once more and it sprang open.

Ross Winslow was visible at once, toppled from the pilot's seat onto the unused copilot's seat next to it. I saw the blood and heard Bonnie's high-pitched voice from the aisle. "What?—What is it?"

I took a deep breath and told Zealand, "Get her out of here, off the plane. Right now." Then I stepped forward and bent over the pilot's seat examining the body. There was no doubt that he was dead.

"What is it, Doctor?"

I turned as Mavis Wing stepped into the cockpit, still wearing her stunt clothes. "Ross Winslow is dead," I said.

"*What?*"

"He's been stabbed to death. Go get Sheriff Lens for me, will you? He's a stocky man over at the edge of the crowd."

Sheriff Lens merely shook his head and stared at me. "What you're sayin' is downright impossible, Doc. Winslow was stabbed to death while he was alone inside this locked cockpit and you're trying to tell me it wasn't suicide?"

"It wasn't suicide," I repeated. "Look at where the knife went in—between the ribs on his left side, toward the back. No suicide would stab himself there. It's an almost impossible angle, certainly unnecessary angle. Besides, when would he have done it? He landed the plane, remember, and taxied up to the crowd. Are we to believe he suddenly decided to kill himself then, by stabbing himself in the back at a nearly impossible angle?"

The sheriff stroked his chin, thinking about it. "Well, that leaves only one other explanation. Zealand and Bonnie Pratt got him to open the door and they killed him together."

"Zealand and Bonnie barely know each other. Why would they conspire to kill Winslow? Besides, you're forgetting the cabin door was locked from Winslow's side. I had to break it in with my shoulder."

"Yeah," he answered glumly.

"We'd better talk to them," I decided. "Whatever happened in that cockpit, they must have heard something."

They were both waiting in the hangar. I spoke with Bonnie while Sheriff Lens questioned Zealand separately. "I didn't hear a thing from the cockpit," she assured me. "You can barely hear yourself *think* in that plane, Sam! It's the noisiest contraption imaginable! Art Zealand told me that on commercial runs they give the passengers cotton to plug their ears."

"The landing seemed smooth from where we stood."

"It was smooth. There was nothing at all unusual until the plane came to a stop and Ross just didn't come out the door." Her composure cracked on the last word and she started to sob.

"Bonnie," I said softly, "I have to ask you this. How serious was it between you and Winslow? You only met him yesterday."

She turned her tear-streaked face to me. "I'd never known anyone like him, Sam. I never believed in love at first sight, but I guess that's what happened to me."

"Did it happen to him too?"

"He said it did. We—we spent the night together."

"I see."

"He told me he wanted to settle down in a town like this, give up barnstorming and raise a family."

"Maybe he told that to lots of girls, Bonnie."

"I don't think so, Sam. I believed him." She wiped her eyes.

"But if you came out here this morning to watch the circus and then discovered he'd lied to you, it might have made you want to kill him."

"Do you think that?"

"I don't know what to think, Bonnie."

She collected herself and dried her eyes. "Well, suspect or not, I still work for a newspaper. I guess I'd better go write this up for Monday's edition."

I left her in the hangar and went in search of the sheriff. When I found him he told me Zealand's story agreed with Bonnie's. The noise of the plane had kept them from hearing anything unusual from the cockpit. "What now?" Sheriff Lens asked, gazing uncomfortably at the cluster of townspeople still waiting at the edge of the field. They'd been told there was an accident and the show had been cancelled, but most of them refused to budge even after the ambulance from Pilgrim Memorial Hospital came and removed the body.

I thought the best thing I could do then was stop Mavis Wing before she took off with her two companions. I told Sheriff Lens what I had in mind and he trailed along. Mavis and the others were in Zealand's office, staying clear of the crowd. I took her aside and asked, "What was your relationship with Ross Winslow?"

She stared hard at me. "I don't know that I need to answer that. You're not the police, are you?"

"No, but I am," Sheriff Lens told her. "Answer the question."

"Maybe I should clarify it," I continued. "Winslow spent the night with a local girl. Might that have made you jealous enough to kill him?"

"Certainly not. And you're forgetting I was up in the sky at the time."

"On the wing of his plane," I reminded her. "He could have slid open the cockpit window to call to you and been killed by a knife you threw, then managed to slide the window closed before he died." I saw the sheriff make a face as I spoke. Even he could see the impossibility of that theory.

"You can't see into the cockpit from the top of the wing," Mavis told us. "Try it if you don't believe me. Besides, I was on the wing for only a few seconds, and visible from the ground. No one saw me throw anything. Throw anything! I was too worried about keeping my balance."

"We'll try it," I assured her, but I knew I was on the wrong track. I turned to Sheriff Lens. "Have you identified the knife?"

He nodded. "Zealand says it was a utility knife from the hangar. Anyone could have picked it up."

"Did you see anyone with a knife?" I asked Mavis Wing.

"No."

"Did you see anything unusual while you were on the wing of the plane?"

"No."

"All right," I said with a sigh. "The sheriff may want to question you again later."

"What about the other two?" Lens asked as we left the office. "Renker and Verdun?"

"Renker was flying Mavis's plane up there, right next to the Trimotor. Verdun was somewhere on the ground. Maybe Renker threw the knife from his cockpit."

"Oh, come on now, Doc—you know that couldn't 'a happened. First of all, that knife's not balanced for throwin', especially not up in the sky with the wind blowin'. And the wound was in the side, around toward the back, and slantin' upward. No knife thrown through the plane's window could have hit him there."

"Of course not," I agreed readily. "I realized that as soon as I said it to Mavis. And that lets Renker off for the same reason. But let's talk to him anyway."

Max Renker was in his mid-thirties, and his blond hair and the scar on his right cheek reminded me of German war aces with university dueling scars. He answered our questions directly, but added little to our knowledge.

"Did you actually see Winslow in the cockpit of the Trimotor?" I asked.

"Sure, I saw him. I waved to him, even. He was alive and well then—but of course he'd have to be, to fly the plane."

"I want to go up on the wing, like Mavis did," I said suddenly.

His eyes widened. "You mean up in the sky?"

"No! On the ground. Can you get me a ladder and help me up there?"

"Sure."

Renker went first and then helped me up onto the wing, some ten feet off the ground. Although the front of the cockpit could certainly be seen, Mavis was right—the angle of the glass prevented a view of the pilot's seat. "That's what I wanted to know," I said. "Let's go back down."

"Wing-walking on the Trimotor is more dangerous than on the Jennies," Renker explained as he helped me down the ladder. "The smaller planes have cables on top we can cling to or brace our legs against. You can't see them from below but they're a big help."

I reached the ground and walked around to the front of the plane. "What's this?" I asked, pointing to a small metal door beneath the cockpit windows on the right side.

"Compartment for luggage and mail sacks. We use it for tools."

"Is there any opening from here to the cockpit?"

"No. Take a look and see for yourself."

I went back inside the plane, walking up the slanting aisle between the rows of wicker seats, then up the few steps to the cockpit door I'd battered open. I checked the windows and noticed each had a little inside latch that was firmly in place. "We modified the cockpit area to our own needs," Renker explained over my shoulder. "The door is placed a bit differently than in commercial planes, and we added those latches so kids wouldn't be climbing through the cockpit windows when the plane's parked overnight at some hick airfield."

"So the door and the windows were latched on the inside," I mused. "And no knife could have been thrown from outside even if a window was open." I turned to Renker in the cramped cockpit. "What about it? You must have some idea how he was killed."

He leaned against the wall next to the door. "Sure. Art Zeland and the girl stabbed him. Ross staggered back into the cockpit, latched the door to keep them out, and died. I hear people can do things like that, even with a fatal knife wound. Isn't that so, Doc?"

"Yes," I agreed. "But it's hard to believe they're both lying. Besides, I don't see any blood by the door, only right by the seat here, as if he was stabbed sitting down."

"Then what are you left with? Suicide?"

"I don't know," I admitted. "Suicide isn't very likely either."

"Well, I sure had no reason to kill him. Ross was the star of the show, he and Mavis. Tommy and I are nothing without them."

"I'd better talk to Tommy," I decided. "He was on the ground—maybe he saw something the rest of us missed."

Tommy Verdun was a small man with short dark hair. He sat in the office wearing a long white duster pulled around him as if to ward off a chill. "I don't know anything about it," he grumbled. "I sure didn't kill him."

"Where were you at the time it happened?" Sheriff Lens asked.

"I don't know when it happened," he answered evasively. "You think he was killed in the air or on the ground?"

"He had to be alive to land the plane," I pointed out.

"Yeah. Well, I was over in back of the hangar, making sure the kids stayed away from my plane."

"Anybody see you?"

"I suppose not," he admitted. "But then nobody seen me kill Ross either."

"Did you kill him?" I asked.

"I told you I didn't. You don't listen good."

"Aren't you supposed to be the clown of this outfit? You're not very friendly for a clown."

"Got nothing to be friendly about, with the boss dead."

I went back outside with Sheriff Lens. "I don't like that fellow," I told him.

"Neither do I, Doc, but that don't prove he killed anyone. We still don't know how it was done." He thought for a moment. "But I got an idea. Maybe there was some sort of mechanical gadget that stabbed him when he sat down in the pilot's seat."

"You're forgetting he took off, flew a dangerous stunt almost touching that Jennie's wingtip, and then landed again. He couldn't have done any of that with a knife in him."

"I guess not," the sheriff agreed glumly. "But what about this guy Verdun? If he was a clown wouldn't he be foolin' with the kids instead of tryin' to chase them away from his plane?"

"A good point," I admitted. "But if he's lying about where he was at the time of the murder—" I stopped, suddenly remembering an earlier conversation. "Let's find Zeland."

The owner of the flying school was in the hangar with Bonnie, seated opposite her and holding her hands. They broke apart as we entered. "Hello, Sam. Bonnie and I were just having a chat."

"So I see. Art, before the killing you asked to see Winslow alone and I heard you say you didn't know what you were getting into when you booked his crew. What was that about?"

Zealand shifted uneasily. "This morning I got a phone call from a friend in Ohio. He told me Winslow and his crew got drunk and smashed up a town out there. Winslow and his wife spent the night in jail."

"His wife?"

"Sure. He and Mavis were married."

Bonnie Pratt flushed deeply and turned away. "Did you know this?" I asked her.

"Art was just telling me. I didn't know it before."

"So there's our motive," I said. "The oldest motive there is."

"Maybe we got a motive, Doc," Sheriff Lens said, "but we still don't have the killer. And you've ruled out every way Winslow could have been stabbed in that locked cockpit."

"Every way but one, Sheriff." I glanced out the hangar door and spotted Tommy Verdun walking quickly across the field toward his plane. "Come on!" I shouted.

I ran out, calling to Verdun, but he broke into a run, perhaps sensing my suspicions. "Try to head him off," I called to the sheriff.

His long white duster billowed out behind him as he ran, and it seemed to slow him down. Finally I was close enough to grab the coattail and I yanked him to the ground. Then the sheriff and I were on top of him.

"So he's our killer," Sheriff Lens said, reaching for his handcuffs.

"No, Sheriff, you don't understand," I said. "Didn't it seem strange to you that Mavis's plane landed at the far end of the field after her act, when the crowd was up here?" I pulled upen Tommy's duster to show the white blouse and knickers underneath. The long blond wig was stuffed in his pocket. "Mavis wasn't on that plane. Tommy walked on that wing in her place while Mavis was in the cockpit of the Tin Goose killing her husband."

I told it all once, after the sheriff had arrested Mavis and taken down her statement. I stood in the center of the empty hangar, feeling a bit like a lecturer, and said, "It was really quite simple—so simple I nearly missed it. After I battered in that cockpit door and sent Bonnie and Art for the sheriff, I bent to examine the body and Mavis suddenly appeared behind me in the doorway. Because I thought she'd been on the wing of that other plane, I never asked what she was doing there, or how she'd made it from the far end of the field so fast. I accepted her presence without even wondering how she'd gotten on the plane ahead of Sheriff Lens."

"How did she get on board?" Bonnie asked. "I didn't see her outside."

"Of course not, because she was on the plane all the time, hidden in the cockpit. Winslow didn't shout for help when he found her there because he never expected she'd kill him. She'd probably had Verdun take her place on other occasions. Winslow told us Verdun sometimes dressed up like a woman for his act, and at that distance the crowd could only see the long blonde hair and the outfit Mavis always wore."

"But why did she hide in the cockpit?"

"To confront her husband with the fact that he'd spent the night with Bonnie. Isn't that right, Mavis?"

She shifted on her chair. "He was always doing it," she answered dully. "I told him I'd kill him if he didn't stop."

"So you hid in the cockpit and confronted him. You probably argued during the flight, with the noise of the plane covering your voices. You stepped behind his seat and brought the knife up into his side. Then you took over the copilot's controls and landed the plane yourself. When I broke the latch and pushed in the door, you simply stood flat against the wall behind it where I couldn't see you. When I bent over you stepped into the doorway as if you'd just come on board."

"I'll be damned," Sheriff Lens muttered.

"It wouldn't have worked if Zealand or Bonnie had remained on board, but you were improvising. It was your only chance."

"But Renker and Verdun musta known she did it," the sheriff said.

"They strongly suspected it, of course. But they'd already lost one star act and if they turned her in they'd have no jobs."

Verdun shook his head. "I didn't know what she was plannin' when I took her place. I'd done it before as a joke. I didn't know she'd kill him."

The crowd had all gone home by the time we finished, except for April and Vera. They were standing out by the Tin Goose, waiting for us to finish. I was sorry April hadn't gotten the plane ride I'd planned for her.

"And that was the story," Dr. Sam Hawthorne concluded. "It was the last flying circus that ever came to Northmont. The era of the barnstormer was just about over. It ended about as quickly as it began. It ended that day for Ross Winslow, one of the great ones."

"In the fall of that same year my folks visited me in Northmont to see how their son the doctor was getting along. It was during hunting season, and their visit was almost spoiled by an impossible killing during a deer hunt."

"But that's for next time."

THE PROBLEM OF
THE HUNTING LODGE

"I think I promised to tell you about the time my folks visited me here in Northmont," Dr. Sam Hawthorne said as he poured the brandy.

"It was the start of deer-hunting season in the autumn of 1930, and I was thirty-four years old. I'd been practicing in town for eight years and it had become more of a home to me than the Midwestern city where I grew up. That was a difficult thing to explain to my father . . ."

We'd always done a great deal of hunting in my youth (Dr. Sam continued), and I suppose it was only natural that my father, Harry Hawthorne, who had retired from the profitable dry-goods store that was his life for nearly forty years, would decide to visit his only son in New England and get in a bit of deer hunting at the same time. My mother came with him, of course, and I was happy to see them both. I hadn't made a trip back home since the previous Christmas, just after Sheriff Lens' marriage, and this was only the second time in my eight years here that they'd come to Northmont.

I met them at the train station and went to help Dad with their baggage.

"You'd think we were staying a month instead of five days," he grumbled. "You know what your mother's like when she travels." Though it was white now, he'd kept most of his hair, and he still had the vigor of a much younger man. My mother, by contrast, had always been on the frail side.

I led them to my new Stutz Torpedo and listened to my father's words of grudging approval. "The doctoring business must be pretty good these days for you to afford a car like this."

"I got a good deal on it," I explained, "from another doctor who needed the money."

"It's too bad about the car we gave you for a graduation present," my mother said, climbing in the front seat.

"It burnt up. I was lucky I wasn't in it," I said, shutting the passenger door and going around to the other side.

We stopped by the office first and I took them inside. "Mom, this is my nurse, April. As I've told you, she's a great help to me."

April had never met my parents and she fussed over them in her best manner. Sheriff Lens dropped by just as we were leaving and gave my father a vigorous handshake. "I'll tell you, Mr. Hawthorne, that son o' yours would make a fine sleuth. He's helped me out on more cases than I care to count."

"Oh?" My mother looked alarmed. "Do you have much crime here, Sheriff?"

"More than you'd think possible," he said with something like pride in his voice. "We needed the gumption of somebody like Doc here to deal with 'em. He's got a mind like that fella Einstein!"

"We'd better be going," I mumbled, embarrassed as always by the sheriff's praise.

"What're you goin' to do while you're here?" he asked my father.

"Oh, a little deer hunting, maybe."

"Good weather for it."

"There's a fellow lives near here that I've been corresponding with," my father said. "Ryder Sexton. I thought we'd drive over and see him one day."

"Oh, Sexton's a hunter, all right! You should see his collection o' weapons!"

"I'm anxious to. He's written me about them."

Sheriff Lens licked his lips. "I'll give you some advice. Go see Ryder Sexton right away—today or tomorrow. Maybe he'll invite you to hunt on his property. He's got some woods an' a pond that're the best deer-huntin' spots in the whole county. He's even got a little huntin' lodge built back on his land, near the pond. He uses it for duck huntin' too."

"Thanks for the tip," my father said. "Be seeing you, Sheriff."

I'd planned a quiet evening for them, but after the sheriff's advice Dad insisted that I phone Sexton after we'd had dinner at my apartment. I knew the man only slightly, though when I put my father on the line it was clear that they were excited at the prospect of a first meeting. The upshot of it was that I agreed to drive my parents over to Sexton's house the following morning.

"I have to see a patient at nine," I told them as I prepared the bed in my spare room, "but I'll be back here to pick you up around ten. Sexton's place is about a twenty-minute drive from here."

Ryder Sexton was the last of our county's old land barons, if the term could ever be used properly in this area of New England. He owned some three hundred acres of property. There were farms that large, of course, but Ryder Sexton was no farmer, not even the gentleman sort. He'd made his money in munitions during the war, and though he no longer had an interest in the Sexton Arms empire his name was still linked to it.

The following morning was crisp and unusually clear for mid-November. I drove along the rutted back roads, pointing out the farms and landmarks. "This fenced-in property is the beginning of the Sexton place," I said.

"It certainly is large," my mother remarked. "Harry, you always knew how to make friends with rich folks."

Father sputtered in mock protest. "I read a letter of his in the *American Rifleman* magazine and wrote him about it. I never knew if he was rich or poor, and I sure never connected him with Sexton Arms."

"He bought this place a few years ago after he sold the company," I explained. "He spends part of the year in Florida and in New York, but he's always up here during hunting season. Sheriff Lens told me about his collection of primitive weapons."

Ryder Sexton himself came to the door to greet us, wearing a fringed deerskin jacket and riding britches. He was a tall, imposing man with a ruddy complexion and steel-gray hair worn in a short military fashion. Seeing him with my father made me think somehow of a reunion of Army officers from the last war, though I knew that Sexton had been busy on the home front and my father's military service had been confined to the local draft board.

Sexton nodded a greeting to me, but he seemed genuinely pleased to meet my father. "I look forward to your letters, Harry. They're more sensible than most of the stuff in the daily papers. And this must be Doris," he said to my mother. "Welcome to Northmont, both of you. Come in, come in!"

I'd never met any of Sexton's family and I was surprised when a young woman appeared with an armload of fall flowers and was introduced as his wife. "There's supposed to be a frost tonight," she explained, "so I've been gathering up the last of them."

Her name was Rosemary, and I guessed her to be maybe thirty years younger than her husband, who was pushing sixty. She was probably a second wife, and attractive, with a direct, friendly manner. I tried to remember if I'd seen her about town, but I didn't think I had—which wasn't surprising, since the Sextons were here only part of the year.

"How's the deer hunting in this area?" my father asked when we were settled down in the paneled living room before a large open fire. "I'd like to give it a try while I'm visiting."

"Fine right now," Ryder Sexton assured him. "Couldn't be better. In fact, I'm going out with a few people tomorrow morning, if you'd like to join us. We hunt here on the property, down by the pond. I have a bit over three hundred acres, with lots of woods. I even have a small hunting lodge down there."

"That's mighty generous of you," Father answered with a smile, quickly accepting the offer.

"You too, Sam," Sexton added, including me as an afterthought. "Your mother can come and stay here at the house with Rosemary while we're out."

I mumbled something about appointments with my patients, but I knew I'd be able to arrange it. The idea of hunting with my father again, as we'd done so many years ago, overcame my momentary distaste for slaughtering deer. "What time will you be starting?"

Sexton thought a moment. "Early. Be out here by seven if you can. My neighbor, Jim Freeman, is joining us and Bill Tracy is coming out from town. Maybe I'll invite Sheriff Lens too. That'll make six of us in all."

Bill Tracy was a real-estate man who'd had some dealings with Sexton, and Jim Freeman was a successful farmer. I knew them both quite well, and had recently doctored Freeman's daughter for the usual childhood illnesses.

"We'll be here," Father assured Sexton. "Now what about your collection? I'm itching to see it."

Ryder Sexton chuckled and led us to an adjoining den where two walls were almost covered by tall glass-doored cabinets. Inside were a number of items, mainly made of wood, and our host gave us a quick description of each. "I've been collecting primitive weapons for years, and though we're here for only a portion of the year I decided this was the best place to house my collection. This first is a cord sling. One of those stones was placed in that pouch and the thing was whirled over your head and released. That's how David killed Goliath. This pellet-bow from India has the pouch fixed between its two strings."

"Unusual," my father murmured. "I never saw one of those."

"These are throwing-sticks used by Australian aborigines. And of course you're familiar with the boomerang. Here's a collection of darts, javelins, and throwing spears. Jim Freeman next door will tell you how he dropped darts from airplanes during the war."

"Notice this wooden spear-thrower from the South Pacific. The spear fits into this socket and the thrower acts like an extra joint in the arm. Eskimos use something similar for harpoons. Here we have some Patagonian bolas, with three balls connected by thongs to a common center. They're generally used to entangle the prey."

I looked ahead at the next cabinet. "These swords seem more recent."

"They're ceremonial swords from the western Pacific islands," Sexton explained. "Notice this club. It's been edged with sharks' teeth to make it quite deadly. I sometimes use it to dispatch wounded deer. And here are some shields of coconut fiber from the same area." He might have gone on for another half hour if his wife hadn't interrupted to say, "Here's Jennifer!" Out the window I saw a young woman in her twenties walking a bicycle into the side yard. "Come on," Mrs. Sexton urged us, "I want you to meet my sister."

We trooped outside and she introduced us as her sister stowed the bike away in an unused henhouse. "Jennifer, this is Harry and Doris Hawthorne— and their son Dr. Sam Hawthorne, from town. They're visiting him this week, and Harry is a friend of Ryder's."

Jennifer seemed delighted to meet us. "Rosemary insisted I come and stay with them for a month, but I really like to see people around. After living in New York, I've become too much of a city girl, I guess."

"You seem quite at home with that bicycle," I remarked.

"Ryder says I mustn't take it on the trails back in the woods. He's afraid a hunter might mistake me for a deer." She pouted prettily. "Would you mistake me for a deer?" she asked me.

"I might," I conceded.

Our departure was delayed by the arrival of Jim Freeman from the neighboring farm. He'd walked over through the fields, a big lumbering man who'd always reminded me more of a wrestler than a farmer. "Weather forecast says we might get a little snow tonight," he told Ryder Sexton. "You gonna run the hose out to your huntin' lodge to keep your water from freezin'?"

Sexton nodded. "I suppose I should." He turned to my father and explained. "I have a tank of water in the lodge for necessities. It comes in handy for brewing coffee or mixing drinks, doing dishes or even flushing the outhouse."

"All the comforts of home," my mother remarked drily. She'd never thought much of hunting, and I remembered how in my youth she'd badgered my father for taking me out to shoot pheasants on a Sunday afternoon.

Ryder Sexton kept a hundred yards of hose coiled around a drum out in back of the barn and he started dragging one end with him as we walked down to his lodge. "I'll show you where we'll be in the morning," he said. "I'll leave the water running slowly all night and then my tank won't freeze up."

He turned to his neighbor. "There'll be six of us in the morning, Jim. Harry and Sam are joining us, and I thought I'd invite Sheriff Lens too."

"Fine."

We strode between two oaks and over the crest of a small hill. Below us, some fifty yards away, was a crude shelter made of rough boards with a roof of tree branches. It stood near the edge of a pond, still and quiet in the morning sun. Sexton gave a yank on the hose and pulled it down the hill, trailing it after him through the short grass. It wasn't much thicker than a garden hose but many farmers bought it in hundred-yard lengths for irrigation purposes.

The hunting lodge was larger inside than it had first appeared, with room for all of us to crowd in easily. Rosemary Sexton and her sister Jennifer had followed along, and with Sexton, Freeman, my folks and me, that made seven of us. The ceiling was low above our heads, but I could stand and walk without stooping. There were firepots, crude chairs, and a table, together with gun racks and even a small icebox where food and beverages could be kept. A metal tank full of water was attached to a shelf along one wall. Sexton ran the end of his hose into it.

"It holds thirty gallons—almost the size of a barrel," he explained, directing his words to my father. "The hose goes in the top. I'll turn the water back on at the pump, just enough to keep it flowing all night. And I'll open this faucet a dribble. The drain empties into the pond."

"There are quite a few holes in your wall," I commented.

"Those are gun holes, Sam," my father was quick to explain. "Right, Ryder?"

"Sure are! Tomorrow morning a couple of us will wait here while the rest of you drive the deer toward us. Then we'll fire through these gun ports and catch 'em as they cross that open space."

"Sounds good to me," Father said enthusiastically.

"It would," my mother muttered.

Jennifer gave a little groan. "Looks as if you and I are going to be cooking venison, Rosemary."

Sexton's wife snorted. "They haven't killed them yet. My money's on the deer."

We strolled back up the hill and watched while Sexton turned on the pump and regulated the flow of water through the hose to the crudely built hunting lodge. Then Freeman headed back across the field toward his farm and I got my folks back to the car. "Seven o'clock," Ryder Sexton called out after us.

That night over dinner my mother admitted that Ryder and his wife seemed nice enough. "For deer hunters," she added.

Father laughed. "I don't think the wife hunts, Doris. Don't tar her with the same brush as him."

"I have to stop by the office," I told them, "in case April left me any messages."

"You go ahead." Mother started gathering up the dishes. "Your father and I better get to bed early anyhow if we're supposed to be up with the chickens."

"Before the chickens, Doris," he corrected her.

I drove down to the office and found only one message of any importance. A farm injury had hospitalized one of my patients, and I drove over to Pilgrim Memorial to see how he was doing. As I was leaving, I ran into Bill Tracy. Bill was always well dressed, with a stiffly starched collar that made him look more like the town banker than a real-estate man. I'd never known him to hunt before, and I had to mention it to him.

"My hunting's no stranger than yours, Sam. How come you're going out there?" he countered.

"My folks are visiting and Dad's corresponded with Sexton. He invited us both to come along. We were out there looking around this morning. It's quite a place."

"Is his sister-in-law still there?"

"Jennifer? Yes, she was around. Lovely girl."

Bill Tracy slid a finger beneath his starched collar. "I think I saw her over at the Freeman place one afternoon last week as I was driving by. I couldn't be sure, though. It might have been Mrs. Sexton. They look a little alike."

"Not close up. Maybe it was one of Freeman's daughters."

"Naw, I recognized that bike Jennifer rides, parked around the side of the house." He winked at me. "And she told me she was bored with country life."

"She implied that much today," I admitted.

"Well, I'll see you in the morning, Sam. Keep your eyes open and you might spot something more interesting than deer."

I was still thinking about that when I got home and found my mother sitting up by the window with a cup of hot chocolate. "I need to relax before I can sleep," she told me. "Not your father, though. He's already snoring in there."

"How's his health, Mom?" I asked, settling down on the sofa by her side.

"Good enough for his age, I suppose. He saw his doctor about some heart palpitations last month. Keep an eye on him during the hunt tomorrow, Sam."

"Of course."

She sipped her hot chocolate and sighed. "I've never liked him hunting. You neither!"

"I haven't hunted in nearly twenty years—not since the last time with him. I'm going along tomorrow because I think he wants me to."

"He likes to think you're still his boy, Sam."

"I guess I always will be. And yours too."

"No, no." She shook her head. "You're a man now. You should be married, with a family."

"I know, Mom."

"When you wrote me about that wedding last Christmas I thought for a minute it was yours."

"Sheriff Lens got married. And he's a lot older than me."

"Don't let it slip by you, Sam. Don't spend all your time treating ill people and doing this detective work of yours and wake up one morning to find you're an old man without anyone to love you."

"Hey," I laughed, "this is pretty serious stuff! Come on, it's off to bed for both of us. I've got the alarm clock set for five-thirty."

"All right," she agreed, and gave me a kiss on the cheek. "But think about what I said."

I lay awake for a time after that, listening to the snoring from the next room and wondering if my mother had anyone to love her.

The morning alarm wakened me from a deep dreamless sleep, and I peered out the window to see a thin coating of snow over the landscape. It was still dark as I heard my folks moving to and from the bathroom and getting dressed.

"Good morning," I called out to them, "we got about a half inch of snow overnight!"

"Good deer-tracking weather!" my father called back.

"Sure is! I'll get us some breakfast."

The road to the Sexton place was virtually deserted as we drove out an hour later. Only a few tire tracks had broken the white mantle of snow, and when we turned into the Sexton driveway I realized that one set of these belonged to Sheriff Lens, who'd arrived ahead of us. The sun was up now, and the sheriff stood by his car with a deer rifle at his side, chatting with Sexton and Jim Freeman.

"Isn't this snow-cover great?" Ryder Sexton exclaimed as he greeted us. "The deer won't have a chance!"

Jennifer came out of the house with wrapped sandwiches for everyone and Rosemary Sexton hurried out behind her to welcome my mother. "Come in the house where you'll be warm—and safe."

Another car pulled into the driveway behind my Stutz and Bill Tracy climbed out, carrying his rifle in a fancy leather case. "Good morning, all!"

I introduced him to my parents and he accepted a sandwich from Jennifer. Then Sexton began issuing orders. "You'll spread out in a half circle with the pond and the hunting lodge as the focus. Stay clear of each other so's you can cover a wider area, then start converging toward the lodge, driving the deer that way. Sam, how about if you stay in the lodge with me?"

I remembered my promise of the previous night to keep an eye on Dad. "I think I'd rather be out in the field if it's all the same with you."

Ryder Sexton shrugged. "Sure. I'll stay down there alone and pick 'em off like in a shooting gallery. Five of you can probably cover a larger circle anyhow."

We tramped back through the shallow snow to the pump house, where he turned off the water he'd had running since the previous night. "Jim, stay here till I disconnect the hose and then reel it in for me. I don't want no one tripping over it and spoiling a good shot."

While Freeman stayed, the rest of us headed for the lodge. Jennifer, wearing only a thin jacket over a sweater and men's workpants, was in the lead with Sexton. "Are you hunting too?" I called out to her.

"I wish they'd let me!"

I fell in step with Sheriff Lens while Bill Tracy brought up the rear with my father. "How's the wife, Sheriff?"

"Good, Doc. I'd better bring home some meat for the table, though, or she'll never forgive me for takin' a whole day off!"

"Damn," Sexton grumbled from up ahead. "I'd forget my head if it wasn't screwed on!" He muttered some instructions to Jennifer and then paused at the top of the rise overlooking the hunting lodge. "And, Jennifer, on your way back tell Jim to start winding up the hose when I give the signal."

"Sure," she said, and started back.

"I like your boots," I told Sexton, admiring the sleek glisten of the new leather.

"Bought 'em in New York. Look at the tread on them!" He showed me the soles, then for the first time he noticed my rifle, an old Winchester I'd had for years. "If you don't mind my saying so, Sam, that's not much of a weapon for deer. I've got an extra up at the house if you'd like it."

"No, no, this is fine for me. I leave the fancy shooting to my father."

"All right, if you say so." He turned to Dad and Bill Tracy and the sheriff. "Look, this little rise pretty much protects the house from stray shots, but even so let's try to keep from firing in that direction. A rifle slug carries a long way and I don't want any broken windows. Or dead wives." He chuckled a bit at the last, to show it was meant as a joke. Then we waited at the top of the rise as he walked down across the virgin snow toward the lodge. He carried the rifle in his right hand and one of Jennifer's sandwiches in his left, stepping over the hose to enter the doorway.

I could see him through some of the gun ports in the lodge walls, pulling the hose from his water tank and dropping it in the doorway. "Pull it in!" he shouted, and I relayed the signal back to Jim Freeman at the pump house. Freeman started turning the drum, collecting the hose as it snaked back through the snow.

When Sexton saw that Freeman had rejoined us, he called out, "Start your circle now. Watch for deer tracks, and drive 'em this way. I'll be ready, and I'll have the coffee brewing too!"

We headed off across the fields, with Tracy and Freeman moving out to the east while the sheriff, Dad, and I fanned out in the opposite direction. I managed to keep my father in sight, and once when he spotted deer tracks I ran over to check them out.

"It's a deer, all right," I agreed. "A big one too, from the looks of it." I trudged along at his side, not bothering to resume my former position. We were on the trail together now, as we'd been so many times in my youth.

He must have been thinking the same thing. "Brings back the old days, don't it?"

"Sure does, Dad."

"Your mother tell you about my heart?"

"She said you've had a few problems. Are you taking some pills?"

"Sure, sure. I'll live to be a hundred. After all, my son's a doctor, isn't he?"

"I only wish I lived nearer to you. What would you think of moving east?"

"To New England? Not a chance! We're Midwesterners. You were too, once."

"I know. But it would be hard to go back now."

"I don't know. Do you think your life is any better here?"

"I enjoy it."

"You like men like Sexton for patients? Rich men?"

"He's not my patient. He's *your* friend, remember."

"Your mother thinks his wife's not happy."

"Why's that?" I asked, guiding our route through the woods so we stayed in line with the deer we were tracking.

"Oh, Rosemary Sexton made some remark about hunting, and about how her whole life seems to be lived around her husband's whims. Doris thought she sounded a little bitter."

"Most women in Northmont would love to trade places with her."

We came upon fresh deer.droppings in the snow and my father signaled for silence. "Quiet now," he whispered. "We're not far behind him."

We came out of the woods, moving around a clump of underbrush, and I saw Sheriff Lens off to the left. He waved and pointed straight ahead, at something we couldn't see. Then suddenly a deer broke from cover about two hundred yards ahead of us, running in the general direction of Sexton's lodge.

"Look at the rack on him!" my father breathed. "Might be a twelve-pointer!"

The deer started to turn toward us and Sheriff Lens raised his rifle for a quick shot. The range was too far for any accuracy, and he must have realized that. He lowered his weapon as the deer changed direction again.

"The wind is from our direction," my father said. "He probably scents us."

"If Tracy and Freeman are in position we've got him trapped. The only way out is past the lodge where Sexton will nail him."

We hurried now, breaking into a trot to keep up with the fleeing animal. Presently the pond came into view, and then the lodge. I could see Freeman just coming over the hill on the other side, and after a moment Bill Tracy appeared too, back toward the house. Both men had seen the deer and had their weapons raised.

"Why don't they shoot?" Sheriff Lens wanted to know, trotting over to join us.

"The buck is so near the lodge Sexton can kill it with an easy shot," my father said. He had his own rifle ready, but the deer kept running, straight as an arrow. It scooted across the clearing, passing not twenty yards from the lodge.

There was no shot.

Then, before anyone realized what was happening, the big buck ran through the shallow water at the edge of the pond, outflanking Freeman. The farmer turned, dropped to one knee, and fired a quick shot. We saw the spout of water where the bullet hit beyond and behind the fleeing deer's path, then it was gone, into the woods beyond the pond.

"What in hell happened?" Tracy yelled, coming down to join us.

Freeman hurried over too. "Why didn't Sexton get him?"

"I don't know," my father replied, and I didn't know either. We all just stood there, staring down at the hunting lodge. There were still only Ryder Sexton's footprints leading into it, but a little column of smoke showed that he'd started the fire for coffee.

My father started down across the snow, following the deer's trail till it passed the lodge, then dropping off to enter through the doorway.

He reappeared almost at once, calling up to me. "Come quick, Sam, something's happened! I think he's been murdered!"

I warned the others to stay where they were and went to have a look. Ryder Sexton was sprawled in the center of the lodge, near the table. He lay on his face and the back of his head was bloody. Nearby was one of the clubs edged with sharks' teeth, from his collection of primitive weapons.

"He's dead, all right," I confirmed. "That thing probably killed him instantly."

"But who, Sam?" my father asked.

I walked to the doorway and called to Sheriff Lens. "I need you, Sheriff, but walk carefully. We don't want to disturb any footprints."

"There aren't any footprints, Doc—except Ryder's own. I been all around the cabin. And the outhouse is empty."

I looked out on the pond side and confirmed what he'd said. The lodge was near the water here, but there were still some ten yards of unmarked snow separating them. Despite my warning, Tracy and Freeman had followed us down, but it didn't really matter. Ryder Sexton's were the only tracks into the lodge, and there were no tracks going out. Whoever had killed him with that primitive club had done it by remote control.

"Someone will have to tell his wife," Jim Freeman said, staring down at the body.

"Who could have done it?" Tracy asked. "A tramp passing through the woods?"

"A tramp who didn't leave footprints?" I asked. "All we saw were the tracks of the deer. Did any of you see footprints?"

They all shook their heads. None of them had. I went outside and knelt in the snow, examining the tracks that Sexton had left. Then we all went back up to the house together, where Sheriff Lens broke the news while we stood grimly by. Rosemary Sexton simply stared at us, uncomprehending. "*Dead?* What do you mean *dead?*"

"We heard a shot," Jennifer said. "Was it a hunting accident?"

"He was killed by a blow on the head," I said. "We don't know who did it." Rosemary Sexton collapsed.

When Jennifer and Jim Freeman helped carry her to her room, I got my bag from the car and gave her a mild sedative. Sheriff Lens was already on the telephone, instructing the operator to ring his deputies and have an ambulance sent out for the body.

I came back into the living room and went over to my mother, who was sitting white-faced in a chair. "What happened, Sam?" she asked me.

"I'm trying to find out," I replied. "Tell me, were either of the women out of the house while we were gone? Mrs. Sexton or Jennifer?"

"No," she answered, then immediately corrected herself. "At least I don't think they were. Rosemary was baking a cake for later and she was in the kitchen part of the time. Jennifer was upstairs for about ten minutes. I suppose either of them could have been out without my realizing it."

I squeezed her hand and went upstairs. Jennifer and Freeman were still with Rosemary. I found another bedroom at the back of the house that faced in the direction of the hunting lodge, but a big red barn stood between the house and the lodge, blocking my view of it.

"Trying to figure out how it was done?" a voice behind me asked. It was Jim Freeman.

"I know it seems impossible, but he is dead. I had a nice theory that the club might have been fired from here, like some sort of mortar shell."

Freeman came over to the window. "This is Jennifer's room. Do you think she did it?"

"I have no idea. I was just checking the view."

Freeman nodded. "During the war I was with the Air Corps in France. They were actually dropping darts, called fléchettes, out of planes onto enemy soldiers."

"That's what I mean. Darts can be dropped from planes, people can be stabbed with arrows. Perhaps clubs can be fired from mortars."

"Not too likely, though," Freeman said.

"No," I admitted, "especially since the roof of the lodge has no large openings in it." I thought of something else. "Have Mrs. Sexton or her sister ever visited your place?"

"Why do you ask?"

"It would be natural, since you're neighbors. Bill Tracy told me he thought he saw one of them over there last week."

Freeman snorted. "Bill Tracy's a gossipy old woman. Sure, Jennifer took a ride over one day. Why not? As you say, we're neighbors."

"But Rosemary Sexton has never been to your place?"

"Can't say never. She may have come with Ryder one evening. But she never came alone, if that's what you're driving at. You think I killed him to get at his wife?"

"I don't think anything right now, Jim. I'm just asking questions."

"Well, ask some others." He turned and walked from the room.

I went back downstairs and found Sheriff Lens conferring with two deputies who'd just arrived. "They're gonna take some flashbulb photographs of the lodge and then remove the body. Is that okay, Doc?"

"Sure. You're in charge."

We walked back through the woods to the hunting lodge with the deputies. The snow was starting to melt in places, but Ryder Sexton's single set of footprints was still clearly visible. "You know, Doc," Sheriff Lens began slowly, "I figure there are just three ways it coulda been done."

I was used to this by now. But Sheriff Lens was generally triumphant when he offered me a possible solution, and there was no triumph in his voice today. "What are those, Sheriff?" I asked.

"The club was thrown or catapulted across the snow somehow."

"He was inside the lodge when he was killed," I pointed out. "Even if we accept the theory that he stuck his head out at the moment the club was thrown and then fell back inside, the club still would have fallen outside in the snow. Besides, those sharks' teeth are what did the damage. A club hurled through the air wouldn't have hit him at that angle with enough force to kill him."

"You thought on that already."

"Yes," I conceded.

"Okay, possibility number two. The murderer walked across the snow in Sexton's footprints, then walked out backward the same way."

I shook my head reluctantly. "His new boots had very distinctive treads. I examined those prints and the treadmarks haven't been blurred or obscured at all. Only Sexton walked across that snow, Sheriff, and he did it only once."

Sheriff Lens took a deep breath. "Well then, Doc, that only leaves my third possibility. Sexton was killed by the first person to enter the lodge, before the rest of us reached it."

"The first person to enter was my father."

"I know," Sheriff Lens said.

We said no more about it then, but walked across the stretch of slowly melting snow to the lodge where the deputies were finishing their work. The body was removed on a suitably covered stretcher, and one deputy moved his camera out to photograph the tracks in the snow before they disappeared.

"I found this on the floor," the other one said, holding out his hand to the sheriff.

"What is it? A feather?"

"Yeah."

Sheriff Lens grunted. "Looks old. Prob'ly left over from the last duck-hunting season."

"Looks more like a chicken feather to me," the deputy remarked. "Maybe someone used it for an arrow."

"Except he wasn't killed with an arrow," the sheriff grumbled. He stuck the feather in his pocket.

When the second deputy had left and we were alone, I said, "My father didn't kill Sexton."

"I know how you feel, Doc, and I'd be the same way. I'll admit he doesn't seem to have a motive—"

"He *couldn't* have killed him. Think about it, Sheriff. How did that club, the murder weapon, get in here? It was up at the house, in Sexton's glass case, and he didn't bring it down. We saw him enter the lodge carrying his rifle and a sandwich and nothing else. I've already shown that he couldn't have left again, even walking in his own tracks, without blurring them."

"Hell, Doc, the killer brought the club with him. That ain't hard to figure out."

"Of course, the killer brought the weapon in. And that means my father is innocent. He certainly didn't walk through the woods with me, and enter this lodge in front of us all, with that long shark-toothed club hidden under his coat. There's no way we wouldn't have noticed."

Sheriff Lens relaxed visibly. "Sure, Doc, you're right. He couldn't have done it."

"Besides, if Sexton was still alive when we approached the cabin he wouldn't have passed up that shot at the deer. He didn't fire at it because he was already dead."

"But where does that leave us?"

"I don't know," I admitted.

"Maybe a bird killed him! That would explain the feather! Or maybe someone with big wings strapped to their arms, soaring over the snow! How's that sound, Doc?"

"Not very likely," I told him gently. We left the lodge and started back toward the house.

"But I might have touched on something when I mentioned concealing the weapon under a coat," I said. "How did the killer approach with that club? Why didn't Ryder Sexton realize what was happening to him in time to fight back?"

"It was concealed somehow."

I snapped my fingers. "In a rifle carrier!"

"Like Bill Tracy has!"

We found Tracy just putting his rifle and case into the car. Sheriff Lens went back for the club and we tried to fit it into the carrier, but without success. With the rifle inside it wouldn't fit at all, and even without the rifle it made a peculiar bulge.

"I didn't even have the case out in the field!" Tracy insisted. "I just had the rifle! You guys are nuts if you think you're pinning this on me!"

"We're not trying to pin anything on you, Bill," I insisted.

He climbed into his car. "You know where to reach me if you got any more questions."

My mother came out of the house as Tracy drove away. "Sam, this whole business has upset your father terribly. I think we should leave as soon as possible."

"Of course," I agreed. "Just let me finish with the sheriff."

Sheriff Lens had gone into the house for a moment, but now he reappeared. "Except for the club none of his weapons are missing from their cases. But I have another idea, Sam. Suppose someone made one of them South American bolas with balls of ice? It coulda been hurled through the door of the lodge and wrapped itself around his neck, bashing his skull. Then the heat from the fire melted the ice balls."

"What about the cord, Sheriff? Did that melt too? And there were no puddles of melted ice on the scene. And what about the teeth marks from the club that really killed him? How do you account for them?" But the fire reminded me of the coffee, and that reminded me of something else. "The water tank!"

"Huh?"

"Come on, Sheriff! I'll explain on the way." He hurried after me as I bounded past the pump house and the barn and up the rise leading to the lodge. "Don't you see? The killer never crossed the snow because he was hidden in there all the time—since before the snow started! If that metal tank will hold thirty gallons of water it'll hold a small adult. He killed Sexton and then resumed his hiding place until it was safe to escape."

We were almost to the lodge now and Sheriff Lens had caught some of my enthusiasm. "Will he still be there?"

"Probably not, but the empty water tank is all the proof we need. The killer would have had to empty it down the drain in order to fit inside, and he couldn't have refilled it later because the hose to the pump house was already disconnected and rolled up."

I'd rarely been so certain of anything in my life. Entering the lodge, I lifted the lid from the tank and plunged my hand inside.

It was filled with water, almost to the brim.

Sheriff Lens tried to console me. "Look, Doc, he could still have hidden in the tank, and just refilled it afterward."

"There was no hose."

"Maybe it's pond water."

"The snow between here and the pond was undisturbed," I reminded him. But just to satisfy us both, I let some of the water run from the tank. It was crystal-clear well water, not from any half stagnant pond.

Back at the house, I began feeling as dejected as when Sheriff Lens had raised the possibility of my father's involvement. There had to be an answer to the crime, but I knew well enough that the longer it went unsolved the less likely a solution became. One suspect, Tracy, had already gone home.

Rosemary Sexton seemed to have recovered somewhat and was back downstairs. She was pale and still a bit slow of speech, perhaps because of the sedative I'd given her. "Tell me how it happened," she said quietly.

"We don't know," I admitted. "He may have been killed by a tramp who'd been sleeping in the lodge."

She dismissed that with a wave of her hand. "Jim Freeman told me he was hit over the head with a club from his own weapons collection. That wouldn't have been a tramp."

My father came into the room in time to hear the end of this exchange. "You mean you think someone he knew killed him? I can't believe that."

"We don't know anything yet," I said wearily.

"He was my friend. I'll do anything I can to find his killer."

My mother intervened. "I think the best thing we can do is go back to town, Harry. Sam will take us."

She was right. It was time to go. But I still couldn't quite let go. "I want to see that weapons case," I said.

"I already checked it out, Doc," the sheriff said.

But I went to the den with its tall glass-doored cabinets. Jennifer followed me there and I asked, "Where did he keep the keys for these?"

"They're open. They were never locked."

I stood and stared at the empty spot in the cabinet where the shark-toothed club from the Pacific Islands had rested, remembering Ryder Sexton's words as he'd shown it to us. Someone had taken that club, crossed the unmarked snow with the wings of a bird, and slain the man.

I stared into the glass, seeing my reflection and Jennifer's next to me. "Let's walk outside," I said.

"The sun's gone in again. It's getting chilly," she said, opening the door.

I helped her down the back steps and we walked toward the out-buildings. "Maybe it'll snow again tonight."

"I feel so helpless," she said.

"We all do. It wasn't until I was looking at that glass case just now that I realized how helpless *I* was. I suddenly knew who killed Ryder Sexton, but I've got no proof that would convince a jury."

"That case told you?"

I nodded. "I remembered what Sexton said when he showed us that club. It was good for dispatching wounded deer in the field, he said. He used it for that, didn't he? And when he said this morning that he'd forgotten something, he was referring to the club. He asked someone to get it and bring it to him at the lodge."

She looked at me questioningly.

"He asked you, Jennifer. You were walking with him and I heard him mutter something to you. Then you went back to the house and got the club for him. The rest of us were off out in the fields and woods by that time, so we never saw you go back out there. The sight of you with that weapon didn't alarm Sexton because he'd asked you to bring it. He even turned his back to you and gave you a perfect target. With those sharks' teeth it didn't take too hard a blow to kill him."

"You're accusing me?"

"It could only have been you, Jennifer. I suppose you did it for the money, so your sister would inherit his fortune and it would be yours too."

"No."

"Yes, Jennifer. My mother told me you were upstairs for about ten minutes—that would have been long enough."

"How did I cross the snow? There were no tracks."

We'd reached the top of the rise and stood staring down at the hunting lodge, peaceful in the autumnal setting. There was still enough of the snow remaining to show us Ryder Sexton's footprints.

"Oh, but there were tracks," I said. "There still are tracks, crying out at us to see them. But like Chesterton's postman they're so obvious they remain invisible. I refer, of course, to the track made by the irrigation hose that ran from the pump house to the lodge. Last night's half inch of snow fell on top of the hose, so when it was rolled up this morning the bare track of it remained across the field, running directly to the door of the lodge."

"You're mad! That hose is only about an inch and a half wide! Even walking on my toes, I couldn't follow its trail without leaving tracks!"

A cold wind was rising and I lifted the collar of my jacket. "You didn't walk on your toes, Jennifer," I said quietly. "You rode your bicycle."

If I had expected the fury of a trapped animal, there was none. She merely closed her eyes and swayed a bit. I put out a hand to steady her.

"You told me he didn't like you riding in the woods during hunting season," I continued, "so obviously it was something you'd done before. Following that narrow line left by the hose wouldn't have been difficult, and if you did edge off it once or twice, the hose itself could have made the marks when it was being dragged back. And of course you carried the bicycle from the henhouse to the pump house where the track began, so it left no new tracks in the barnyard. You probably held the club under your arm as you pedaled, and you followed the same track coming back. As long as you stayed in it there was no snow to record the tread of your bicycle tires. You left no clues, except for a single old chicken feather that must have stuck to the bicycle in the henhouse. That feather was all the confirmation I needed once I remembered you putting the bike away there yesterday."

"It wasn't the money." She spoke at last. "That had nothing to do with it. He was damned cruel to my sister. You must have noticed how unhappy she is. Sometimes he even beat her when he was drunk. She wouldn't leave him, so I did her the biggest favor I could. I killed him."

"Will you tell the sheriff that?—If you don't, I will."

We went back to the house and I left with Mom and Dad while Jennifer spoke to Sheriff Lens. On the way to town we caught sight of that big twelve-point buck running at the edge of the woods. My father wanted me to stop so he could get a shot at it, but I kept on driving.

"That was the last time my parents visited me in Northmont," Dr. Sam Hawthorne concluded. "They said city life was a whole lot safer. Look here—the bottle's empty. But I'll have a fresh one next time you drop by. I'll tell you about the time Sheriff Lens finally solved a mystery all by himself."

THE PROBLEM OF
THE BODY IN THE HAYSTACK

"This time I promised to tell you about the case Sheriff Lens solved by himself," Dr. Sam Hawthorne said as he filled the glasses from a newly opened bottle of brandy and settled down in his favorite chair. "Oh, I solved it, but he beat me to the solution. I'm gettin' ahead of my story, though. This all happened during an especially quiet time in Northmont. We'd gone eight months without a murder or a serious crime . . ."

It was in July of 1931 (Dr. Sam continued), a time of deep depression for the country but a peaceful, almost listless summer for our town. The biggest excitement was a black bear that seemed to have taken up residence in Holland Woods and was preyin' on farmers' livestock. By this time Northmont had its own veterinarian, a pleasant chap a few years younger than me whose name was Bob Withers. He'd been kept busy patching up the animals lucky enough to have survived the bear's attacks and putting others out of their misery.

This day I'd been over to Pilgrim Memorial Hospital checking on one of my patients who'd just given birth to twins and another who'd had minor surgery. It was a hot, humid afternoon of the sort that often produces a summer thunderstorm in our part of the country, so as I drove back along Cob Hill Road I wasn't surprised to see farmers covering their haystacks with canvas tarpaulins to guard against a sudden downpour.

I recognized the tall, gaunt frame of Felix Benet driving stakes into the ground to anchor one of his tarps, and I pulled the Stutz up to the side of the road to speak to him. Felix was over six feet tall and wore a wide-brimmed hat in the field to keep the sun off his fair complexion. I told him once he had to keep moving or people might mistake him for a scarecrow at a distance. He was a taciturn man by nature, though I could usually get a smile and a few words out of him. He'd been farming his land for as long as I'd been in Northmont, and with better than three hundred acres his was one of the largest farms in the county.

"Keeping the hay dry, Felix?" I called to him, jumping a little ditch to walk out and join him.

"Tryin' to," he responded. He put down the sledgehammer and wiped his sweaty palms on the front of his bib overalls.

"Seen anything of the bear lately?"

He spit out a wad of chewing tobacco and took off the big straw hat for a moment to mop his brow. His answers were always slow in coming, as if they had to filter through some inner mechanism "Too much. He killed one o' my pigs last night. Doc Withers is up to the house now."

"Sorry to hear that." I squinted into the afternoon sun and saw the vet's horse-drawn wagon standing near the Benet farmhouse. "Maybe I'll stop by and say hello to Bob."

"Tell Sarah I'll be home presently. Just got one more haystack to cover after this one and that's up near the house. I'll do that later." It was a long speech for him, and he lapsed into silence again, spitting on his hands and lifting the sledgehammer to continue driving pegs around the base of the stack. I watched for a moment and then walked back to the car.

At the farmhouse I pulled into the driveway behind Bob Withers' wagon full of vet equipment, causing his horse to prance about nervously. The screen door was unlatched, and when no one responded to my knock I walked right in. Country doctors were used to doing that. The first thing I saw was Sarah Benet tussling with someone on the sofa, and by that time it was too late to back out and come in again.

Bob Withers got quickly to his feet, adjusting his clothing and looking sheepish. "Hello, Sam. I didn't hear you."

"I knocked," I assured them.

Sarah Benet was a good deal younger than her husband, but she was older than Withers by some ten years. She stood up, brushed the soft brown hair from her eyes, and said, with all the composure in the world, "What can I do for you, Doctor?"

"I was just chatting with Felix down the road and he told me Bob was here. You had another bear attack last night?"

"Killed one of our pigs and slashed another with its claws," she answered. "Dr. Withers just finished treating it."

Withers seemed anxious to get me out of the house. He guided me toward the door. "We've got to do something to stop that bear, Sam, or one of these times he'll get himself a human victim. Can't Sheriff Lens round up a posse to hunt him down?"

We stepped out on the porch and down to the dusty driveway. Bob Withers was a bit shorter than me, but his legs moved fast, urging me away from the house. For a moment I was afraid he might comment on the scene I'd witnessed, and I tried to prevent that by chattering on about the bear. "The sheriff hunts deer in season but somehow I can't imagine him going after a bear," I said. "Did it come all the way into the pigpen?"

"Sure did—come on, I'll show you."

It was along one side of the barn, about a hundred feet from the house, and as we neared it I could see the place where the fence had been knocked down. "Probably come back tonight, too," Withers commented, "since he knows there's food here."

"That might be worth a call to the sheriff," I admitted. "Maybe I'll use the phone in the house."

As I turned back, he started to say something else. "Sam, I'd—"

"Yes, Bob?"

"Nothing. You'd better call the sheriff." He went over to see how the injured pig was coming along.

When I reentered the house, Sarah called out from the kitchen. "Bob?"

"No, Mrs. Benet, it's Dr. Hawthorne. Could I use your telephone to call Sheriff Lens?"

She came into the parlor, her face white with fright. "What is it? Felix didn't—"

"It's just about the bear," I hurriedly assured her. "Bob thinks it'll be back tonight, and maybe the sheriff could set a trap for it."

"Oh! Certainly. The phone is right in here."

I cranked it up and gave the operator the sheriff's number. When he came on I told him the situation with the bear. "I suppose I could come out an' lend Benet a hand with it tonight," he agreed. "Bears are a bit outa my line, but folks have been raisin' a fuss about it, and there's an election comin' up in a few months."

I chuckled. "That would make a great campaign poster, you standing next to the bear's body with your foot restin' on it. Like Teddy Roosevelt."

"Yeah," he said, warming to the idea. "Tell 'em I'll drive out after supper."

I hung up and repeated the message to Sarah Benet.

There was a noise from the back of the house and I thought it was Felix returned from the fields, but it was only Hal Perry, the fellow who was something between a hired hand and a tenant farmer on the Benet place. He had his own little house out across the field and farmed part of the land himself, but he also helped out with chores and lent a hand to Felix at planting and harvest time. I'd always considered him something of a mystery man, keeping to himself as if he were hiding out from something.

" 'Lo there, Doc," he greeted me. "Somebody sick?" He reached into his overalls for a plug of tobacco.

"No, I stopped by to talk with Dr. Withers about the bear. You seen anything of it out your end of the field?"

"Saw tracks in the dirt, that's all. He's a big one if you ask me—big and mean." Perry lumbered away, ducking his head of thinning black hair to clear the door frame to the kitchen.

Sarah Benet waited till he was out of earshot, busy getting water at the pump, and said to me, "What you saw in here before—"

"I didn't see a thing, Mrs. Benet," I assured her.

"Thank you," she said softly and turned away.

I went back outside just as Felix came in from the field. "You still here, Doc? How about stayin' for supper?"

"No, I wouldn't want to put your wife to the bother."

"No bother at all! Maybe Doc Withers will want to stay, too. You fellas can talk about the differences between treatin' horses and people."

"Horses have four legs," Withers said, coming up to join us. "That's the only difference."

"There's one other," I observed. "Horses can't tell you what's wrong with them."

"Sometimes people can't either, at least not so's you can understand them," Bob Withers replied.

Sarah came out on the porch then and Felix insisted she set two more places at the table. The Benets had no children so most times there were only the two of them, plus Hal Perry, for meals. I felt a bit awkward about staying under the circumstances, but Withers seemed glad to have me along.

We sat around the big oak table in the kitchen while Sarah finished baking a ham and served it to us. I was used to dinner invitations from my patients, but this was only the second time I'd dined with the Benets. The supper conversation seemed strained, though I may have imagined it. We were just starting dessert—one of Sarah's famous raspberry pies—when there was a noisy interruption. A Model T Ford had pulled into the driveway behind my Stutz, hitting lightly against my bumper as it came to a stop.

Felix and I both went out on the porch to see what had happened. There was no damage to my car, but I was a bit annoyed when the driver of the Model

T—a short man with a bristly black mustache—made no effort to apologize. In fact, he ignored me altogether and spoke to Felix instead. "You don't remember me, do you?"

Benet stood frozen to the top step of the porch. "I remember you, Rawson," he said, his lips barely moving. "What brought you back here?"

A smile formed beneath the mustache, but there was no humor in it. "I'm just out of prison, Felix. Nine long years. Remember I told you I'd come to see you when I got out?"

"Get off my property, Rawson," Felix Benet said quietly.

"Oh, come on—you don't scare me any more!"

Benet turned his head and called, "Hal, come out here!"

Hal Perry came through the screen door and joined us on the porch. Perry was a big man and looked as if he could break Rawson in two, though he made no threatening move. Rawson kept on smiling. "This your latest bodyguard, Felix? Is he livin' back in my house?"

"I'm telling you again—get off my property."

"You heard him," Hal Perry said.

Rawson seemed to hesitate, debating his next move. Finally he decided to back off. "All right, but you haven't heard the last of me, Felix. Next time I'll come around when you're alone. And it'll be soon." He got in the car and backed out of the driveway.

"What was that all about?" I asked Benet as we returned to the table.

"I guess it was just before you came to Northmont, Doc," Felix said, reseating himself and tucking in his napkin. "I've always tried to help people. Like ex-convicts. Give them another chance at life. Jake Rawson was one I helped. He lived in the little house out in back where Hal is now. Farmed his own little land and helped me with the chores. He was on parole from a twenty-year manslaughter sentence. Killed his former employer in a fight. He had nine years left to serve when they let him out. Things were fine for a while, but one night he got drunk and went after Sarah. I don't know what he intended, but I couldn't take any chances after that. I turned him in to his parole officer and he was sent back to prison for the rest of his term. He swore he'd come after me when he got out."

"I never thought we'd see him again," Sarah said. "That's a long time to hold a grudge." She was staring at her plate, unable to meet our eyes.

"He won't be back," Perry said. "I know his type." For the first time it occurred to me that Perry too might be an ex-convict.

"I hope you're right," Benet said. "He was nothing but a troublemaker."

Bob Withers glanced out the kitchen window. "Here comes Sheriff Lens. Maybe you'd better tell him about it."

The sheriff had indeed arrived, as promised, and parked his car behind mine. When he came in, he carried a rifle under one arm. "Here I am," he announced. "Loaded for bear."

We were all silent for a moment and then Sarah Benet spoke up. "We've had some other trouble here, Sheriff. My husband has been threatened." She told him about Rawson's visit.

Of course Sheriff Lens had been in Northmont longer than me, and he remembered the earlier trouble with Jake Rawson. "We sent him back to prison once, and we can do it again if he tries anything." He accepted an offer of Sarah's raspberry pie and dug into it with unconcealed relish. Then except for Sarah and Bob we all trooped outside.

For his part, Felix Benet tended to downplay Jake Rawson's visit. He was more interested in the problem of the bear. "You plannin' to spend the night and help us get him, Sheriff?"

"Sure am."

"I figure if you're on the back porch, with a good view from the pigpen all the way out to that nearest haystack, and Hal is over at his house the other side of the field and I'm in the barn, we can get him in a crossfire if he comes back."

"Just make sure you don't shoot each other," I cautioned.

The early evening sun, already low in the western sky, was beginning to disappear behind a threatening black cloud and this reminded Benet of an unfinished task. "Damn it, Hal, I forgot to cover that last haystack. We'd better get right at that before it rains."

Sheriff Lens and I went back in the house where Withers and Sarah were deep in conversation. It seemed an appropriate time for me to depart. I thanked her for the delicious supper and then asked the sheriff to move his car so I could get out. "I'll be leaving soon, too," Withers said.

Sheriff Lens nodded. "I'll park out on the road and leave the driveway clear." We chatted with Sarah a few more minutes and then left.

As the sheriff and I walked out to our cars, I saw Felix Benet out in the field with his straw hat on once more, securing the tarpaulin over the haystack nearest the house. "Goodbye, Felix!" I yelled. "Good luck tonight!"

He waved and went back to his work. As soon as the driveway was clear, I got in my car and backed out. By that time Felix had finished tying down the tarp and was heading over toward Hal Perry's little house at the other end of the field.

The sky had darkened considerably and the first drops of rain fell as I drove back to town. Along the way I passed Jake Rawson's Ford parked in a patch of tall weeds off the road. He was nowhere in sight.

I was in bed by midnight, dreaming of haystacks and bears, when the telephone awakened me. It was not an unusual sound for a doctor to hear in the night and I rolled over to answer it, expecting to hear one of my patients or perhaps my nurse April with news of some accident.

Instead I heard a barely recognizable voice whispering, "Doc, this is Felix Benet. I need help."

"Is it the bear?" I asked.

"No, it–" Then the phone went dead.

I called the Benet house at once and waited while the phone rang several times. Finally Sheriff Lens answered and I asked where Benet was. "He's in the barn, Doc. I saw him go in hours ago. No sign of the bear yet."

"There's no telephone in the barn, is there?"

"No."

"Because Benet just called me from somewhere. He sounded as if he was in trouble."

"I'll go check on him and call you back, Doc."

I sat on the bed waiting for the call, almost fearing what Sheriff Lens might find in the barn. But when he called back five minutes later he said, "Benet's not in the barn and Sarah says he's not upstairs either. Do you think something's happened to him, Doc?"

"I don't know. I'd better drive out and see. Check with Perry in the meantime—he might have seen something."

"You think Rawson came back?"

"He never left. I spotted his car about a mile down the road on my way home."

"You shoulda called us."

"I didn't think he'd try anything with you on the scene, Sheriff. I'll be out soon."

The rain hadn't amounted to much and now a full moon had replaced the clouds, bathing the landscape in a soft glow. I enjoyed driving on nights like this, when the roads were empty and visibility was good. As I neared the spot where I'd seen the Ford, I searched for it among the weeds, but if it was still there it had been pulled further into the woods, out of sight in the darkness. Around the next bend the Benet farm came into view.

I'd expected to find Sheriff Lens out in front to greet me but he was still at his post on the back porch, single-mindedly watching for the bear. Hal Perry was with him now, and Sarah came to the door in a bathrobe as I arrived.

"Any sign of Felix, Sarah?" I asked.

"No. I'm worried, Dr. Sam."

"We'll find him," I said with more assurance than I felt.

I went out back to talk with the sheriff and Hal Perry.

"Hal hasn't seen anything of him since he went to the barn," Sheriff Lens told me. "I suppose he might have heard some noise and gone into the woods after the bear."

"Or Jake Rawson," I said.

But Perry shook his head. "He wouldn't have gone alone."

"Tell me everything that happened after I left."

Sheriff Lens shrugged. "Nuthin' happened, Doc. Benet finished covering that haystack there—"

"I was still here then. I saw that."

"—and walked around in the field a bit before the rain. He went over toward Perry's place and called out something to him."

"What was that?" I asked Perry.

"He just wanted to make sure I was in position with my rifle. It was gettin' on toward dark and we wanted to be ready for the bear. I called back that I was there."

"Did he go into your place?"

"No, just stood about fifty feet away and called to me. I didn't come out, either. Just told him I was set. Then it started to rain and he headed back toward the barn."

Sarah was listening from the doorway and I turned to her. "He didn't come back to the house, Sarah?"

She hesitated before replying. "No. I haven't seen him since supper."

"How long did Withers stay?"

"Only a few minutes after you left."

"And none of you saw anything of Felix after he entered the barn."

"Not a thing," Perry confirmed.

"So Jake Rawson or someone else could have sneaked up on him in there."

"You're forgettin' the phone call," Sheriff Lens said.

It was Perry who interrupted us then, pointing out across the moonlit field. "I saw something move! Maybe it's Felix!"

I strained my eyes and saw the shadows shifting slightly at the edge of the woods. "Something's out there," I agreed, lowering my voice.

After another minute Sheriff Lens whispered, "I think it's the bear!"

It came across from the far end of the field, moving with that lumbering motion one associates with bears. At that distance it was only a black form, an animated shadow that had detached itself from the woods, but there could be no doubt it was the bear. "Headin' for the pigpen," Perry said. "I'll try to circle around him. When he reaches the pen, you fire first, Sheriff. If you miss, I'll have a shot before he can get back to the woods."

The bear kept coming until it was about a hundred feet from the barn. Then, inexplicably, it changed course and headed for the haystack instead. "Where's he goin'?" the sheriff wanted to know.

"Sniffing around at the haystack," I said. "Can you hit him from here?"

"I'd like to get a bit closer." He moved slowly, carefully, off the porch.

I was afraid the bear might sense his approach, but the beast was now actually clawing at the canvas tarpaulin over the haystack. Sheriff Lens had halved the distance between them before the bear finally turned from its task. Then the sheriff dropped to one knee, sighted quickly, and fired. An instant later Hal Perry fired from the orchard. The bear gave a massive growl, turning first one way and then the other. Sheriff Lens had time for a second shot before the beast finally turned toward the woods. It ran perhaps twenty feet before it collapsed and lay still.

"Good shooting," Perry told the sheriff as we converged on the bear.

"You, too. Better give him one more in the head to make sure."

Perry fired a final shot and then we moved in closer. The bear, a big black one weighing perhaps two or three hundred pounds, was indeed dead. "There's your campaign picture, Sheriff," I said.

Sarah Benet came out across the field to join us. "Any sign of Felix?" she asked.

"Not a thing," Sheriff Lens told her. "If he doesn't turn up by daybreak we'll send a search party into the woods."

But I had another idea. "You go back to the house now, Sarah," I told her gently. "That bear's not a pretty sight."

When she reluctantly departed, the two men turned to me. "What are you thinkin'?" Perry asked.

"That haystack. I want to see what the bear was after under that tarp."

We worked silently in the moonlight, untying the ropes that held it in place. There seemed to be nothing but hay beneath it, until I had them pull the tarpaulin off to one side. Then, prodding gently with their rifles, they found the body near the top of the stack.

It was Felix Benet. The row of wounds across his chest indicated he'd been stabbed with a pitchfork.

By that time it was nearly two in the morning, but there were things that had to be done. The hardest was breaking the news to Sarah. Her tears seemed genuine enough, but I couldn't be certain after what I'd seen earlier.

"I have to ask you some questions," I said. "It might be easier talking to me than to the sheriff."

"You think I had something to do with this?"

"No. Not directly."

She caught my meaning at once. "Bob! You think it was Bob?"

"I didn't say that. But maybe you should call and tell him. It would look good if he was here."

Sheriff Lens came in while she was talking to him on the phone. "What's that?"

"I thought Bob Withers should be here."

"Doc Withers? What for? The bear don't need him."

"He was here earlier. He's a suspect."

The sheriff shook his head. "You know somethin', Doc—this here's another one of your damn impossible crimes."

"How come?"

"We all saw Felix coverin' that haystack with the tarp. And now he's dead inside it. But, damn it, Doc, I was sittin' on that back porch every minute after you left, watching for the bear—even before it got dark. There's no way anyone could have killed Felix and put his body in there. Hell, they'd have to untie the tarp and take it all the way off to get the body up near the top like that."

"Well, you probably went to the outhouse for a minute."

"No, sir!"

"Or back into the kitchen for more coffee."

"No, I didn't!"

"Maybe you dozed off for a few minutes."

"I was wide awake the whole time!" he replied indignantly. "Listen, you saw the trouble it took three of us to get that tarp untied and off the haystack. The killer woulda had to do the same, and then put it back on again."

"There are a couple of other possibilities," I pointed out. "The far side of the haystack was out of sight from the porch the whole time. And even though the moon is bright, it *was* night. The killer could have dragged Benet's body across the field, keeping the haystack between himself and the house, and then just shoved the body under the edge of the tarp."

"You know better than that, Doc. Felix was way up near the top of the stack. And that field out there is still a little damp from the rain. It don't show footprints too well, but it sure would show signs of a body bein' dragged across it—even if that could have been done without me or Hal seein' it. Hal was watchin' the field from the other direction—he'd have seen anyone comin' up on the haystack from behind."

"What *about* Hal?" I asked the sheriff. "What's his background?"

Sarah Benet had finished her phone call to Withers and joined us in time to answer. "Felix always tried to help the unfortunate. He kept that little house back in the field for former convicts trying to start a new life. Jake Rawson didn't turn out too well, but I urged him to try again. Hal's been with us nearly nine years now without a problem."

"What was he in prison for?"

"Not manslaughter like Rawson, I can assure you. Some sort of theft or embezzlement."

"Is there a phone in his house?"

"No. He comes up here when he needs one."

"What's this about a phone?" the sheriff asked.

"Remember I told you? Felix called me from somewhere before he died. It's beginning to look like it had to be from this house."

"I was right on the back porch. I'd have seen him."

"Maybe not, Sheriff. He could have circled around to the road and come in the front."

"Why would he go to all that trouble to call for help when I was sittin' on his back porch with a rifle—all the protection he needed?"

"I don't know," I admitted. "Look, let me try something. This phone has to be cranked, and I want to see if the sound of it would carry to the back porch or upstairs. You two go to where you were earlier."

I tried cranking the phone three times, but the sound didn't carry upstairs or through the back door. The call could have been made from the house without their knowing. But that didn't prove it had been.

Next I phoned the hospital to send an ambulance for Felix's body. I wanted to examine it as soon as possible, to try to determine how long he'd been dead. Then I went outside to talk with Hal Perry. "You were in trouble with the law once," I said.

"Yeah. I served some time. Stole some money from a place where I worked. But Felix was awful good to me here. He really cared about seein' I got a fresh start."

I was about to ask him something else when we both heard a noise from the barn. "Come on!" I said, breaking into a run. It wasn't the sort of noise animals make—more the sort a person makes knocking over some rakes and pitchforks.

"I have a gun!" I shouted into the barn. "Come out with your hands up!"

After a moment's silence, a figure emerged from the shadows. It was Jake Rawson, dressed as he had been earlier that evening. He lowered his hands when he saw us more clearly. "You don't have no gun at all. I fell for the oldest trick in the world."

"What are you doing back here, Rawson?"

He squinted at me in the dim light. "You're the doc, ain't you? Well, I just come back to settle an old score with Benet."

"Looks like you did that all right. We found his body in the haystack."

"What? I don't believe it."

"It's true," I assured him. "And you're the number one suspect."

"I didn't come here to kill him—just give him a few good fists in the face for getting my parole revoked. You think I'd be dumb enough to announce myself like I did if I meant to kill him?"

"Maybe. I've no idea how smart you are." I turned to Perry. "Let's bring him back to the house."

Just as we reached the side porch, headlights targeted us and a car pulled into the driveway. It was Bob Withers, driving his Packard instead of the horse and wagon filled with equipment he'd had earlier.

"What's happened?" he asked. "Sarah said someone killed Felix." He glanced at Rawson, then suddenly recognized him. "Did he do it?"

"We don't know," I replied. "There's a problem as to just how it was done."

"Sarah said it was with a pitchfork."

My mind raced back, trying to remember if I'd mentioned the apparent murder weapon to her. Yes, I was pretty sure I had. "That's right," I agreed. "But the body was on a haystack, under a tarpaulin. We don't know how it got there."

We went into the house and Withers made some effort to comfort Sarah. I couldn't hear what he said to her, but a few moments later I saw her go into the pantry. The door didn't close completely behind her and I could see her take something from a shelf, dropping it into the wastebasket. I waited until she returned and then managed to slip through the kitchen to the pantry. I retrieved the small package from the wastebasket and slipped it into my pocket without looking at it.

When I returned to the parlor, the ambulance from the hospital was just pulling into the driveway. Sheriff Lens directed the attendants to the body, saying to me, "We can search the area and take some pictures by daylight. There's nothing to see right now."

I nodded. "I want to examine the body more thoroughly. I'm going to follow the ambulance to the hospital and look it over. Then I'll get back here and let you know if I found anything."

"I won't be staying around too long myself. Perry can deal with the dead bear in the morning." He frowned and looked at me. "What do you think, Doc? How did the body get in the haystack?"

"You know my methods, Sheriff," I said, paraphrasing one of those popular fictional detectives. "You think about it."

Sheriff Lens looked unhappy. "Is there anything special you could point out to me?"

I smiled and said, "The curious incident of the bear in the night-time."

"Huh?"

"And the bushy mustache of Mr. Jake Rawson."

"What in hell are you talkin' about?"

"Think about it, Sheriff," I repeated, and went out to my car.

It was hardly necessary to examine Felix Benet's body at the hospital, but I wanted confirmation of what was only a theory. He still wore the clothes he'd had on earlier, except for the hat, but in death he seemed somehow smaller. The body was already cold when I examined it, and rigor mortis was well advanced. That was as I had expected.

I was pretty sure I knew then what had happened, and I knew I'd have to tell Sheriff Lens. I telephoned the jail, hoping he might have gone back there, and he answered the phone. "Hello, Doc. I still haven't figured out those clues you gave me."

"Maybe I'll drop over and explain them, Sheriff. It looks like neither of us is going to get much sleep anyway."

"Well, you don't have to, Doc. Not really. See, I solved the case without them."

"What?"

"I arrested the killer a little while after you left, and I got a full confession."

"I'll be damned!" I said. "I'll be right over."

He was sitting in his office at the jail, beaming all over. "I finally solved one on my own, Doc."

"Tell me about it."

"First off, you tell me what you meant by them clues. What about the bear in the nighttime?"

"All right. The bear was attracted by the scent of Benet's dead body. To me that indicated that Benet had been dead for a while—a few hours, anyway. A freshly killed body under that tarpaulin probably wouldn't have given off enough odor to attract the bear."

"Maybe," Sheriff Lens said uncertainly. "What about the mustache?"

"Rawson's bushy mustache was the best proof he was telling the truth about his intention to beat up Benet rather than kill him. He never would have been allowed to grow that mustache in prison, so it told me he'd been out for several weeks or maybe months. That didn't sound like a man obsessed with killing the person who sent him to prison. Revenge, yes, but not a driving obsession, or he wouldn't have waited those weeks or months."

"Yes," the sheriff agreed. "I can see that."

"So who did you arrest?"

He grinned at me. "You mean you don't know, Doc?"

"It's your solution, Sheriff. I want to hear you tell it."

"Well, the whole impossibility came about because we didn't know what time Felix was killed. Nobody had to take that tarpaulin off the haystack or sneak the body up under it. Felix was dead when the tarp was first put on. He was dead before you left the farm last evening."

He had it. He had the answer and he'd come up with it by himself. "But we both saw him alive."

"No we didn't, Doc. We saw the killer wearin' Benet's big straw hat to hide his face and the color of his hair. Benet left the house and walked out to that haystack, and the killer, dressed the same, in overalls, stuck him with a pitchfork. Then he put on the hat, hoisted the body up into the haystack, and pulled the tarpaulin over it—in a matter of minutes, with no witnesses. The actual murder probably happened on the far side of the haystack, out of view of the house."

"And which one imitated him?"

"You know that as well as I do, Doc. It couldn't have been Sarah, certainly. Or Bob Withers, who's shorter than you. Or Jake Rawson, another short man. It could only have been Hal Perry, who's tall like Benet—so tall, in fact, he has to duck his head goin' through doorways."

"Yes," I agreed. "It was Perry. Did he tell you his motive?"

"Sure. He'd been robbin' Felix for years, skimming off some of the money when he took produce to market. Benet grew suspicious and Perry was afraid he'd be sent back to prison. When Rawson arrived on the scene, he saw the perfect opportunity for a scapegoat. He killed Felix with a pitchfork there by the haystack and then put on his hat. From a distance we thought it was Felix covering the stack with a tarpaulin. He was only trying to hide the body till early morning, when he planned to carry it into the woods where it would look like Jake Rawson had ambushed Felix. But the bear sniffed it out first."

I nodded. "Perry was wearing overalls like Benet, and with the straw hat to hide his face and black hair he passed for him at that distance. He waved to me when I left but didn't speak. You said he walked toward the little house and called—pretended to call—to Perry. But Perry supposedly stayed in the house, so you never saw them together. Then he went to the barn. At midnight he slipped into the house through the front door and phoned me, whispering to make me think it was Benet and that he was still alive at that time. Then he slipped out again and back to his place before I phoned and talked to you."

"What if we'd gone to the barn earlier—Sarah or me?"

"He'd simply have said Benet went off into the woods. It was a pretty safe scheme, except for the bear sniffing out the body. But how'd you figure it was Perry?"

The sheriff smiled proudly. "It was that straw hat, o' course. Felix wore it to keep the sun off, but there was no sun when he went out to cover that last haystack. Remember those dark clouds? I asked myself why he was wearin' the hat. Later it dawned on me."

I went to Felix Benet's funeral two days later, and after the service I went back to the Benet farm one more time. Bob Withers was there, and some of the neighbors and friends of the dead man. When I had a chance to be alone in the kitchen with Sarah I took a small packet from my pocket and showed it to her in the palm of my hand.

"I saw you throw this away the other night," I said quietly.

"What?" She made a grab for it but I closed my fist in time.

"It's a sample of a new kind of rat poison for veterinarians to use around barns where there's a rat problem with livestock. Bob Withers gave you this, didn't he? And after we found Felix's body you decided you didn't need it after all."

"I—" She tried to speak but her voice seemed to have deserted her.

"Poor old Felix. There were so many people who wanted him dead."

I went out to the car and drove home. That night I flushed the rat poison down the toilet.

"So that was how Sheriff Lens solved the problem of the body in the hay stack," Dr. Sam Hawthorne concluded. "Hal Perry got twenty years to life in prison, and Sarah married Bob Withers. She sold the farm, he turned his practice over to another vet, and they moved away. I never heard what became of them.

"A few months later. I took a little vacation for myself. But you can't get away from murder, as I learned when I spent a night in a lighthouse and tangled with a ghostly pirate. But that'll be next time you come for a visit and a little libation."

THE PROBLEM OF
SANTA'S LIGHTHOUSE

"You say you'd like a Christmas story this time?" old Dr. Sam Hawthorne said as he poured the drinks into fine crystal wineglasses. "Well, the holidays are approaching, and as it happens I've got an adventure from December of 1931 that fills the bill nicely. It didn't happen in Northmont, but along the coast, over toward Cape Cod . . ."

I'd decided to take a few days off (Dr. Sam continued), and took a drive by myself along the coast. It was something of a treat for me, since vacations are rare for a country doctor. But now that the Pilgrim Memorial Hospital had opened in Northmont, some of the pressure was off. If people couldn't reach me in an emergency, the hospital was there to minister to their ills.

So off I went in my Stutz Torpedo, promising my nurse April I'd telephone her in a few days to make certain everything was under control. It was the first week in December, but winter hadn't yet set in along the New England coast. There was no snow, and temperatures were in the forties. Along with every other part of the country, the area had been hard hit by the Depression, but once I'd passed through the old mill towns and headed north along the coast I saw less poverty.

Not far from Plymouth, a sign nailed to a tree caught my attention. *Visit Santa's Lighthouse!* it read, and although such commercial ventures to attract children are commonplace today, they were still a bit unusual in 1931. I couldn't imagine a lighthouse whose sole function was to entertain tots in the weeks before Christmas. But then I noticed that the word *Santa's* had been tacked on over the original name. It was enough to make me curious, so I turned down the road to the shore.

And there it was, sure enough: a gleaming white structure that rose from the rocky shoreline and proclaimed across its base, in foot-high wooden letters, that it was indeed Santa's Lighthouse. I parked my car next to two others and walked up the path to where a bright-faced girl of college age was selling admissions for twenty-five cents. She was wearing bright Christmasy red.

"How many?" she asked, peering down the path as if expecting me to be followed by a wife and children.

"Just one." I took a quarter from my pocket.

"We have a special family rate of fifty cents."

"No, I'm alone." I pointed up at the sign. "What's the name of this place the rest of the year?"

"You noticed we changed the sign," she said with a grin. "It's really Satan's Lighthouse, but there's nothing very Christmas-sounding about that. So we took the 'n' off the end of Satan and moved it to the middle."

I had to chuckle at the idea. "Has it helped business?"

"A little. But with this Depression and gasoline twenty-five cents a gallon, we don't get many families willing to drive here from Boston or Providence."

A bulging, padded Santa Claus appeared at the door just then, mumbling through his beard, "Lisa, you have to do something about those kids. They're pulling the beard and kicking me!"

She sighed and turned her attention to the Santa. "Harry, you've got to show a little patience—you can't expect me to go running in to rescue you every time they give you any trouble."

I said, "He's not so good at this Santa Claus business."

"He's much better as the pirate ghost," she agreed.

"The pirate ghost is a feature of Satan's Lighthouse?"

She gave a quick nod and offered her hand. "I'm Lisa Quay. That's my brother, Harry. There's a legend that goes with this place—I guess it's why our father bought it."

"Buried treasure."

"How'd you guess? Pirates are supposed to have put up a false light here to lure ships onto the rocks and loot them, just as they once did off the coast of Cornwall. That's why it was called Satan's Lighthouse. When a real lighthouse was built years later, the local people called it by the same name. But of course there aren't pirates any more—except when my brother puts on his costume."

I introduced myself and she told me more about the region. She was an open, unassuming young woman who seemed more than capable of taking care of herself—and her brother, from what I'd seen. "Is your father here, too?" I asked.

She shook her head. "Daddy's in prison."

"Oh?"

"He was convicted of some sort of fraud last year. I never fully understood it, and I don't believe he was guilty, but he refused to defend himself. He has another year to serve before he's eligible for parole."

"So you and your brother are keeping this place going in his absence."

"That's about it. Now you know my life story, Dr. Hawthorne."

"Call me Sam. I'm not that much older than you."

Four unruly children came out of the lighthouse, shepherded by a frustrated Santa Claus. I watched while they piled into a waiting car and drove off with their parents. "Anyone else inside now?" Lisa asked her brother.

"No, it's empty."

"You're not making any money by my standing here," I decided, plunking down the quarter I was still holding. "I'll have a ticket."

"Come on," Harry Quay said. "I'll show you through."

The lighthouse was a slender whitewashed structure with rectangular sides that tapered toward the top, where a railing and walkway surrounded the light itself. I followed Quay up the iron staircase that spiraled through the center of the structure. The padded Santa suit didn't slow him down and he made the first landing well ahead of me. I was short of breath and welcomed the pause when he led me to a room that had been converted into a Santa's workshop.

"We bring the kids up here and give them inexpensive little toys," he explained. "Then we go the rest of the way up to the light."

"What's the room used for the rest of the year?"

"Originally it was the sleeping quarters for the lighthouse crew—generally a keeper and his wife. Of course, Lisa and I don't live here ourselves. We use the room for the pirate's den when it's not Christmas."

I glanced at the spiral staircase, anxious to get the rest of the climbing behind me. "Let's see the top."

We went up another dozen feet to the next level, where a rolltop desk and wooden filing cabinet had been outfitted with signs indicating it was Santa's office. The nautical charts of Cape Cod Bay on the walls were festooned with streamers proclaiming a landing area for Santa's reindeer-powered sleigh. There were powerful binoculars and a telescope for observing passing ships, and a two-way radio for receiving weather reports or S.O.S. messages.

"I have to watch the kids every minute up here," Harry Quay said. "Some of this equipment is valuable."

"I'm surprised it's still here if the lighthouse is no longer in use."

"My father kept them for some reason. He used to sit up here at night sometimes. It was a hobby of his, I suppose. That's why he bought the place."

I gestured toward the ceiling of the little office. "Does the light up above still operate?"

"I doubt it. I haven't tried it myself."

We climbed the rest of the way to the circular outside walkway that went around the light itself. A metal railing allowed me a handhold, but one could easily slip beneath it and fall to the ground. "You don't bring the kids up here, do you?"

"One at a time, with me holding their hand. I'm very careful."

I had to admit it was a magnificent view. On the bay side the land fell away rapidly to the water's edge, and as far as I could see the chill waters were casting up rippling whitecaps before the stiff ocean breeze. The curve of Cape Cod itself was clearly visible from this high up, and I could even make out the opposite shoreline some twenty miles across the bay.

But at this time of the year night came early and the sun was already low in the western sky. "I'd better get going if I want to reach Boston tonight," I said.

"Why go that far? There are plenty of places to stay around Plymouth."

We went back downstairs and met Lisa at the workshop level. "Did you enjoy the view? Isn't it spectacular?"

"It certainly is," I agreed. "You should double your prices."

"No one comes as it is," she replied with a touch of sadness.

"If the light still works, turn it on! Bring in some customers in the early evening."

"Oh, the coast guard would never allow that." She bustled about the workroom, picking up a few candy wrappers dropped by the children, retrieving a reel of fishing line and a set of jacks from one corner. "You find the darnedest things at the end of the day."

"Your brother says there are some places I could stay in the Plymouth area."

"Sure. The Plymouth Rock is a nice old place, and the rooms are clean." She turned to her brother. "Let's close up for the night."

"I'd better make sure everything's shut upstairs," Harry said.

"I'll go with you."

I started down the spiral staircase to the ground floor. I waited a few minutes, thinking they'd be following soon, but I became restless. The lighthouse had been a pleasant diversion, but I was anxious to move on.

"Wait a minute!" Lisa Quay called out as I started down the path to my car. She was at one of the middle windows, and I paused while she came down to meet me.

"I didn't mean to leave without saying goodbye," I told her, "but it's getting dark and I should be on my way."

"At least wait for Harry. He's taking off his Santa Claus suit. He'll be down in a minute."

I strolled back with her while she closed up the foldaway ticket booth and stowed it inside the lighthouse doorway. "If this weather holds out, you should get some crowds before Christmas."

"I hope so," she said. "Those four kids you saw were the only customers we had all afternoon."

"Maybe you could offer a special group-rate for—"

"What's that?" she asked suddenly, hurrying back outside. "Harry?" she called out, looking up. "Is that you?"

There was some sort of noise from above us and then Lisa Quay screamed. I looked up in time to see a figure falling from the circular walkway at the top of the lighthouse. I sprang aside, pulling her with me, as Harry Quay's body hit the ground where we'd been standing.

Lisa turned away screaming, her hands covering her face. I hurried over to her brother, my mind racing through the possibilities of getting fast help if he was still alive.

Then I saw the handle of the dagger protruding from between his ribs and I knew that help was useless.

"I don't believe in ghosts," she said quite rationally as we waited for the police to arrive. I'd used the lighthouse radio to call the coast guard, who promised to contact the state police for us. While I was inside, I'd looked in both rooms and even inside a little storeroom, but the lighthouse was empty. There was nothing on the walkway to indicate anyone else had been there, nothing on the spiral staircase to point to an unseen visitor.

"We don't have to believe in ghosts," I told her. "There's a logical explanation. There has to be. Have you ever seen that dagger before?"

"Yes. It's part of his pirate costume. The storeroom—"

"I checked the storeroom. I saw the costume hanging there. No one was hiding."

"Well, I don't believe in ghosts," she said again.

"The police will be here soon."

She fastened her hand on my arm. "You won't leave, will you? You won't leave before they come?"

"Of course not." I'd moved her away from her brother's body, so she'd be spared the sight while we waited for the police. I could see she was close to hysteria and might need my professional services at any moment.

"Without your testimony they might try to say I killed him," she said. "Even though I had no reason to."

"I'm sure they wouldn't say that," I tried to assure her.

"But no one else is here! Don't you see how it looks?"

"You were down on the ground with me when he was stabbed. I'll testify to that."

"Suppose I rigged up some sort of device to throw the knife at him when he stepped out onto the walkway."

I shook my head. "I was up there with him shortly before he was killed. And I went up there again a few moments ago. There was no device, and nothing left over from one. There was nothing at all on that walkway."

"Then what killed him? Who killed him?"

Before I could respond, we saw the headlights of two police cars and an ambulance cutting through the early darkness. I had plenty of time to tell my story then, and Lisa told hers. They walked around with their flashlights, examining the body, asking questions, going through the motions. But it was clear that they didn't want to deal with a pirate ghost, much less any sort of impossible crime. I fondly wished for old Sheriff Lens back in Northmont. At least he could keep an open mind about such things.

"Did your brother have any enemies?" one officer asked Lisa.

"No, none at all. I can't imagine anyone wishing him harm."

"Can you tell me why he's wearing this false beard?"

"He'd been playing Santa Claus for the children. He was changing out of his costume when it happened."

The officer, a burly man named Springer, turned to me next. "Dr. Hawthorne?"

"That's correct."

"You say you were just passing through, not bound for any particular place?"

"Just a little vacation," I explained. "I practice in Northmont, near the Connecticut state line. The sign attracted me, and I stopped for an hour or so."

"Ever know the deceased or his sister before?"

"No."

He sighed and glanced at his pocket watch. Perhaps he hadn't had supper yet. "Well, if both of you are telling the truth, it looks like an accident to me. Somehow he slipped and fell on the knife up there, and then toppled off the walkway. Or else he killed himself."

"That couldn't—" Lisa started to say, but I nudged her into silence. The officer seemed not to notice.

As the body was being taken away, she said, "I'll have to notify Father."

"How do you go about that? Where's his prison?"

"Near Boston. I'll phone a message tonight and go there tomorrow to see him."

I made a decision. "I'd like to go with you."

"What for?"

"I've had a little experience in solving crimes like this. I may be able to help you."

"But there are no suspects! Where would you begin?"

"With your father," I said.

I slept surprisingly well in my room at the Plymouth Rock, and awoke refreshed. After a quick breakfast, I picked up Lisa at the small house in town she'd shared with her brother. "The police called this morning," she said. "They want us both to come in and make statements about what happened."

"We'll do it this afternoon," I decided. "Let's see your father first."

"What do you hope to learn from him?"

"The reason why he's in prison, among other things. You seem reluctant to talk about it."

"I'm not reluctant at all!" she bristled. "Until now I didn't really feel it was any of your business. Daddy brought us up after Mother died. What happened to him was a terrible thing. He's in prison for a crime he didn't commit."

"You said something about a fraud."

"I'll let him tell you about it."

Because of his son's death, we were both allowed to see Ronald Quay together. He was a thin man, who looked as if he might have aged overnight. His pale complexion had already taken on the look of endless incarceration, even though Lisa said he'd been locked up for only a year. She cried when he was led into the room, and the guard stood by awkwardly as they embraced.

"This is Dr. Sam Hawthorne," she told her father. "He was at the lighthouse with us when it happened."

He wanted details and I told him everything I knew. He sat across the table, merely shaking his head.

"I've done a little amateur detective work back in Northmont," I told him. "I thought I might be able to help out here."

"How?"

"By asking the right questions." I paused, sizing up the man almost as I would diagnose a patient's illness, and then I said, "You're in prison for committing a crime, and now the crime of murder has apparently been committed against your son. I wonder if there could be a relationship between those two crimes."

"I don't—" He shook his head.

"I know it seems impossible that anyone could have killed Harry, but if someone did they had to have a motive."

"He didn't have an enemy in the world," Lisa insisted.

"Perhaps he was killed not for what he was like but for what he was doing," I suggested.

"You mean playing Santa Claus?"

"You said he played a pirate, too. And he was struck down with a pirate's dagger."

"Who could possibly—?"

I interrupted her with another question for her father. "Were you engaged in any sort of illegal activity at the lighthouse?"

"Certainly not," he answered without hesitation. "I've maintained my innocence of these charges from the beginning."

"Then the fraud charges somehow involved the lighthouse?"

"Only in the most general way," Lisa replied. "At one point we tried to set up a corporation and sell shares of stock. A Boston man went to the police and accused my father of fraud because Daddy claimed he had a million dollars to build an amusement park."

"Did you ever claim that?" I asked him.

"No! Harry suggested once that we put in one of those miniature golf courses that are all the rage, but I was against even that. Certainly no one ever mentioned a million dollars."

"They must have had evidence of fraud."

He looked at his hands. "A stock prospectus we had printed, just for test purposes. It wasn't supposed to get out. Lisa can tell you we don't even own much land around the lighthouse—We couldn't have built an amusement park there even if we'd wanted to."

Lisa sighed. "That's exactly the argument the prosecutor used to convict you, Daddy."

I was aware that he'd neatly avoided the main thrust of my question by bringing up the fraud conviction. "Forget the fraud charges for the moment, Mr. Quay. What about other activities at the light-house?"

"I don't know what you mean," he said, but his eyes shifted away.

"The two-way radio. The powerful binoculars. The telescope. They were used to locate and contact ships offshore, weren't they?"

"Why would I–?" he began, then changed his mind. "All right. You seem to know a great deal."

"What were they landing at the lighthouse? Illegal whiskey from Canada, I imagine."

Lisa's eyes widened. "Daddy!"

"I needed money from somewhere, Lisa. Using that lighthouse for pirates and Santa Clauses was a losing proposition from the beginning."

"You told Dr. Hawthorne there'd been no illegal activity there."

"Prohibition is an unjust and unpopular law. I don't consider that I acted illegally in helping to circumvent it."

"What happened after you went to prison?" I asked. "Did Harry continue the bootlegging activities?"

"He knew nothing about it," Quay insisted.

"And yet the radio and telescope are still in place, a year later."

"He was sentimental about moving them," Lisa explained. "He wanted everything just as it was for when Daddy came back."

"You must have dealt with someone on this bootlegging operation, Mr. Quay. Couldn't that man have contacted Harry and struck a deal with him after your imprisonment?"

Ronald Quay was silent for a moment, considering the possibility. "I suppose so," he admitted at last. "That would be like him. And it would be like Harry to accept the deal without telling anyone."

"I need the name, Mr. Quay."

"I–"

"The name of the man you dealt with. The name of the person who might have contacted your son to continue with the setup. Because that might be the name of his murderer."

"Paul Lane," he said at last. "That's the name you want." The words had been an effort for him to speak.

"Who is he? Where can we find him?"

"He owns some seafood restaurants along the coast. I can give you an address in Boston."

As we parked my Stutz Torpedo along the Boston docks a few hours later, Lisa said, "Sam, how come you're not married?"

"I've never met the right woman at the right time, I guess."

"I want to ask you something–a very great favor."

"What is it?"

"Could you stay here with me until after Harry's funeral? I don't think I could get through it alone."

"When—?"

"Day after tomorrow. You could leave by noon if you wanted to. They'll let Daddy come down from prison with a guard, and there'll be some aunts and uncles. That's all. We're not a big family."

"Let me think about it. Maybe I can."

Lane's Lobsters was a seafood restaurant that also sold live lobsters for boiling at home. A grey-haired man behind the lobster tank told us Paul Lane's office was upstairs. We climbed the rickety steps to the second floor and found him sitting behind a cluttered desk. He puffed on a fat cigar that gave him the look of a minor politician.

"What can I do for you?" he asked, removing the cigar from his mouth.

"We're interested in some lobsters," I said.

"The retail business is downstairs. I just handle wholesale up here." He gestured toward an open ice-chest full of dead lobsters.

"That's what we want—wholesale."

He squinted at Lisa. "Don't I know you?"

"You may know my brother. Harry Quay."

Paul Lane was no good at hiding his reaction. After the first shock of surprise he tried to cover it with a denial, but I pressed on. "You run a bootlegging operation, Lane, and you involved her father and brother in it."

"Go to hell! Get outa here!"

"We want to talk. Somebody killed her brother last evening."

"I read the papers. They say it was an accident."

"I was there. I call it murder."

Paul Lane's lip twisted in a sneer. "Is that so? If you two were alone with him, then you must have killed him."

I leaned on the desk between us. "We didn't come here to play games, Mr. Lane. I think you approached Harry after his father went to prison on that fraud rap. You wanted to continue bringing your Canadian whiskey ashore at Satan's Lighthouse, and you needed Harry's cooperation. Isn't that right?"

He got up from his desk and deliberately closed the lid on the ice-chest. "I don't know what you're talking about, mister."

As a lobsterman or a bootlegger, he might have been pretty good, but just then he was being a bit too obvious. When he sat down again I lifted the lid and picked up one of the cold lobsters.

"What in hell are you doing?" he bellowed, coming out of his chair.

I turned the lobster over. Its insides had been hollowed out to make room for a slim bottle of whiskey. "Neat," I said. "I'll bet that's a popular take-out item at your restaurants."

Before I realized what was happening, his fist caught me on the side of the head. I stumbled back against the ice-chest as Lisa screamed. Two tough-looking seamen barged in, attracted by the noise. "Get them!" Lane ordered. "Both of them!"

I was still clutching the dead lobster and I shoved it into the nearest man's face. "Run!" I shouted to Lisa. Lane was out from behind his desk, trying to stop her, when I shoved him aside and followed her out the door. Then all three of them were after us and I felt one beefy hand grab at my shoulder. We made it halfway down the stairs before they caught us, and I tripped and stumbled the rest of the way to the ground floor, landing hard on my chest.

I looked up and saw one of the men take out a knife. Then I saw someone from the restaurant grab his wrist.

I recognized Springer, the state police officer who had questioned us. "Having a little trouble here, Dr. Hawthorne?" he asked.

I'd cracked a rib falling down the stairs, and while it was being taped up Springer explained that he'd gone to the prison to question Ronald Quay, arriving just as we were leaving. "You seemed in such a hurry I decided to follow along. You led me here."

The Boston police and agents of the Prohibition Bureau had taken over Paul Lane's operation, seizing hundreds of barrels of good Canadian whiskey. My last glimpse of Lane was when a cop led him away in handcuffs. "Did he kill my brother?" Lisa asked.

"Not personally, but he probably ordered it done. I can't name the actual killer, but I can give you a description of him and tell you how I think the murder was committed."

"I hope you're not going to say somebody threw the knife from the rocks all the way to the top of that lighthouse," Springer said.

"No," I agreed. "It's much too tall for that. And that pirate dagger is too unbalanced to have been fired from a crossbow or anything similar. The killer was right there with Harry when he died."

"But that's impossible!" Lisa insisted.

"No, it isn't. There was one place in that lighthouse we never searched, one place where the killer could have been hidden—the rolltop desk in the office on the top floor."

"But that's absurd!" Lisa said. "It's hardly big enough for a child!"

"Exactly—a child. Or someone dressed as a child. Remember that carload of children that arrived just before me? Didn't you think it odd the parents remained in the car—especially since the lighthouse offered a family rate? Four children came out, but I'm willing to bet that five children went in."

Lisa's eyes widened. "My lord, I think you're right!"

"One stayed behind, hidden in that rolltop desk. And when Harry came back upstairs to close up, he did his job. He was a hit man hired by Paul Lane, who'd had a falling-out with your brother over the bootlegging business. I think we'll find enough evidence in Lane's records to verify that."

Springer was frowning. "You're telling us a child was the hit man?"

"Or someone dressed as a child," I said. "Someone small—maybe a midget."

"A midget!"

"What better hit man to kill a Santa Claus than a midget dressed as a small child? Five children entered the lighthouse but only four came out. No one thought of the missing child. The supposed parents drove away, leaving a hidden killer awaiting his opportunity."

"All right," Springer said with a nod. "If Lane has a midget on his payroll it should be easy enough to discover." He started out and then paused at the door with a slight smile. "I checked up on you. Sheriff Lens back in Northmont says you're a pretty fair detective."

When he had gone, Lisa Quay said simply, "Thank you. It won't bring him back, but at least I know what happened."

Two days later I was at Lisa Quay's side as her brother was buried beneath the barren December trees of the Plymouth cemetery. As we were walking to the car, Springer intercepted us. "I thought you'd like to know that we have a line on a very short man who worked as a waiter last year in Paul Lane's New Bedford lobster house. We're trying to locate him now."

"Good luck," I said. "I'm heading home today."

My car was back at the funeral parlor and I said goodbye to Lisa Quay there. "Thanks again," she said. "For everything, Sam."

I'd been driving about an hour when I saw the boy fishing off a bridge over a narrow creek. My first thought was that December wasn't likely to be a good fishing month.

My second thought was that I'd made a terrible mistake.

I pulled the car off the road and sat for a long time staring at nothing at all. Finally I started the motor and made a U-turn, heading back the way I had come.

It was late afternoon when Santa's Lighthouse came into view, much as it had been that first day I saw the place. Lisa's car was parked nearby, but no others. The lighthouse was still closed to visitors. I pulled in next to her car and got out, walking up the path to the doorway. She must have heard the car and seen me from the window, because she opened the door with a smile.

"You've come back, Sam."

"Just for a little bit," I told her. "Can we talk?"

"About what?" She was flirting, seductive.

"About Harry's murder."

Her face changed. "Have they found the midget?"

I shook my head. "They'll never find the midget because there never was one. I made a mistake."

"What are you talking about?"

"We kept saying there were no suspects, but of course there always was one suspect. Not the least likely person but the most likely one. You killed your brother, Lisa."

"You're insane!" she flared, trying to close the door on me. I easily blocked it with my foot, and after a moment she relaxed and I stepped inside.

"The more I thought about it, the more impossible the midget hit man became. Those kids were raising a fuss, pulling Santa's beard and otherwise calling attention to themselves. That's hardly the sort of thing our killer would have allowed. The success of his scheme as I imagined it depended upon their group being unnoticed and uncounted." Lisa stood with her arms folded, pretending to humor me.

"Then, too, there was the matter of the murder weapon. A hit man would certainly bring his own weapon, not rely on finding a pirate dagger in a storeroom."

"Third point: how did the killer lure Harry out onto that walkway, especially when he was still removing his costume and had the beard on?"

"He might have been stabbed in the office below," Lisa said, her voice a mere whisper.

I shook my head. "No midget could have carried Harry's body up that ladder. He went up there by himself, with his murderer, and with the fake beard still on, because it was someone he trusted."

"You're forgetting I was with you when he was killed."

"Correction—you were with me when his body fell from the walkway. An hour ago on the road I passed a boy fishing off a bridge. And I remembered you picking up a reel of fishing line in the workroom. It hadn't been left by a child at all. You simply needed it for your scheme. You went back upstairs, called your brother up to the walkway on some pretext, stabbed him, and left his body right at the edge where it could easily be slid beneath the railing. You tied one end of the fishing line to his body and dropped the other end over the side of the lighthouse to the ground. It was nearly dark at the time, and I didn't see it when I went out. You called me back because you needed me for your alibi. I suppose you'd been waiting for days for the right person to happen along just at dusk. You pulled on the line and Harry's body rolled off the catwalk, nearly hitting us as it fell to the ground."

"If that's true, what happened to the fishing line?"

"I missed it in the dim light when I examined the body. Then when I went upstairs to radio for help, you simply untied it from the body and hid it away."

"Why would I kill my own brother?"

"Because you discovered he was responsible for sending your father to prison. It was Harry who printed that phony stock prospectus and tried to defraud investors with dreams of an amusement park. Your father was covering up for him. When you learned about that, and learned that Harry was involved in the bootlegging scheme with Paul Lane, it was more than you could bear."

The fight had gone out of her. "At first I couldn't believe the things he'd done—letting Daddy go to prison for his crime! And then this thing with Lane! I—"

"How did it happen?" I asked quietly.

Her voice was somber. "I waited a week for someone like you to come by—someone alone. Then I called him up there and gave him one last chance. I told him he had to confess to the police and get Daddy out of prison or I'd kill him. He laughed and made a grab for the dagger and I stabbed him. I used the fishing line just like you said. It was strong but thin, and almost invisible in the fading light." She looked away. "I thought I was lucky you came along, but I guess luck doesn't run in the family."

"You have to tell Springer," I said. "He's looking for that waiter. If you let an innocent man go to prison, you'd be as wrong as your brother was."

"All that planning," she said. "For nothing."

"That was how it ended," Dr. Sam concluded. "I wasn't particularly proud of my part in the affair, and I never told the folks back in Northmont about it. When my nurse April asked about the tape on my ribs I told her I'd fallen down. But by the time Christmas came we had snow, and it was a merry holiday for all of us. Then early the following year came that business at the cemetery—which *didn't* involve a ghost. But that's for next time."

A DR. SAM HAWTHORNE CHECKLIST

BOOKS

Diagnosis: Impossible, The Problems of Dr. Sam Hawthorne. Norfolk: Crippen & Landru Publishers, 1996. Contains Dr. Sam's first twelve cases.

More Things Impossible, Further Problems of Dr. Sam Hawthorne. Norfolk: Crippen & Landru Publishers, 2006. Contains Dr. Sam's next 15 cases.

INDIVIDUAL STORIES

All of Dr. Sam Hawthorne's reminiscences were first published in *Ellery Queen's Mystery Magazine* [EQMM]. Dates when the events took place are recorded below in brackets.

"The Problem of the Covered Bridge" [March 1922]. EQMM, December 1974.
"The Problem of the Old Gristmill" [July 1923]. EQMM, March 1975.
"The Problem of the Lobster Shack" [June 1924]. EQMM, September 1975.
"The Problem of the Haunted Bandstand" [July 1924]. EQMM, January 1976.
"The Problem of the Locked Caboose" [Spring 1925]. EQMM, May 1976.
"The Problem of the Little Red Schoolhouse" [Fall 1925]. EQMM, September 1976.
"The Problem of the Christmas Steeple" [December 25, 1925]. EQMM, January 1977.
"The Problem of Cell 16" [Spring 1926]. EQMM, March 1977.
"The Problem of the Country Inn" [Summer 1926]. EQMM, September 1977.
"The Problem of the Voting Booth" [November 1926]. EQMM, December 1977.
"The Problem of the County Fair" [Summer 1927]. EQMM, February 1978.

"The Problem of the Old Oak Tree" [September 1927]. EQMM, July 1978.

"The Problem of the Revival Tent" [Fall 1927]. EQMM, November 1978.

"The Problem of the Whispering House" [February 1928]. EQMM, April 1979.

"The Problem of the Boston Common" [Spring 1928]. EQMM, August 1979.

"The Problem of the General Store" [Summer 1928]. EQMM, November 1979.

"The Problem of the Courthouse Gargoyle" [September 1928]. EQMM, June 30, 1980.

"The Problem of the Pilgrims Windmill" [March 1929]. EQMM, September 10, 1980.

"The Problem of the Gingerbread Houseboat" [Summer 1929]. EQMM, January 28, 1981.

"The Problem of the Pink Post Office" [October 1929]. EQMM, June 17, 1981.

"The Problem of the Octagon Room" [December 1929]. EQMM, October 7, 1981.

"The Problem of the Gypsy Camp" [January 1930]. EQMM, January 1, 1982.

"The Problem of the Bootleggers Car" [May 1930]. EQMM, July 1982.

"The Problem of the Tin Goose" [July 1930]. EQMM, December 1982.

"The Problem of the Hunting Lodge" [Fall 1930]. EQMM, May 1983.

"The Problem of the Body in the Haystack" [July 1931]. EQMM, August 1983.

"The Problem of the Santa's Lighthouse" [December 1931]. EQMM, December 1983.

"The Problem of the Graveyard Picnic" [Spring 1932]. EQMM, June 1984.

"The Problem of the Crying Room" [June 1932]. EQMM, November 1984.

"The Problem of the Fatal Fireworks" [July 4, 1932]. EQMM, May 1985.

"The Problem of the Unfinished Painting" [Fall 1932]. EQMM, February 1986.

"The Problem of the Sealed Bottle" [December 5, 1933]. EQMM, September 1986.

"The Problem of the Invisible Acrobat" [July 1933]. EQMM, Mid-December 1986.

"The Problem of the Curing Barn" [September 1934]. EQMM, August 1987.

"The Problem of the Snowbound Cabin" [January 1935]. EQMM, December 1987.

"The Problem of the Thunder Room" [March 1935]. EQMM, April 1988.

"The Problem of the Black Roadster" [April 1935]. EQMM, November 1988.

"The Problem of the Two Birthmarks" [May 1935]. EQMM, May 1989.

"The Problem of the Dying Patient" [June 1935]. EQMM, December 1989.

"The Problem of the Protected Farmhouse" [August or September 1935]. EQMM, May 1990.

"The Problem of the Haunted Tepee" [September 1935]. EQMM, December 1990.

"The Problem of the Blue Bicycle" [September 1936]. EQMM, April 1991.

"The Problem of the Country Church" [November 1936]. EQMM, August 1991.

"The Problem of the Grange Hall" [March 1937]. EQMM, Mid-December 1991.

"The Problem of the Vanishing Salesman" [May 1937]. EQMM, August 1992.

"The Problem of the Leather Man" [August 1937]. EQMM, December 1992.

"The Problem of the Phantom Parlor" [August 1937]. EQMM, June 1993.

"The Problem of the Poisoned Pool" [September 1937]. EQMM, December 1993.

"The Problem of the Missing Roadhouse" [August 1938]. EQMM, June 1994.

"The Problem of the Country Mailbox" [Fall 1938]. EQMM, Mid-December 1994.

"The Problem of the Crowded Cemetery" [Spring 1939]. EQMM, May 1995.

"The Problem of the Enormous Owl" [August-September 1939]. EQMM, January 1996.

"The Problem of the Miraculous Jar" [November 1939]. EQMM, August 1996.

"The Problem of the Enchanted Terrace" [October 1939]. EQMM, April 1997.

"The Problem of the Unfound Door" [Midsummer 1940]. EQMM, June 1998.

"The Second Problem of the Covered Bridge" [January 1940]. EQMM, December 1998.

"The Problem of the Scarecrow Congress" [late July 1940]. EQMM, June 1999.

"The Problem of Annabel's Ark" [September 1940]. EQMM, March 2000.

"The Problem of the Potting Shed" [October 1940]. EQMM, July 2000.

"The Problem of the Yellow Wallpaper" [November 1940]. EQMM, March 2001.

"The Problem of the Haunted Hospital" [March 1941]. EQMM, August 2001.

"The Problem of the Traveler's Tale" [August 1941]. EQMM, June 2002.

"The Problem of Bailey's Buzzard" [December 1941]. EQMM, December 2002.

"The Problem of the Interrupted Séance" [June 1942]. EQMM, September/October 2003.

"The Problem of the Candidate's Cabin" [October-November 1942]. EQMM, July 2004.

"The Problem of the Black Cloister" [April 1943]. EQMM, December 2004.

"The Problem of the Secret Passage" [May 1943]. EQMM, July 2005.

"The Problem of the Devil's Orchard" [September 1943] EQMM, January 2006.

More Things Impossible

More Things Impossible, The Second Casebook of Dr. Sam Hawthorne by Edward D. Hoch is set in 11-point Goudy Old Style on 13.5-point leading (for the text). It is printed on sixty-pound Natures acid-free paper. The cover painting is by Carol Heyer and the design by Deborah Miller. The first edition was printed in two forms: trade softcover, notchbound; and two hundred thirty copies sewn in cloth, signed and numbered by the author. Each of the clothbound copies includes a separate pamphlet, *The Bad Samaritan* by Edward D. Hoch. *More Things Impossible* was printed and bound by Thomson-Shore, Inc., Dexter, Michigan and published in June 2006 by Crippen & Landru Publishers, Inc., Norfolk, Virginia.

CRIPPEN & LANDRU, PUBLISHERS

P. O. Box 9315, Norfolk, VA 23505
E-mail: info@crippenlandru.com; toll-free 877 622-6656
Web: www.crippenlandru.com

Crippen & Landru publishes first edition short-story collections by important detective and mystery writers. The following books are currently (May 2006) in print in our regular series; see our website for full details:

The McCone Files by Marcia Muller. 1995. Trade softcover, $19.00.

Diagnosis: Impossible, The Problems of Dr. Sam Hawthorne by Edward D. Hoch. 1996. Trade softcover, $19.00.

Who Killed Father Christmas? by Patricia Moyes. 1996. Signed, unnumbered cloth overrun copies, $30.00.

My Mother, The Detective: by James Yaffe. 1997. Trade softcover, $15.00.

In Kensington Gardens Once by H.R.F. Keating. 1997. Trade softcover, $12.00.

Shoveling Smoke by Margaret Maron. 1997. Trade softcover, $19.00.

The Ripper of Storyville by Edward D. Hoch. 1997. Trade softcover. $19.00.

Renowned Be Thy Grave by P.M. Carlson. 1998. Trade softcover, $16.00.

Carpenter and Quincannon by Bill Pronzini. 1998. Trade softcover, $16.00.

Not Safe After Dark by Peter Robinson. 1998. Trade softcover, $17.00.

Famous Blue Raincoat by Ed Gorman. 1999. Signed, unnumbered cloth over-run copies, $30.00. Trade softcover, $17.00.

The Tragedy of Errors by Ellery Queen. 1999. Trade softcover, $19.00.

Challenge the Widow Maker by Clark Howard. 2000. Trade softcover, $16.00.

Fortune's World by Michael Collins. 2000. Trade softcover, $16.00.

Long Live the Dead by Hugh B. Cave. 2000. Trade softcover, $16.00.

Tales Out of School by Carolyn Wheat. 2000. Trade softcover, $16.00.

Stakeout on Page Street and Other DKA Files by Joe Gores. 2000. Trade softcover, $16.00.

The Celestial Buffet by Susan Dunlap. 2001. Trade softcover, $16.00.

The Old Spies Club by Edward D. Hoch. 2001. Signed, unnumbered cloth over-run copies, $32.00. Trade softcover, $17.00.

Adam and Eve on a Raft by Ron Goulart. 2001. Signed, unnumbered cloth overrun copies, $32.00. Trade softcover, $17.00.

The Sedgemoor Strangler by Peter Lovesey. 2001. Trade softcover, $17.00.

The Reluctant Detective by Michael Z. Lewin. 2001. Signed, numbered clothbound, $42.00. Trade softcover, $17.00.

Nine Sons by Wendy Hornsby. 2002. Trade softcover, $16.00.

The Curious Conspiracy and Other Crimes by Michael Gilbert. 2002. Signed, numbered clothbound, $42.00. Trade softcover, $17.00.

The 13 Culprits by Georges Simenon. 2002. Trade softcover, $16.00.

The Dark Snow by Brendan DuBois. 2002. Signed, unnumbered cloth overrun copies, $32.00. Trade softcover, $17.00.

Come Into My Parlor: by Hugh B. Cave. 2002. Trade softcover, $17.00.

The Iron Angel and Other Tales of the Gypsy Sleuth by Edward D. Hoch. 2003. Signed, numbered clothbound, $42.00. Trade softcover, $17.00.

Cuddy – Plus One by Jeremiah Healy. 2003. Trade softcover, $18.00.

Problems Solved by Bill Pronzini and Barry N. Malzberg. 2003. Signed, numbered clothbound, $42.00. Trade softcover, $16.00.

A Killing Climate by Eric Wright. 2003. Signed, numbered clothbound, $42.00. Trade softcover, $17.00.

Lucky Dip by Liza Cody. 2003. Signed, numbered clothbound, $42.00. Trade softcover, $17.00.

Kill the Umpire: The Calls of Ed Gorgon by Jon L. Breen. 2003. Trade softcover, $17.00.

Suitable for Hanging by Margaret Maron. 2004. Trade softcover, $17.00.

Murders and Other Confusions: by Kathy Lynn Emerson. 2004. Signed, numbered clothbound, $42.00. Trade softcover, $19.00.

Byline: Mickey Spillane by Mickey Spillane. 2004. Trade softcover, $20.00.

The Confessions of Owen Keane by Terence Faherty. 2005. Signed, numbered clothbound, $42.00. Trade softcover, $17.00.

The Adventure of the Murdered Moths and Other Radio Mysteries by Ellery Queen. 2005. Numbered clothbound, $45.00. Trade softcover, $20.00.

Murder, Ancient and Modern by Edward Marston. 2005. Signed, numbered clothbound, $43.00. Trade softcover, $18.00.

More Things Impossible by Edward D. Hoch. 2005. Signed, numbered clothbound, $43.00. Trade softcover, $18.00.

FORTHCOMING TITLES IN THE REGULAR SERIES

Murder! 'Orrible Murder! by Amy Myers
The Mankiller of Poojeegai and Other Mysteries by Walter Satterthwait
A Pocketful of Noses: Stories of One Ganelon or Another by James Powell
Thirteen to the Gallows by John Dickson Carr and Val Gielgud
The Archer Files: The Complete Short Stories of Lew Archer, Private Investigator, Including Newly-Discovered Case-Notes by Ross Macdonald, edited by Tom Nolan
Quintet: The Cases of Chase and Delacroix, by Richard A. Lupoff
A Little Intelligence by Robert Silverberg and Randall Garrett (writing as "Robert Randall")
Hoch's Ladies by Edward D. Hoch
Attitude and Other Stories of Suspense by Loren D. Estleman
Suspense – His and Hers by Barbara and Max Allan Collins
[Untitled collection] by S.J. Rozan

CRIPPEN & LANDRU LOST CLASSICS

Crippen & Landru is proud to publish a series of *new* short-story collections by great authors who specialized in traditional mysteries:

The Newtonian Egg and Other Cases of Rolf le Roux by Peter Godfrey, introduction by Ronald Godfrey. 2002. Trade softcover, $15.00.

Murder, Mystery and Malone by Craig Rice, edited by Jeffrey A. Marks. 2002. Trade softcover, $19.00.

The Sleuth of Baghdad: The Inspector Chafik Stories, by Charles B. Child. 2002. Cloth, $29.00. Trade softcover, $17.00.

Hildegarde Withers: Uncollected Riddles by Stuart Palmer, introduction by Mrs. Stuart Palmer. 2002. Cloth, $29.00. Trade softcover, $19.00.

The Spotted Cat and Other Mysteries by Christianna Brand, edited by Tony Medawar. 2002. Cloth, $29.00. Trade softcover, $19.00.

Marksman and Other Stories by William Campbell Gault, edited by Bill Pronzini; afterword by Shelley Gault. 2003. Trade softcover, $19.00.

Karmesin: The World's Greatest Criminal – Or Most Outrageous Liar by Gerald Kersh, edited by Paul Duncan. 2003. Cloth, $27.00. Trade softcover, $17.00.

The Complete Curious Mr. Tarrant by C. Daly King, introduction by Edward D. Hoch. 2003. Cloth, $29.00. Trade softcover, $19.00.

The Pleasant Assassin and Other Cases of Dr. Basil Willing by Helen McCloy, introduction by B.A. Pike. 2003. Cloth, $27.00. Trade softcover, $18.00.

Murder – All Kinds by William L. DeAndrea, introduction by Jane Haddam. 2003. Cloth, $29.00. Trade softcover, $19.00.

The Avenging Chance and Other Mysteries from Roger Sheringham's Casebook by Anthony Berkeley, edited by Tony Medawar and Arthur Robinson. 2004. Cloth, $29.00. Trade softcover, $19.00.

Banner Deadlines: The Impossible Files of Senator Brooks U. Banner by Joseph Commings, edited by Robert Adey; memoir by Edward D. Hoch. 2004. Cloth, $29.00. Trade softcover, $19.00.

The Danger Zone and Other Stories by Erle Stanley Gardner, edited by Bill Pronzini. 2004. Cloth, $29.00. Trade softcover, $19.00.

Dr. Poggioli: Criminologist by T.S. Stribling, edited by Arthur Vidro. 2004. Cloth, $29.00. Trade softcover, $19.00.

The Couple Next Door: Collected Short Mysteries by Margaret Millar, edited by Tom Nolan. 2004. Trade softcover, $19.00.

Sleuth's Alchemy: Cases of Mrs. Bradley and Others by Gladys Mitchell, edited by Nicholas Fuller. 2005. Trade softcover, $19.00.

Who Was Guilty? Two Dime Novels by Philip S. Warne/Howard W. Macy, edited by Marlena E. Bremseth. 2005. Cloth, $29.00. Trade softcover, $19.00.

Slot-Machine Kelly by Dennis Lynds writing as Michael Collins, introduction by Robert J. Randisi. 2005. Cloth, $29.00. Trade softcover, $19.00.

The Detections of Francis Quarles by Julian Symons, edited by John Cooper; afterword by Kathleen Symons. 2006. Cloth, $29.00. Trade softcover, $19.00.

The Evidence of the Sword by Rafael Sabatini, edited by Jesse F. Knight. 2006. Cloth, $29.00. Trade softcover, $19.00.

The Casebook of Sidney Zoom by Erle Stanley Gardner, edited by Bill Pronzini. Cloth $29.00 Trade softcover, $19.00.

FORTHCOMING LOST CLASSICS

The Trinity Cat and Other Mysteries by Ellis Peters (Edith Pargeter), edited by Martin Edwards and Sue Feder

The Grandfather Rastin Mysteries Lloyd Biggle, Jr., introduction by Kenneth Biggle

Masquerade: Nine Crime Stories by Max Brand, edited by William F. Nolan, Jr.

The Battles of Jericho by Hugh Pentecost, introduction by S.T. Karnick

Dead Yesterday and Other Mysteries by Mignon G. Eberhart, edited by Rick Cypert and Kirby McCauley

The Minerva Club, The Department of Patterns and Other Stories by Victor Canning, edited by John Higgins

The Casebook of Jonas P. Jonas and Others by Elizabeth Ferrars, edited by John Cooper

The Casebook of Gregory Hood by Anthony Boucher and Denis Green, edited by Joe R. Christopher

Ten Thousand Blunt Instruments by Philip Wylie, edited by Bill Pronzini

The Adventures of Señor Lobo by Erle Stanley Gardner, edited by Bill Pronzini

Lilies for the Crooked Cross and Other Stories by G.T. Fleming-Roberts, edited by Monte Herridge

SUBSCRIPTIONS

Crippen & Landru offers discounts to individuals and institutions who place Standing Order Subscriptions for its forthcoming publications, either all the Regular Series or all the Lost Classics or (preferably) both. Collectors can thereby guarantee receiving limited editions, and readers won't miss any favorite stories. Standing Order Subscribers receive a specially commissioned story in a deluxe edition as a gift at the end of the year. Please write or e-mail for more details.